# Change of Plans

# CINDY RAS

## A ROMANTIC COMEDY

*Thank you for picking up my book! This is a revised edition of Change Of Plans. It took me over two years to get my book published, and in that time I've grown as a writer. I felt that there were chapters I wanted to add and change. While Ember and Colton's story remains the same, this version is one I love even more.*

"I temporarily lost my hope in love, and it was temporary, thank goodness."
- Shania Twain

# CHAPTER ONE

## EMBER

I'm fixated on the woman in front of me, her hair reminiscent of Tina Turner's iconic style. She exhales with an exasperation that seems to have built up over time. It's not the fleeting annoyance of the moment, but a deeper frustration born from life side-swiping you too many times.

My eyes follow her fingers as they tap a rhythm against her arm. A wedged toe joins in when she shifts her weight, and my fingers begin drumming the same beat against my thigh. She twists her body my way with a sigh.

"Can you believe this?" Her hand gestures to the line of ladies ahead of us.

Her eyes widen, a clear invitation to join forces and bond over mutual annoyance. Normally, I avoid all forms of small talk, but this moment feels important. I know I should throw out an "Oh my gosh, I know, right?" But I'm frozen, staring at the name *Deiondre* tattooed in large swirling letters on her chest.

My brain short-circuits. Etiquette has abandoned me, while her eyes implore me to utter some form of agreement.

I should say something. The longer the silence grows, the more vital my response becomes. We either link arms—comrades against the injustice of waiting our turn like cattle—or I earn another social faux pas.

And as much as I'd rather avoid the threat of meaningless chitchat, I get the feeling she believes women should have each other's backs while standing in line to pee.

Her eyebrows raise a millimeter with every second I stretch the silence, her judgment growing with my lack of response. Yup, serious judgy brows.

I've majorly botched an encounter with a stranger that should've been no big deal. But my mind is too busy to formulate an appropriate response—it's occupied with compiling a list of questions about the man whose name she showcases so permanently. My eyes catalogue the intricate detail of the lettering above her bosom.

I know she's waiting for my reply, but my curiosity takes over, and my own question leaps out.

"How's Deiondre?"

"At the bottom of a lake, I hope." She says with another eye roll.

"Sorry," I say, making an eek face and hoping she senses the sincerity in my lame, one-worded response. "Did you at least... key his car or something?"

"Or something." She grins with a short throaty chuckle.

I want to ask what that something is, hoping for some tips. But the restroom door swings open, revealing a small cleaning supplies cart, followed by its user.

"Sorry for the wait, ladies. Toilet was clogged, but it's all fixed now."

*It's all fixed now.*

The phrase echoes mockingly in front of me.

I wish I could say the same about my life, but I'm still at the plunging part, hoping to hear that delightful gurgle signaling things are flowing again. At least I can say I've recognized the problem and am doing something about it, though it doesn't make the plunging part more pleasant.

Tina Turner hair disappears into the restroom, and I shift on my feet, praying my date doesn't interpret my extended bathroom break the wrong way.

When my turn finally comes, I do my business, struggling to stifle my usual bathroom paranoia.

I wash my hands and pause to give myself a good stare in the mirror.

"You can do this, Em. It's for a good cause."

That cause is my own sanity, self-care, or whatever you want to call it. But I've boarded this train, and there's no getting off now.

I make it back to my seat, slightly embarrassed that I had to excuse myself five minutes after arriving. Balancing hydration and bladder capacity is a skill I have yet to master.

"Sorry for the long wait. There was an issue with the ladies' restroom."

There's a euphemism if I ever heard one. It's like telling someone I'm out on this blind date willingly and that my life is going exactly how I want it to when in reality, it's all a bunch of poo.

"Your eyebrows are very symmetrical."

*Ooookay. Did not see that one coming.*

I cough lightly, faking a throat clear. "Thank you," I say, partly to my date, partly to the waiter who just arrived. I squint my eyes to read our server's name tag as he places our drinks.

*Paul.* I would have guessed Kenneth, but I guess Paul it is.

He has a Kenneth look about him.

"So you agree?" my date asks, narrowing his eyes like I'm a puzzle he's trying to solve.

"What's that?"

I'm trying the old "Oh, I didn't hear you" to move this awkwardness along, but Mr. Sweaty Pits isn't taking the hint.

"You agree your eyebrows are symmetrical?"

"Uh—I guess, yeah. I haven't given them too much thought."

I sip my water while my eyes dart around the busy restaurant, looking for just an ounce of sympathy. Where's my Tina Turner friend? We bonded, right? Surely there's a kind soul who can sense that I'm just a helpless woman needing to be rescued from a blind date that is *not* going well. The evening seems to be yo-yoing between two extremes of awkwardness and boredom, unable to decide which torturous vibe to settle on.

"Interesting," Jerry, a.k.a. "Sweaty Pits," says. His eyes bore into mine as he sniffs his wine creepily. His gaze hasn't left me for a second.

Why is he so sweaty? He looks like he just wrestled a bear, and not in a sexy way. He doesn't seem nervous. Maybe sweaty is his natural state? I wrinkle my nose at that thought.

He's still staring.

I'm going to be murdered tonight. He's plotting my demise, and I'm too polite to object.

"So you're a dentist?" I try to redirect.

*How 'bout we stop with the murder stares, Jerry.*

"That's correct." He steeples his fingers. Guys must think this is some attractive power move, but all I'm getting is Mr. Burns from The Simpsons.

"You know, there's a lot I can tell about a woman based on her teeth. I know you don't bite your nails. Which is good, because that's a deal breaker for me. Yeah…" He leans forward, baring his gums like he wants me to mirror his expression. "You've got great teeth. I can tell you floss, too."

My eyes crinkle. A tight-lipped laugh is all I can muster while I take another stalling sip of water. I purposefully avoid saying thank you because I don't want another Regina George moment like the eyebrow-gate that just happened.

My neighbor, Cynthia, set me up on this date with her boyfriend's cousin. We have very different definitions of cute. Her exact words were, "Oh my gosh, you'll love him. He's a big-shot dentist in Houston, and so cute!"

Our server returns, and I try desperately to silently communicate my concerns with my eyes.

Jerry buries his face in the menu, and I up my plea for help, but Paul is giving me nothing.

*Come on, Paul! Spill the wine, tell me I have a phone call, announce there's a fire! I'll take anything! Can't you see that I'm a damsel in distress?*

I normally wouldn't even dare think those words, but just this one time, I'd accept a little help if it meant a quicker escape and avoiding my untimely murder.

Paul maintains his ignorance and asks if we've decided what to order.

*I'm on to you, guy.*

Jerry's menu closes with a snap. "I'll have the fish, and the lady will have the risotto."

He didn't.

He did *not* just order for me.

Flashbacks from the countless times when I wasn't allowed a say in what I wanted swarm me.

Out of habit, my thumb finds the curve of the fork, pressing my forefinger onto each tine.

It's a soothing action I've picked up while enduring one too many meals suffocated with tension.

The unpleasant memories return, but like the indents on

my finger, I know they'll recede. I'm choosing not to cower anymore.

In my head, I'm removing my earrings and telling Paul to hold my handbag, ready to launch toward Jerry in a fit of rage.

But I hate confrontation. My palms sweat and itchiness tingles my neck just thinking about it.

I'm also starving. If I throw a fit and leave, I'll leave hungry, and the very least I can aim to get out of this date is a decent meal. "Actually, Paul, I'll have the burger—extra bacon."

Jerry's eyes bug out like I've just asked if dentists are real doctors. I smile at Paul, then at Jerry, daring him to say something. A tiny part of me hopes he'll show a smidgen of remorse, but he's determined to avoid any redeeming qualities. He only nods at Paul like he's permitting him to indulge the silly little woman in front of him.

The rest of the date doesn't go any better. I'm beginning to regret the "I'm open to blind dates" line I've been reluctantly sprinkling around.

I barely survive the evening—asking Jerry vague questions about his job and family to pass the time, the small talk nearly killing me. Each round of back and forth crushes my soul a little more.

Jerry has no problems talking, leaning forward as he does. I should probably feign mild interest.

This must be the good part of the story.

"You can detect a lot of health issues based on the odor coming from someone's mouth, fishy odors in particular."

"Mm-hmm, that's fascinating," I mumble.

*Nope. Gross.*

We're nearing the end of the date, and I deserve a prize for not stabbing my own eyes out. I inhaled most of my burger, but a couple of bites and half a handful of fries still sit on my plate. I could have finished it, but if leaving some morsels helps me escape this nightmare sooner, then I'm willing to make the sacrifice.

Paul deserves an award too for his commitment to being unhelpful.

My last attempt at being spared Jerry's monologues about things he's found in patients' mouths was to pass a plea for help written on a napkin to my buddy, Paul. He was no help. My shoulders slumped when he scrunched my "Please save me from the worst blind date EVER!" note into a ball and shoved it in his apron pocket. It was heartbreaking, a knife to the chest after the Houdini act I performed fishing a pen out of my bag and scribbling on my napkin without Jerry noticing as he got disturbingly intimate with a toothpick.

He lifts his hand in the air. He must finally be ready to release me from this torture because he's waving dearest Paul over.

Paul arrives, and I narrow my eyes. He still can't read my death glares. Jerry gestures something with his hands, and I assume he's going to make the pen-on-paper hand signal, the infamous *check-please*.

But no. He's making a square shape.

"Can I get a to-go box? Oh, and a split bill?"

I'm confused.

Jerry's plate is empty.

Wait, did he just say "split bill"?

What is *happening*?

Paul scurries away, and Jerry briefly glances at me, pointing at my food while he opens the calculator app on his phone. "You're done eating, right?"

My mouth hangs open. I tilt my head, looking to the side then back at Jerry.

"Uh...yeah?"

The shock of the past thirty seconds is a lot for my brain to process.

This date has been a doozy, but a small part of me relishes the crazy. Telling my best friend Ivy about all the insane things I endured will be a dollop of joy in the cruel world of blind dating. A gloriously tanked date is just fuel for our cause.

"You don't mind if I take the rest of your food home, do you?"

I frown, my mouth trying to form words, but unable to pick the right ones. Too much time passes.

"Well, do you?"

"Is it...for your dog or something?"

His brows form a V, and he's looking at me like I'm the weird one.

"No. I told you, I don't have a pet," he says with indignation, like I haven't been paying enough attention to him.

I snap my mouth closed as I hear my mother's voice in my head, telling me to stop catching flies.

I feel like standing up and asking the room, "Do you see what I'm dealing with here?" I can even picture executing it in a near-perfect Jerry Seinfeld voice.

"Okay...um...yeah, I guess that's fine if you...take it." Honestly, I don't have the energy to dig into this. The stress of the evening has reached a level I can't disguise with humor anymore. I grab my purse from beneath the table and leave some cash beside my plate.

"You know what, I'm just gonna head home. Thanks for the company...I guess. I..." I shake my head as I trail off, still at a loss for words.

"Oh, you don't wanna go for a walk or get some dessert somewhere?"

Wow. He's very optimistic about the way this has panned

out. My chair squeaks as I bolt up, and I have to grab it before it topples over.

"That's okay, I've got an interview in the morning. I should turn in early tonight. This was...an evening...out."

*Smooth.* State the obvious. No need to sugarcoat it. "I'll tell Cynthia you said hi."

I slide my handbag over my shoulder, gripping the strap tightly. I manage a small wave and hastily order an Uber while I head toward the exit before Jerry can respond.

My steps quicken, and I release a breath as I make it out of the restaurant doors and into the cool night air.

I hate blind dates.

Only four more to go.

# CHAPTER TWO

## EMBER

I crash through my apartment door, dropping my handbag and coat on the entryway table. Things roll out of my purse, hitting the floor, but I don't care; my sweatpants are calling.

The TV blares obnoxiously, and I rush for the remote, patting my cat on the head and giving him a rough little back rub.

"What ya watching, buddy?"

My cat watches TV. He has a screen-time problem. He's not random about what he watches either. His full name is *Nicolas Cage* because the day I moved here, he waltzed into my apartment like he owned the place, perched himself on the arm of my sofa, and stayed until the credits of *National Treasure* rolled across the screen. I think that was what hooked him—the enigma that is *Nicolas Cage*. Since that day, he's made himself at home, and I haven't sent him away. He'll knead that darn remote till he's found a show to match his mood. Unfortunately, he stomps on the volume buttons too.

He must be feeling cheery tonight because he's chosen a cooking show. I avoid him on days when he chooses true crime.

He's a cool cat, but it's also possible he's committed a few crimes and I can't confidently say that he hasn't gotten away with murder.

I leave him to change and wash my face, tying my hair in a messy bun. (Because is there any other way? It's the hair equivalent of removing a bra.)

Comfy status has been attained. Sugar must follow.

With a bowl of ice cream in hand, I settle into the space on my couch that's molded to my shape. It hugs me as I sink into its lumpy cushions. A grin springs across my face, and I bask in the luxury of slouching without having to worry about anyone correcting my posture.

That first scoop of deliciousness melts in my mouth, and I sigh heavily. I'm so grateful for this space. Having my own apartment has given me a sense of security I didn't know I craved, and making it my own with a colorful collection of thrift store finds has been so much fun.

If these walls could talk, they'd tell you a very short, sad story, though: *Twenty-five-year-old spinster attempts to eat her weight in ice cream.*

Even with their slightly judgmental tone, I've come to love the walls and the people surrounding them.

A rapid succession of knocks echoes through my door, accompanied by hushed voices, the occasional "shh" of an old lady, and what sounds like playful jabs, judging by the chorus of "ouches." I approach the door with quiet steps, pressing my ear against it to eavesdrop on the unfolding comedy spectacle beyond, determined not to disrupt the hilarity.

"Calm down, Gail. The girl won't divulge anything with you acting like Barbara Walters gettin' ready to interview Oprah."

"Oh, hush. We both know you're the Oprah in this friendship. And I am calm, I just had too much rum cake after dinner. Ssshhh, I think she's coming."

"Ow! Why are your elbows so sharp?"

I swing the door open and Gail yelps, hands flying up to her chest.

"Gail. Opal. It's been a full ten minutes since I got home. You're getting slower," I greet them with my hands on my hips.

Opal side-eyes her companion as she makes her excuse. "This one had some rum to finish."

Gail elbows her harder. "Rum *cake*. I had rum *cake*, and you had some too." She spears Opal with a deadly look, silently threatening to hide her prune juice again.

The flowery scent that seems to embody every fiber of their clothes gently flows into my apartment. It's not an artificial odor, but one that comes from hours spent tending to and growing hundreds of potted flowers.

Since moving in two months ago, I've learned that Opal and Gail—best friends in their seventies—have made it their mission to fill every possible corner, wall, and nook surrounding the apartments with flowers. There's a rumor that it began with a bet that they've long since forgotten when they inadvertently discovered their green thumbs. Either way, I find myself living within a Disney painting, the courtyard, and now my apartment filled with vibrant colors growing out of each pot they've planted. I'm half-expecting mice to show up and offer to sew my clothes.

I immediately told them upon moving in that I would one hundred percent kill any plants they entrusted to my care. Gail and Opal must have taken my threat seriously, because they make it a habit to pop in for regular chats and tend to the plants, making certain I haven't had to endure the shame of anything dying on my watch.

"So, how'd it go? This one show any promise?" Opal asks, hope in her nosey, kind eyes.

I click my tongue. "Unfortunately not. This one was a giant *hell no*."

Groans and "whats" and "whys" follow. I give them a summary but tell them to wait for the blog for the juicy parts.

Opal shakes her head. "Well, that's a shame, dear. I hoped this one would be a second dater at least," she says with genuine regret in her voice.

I shrug, brushing off the remnants of disappointment. I'm not enduring these dates to find love. My only motivation is Hawaii. "It's okay. I mean, it's not like I expected Prince Charming from these stupid dates. That wasn't the goal, so it's fine. I'm fine."

Gail peers over my shoulder, her eyes fixed on the TV. "At least Nicolas is in a good mood."

"Yup." I nod.

"Such a sweet boy." Gail coos. She's just glad he's stopped digging up her petunias. They sandwich me in a hug, transferring their flowery scent as they pat my back and leave with promises of tea in the courtyard soon.

I plop my butt back down onto the sofa and slurp my melted ice cream while Guy Fieri goes to flavor town. The nation might crumble if that man changed his hairstyle.

My phone vibrates on the coffee table, making me jump. I glance at the caller ID, though it's pointless. My best friend Ivy is the only one who calls. Not to mention, I've blocked all the others.

"Hey, Vee," I mumble over a giant scoop of Tillamook.

"How much?"

"What are you talking about?"

"Pfff, how much?"

"Just one pint,"

"The date was a bust?"

"How many weirdos live in Aster? The statistics are shocking. Is it something in the water that draws them here?"

"Man, I love the weirdos. They make for the best articles. Hit me with it. What happened? Did he bring his mom?"

That did happen once, but thankfully not today. Let me tell you, it gets really weird when a man's mom wipes her son's chin while sitting next to his blind date.

Why all the blind date talk? Hold on to your seats, ladies and gentlemen, because this one's a doozy. I should premise this by stating that a blind date, let alone seven of them, is not something I would ever willingly subject myself to.

Enter the well-meaning best friend. When said best friend witnesses her BFF end a bad relationship, she gives advice to help her out of the bucket 'o pain she's waddling around in like a fly stuck in water. It's me. I'm the fly.

Together, we lamented all the duds out there and joked that it would be amazing if we received compensation for terrible dates. I would have been consoled with a tattoo with the quote, *"What are men, compared to rocks and mountains?"* But Ivy beat me in a staring contest—more like declared herself the winner—and decided that we would each go on seven (why even?) blind dates, which we'd chronicle in our blog, using the money it filtered in to escape to Hawaii next year.

And since Ivy ensures I don't live a life of a complete hermit with more cats than mismatched mugs in my kitchen, I let her drag me out into the world now and again.

"Your last post was hilarious, Em. I *cannot* believe he called you 'The wifing type'!"

Yeah. That was the cherry on top of *that* weird date. Don't get me wrong, I'm not like one of the cast members on *Seinfeld,* looking for the tiniest thing to nitpick about a person. I just seem to date legitimately weird men. Some have made me cringe, some have made me laugh (again, not in a good way), and a few have even elicited some tears.

"Well, tonight's date is right up there on the cringe scale. Maybe even top three."

"Tell me everything," her voice cracks as she tries to hide her amusement at my expense. "Wait, was this the guy your neighbor set you up with?"

"Yup. Her boyfriend's cousin. She should do more research on that family line before she commits. Some crazy mixed in with those genes."

"Spill."

"Okay, so he greets me and, two minutes later, launches into a speech about how strongly he believed in treating men and women as equals with all the conviction of a Kanye rant, which is also why he didn't stand or pull out my chair when I arrived."

"Solid first impression."

I give Ivy a summary of the rest of the night, leaving her in hysterics. I knew this one wouldn't disappoint.

"I'm a magnet for Aster's freaks. I should introduce these guys to each other so they can start a club or support group."

"You took one for the team."

"One? At this point, I'll be shocked if I ever come across a normal man," I lament.

"Normal is boring."

"I dunno. If boring means dating a nice guy who doesn't think the world owes him something and isn't determined to lord his control over others, then sign me up!"

"Em, I get it. I'm sorry. I just think you could do with the *teensiest* bit more risk in the dating department. But this is good. Diving back into the dating pool is the first step to finding a nice guy. And you deserve to be happy. Especially after—"

"Yeah...well, I'm only doing this for Hawaii," I insist. I'm so not ready for an actual relationship right now. I still believe in true love, but I have other things to focus on before I jump back on that bucking horse.

"He hasn't contacted you again? Because if he has, I'll—"

"I don't wanna talk about it, Vee. Let's just focus on Hawaii."

Just thinking about him knots my stomach as my eyes flick to the latch on my door.

"I'm sorry, Em."

I change the subject, not wanting to go to bed with that yucky feeling. "Well, Hawaii is calling, and the worse the dates, the better."

"True. Hey, don't you have a job interview in the morning?"

Oh, did I not mention that I'm currently unemployed, too? Yup, add that to the list of things I've got going for me.

"Yeah," I say, adding excitement to my voice. "I'm hopeful about this one. I've already had a phone interview for it. So tomorrow is just to meet in person to see if I'll be a good fit. It's actually just a few streets down from here, for that adventure company."

"Shania would be proud," Ivy declares, and I can hear the smile in her voice.

My eyes find the framed Shania Twain poster next to my TV. "She would," I agree softly.

We make plans to meet up for coffee and say goodbye. Then I change into my favorite PJs and get ready for bed, hoping tomorrow ends better than today.

# CHAPTER THREE

## EMBER

I spent the night overthinking every minor detail I needed to remember for my interview, finally falling asleep around one in the morning. It wasn't the worst night, but I could have done without the paranoia about my outfit choice or second-guessing whether I put the dryer on again.

Why don't dryers have longer cycles?

while I should have been sleeping, I made a mental pros and cons list to decide which shoes to wear. I plan to walk since the offices are just a few blocks from my apartment. And if I can walk somewhere, I will. It's cheaper than Uber.

At some point in my overthinking, I circled back to my shoes and how none of mine that say, "I'm a responsible woman who absolutely wears heels regularly," would get me further than a few yards without blisters.

Should I wear sneakers and swap them out before walking in? What do I do with my sneakers then? Take an oversized handbag to stash them in and risk looking like a crazy bag lady? I eventually decided to walk in a pair of flat pumps and switch to my power heels just before entering the building. Pumps are less comfortable than sneakers, but they're easier to hide in a tote without looking like a kleptomaniac.

I spend more time getting ready than usual because I believe in the importance of first impressions. The woman in the mirror looks good. It's not my usual style, but I figure corporate casual is what's expected. I'm wearing a pair of thrifted, high-waist black slacks and a cream satin blouse. It feels good to choose my own clothes again. While this is more formal than what I'm comfortable in, at least it's something *I* chose. There's nobody here to comment on how it washes out my skin or fits weirdly.

I sigh, releasing all those ugly memories.

I'm confident. *Ready.*

This has to work. I can't handle another job rejection, though they're easier to stomach than the interviews. Talk about a situation full of awkward potential. It turns out half of a marketing degree doesn't put me in the hirable category.

I've applied to so many jobs that twirling a sign while wearing a Statue of Liberty costume is looking like my only option. And let me tell you, I do not have the dance moves to see that through.

"You've got this, Em."

I've reached the encouraging-myself-out-loud phase.

I grab the protein smoothie I'd pre-made before my date last night because I couldn't risk a mess this morning with my track record. I'm also a low-blood sugar disaster waiting to happen if I don't eat within an hour of waking up.

Again, unwanted memories seep through, reminding me of how I used to hide that unfortunate struggle.

Nope, none of those thoughts today. *Especially* today.

I finish my smoothie and turn to gaze at my Shania Twain poster on the way out. I need all the Shania magic today.

Cherished memories wash over me this time, making me

smile. I'm so grateful for Ivy's mom introducing us to the enchantment of Shania, the three of us dancing in their living room, hairbrushes in hand. Those moments were so contrasted with my own home life that they forever cemented Shania as an emblem of freedom in my heart. She became the embodiment of everything I still tell myself I'll fight to become. I may be a little bit obsessed, but I only have one poster of her, so there's no need for therapy just yet.

"Wish me luck, Nicolas!" Shoulders back, deep breath in. I lock my door, giving it a little fist bump afterward. I treasure my cute little apartment. The feeling of safety isn't something you truly appreciate until you don't have it anymore.

My cheeks lift with contentment on my way down the hallway of flowers as I review my mental checklist one last time. Positive attitude? *Check.* Printed, but sad, resume? *Check.* Emergency snacks? *Check.* Power heels in my bag? *Check.* Awkwardness tightly tucked away? We'll see about that one.

*Let's go girls!*

# CHAPTER FOUR

## COLTON

Grinning like a proud parent, I navigate onto the street where my company stands tall. However, my gaze, initially fixed on the building with adoration, is soon captivated by a graceful figure hopping along the sidewalk, drawing my attention away.

I chuckle as I watch her muttering to herself, caught in the midst of an uncoordinated effort to remove a shoe while maintaining her hop-walk.

My mind floods with a barrage of questions as I slow my pace, attempting to avoid any semblance of creeping, yet unable to tear my gaze away. She exudes a blend of frustration and beauty and I'm incapable of looking away.

I'm vaguely aware that I might be coming across as a lurker, yet I can't look away. I also need to focus on the road while I'm driving, but this woman has opened the page of a story and shoved my face in it.

Another shoe emerges from her bag, and a sense of triumph washes over me as I receive a new piece of the puzzle. With flat shoes off and fancy ones on, it seems like some sort of before-work shoe switch is taking place.

Who is this woman? My curiosity and fascination with the narrative of someone's life are what makes me good at my job, but something about this beautiful hopping woman draws me in.

I drive past, puffing out my lips. My speed would have entered the creep zone if I'd slowed down more. She's a shrinking figure in my slightly crooked rearview mirror as I turn into our private parking. Something tugs at me to root for her.

I risk one more glance.

She did it! My smile doubles as I celebrate her successful shoe swap. My joy at witnessing her wardrobe juggle is slightly overshadowed by the realization that I have no way of finding out more about her.

As I maneuver my Grandpa's 1973 Ford F250 into its familiar spot, I push aside those lingering thoughts. Removing my sunglasses, I slip them into the same weathered space where he used to toss his hat before settling into the driver's seat of this vintage truck, now mine. Inside the cab, the lingering scent of his freshly polished boots wraps around me like a comforting embrace, the truck holding onto his memory as tightly as I am.

Sure, I can afford a new vehicle. The company I started from scratch has made me a wealthy man. But looking after and driving this truck helps ease a bit of my guilt now that my grandfather's gone.

Posters of happy, smiling couples in a variety of locales greet me from the lobby's white walls. My vision for the space that houses The Adventure Project was to embody the spirit of adventure my grandad radiated his whole life. The space is open, light, and inviting, having been renovated to encourage creativity and teamwork. Natural wood and sleek whites cover every surface, as well as a concerning amount of plants.

Pushing through the lobby doors, I smile at our receptionist. "Good morning Mrs. Sullivan."

At fifty-two, she's the oldest employee by far, but I'll be screwed if she ever leaves. Her experience is invaluable, and she keeps us all on our toes. She's wearing her light brown hair in its trademark neat twist and dressed in a floral print that only hints at her softer side.

"Mr. King, I keep telling you to call me Maggie."

I turn to face her while I continue walking backward toward my office. "No can do, Mrs. Sullivan." We do this same dance every few days. She tries to get me to call her by her first name, and I charm her into a bashful grin.

"Oh, you!" She blushes, swatting her hand as I push the door open with my back.

Ethan gives me a chin lift and finger guns as I pass his office. "Big bro, looking sharp."

"You could at least look busy, Eth," I say before turning into my office.

With half of one wall made entirely of glass, I still catch glimpses of him as I settle at my desk. I ignore his return gesture since it's far less polite than finger guns. Little brothers have an inborn drive to piss off their siblings.

I get right to scanning emails, flagging ones that need my immediate attention. There's a light tap on my door before it opens slightly.

"Good morning, Colton."

"Hey, Lemon, what's up?"

She taps her red fingernails rhythmically against the door, her body arching in a seductive pose. Her chin tilts in a practiced pose, making me think she read this move in a magazine somewhere.

"Lisa said to remind you she won't make the meeting this morning. She's got one more interview."

"Thanks. I'll see you in there in a minute."

"Okay...um...see you in there." Her eyes drop down and then back up as she retreats with a coy lift of her mouth. I know she's trying to bridge the gap and turn our working relationship into something more, but I promised myself that I would keep this business as my focus—not that Lemon is my type, anyway. I'm sure she's used to guys falling at her feet with her blonde hair and Southern charm. But it's just not my thing. Hopefully my lack of response sends the message that I'm not interested.

I'm shuffling papers on my desk when my phone rings. "Colton."

"Why d'you answer your phone like that?" My brother's lazy voice drips with the tone of reproval only a sibling can master.

"Like what?"

He ignores my reply. "I saw Lemon leaving your office. You finally ask her out?"

My eyes close, and I pinch the bridge of my nose. "Ethan, if I'd known hiring my brother would involve so much meddling, I might've reconsidered."

"Ha, it was me or Tom, the guy who spits when he talks. I still have his interview details on file. I can call him if you're in the mood for the next subscription box to be saliva-themed."

"I'm gonna look into that adoption theory. We can't be related."

"Colt, stop being the buttons on my fancy green shirt. You need to go on a date."

I tap my pen on my desk, preparing for this conversation to go nowhere.

He's calling me difficult yet he's the one that makes weird metaphors to get his point across. But I'm not willing to move the boundaries I've set. "You mean the shirt you stole from me."

"Fine, but I saved that shirt from a life of drudgery and wore it on a date like the fashion gods intended."

"Drudgery?" My turn to make fun of him. Ethan has always been a reader, but the old English words he throws out are easy ammunition when I need to irritate him.

He scoffs. "Yes, drudgery, the abyss that is the dark recesses of the back of your closet. Shame on you. That shirt deserved better, so I stepped in."

If I don't steer this conversation, we'll still be talking about nothing in two hours. It's a special gift we have.

"Don't you have work to do?"

"Lemon seems like a fun person. I heard she likes rock climbing." And we've circled back to things I don't want to discuss. I lean forward, shaking my head at the smirk he wears with his feet crossed on his desk.

"I can't afford distractions right now, Eth. The last subscription drop was a success, but we've got a lot of work to do before the next one. You know how much this means to me, man. Besides, why would I look for a relationship right now? I'll be leaving for months, maybe even a year."

He looks taken aback, his frown deepening. "That long?"

"Maybe," I shrug with heaviness. "If I decide to go ahead with this plan, then I'll be in Salt Lake City for at least six months. But I've done this before, and I know getting a new company up and running can take longer than that."

"Colt..." The humor has left his voice. "I know you're trying to atone for something. But Gramps was proud of you. He wouldn't want you working yourself like this. It's okay to have a personal life. Let me take on more. I can shoulder some things."

"Thanks, Dr. Phil. Can I get back to work now?"

He sighs again. "Yeah, I'll see you in the meeting."

We hang up, and I give him my annoyed big-brother stare

as I rise from my seat. I love him, but I doubt we'll ever see eye to eye when it comes to our convictions on dating and relationships.

Bright morning sun floods the boardroom as I walk in. It's my favorite kind of light, the kind that splays through large windows and makes the space feel warm and inviting.

I claim a seat on one of the velvet sofas. It's an unconventional setup for a boardroom, but it's functional.

Behind me, the clicking of heels on hardwood gets louder. *Lemon.* Her advances are becoming more annoying than anything, and I'm starting to worry about whether she's working here for the right reasons. I hope she's just really driven and goes for what she wants, but time will tell.

I pull at the knees of my faded jeans before sitting while our small products team filters in. At the moment, there are only five of them, though they've formed a sort of work-family over time.

Jed has been my longest-standing employee. We shared the same classroom from elementary to high school, and we even teamed up on the baseball field. While I pursued my dreams beyond Aster, Jed opted to stay close to home, settling down and starting a family. He was hustling as a car salesman until I convinced him to join me in launching The Adventure Project. With his dependable character and fearless spirit, I knew I needed Jed's boldness beside me as I dove headfirst into building a new company.

Mallory and Lisa were my next hires once the company started growing. I eventually begged Ethan to work for me a few days a week while his house-flipping business was in its earlier stages. I needed someone I could trust; he needed another job that still allowed him to do what he loved.

Lemon was the last hire after the workload got too much for

the four of them, and now we're back at that point, hence Lisa's interviews today.

Plush blue couches hug bodies as everyone claims a seat. It's an unconventional setup for a boardroom—no giant table or stiff chairs here. But if we're going to brainstorm and talk our way through ideas for hours at a time, I want us to be comfortable while we do it. We're not riding around on scooters or taking slides to get to different floors, but I believe in a space that encourages discussion and fosters creativity.

Gramps would have liked that the room was more like a living room than a boardroom, although he'd probably have something to say about the color of the furniture or all the plants invading the place.

"Hey guys, have a seat." I tell the group. "Mallory, if you're good to go, you can start when everyone's settled,"

In the room, there's just one two-seater couch amidst the longer sofas. As I notice Lemon casting that familiar look, hinting at her intentions to cozy up, I swiftly relocate my files to the space beside me, quietly staking my claim on the entire couch.

Ethan gives me a knowing smirk. For a moment, I regret not having the typical boardroom setup, if only to kick my brother's shin under the table.

Mallory clears her throat, making quick eye contact with each of us as she speaks. "Right. Lisa is interviewing someone, so it's just the five of us. She'll join us if she can."

The team members toss out stats and numbers, interspersed with nods, back pats, and the occasional "well done" and "good job, guys."

I offer my usual congratulations for working so hard. "I appreciate all the hours that went into making this a success," I say, a proud smile tugging up at the corners of my lips. The level of excellence and the quality of our product is truly impressive. As much as our team is still finding its feet, for the most part, they've avoided any significant setbacks without any casualties along the way.

"Next season's boxes need to top that. We need fresh ideas if we want to give people the best adventures of their lives. Jed, why don't you share the themes we discussed?"

An hour passes, and we take turns scribbling every concept onto a giant whiteboard. By the end, it looks like the psychotic ramblings of a madman. Words in bubbles and branches form a web of thoughts that would be concerning out of context. The assortment of handwriting that would cause anxiety in any other setting somehow works, forming a creature of ideas spreading its uneven tentacles across the board.

I love seeing all the possibilities for adventure. It reminds me that I'm doing something good, allowing people to create memories.

"Okay, that looks great so far. You'll break into teams of two as usual, once the new hire is acclimated. And then next week we're doing adventure tests."

A chorus of elation follows the announcement. Once per quarter, I take time with my creative team to test our products. It promotes team building while we conduct research and evaluate the customer experience of our adventures.

After they settle, I continue. "We'll be paying specific attention to the quality of the supplies we decide to send out with each box. Mallory, will you recap so everyone's clear on their projects?"

She summarizes what we hashed out on the board, but my attention is drawn to the hallway.

I recognize that hair.

Shoe-shuffle lady.

"I'm sorry, Colton, did you say something?"

A slow smile builds on my face, but the awkward silence in the room pulls me back.

*Crap.* I said that out loud.

I clear my throat and tug at my shirt collar. "Nothing... sorry. Carry on." As Mallory continues, I force a tight-lipped smile and reach for a water bottle, trying to focus. But the puzzle pieces begin to connect. Is shoe shuffle lady the new hire?

Mallory's voice fades into my consciousness again. "We'll meet later this week to fine-tune these. Lemon, you'll be paired with the new hire in a few weeks to show them our full product procedure. Oh, and there's a box of pastries by the coffee. I was told some of you need to eat, or you'll get grumpy." Her eyes are big, and she's smirking at Ethan and me as she says it.

I like to think I'm rarely grumpy. Gramps lived his life with the kind of optimistic approach that made every obstacle surmountable. He instilled the same attitude in my dad, and I hope he'd look at me and say I inherited that part of him too.

Ethan gives her a mock salute as he and Jed beeline toward the coffee bar. I lean to peer around some of the plants, trying unsuccessfully to see inside Lisa's office. The walls in this building are fifty percent glass, but the one time I want that to work in my favor, it doesn't.

Lemon and her overpowering perfume edge closer, her eyes following the path of my stare. She brushes a hand on my forearm, but when I pull away, she doesn't look even a little deterred. Instead, she perches on the back of the sofa and moves even closer.

"So, Colton, I've been here two months and still don't know the best places to grab lunch. Maybe you could show me?"

Ethan grins at me from behind her, shoving a pastry in his mouth. My eyes narrow at him before shifting back to Lemon.

"Mrs. Sullivan usually orders my lunch. You should ask

her. She'll have the best recommendations." I keep my voice friendly, not wanting to embarrass her.

She bites the corner of her lip, and I'm not sure whether she's disappointed or if she's just trying to flirt again. "Okay, yeah, thanks. I'll ask her." When she twirls her hair around her finger, I have my answer. No disappointment, only more determination.

This has been sufficiently uncomfortable. "Good meeting, guys." I lamely announce to the room as I retreat to my office. Ethan follows me inside as I take a seat.

"Heard of knocking?"

"Knocking is for acquaintances. I've seen you naked. Also, we have the same parents, and I know you have pajamas with teddy bears on them."

"You have the same pajamas."

"That's beside the point. You gonna take Lemon out for lunch?" He wiggles his eyebrows but wisely takes a step back, suspecting I might punch his arm for being annoying.

"Ethan, I'm not interested in Lemon. Can we close the file on that topic, please?"

"Okay, well, you know my stance on this. Oh, and Jed said you left before he could tell you that the new paper samples arrived. He wants you to look at them."

"Thanks," I say, rising from my seat. I might as well walk over there now...and maybe peek into Lisa's office while I'm at it.

Ethan tosses something at me as I round my desk. "Mrs. Sullivan says eat this."

"You'd make a good delivery boy if this job tanks."

He leaves but not before punching me in the arm.

# CHAPTER FIVE

## EMBER

I never know how to sit at these things. It's like my body forgets how to be normal. I'm perched on the end of the chair, my back straight and my fingers twisted in knots. At least my hands are hidden so Lisa, my interviewer, can't see my nervous fidgeting.

Does anyone actually enjoy interviews? I psyched myself up this morning, my power heels doing their Elle Woods magic. But now that I'm here, I'm sweating in places it's too early to sweat in. And I seem to be overdressed. Lisa looks like she could be headed to the beach or the movies in her relaxed jeans and Patagonia tee.

Is this a bad omen? It took a lot for me to apply for this job, and I don't know how I'll recover if this doesn't end well. If I could wave a wand and skip all the awkwardness of the interview and the first few weeks in a new environment, I would.

*It's better than waving a sign.*

I should've picked a career that lets me work from my couch.

Thankfully the people I've met so far seem genuinely friendly. Mrs. Sullivan was just the sweetest, and Lisa isn't giving off intimidating vibes, which is helpful for my already fragile nerves.

Her mouth purses to the side while she reads through my resume. This is the part where the cartoon Ember visibly and loudly gulps. My resume isn't impressive. Her squinty eyes confirm.

"So Ember, I'm going to be honest, your qualifications aren't extensive—"

*Told you.*

"But your experience can make up for that."

*Be still my heart!* I perk up, sitting straighter in my chair again.

"As you know, this is a creative position. We're looking for someone who can bring a unique set of ideas and perspectives. Can you convince me that's something you can add to this team?"

Wow. No pressure.

Flashes of the past six months roll through my mind. *Heartbreak. New city. Job interviews. Blind dates...*

"Well...my friend and I—we have this blog...It sort of chronicles all the failed blind dates we've been on. That feels like a lifetime's worth of adventure," I laugh nervously. "It's not always pleasant, but I've learned a lot from the experience. And it's given me a unique perspective on what people enjoy doing. I grew up in a small town, and moving away has led me on a lot of new adventures too."

This is such a long shot that I might as well tell her "thank you and goodbye". But to my surprise, her smile grows as I continue talking.

"Sounds like you're not afraid to try new things."

Oh, Lisa. If only she knew the guts it takes for me to put myself out there each time. A questionable dose of peer pressure from my BFF and a desire to stick my toes in some white sand while drinking a froofy drink are what got me into this blind date situation—not guts, and certainly not confidence. In those aspects, I'm seriously lacking. And moving towns was a matter of survival, not adventure. But Lisa doesn't necessarily know any of this, and I need a job, so I'm rolling with it.

"The comments and feedback from our readers about their own experiences have given me a lot of different perspectives too."

That sounded insightful. *Take that, Statue of Liberty outfit!*

A few minutes later, Lisa looks triumphant as she sticks her hand out across the desk. "Welcome to The Adventure Project team, Ember."

I scoot a little further on my chair. Any more and I'll fall off. "I'm...I'm hired?" I dazedly shake her hand, hesitant to believe my luck may be changing. Did I really just manage to land a job that doesn't require acrobatic skills?

Lisa flashes her white teeth, a bit of relief in the way her shoulders relax. "You are. I think you'll be a great addition to this company."

Would it be too dorky to squeal with happiness? I can feel all the anxious butterflies in my stomach breathing a sigh of relief because they've been told to stand down. *At ease, boys. She's got the job. You can take a break for now but don't get too comfortable. She's bound to find herself in some new anxiety-inducing scenario soon.*

Lisa stands, and I follow her in a happy daze. "If you're up for it, I'll introduce you to our CEO and the products team you'll be working with. They should be wrapping up their meeting any minute now."

"Sure, that sounds great." I follow Lisa as our collective footsteps create a beat on the hardwood floors. She leads me to a room that looks like an Ikea living room display—also, so many plants. It reminds me of my apartment, and I half-expect

Gail and Opal to pop out from around the corner to water everything.

"Actually, can I use the restroom first?" I need a minute to collect myself before meeting more people. I'm still a little shocked at how this is all panning out.

"Of course. You can meet me in this room when you're done. You remember where the restrooms are?"

"Yes." *Nope.* "I'll just be a few minutes," I assure her. *Assuming I don't get lost.*

Lisa's lips tug up with kindness as she heads into the Ikea room. I turn, trying to recall where those restrooms might be.

I'm horrendous with direction, but I seem to be making a good first impression, so I'll be keeping that deficit to myself for now. My thoughts are still a mashup of navigation struggles and mild shock over getting a job. The restrooms were just around the next corner on the left, I'm sure. I glance behind me and frown. Okay, maybe seventy-five percent sure about that.

I'm still having second and third thoughts about the restroom location when I round the corner, squeaking out something between a yelp and a gasp when I get the fright of my life. I could kiss the ground in gratitude that I manage to stop a second before colliding with the broad chest I'm now facing.

My eyes close and my hands fly to my collar, making me look like my grandmother when someone mentions consenting adults knockin' boots.

"I'm so sorry! You scared the crap out of me," I breathe out.

I open my eyes again, and my skin tingles when I take in the man standing before me, the one wearing a perfect broody frown like he studied a GQ magazine. My muscles release a smidgen of tension at the concern etched between his brows. He's tall with perfectly mussed, dark blond hair. His shoulders are strong, and the way he's cradling something in his hands highlights the definition in his arms. I suspect the T-shirt he's wearing must be one of those fancy, expensive ones because of the way it fits him so well. My eyes dart down to the jeans completing his casual style as my brain struggles to categorize him.

*Does he work here?*

That fright must have scrambled my brain even more than I thought because it's the only explanation for what I say next.

"Ohmygosh! Is that a hamster?"

He still hasn't spoken when he lifts a perfect eyebrow, glances down at his hands, then brings his eyes back to mine, as the corner of his mouth lifts. He stares at me with a smirk on his too-handsome face, as if he knows something I don't.

And then the Adonis speaks, his deep voice laced with humor. "It's a muffin."

*Kill me now.*

"Oh, so *not* a hamster, then. Well, I'm just gonna find a cliff to jump off," I squeak, hitching a thumb behind me.

*I'd like one order of a hole in the ground to swallow me up, please.*

Why did my brain see a hamster, for crying out loud?

*Great first impression, Em.*

Maybe I'm having a stroke. I take a small step back as I flatten my lips together, making small nods with my head.

This is going swimmingly. And because I can't leave without adding some extra awkwardness, I point a finger gun at him and make a clicking sound as I turn to attempt a swift exit. But before I can escape or disguise the flush covering my face, I feel his hand gently wrapping around my elbow.

"I'm afraid I can't let that happen."

*Yeah, that's what I was afraid of.*

My eyes are pinched shut as I pivot to face him. I'm not ready to open them, since I don't know how to escape this situation without further mortification. Not to mention, the butterfly sergeant in my tummy is rallying the troops again. *Attention boys! Flutter! She's talking to a hot man. More fluttering! She's already made a fool of herself! This is not a drill!*

My eyes pop open, and whoa. I'm caught off guard again by how attractive this man is. His jawline is such a thing of beauty that it's messing with my head. "I'm sorry about the hamster thing. It looked like a hamster for a second, but I can see now it's clearly *not* a hamster."

*Stop saying hamster, Ember.*

His mouth angles with a half-grin, and dammit if it's not the nail in my coffin.

"I hope you're not committed to that whole cliff-jumping thing. Lisa would kick my butt for making her go through the trouble of finding someone else to hire again."

"Well, it's that or buying a one-way ticket to a remote island, but if you can forget the last two minutes ever happened, then I guess I could reconsider."

He clenches his teeth, sucking in air with a regretful smile, then leans a large shoulder against the wall. It's unfair how smooth he makes it all look.

"And here I was, looking forward to sharing the hamster story with my grandkids one day. But Lisa can be scary when I make extra work for her, so I'll agree to your terms."

Pushing off the wall, he sticks his hand out toward me. "It's a pleasure to meet you. I'm Colton King, and I don't own a hamster."

*Shake the man's hand, Ember.*

*He's an attractive guy, not a raccoon.*

Wait...King...

*Crap.*

He's my boss.

Of course he's my boss. Because I'm an overachiever when it comes to embarrassing situations.

I rush to shove my hand into his, trying not to let the contact distract me. "Ember Hayes."

He releases my hand and takes a small step back, but that darn smile is still there. "I'm assuming Lisa gave you the job, seeing as you're roaming the halls?"

Now my grin matches his. "She did. I'm excited to get started." Even though I have no idea what I'm doing.

Colton is about to say something else, but Lisa's cheery voice interrupts.

"Oh, there you are. I was coming to check on you. Great, I see you've met Colton. If you're ready, I'll introduce you to the rest of the team."

"Uh, sure, I'll follow you."

I spend the next thirty seconds telling myself to calm down. It's not like I've never seen an attractive man before, and I can't afford to let my reaction to my new boss's smile ruin this opportunity.

*You've never seen one who had this effect on you, though.*

# CHAPTER SIX

## COLTON

I follow Lisa and Ember, still clutching the hamster muffin.

*That was cute.*

There's no way I could eat this thing now. I might have, but also *definitely* did squash it beyond being edible to avoid colliding into the alluring shoe-shuffle lady who is now my employee.

We pass the kitchen, and I drop the mangled muffin on the counter that's right beside the door. Ember catches me in the act as I turn back to follow them, and the way her lips curl into a smile tells me she saw what I just did.

I try to ignore what that lift of her mouth does to my insides.

Also, note to self: Stop calling her "shoe-shuffle lady."

We enter the boardroom, and Lisa introduces Ember to the group. The product team is the one I work with most closely, so it's important that everyone gets on well. We have just under fifty employees in total, but these are the faces I see regularly.

And then it hits me that the alluring woman from this morning is my employee. There's no reason to think anything of it...right? I'll be fine focusing on my company, as I always have. Women have never been a distraction for me. My only concern is that she assimilates nicely with the group's dynamics. The company has grown quickly, and I need this small team to work well together. It wouldn't be a good idea to blur any lines.

So far, things have been going okay with employee relations, besides being unsure whether the last hire, Lemon, is the right long-term fit for the team. Hopefully, everything will be resolved, Ember's addition will go smoothly, and Lemon's flirting will stop.

I watch the interactions carefully, noticing how Ember seems to be getting along well with everyone from the start. Ethan sidles up next to me, his mouth quirked in one corner.

"What?" I snap, but it's more of a "back off" warning than an actual question.

That smirk he's wearing is dangerous. It usually means he's plotting something that will inevitably end up in a mess or more work for me. His shoulder bumps mine. "The new girl is cute."

"She's a woman, not a girl. Do I need to send you to HR for training again?"

"You know what I mean. I'm surprised you even noticed she's a woman. I was beginning to think you were a robot."

"This again? Can we fast forward to the part where I tell you to shut it, and you punch me and leave me alone?"

"Sure, but I saw the way you looked at her. There sure are some pretty fish in this pond," he replies smugly.

*For the love...*

"Ethan." I rub my forehead and drag my hand down my face.

He steeples his fingers and wiggles them. I've got to distract him before he gets to the planning stage of his matchmaking schemes.

I force a laugh, attempting to convince him that I'm perfectly at ease and not at all unsettled by the quirky brunette Lisa just hired. "This place needs my focus. And I told you, I'm too busy for a relationship. Even if I were ready for one, I don't think my employee pond would be the most appropriate place to go fishing."

"It's the perfect pond. You're in this pond all the time. You never visit any other ponds."

"Did you bump your head? Stop saying pond."

He turns his troublemaking face and looks me straight in the eyes. "*Pond.*"

"You're an idiot. Get back to work."

He walks away, laughing as he says, "This is gonna be fun."

Honestly, that's what I'm afraid of.

# CHAPTER SEVEN

## EMBER

"Let me help you with that," Ethan says.

"Nope, I've got it," I breathe, struggling to haul the five grocery bags I barely manage to lift from the trunk.

He watches with raised eyebrows and a slow blink. He doesn't think I can do it.

*Ha! I'll show him.*

But I suppress a moan, my fingers and shoulders burning with the weight. I have no idea why we needed so many groceries for a milkshake adventure. These muscly men don't know how to shop conservatively.

Colton rounds the corner, ending the phone call he answered as we parked outside his parents' home. I'm not freaking out at *all* about meeting their mom, by the way. My raised heart rate is purely the result of drinking too much coffee this morning.

He wears a scowl as he takes in the scene. His phone slides into his pocket while an upturned palm gestures my way. "What the heck, Eth! Why is she carrying all the bags?"

Ethan raises his hands like he tried to help a porcupine cross the road but it hissed at him. "She said she had it."

"*She* is standing right here," I grunt from the porch. And if I stand here any longer, my arms will pop out of their sockets like a tortured doll. It feels like I'm carrying fifty watermelons in each hand, but I refuse to put the bags down. Not after I made such a fuss over doing it myself. It's a matter of principle.

*Suck it up, Hayes.*

"The door?" I say, trying hard not to sound like I'm dying or that my hands are about to fall off.

Colton stomps up the steps, muttering to his brother as he passes him. When he reaches the top step, he rings the doorbell before using his large hands to pry the bags from mine. I shoot him a glare, even though I immediately roll my aching shoulders. Yes, my fingers are also happy not being threatened with amputation, but I could have done it.

My chin juts out in protest, and I'm still thinking about throwing out an "excuse me" when the front door swings open.

An ethereal woman with grayish-blonde hair greets us, her wide smile making me frown.

"Boys! Oh and who is this beautiful thing? You didn't tell me you were bringing a guest!" She swats Colton's arm before folding me into a hug that sets off my fight-or-flight response. And I am solidly on the *flight* side of that camp, except I'm currently being held hostage and can't execute my body's instinct to escape. My family aren't huggers. Is this normal?

"Hey, Mom, be right back," Colton chimes as he disappears into the house. Ethan places a kiss on his mother's cheek while I'm still frozen in her arms, taken aback by this unexpected predicament. It takes me a second to decide I should do something with my hands, so I lift one and robotically pat the back of the lady who's hugging me like I'm hers.

Just as fast as the hug began, it's over. I'm released, and my face is cupped in warm hands. "I'm Jeanie."

Colton appears at her side, "Sorry, Mom, this is Ember. Ember, this is our mother, Jeanie." He turns to her, but his words are meant for me. "I had to put a few heavy bags down in the kitchen."

"Oh, no worries, sweetheart. Come in, come in." She herds us all inside, and I follow her cheery chatting. We reach a kitchen that's so exquisite I expect Ina Garton to pop out and tell me to use only *good* olive oil. Beautiful white countertops and cream cabinets form an L-shape, perfectly angled to receive the sunlight spilling through the wide, arched windows. In the middle is an island with more than enough space for a life raft that could sustain both Jack and Rose.

"So, you need to use my kitchen?" she asks, going to the fridge and taking out a pitcher of tea.

Honest-to-goodness flower petals are meandering inside of it.

I'm not sure what alternate universe I've walked into, but this whole scenario is freaking me out. Not only am I in my boss's parents' home, but the huge house is peppered with so many personal touches. It's not a museum and I didn't know wealthy people had *normal*-looking homes. The genuine warmth in the atmosphere is a shock to my system.

Today is the first day of a week of adventure tests. It serves two purposes: team building, as well as getting a feel for the activities in the subscription boxes.

We've been split into two groups for this one, with Lisa, Jed, and Lemon forming one team, while I've been assigned to the brawny brothers. Mallory couldn't make it, so we're evenly split.

The subscription boxes come with a premium book featuring a unique date idea on every page, along with a designated space for attaching a printed photo. Each box offers the option to include an instant Polaroid camera and any necessary supplies for the planned activities of the date.

If I were in a relationship, I'd want one of our boxes. I'm all for dinner and a movie, but you can't be apathetic about fun in a relationship.

It's pretty clear my last relationship lacked all of that. Somewhere along the line, I also seemed to misplace the art of having fun. Perhaps that's why I find myself idolizing Shania Twain. Her on-screen personas exude such carefree energy, always up for an impromptu road trip with her girlfriends. Today feels like a good opportunity to practice loosening up a bit.

"Yeah, thanks for letting us take over," Colton's voice brings me back. "We're making milkshakes. I don't have a smoothie machine, Ethan's kitchen isn't done, and Ember's is too small."

That's not exactly true. I could squeeze two giant men into my kitchen. But something about having people in the space that's become my sanctuary tightens my chest.

Jeanie fills three glasses with tea, the ice clinking as she hands one to each of us.

"You can hang around, Mom. You don't have to leave."

"Oh, thank you, Colt, but I'm meeting Sheri for book club. I'll be back in an hour to taste your creations, though." Jeanie leaves after a gentle pat on my hand and cheek kisses for her boys.

I frown, watching her float away. I keep waiting for someone to utter a snide remark or passive insult, but it hasn't happened, and Colton looks like he genuinely wanted his mom to stay.

Is this some kind of interactive-theater art piece? This can't be normal.

Being in Colton's family home feels oddly unfamiliar.

Compared to other teams I've been a part of, this one seems less formal, which isn't necessarily a bad thing. However, the overwhelming friendliness of everyone here leaves me questioning if there's something wrong.

I also realize Colton's so out of my league that it isn't even funny. That small fact is surprisingly comforting because it means I have no reason to worry about the temptation of any inter-office canoodling. Colton would never be interested in someone like me.

Today's adventure involves concocting a new milkshake flavor. Our mission: to recruit a brave taste-tester for our DIY creations and crown a champion. As the ingredients are spread out on the kitchen island, I can't help but notice a stark contrast between my modest selection and the hodgepodge amassed by the guys. While I opted for refined flavors to complement the classic vanilla, Ethan and Colton seem to have taken a more...adventurous approach.

Colton fiddles with the Polaroid camera that we're supposed to use to document each adventure, setting it beside our ingredients, and then handing me the blender jug.

Narrowed eyes squint toward my modest huddle of supplies.

"You can go first, Ice. Yours can sit in the fridge while we blend ours afterward."

"*Ice?*"

Ethan's tossing nuts into his mouth, chuckling while Colton's lip pouts to the side. "Looks like you've got a pretty vanilla theme going there. I'm not sure it'll earn you a win, but it seems fine...*safe,*" he declares with folded arms and a shrug of his shoulders.

Tha man is goading me. A challenge lights his eyes.

I lift one brow.

*Bring. It. On. Mr. Sexy Face.*

Wait—Nope. We'll not be acknowledging any sexiness, *Mr...Man Face.*

I'll work on that one.

"Vanilla is a classic for a reason." I cross my arms in response. This man is bringing something out in me that usually lies very, very dormant.

"Not disagreeing with you." Colton responds, his voice dripping with smugness.

I open the bag of pecans, throwing one at Colton. He doesn't even flinch when it bounces off his solid chest. Ethan watches, laughing while shoveling more food into his mouth. I throw a pecan at him too, which he dodges just in time.

It's scary how easy Colton makes it to forget that he's my boss. So much teasing and joking happens at the office, but I thought it was just the vibe there, that this is what happens while the team is hanging out and discussing fun things.

But I think it's Colton. He's the one that puts people at ease. He and Ethan have set a tone of camaraderie that's infectious.

"Whatever—" I eye their stash of ingredients, looking for inspiration for their own stupid nicknames. "Hang on, who bought bacon?" I frown at the weird assortment of ingredients. "Ew, salt and vinegar chips? Nope...gross. That can't go in a milkshake."

"Afraid to live on the wild side?" Colton chirps.

"I'm afraid you'll make your mother hurl when she tastes your witches' brew."

I don't know what's happening to me. I'm never this sassy. Maybe I was, once upon a time, but that girl was shushed a long time ago.

"Okay, new rule," Colton says with a sneaky glint in his

eyes. "Before we mix our milkshakes, the person to your right gets to either add or remove one ingredient from your recipe."

Ethan immediately agrees, seemingly unfazed that Colton is threatening to grip the tablecloth of our neatly organized table setting.

I like rules. And rule-lovers are not fans of change.

This isn't a big deal. I take a deep breath in, telling myself I can roll with this.

It takes effort to sound apathetic when I respond. "Fine."

"Great." He beams like he's proud of my decision. I don't like that look. It threatens the very clear walls I'm trying to keep intact. I'm only doing this to finish the task as quickly as possible.

We write our recipes on paper and I'm rather proud of what we come up with.

"Ember, what you got?" Ethan asks.

"Vanilla ice cream," my eyes flicker to Colton, finding the tiniest curl of his mouth. "With milk, pecan nuts, and maple syrup. I'll blend it finely so it's not gritty."

Ethan turns to Colton like he's the host of a game show. "What's your trump card, Colt?"

Colton says nothing. I watch as he slowly unfolds his arms while I try hard not to notice how nice they look. I fail. I'm pulled back to reality when he places an index finger on the package of bacon, sliding it my way.

*No!*

My jaw slackens as I gasp, eyeing the bacon like it's a spider he just dared me to pick up. There's a reason milkshakes are sweet. Bacon does not fit into that category. Sure, slap it on some waffles, but it does not belong in anything that'll be consumed through a straw. When my eyes return to his face, he's got the Polaroid pointed my way. I'm mortified when I hear it click before I shut my mouth. The man just documented me gaping like a fish.

"What are you—you can't...*Bacon?* Seriously?"

"It'll work. Trust me."

He doesn't know how difficult that is for me. I purposefully avoid situations where my trust needs to be put in others. I exhale, reminding myself that this is meant to be fun.

"Fine, but if your mother gags, I'm blaming you."

Colton goes about frying the bacon while I add ingredients to my jug. I feel like an intruder, watching him and Ethan joke with each other. Ethan keeps stealing bacon, and Colton repeatedly scolds him, claiming that it hasn't reached *peak crispiness* yet.

Eventually, he places three strips of perfectly fried bacon on a plate, pushing it my way. I look sadly at my perfectly measured ingredients, hating that I'm about to taint them with a savory trespasser.

Ethan and Colton watch as I eat one of the three pieces, then hold the other two above my jug. "Here goes nothing."

"Bacony goodness," Ethan hums. I shake my head, still unconvinced that this is a good idea.

I blend my milkshake and pour it into four Solo cups. I carry them to the fridge and Colton washes the jug and begins adding his watermelon-peach concoction. That's why the darn grocery bags were so heavy—one of them actually contained a watermelon.

"What's my punishment, Bro Mein?" Colton asks.

Ethan rubs his hands together, resting the tips of his fingers against his mouth. He pauses, then looks at Colton like he's on the cusp of a world-changing decision. "Gummy worms."

I throw my hands up, half spinning around. "You've got to be kidding me!"

"Don't knock it till you've tried it, Firecracker," Ethan says with a shrug. What is it with these two and the nicknames? He turns to Colton, raising a questioning brow. I'm praying Colton sees some common sense and vetoes that decision. We should have discussed vetoes.

"Done," he says. No argument.

I can't hide the disgusted look as I shake my head. "This won't end well."

Colton blends everything while I watch the two of them act like they're a couple of kids mixing mud pies. Their relationship seems so outlandish. But then again, I've never had siblings. The closest thing I have to a sister is Ivy, but our time together was limited while we were growing up. The dynamic unfolding before me feels like I'm witnessing an alien species. There's a sweetness to it, stirring up a sense of nostalgia for something I never had. It's like my heart is sad about observing something I missed out on.

Colton adds his milkshake to the fridge and a shudder runs over my shoulders when I read Ethan's recipe: chocolate, almonds, vanilla ice cream. Sounds delicious. But it's the last ingredient that is slightly offensive. I don't mind salt and vinegar chips on their own, but I can't fathom their addition to a sweet drink.

I look down at the chips and back up to Ethan's puppy dog eyes.

It's a stand-off, but he knows I hold all the power. Do I play it safe or take a wild chance and possibly throw up afterward?

"Don't do it, Flamethrower," he says.

More nicknames. I've got some catching up to do.

I can feel laughter bubbling up as I take in their serious faces. I roll my lips, nostrils flaring as I try to squash it back down. Ethan's fake lip tremble is my undoing.

"Fine! Keep your weird chip ingredient. And add chocolate syrup. You'll need it to overpower the salt."

Ethan and Colton both raise their hands, shouting exuberantly like they've just witnessed a game-winning touchdown.

It's a weird and disorienting feeling, being celebrated so purely. But I think I could get used to it.

---

# CHAPTER EIGHT

EMBER

This is fake, right? Nobody's mom is this sweet. I feel like I've accidentally walked onto the set of a sitcom.

Jeanie returned from her book club, just as Ethan finished blending his monstrosity of a milkshake. She began doling out more hugs the moment she swooped into the kitchen with her joyful joyousness. I had a two-second warning this time, which prevented me from turning into a troll statue when she wrapped her arms around me in motherly tenderness. Unfortunately, I couldn't completely avoid making a fool of myself and choked on my spit mid-hug when the warmth of her arms caught me off guard.

The three of us stand facing her on one side of the island while she sits on a barstool, smiling like we're royalty about to bestow a blessing on her peasant head.

My eyes dart to Ethan and Colton, gauging their reception of her eagerness. They seem to receive it with ease, so this must be a normal interaction.

It creeps me out. There's also a niggle of jealousy, but I shrug it off. It must have been pure torture to grow up living with someone who radiates this much happiness. I bet it made them sick, you know, with all that affection and encouragement. It's borderline child abuse.

Three cups of questionable contents sit before each of us. Colton picks up the first smoothie, and Jeanie is already bursting with excitement. "This one is a watermelon-peach blend with a subtle hint of gummy-bear."

There's so much pride in his expression, it'll be a miracle if Jeanie doesn't figure out this one is his. She claps her hands in anticipation, giving me a wink before picking up the offending concoction.

"Bottoms up," Ethan says after he taps his cup to Colton's.

We sip, tentatively. Frowns and mouth-smacking fill the room.

Jeanie is the first to speak. "It's—interesting," she offers before she chases it with a large gulp of water. "Maybe a tad too sweet, but I give it an A for creativity." She's the sweet one–this drink is diabetes in a cup.

Colton puffs his chest out, throwing a smug look my way. A smile creeps across my face when I catch it, and I shake my head.

He lifts the next drink. "This delicacy is a smooth blend of vanilla, maple syrup, and pecan nuts..." Then he pauses for dramatic effect, and the sneak dares to flicker his gaze to me before he continues. "And bacon."

*Oh, for Pete's sake.*

Jeanie lifts her eyebrows, the corners of her mouth dipping like she's impressed. This is the strangest workday of my entire life. I roll my eyes and take a generous gulp.

I wish I could say that it was repugnant and that I immediately gagged, but that would be a big, fat lie. The way the flavors complement each other so well catches me by surprise.

"Wow, that's actually really good," I admit, finding Colton's eyes and thinking I'd get another smug smile in return. Instead, his expression is gentle and confusing. It's a little tap on my shoulder and a whisper that says not all men are dirtbags.

*Doesn't matter. It's insignificant.*

Even if he were a saint, I have my reasons for staying away —good reasons. I shouldn't be thinking about my boss in any way besides professionally. Given, that's a little hard to follow when I'm throwing nuts at him and he's daring me to add bacon to a made-up drink. But I'm an adult and perfectly capable of redirecting my thoughts.

"Oh, that *is* good," Jeanie agrees with a frown. She's just as surprised as I am. I look over at Ethan and burst into laughter when he and Colton race to finish theirs.

Ethan releases a contented sigh. "Bacon makes everything better."

Then Colton introduces the last contender, which garners a skeptical look from his mother.

The three of them raise their cups, their sips far less generous than before, and immediately scrunch up their faces and shut their eyes. My stomach sours just watching them.

"Do I have to?" I whine. Maybe I'll get a pass on this last one.

Colton slams his cup down as if he's just downed a pint of beer. A tan forearm swipes across his mouth. "You've come this far. Don't back out now, soldier."

He's right. I have to do it. Part of moving away from home was to force myself to try new things and have more fun, and this is the most basic form of that. Backing out would be wimpy.

Before I can overthink it, I throw back a swig, swallowing as quickly as possible. I wouldn't call it pleasant, but the aftertaste isn't as repulsive as I expected.

Colton raises a hand, offering a high five. I slap my palm to his, annoyed by the jolt of awareness that comes with it.

"Alright, Momma," Colton begins. "Who gets bragging rights? Tell us which one is the best."

"Oh, the bacon-maple one for sure. I just loved that one so much!" she responds, without hesitation. Her southern accent seems to thicken when she's excited, making her even more endearing. It's like she tries to reign it in, but once something sparks that infectious joy, she loosens up and feels free to be herself.

"Well, you can congratulate Ember, then," he says with a huge grin. "That one was hers."

Jeanie rounds the island, embracing me again. It goes on no longer than the previous ones, but it hits me in the chest just the same. Every hug she gives seems to stir up something different: alarm, longing, peace. I'm still awkward as heck each time, but with enough exposure, I reckon I might start to crave those hugs.

*Dangerous territory, that.*

# CHAPTER NINE

## COLTON

We're playing dodgeball but with a twist. Instead of a ball, we've filled nylon stockings with paint powder and tied the ends. We're all wearing black shirts, so the hits will show. And the teams consist of guys versus ladies.

It's good to be in a group setting because having Ember in my parents' home yesterday was the weirdest worlds-colliding feeling ever. I've never done anything social that included both my coworkers and my family—aside from Ethan, obviously. There's no getting rid of that guy.

Today will be good for refocusing. I've got a plan to make the next two quarterly subscription releases a success, and then it's on to the next venture. I don't have time to think about Ember fitting into my mom's kitchen so well that I could imagine her there every weekend, or to micro-analyze her expressions or the way I enjoyed watching her loosen up and have fun.

Like I said, I don't have time for any of that. Any consideration of those things was a lapse in concentration, and that's all.

Ethan gathers everyone before explaining the rules. "Once

you're hit, you're out. We'll play three rounds, using a different color for each. The first team to take out the other team wins. No hits above the shoulders and wear your goggles at all times. Questions?"

A series of "nopes" choruses through the group. My eyes catch Ember and catalog her outfit. Everyone else is dressed in plain black, except for her. She's wearing black leggings and a black tank top with Shania Twain's face on it. My mouth tugs with a half smile that I quickly wipe off. There's no need to notice anything special about my employees besides their work efforts. It shouldn't matter that she looks that cute, bouncing on the balls of her feet.

At first glance, she seems excited, but when I take in the way she's chewing on her lip, I get the feeling it's nerves. And not the good kind.

But none of that should matter to me. She's got other women around if she needs anything.

"You're going down!" Lisa shouts as our teams separate to gather at opposite ends of the small open field that sits next to Aster's paintball property.

"Three minutes till game time!" We hear John, the paintball manager and today's referee, call out. Kyle is joining us from our finance department to make our teams even. He's a scrawny twenty-something-year-old who looks like he shuns the sunlight–great with numbers, but it's safe to say this isn't his forte. Maybe it'll be good for him...if he doesn't pass out.

The four ladies huddle together, and Jed looks at Ethan, Kyle, and me with a battle-ready face.

"What's our plan?" Jed asks, standing feet apart and arms folded. If it weren't for the tote bag of powder-filled pantyhose balls hanging across his chest, he'd look like a soldier planning for war.

Ethan shrugs like he doesn't understand the question.

"Dude, what do you mean? They're ladies. I doubt they practice throwing anything besides a fit. We've got this. We just attack. Simple." He turns to me with a small headshake, like this is a no-brainer.

Jed turns my way, gesturing toward Ethan with his palm up and a deadpan expression.

"I know." There couldn't be more exasperation in my voice. For the millionth time, I question why I hired Ethan. "He was dropped on his head as a child. Ethan, keep your mouth shut—you're not allowed to talk from here on out. You're lucky none of them heard that. Jed, what ya got?"

Jed runs us through a schoolyard strategy, and we break our huddle to take our positions. The ladies all have one hand in their circle and they do a chant before shouting, "Beyonce for life!" and breaking apart. The dirty looks they shoot us as they scatter around the field are surprisingly scary.

"Why didn't we make up a chant?" Ethan frowns.

"Would you like to join their team?"

"They look pretty fierce, but I'll wait to see how helpful Kyle is before making my decision."

I turn to see Kyle gaping with offense. Ethan throws his head back and laughs, then grabs Kyle in a rough side hug around the shoulder.

Kyle straightens, pushing his sleeves higher up his arms. "I may not be able to throw as well as the girls, but I can blind them with my reflective skin."

"It's good to know your strengths," Ethan says with a pat, then resumes his place.

John counts us down and blows the whistle to begin. We've each got four nylon balls, and Jed has used all of his within the first ten seconds.

The first two he aims at Lemon, but she dodges them easily. The third he hurls towards Mallory, deciding Lemon is too agile to waste his ammo. Mallory squeals, covering her face with her arms, but twists out the way just in time. Then she jumps behind Lisa, holding her like a human shield, and Jed hits his mark.

Lisa growls and walks off to the side, plopping down.

"I'm so sorry, Lis!" Mallory shouts.

Ember and Lemon run at us from either side, and both hit Kyle at the same time. While the girls raise their arms in triumph, Ethan and Jed use the celebratory distraction to take them both out. Before they bring their hands down, their stomachs are both covered by pastel yellow blobs, and frowns and gaping mouths replace their happy shouts. I'm too busy watching this all happen to even move.

Ember looks down at her shirt then spears a death glare at Ethan. "You shot Shania!"

"She'll survive." He retorts, laughing at her.

Lemon floats to the sideline, but Ember looks genuinely peeved. Not for the first time, I wonder if she's an only child.

Nope, doesn't matter. I don't need to know her life story or what makes her pretty head tick.

Although, the fact that I find her grouchy face kind of adorable may be problematic.

Mallory gives the next fifteen seconds a great effort, but by the end, she gets decorated in yellow polka dots, while Jed, Ethan, and I are still standing.

"Guys' game. Switch out your ammo!" John shouts after a whistle blow.

We load up with new balls, and the ladies' collective glare becomes even scarier.

"Kyle, you're at the back this time. Wave your arms around," Ethan explains, gesturing like a crazed octopus. "Distract them like that shiny vampire. Open some buttons on your shirt a little."

Kyle plants his feet and uses his thin arms to mimic Ethan's wavy movements.

"Add more crab. Yeah, like that, side-to-side with your legs. Evasive maneuvers," Ethan coaches.

I roll my eyes and laugh, catching Ember's pursed lips when John blows his whistle. The day has been fun so far, but Ember's serious expression tells me she wouldn't say the same. I'll catch her after this round and check in—a strictly platonic, employer/employee check-in. Routine, really, like a mental health check-in. Perfectly standard procedure.

Lisa also means business this round. She feigns an injury, taking advantage of Jed's pause for concern to take him out. He's not happy, but he handles it with Jed-like grace.

The ladies set their sights on Kyle next. He's sprinting back and forth in front of us like a crazy person. Ethan hits him with one of his balls, and I figure there's only a ten-percent chance it was accidental. Kyle turns, palms up, face aghast.

Ethan grins with clenched teeth, only slightly apologetic. "Sorry dude, your moves were distracting me."

Zero percent accidental.

All four ladies are still untouched. They zone in on me like a pack of zombies. I have no chance of survival. Ethan manages to take Mallory out, but I'm still pummeled by three balls.

The ladies jump up and down in celebration until Mallory shouts a reminder that they're still in the game. Lisa dodges two of Ethan's attacks. He makes a hero's attempt to take them down, diving as he throws his last ball at her.

He crashes to the ground. Lisa is hit, but Ethan's down, unarmed. Lemon is closest, but her toss sails wide right and misses the target.

"Throw me a ball!" Lemon shouts to Ember. Ember hesitates for a second, her mouth a flat line. She only has one ball left, and Ethan is rising to his feet while she hesitates. But then, something fierce and stubborn and beautiful swirls in her eyes. I don't want to notice the struggle I see there, but I do, and I can't help how alluring I find her, once again.

This much curiosity is dangerous, though. It threatens too many plans. And I'm still not sure what to do about it.

# CHAPTER TEN

## EMBER

Ethan shot Shania—in the face. I have to be the one that makes him pay.

It's not blood I'm after; I'm not a monster. But I'll be damned if I let Lemon have this moment, a moment moving in slow motion, sticky and slow like wading through mud.

It'll probably end poorly, but I have to take this shot. The first round was a giant flop. I'm not wasting the chance to prove myself.

I'm ninety-two percent sure I can make it, though most of that confidence is the result of consuming a concerning amount of sugar and caffeine in conjunction with the Martha Stewart podcast interview I listened to on the way here this morning.

Lemon's bugging her eyes at me. "Ember! Throw me a ball!"

I tune her out as I swing my arm back, but just like my fickle confidence, my throwing skills suck. The ball swooshes between Lemon and Ethan, hitting the ground with a shamefully anticlimactic plop.

Ethan is up, gathering ammunition while Lemon shrieks at

both of us. She's irate as she reminds me that catching Ethan unarmed and on the ground was a fluke. I've wasted that magical combination of circumstances in our favor, the only sliver of a chance our team had to win.

I sigh as I lean down to pick up more ammunition, facing the embarrassing truth that I'm the one who's *literally* dropped the ball. I'm still stuck in my head by the time I whip around, hoping to salvage the dregs of this round, but it looks like Ethan has already taken Lemon out and has turned his sights back to me.

I squeal, flinging two balls his way, but again, I clearly can't throw well enough to hit anything. He catches one of my balls and takes a step back as he aims, and the smug look on his face says I'm no doubt a goner.

He throws.

I jump.

I cover my face with my hands, and Shania gets another plop, right in the kisser.

"Stop hitting Shania, Ethan!" I laughingly growl out.

"All right, water break, then round three!" John shouts after another shriek of his whistle.

I shuffle over to Lemon while the group grabs water bottles.

I don't want to do this, but I know I owe her an apology. I messed up. I wanted so badly to win, not for the team, but for myself. That sounds selfish. It is selfish. And I let my team down.

"Hey, Lemon," I begin. I'm just going to get this over with before my stomach coils itself into a tight spring. "About not passing you the ball. I should have. It was selfish, and uh...I'm sorry."

She's taken aback, and her eyes squint into little slits like she's looking for an ulterior motive for my apology.

Either she finds her answer or decides I'm not worth the

effort to figure it out, and her eyes do a little roll before she continues walking with a tight smile. "It's fine, but remember, we're on the same team." And she stomps off, going to stand next to Colton.

Colton, whose eyes I've felt on me all morning, is watching our exchange intently. But I'm choosing to ignore it.

I grab a bottle and wander a few yards away, sitting on a hay bale with my back to the group. Sometimes I just don't feel like peopling, and I've definitely reached my limit for the day. The pressure to live up to being as strong and capable as I pretend to be has started to overwhelm me, and I know I need to step away and decompress without an audience. The fact that I can still sense Colton's gaze following me isn't making it any easier, though. He's probably doubting my ability to make any valuable contributions to this team, and definitely not staring at me for any other reason. That possibility is a dream I can't even allow to breathe, so I'll starve it of air until it fades away.

*Good plan.*

"Not a fan of team sports, huh?"

I startle, spilling water down Shania's face. Poor girl—she's been through it today.

"Jeez, Colton. Sneak up louder, will you." I'm still unsure where this sassiness comes from when I'm around him. "And I'm perfectly happy with team sports."

He eyes me with a softness that makes me want to throw a towel over his head. I don't need to be handled with care or figured out. That look says he's attempting to be understanding, kind words brewing in that kissable mouth, and I'll have none of it.

"I'll take you down next round, Boss Man," I say with a strained smile.

Those eyes. They still singe me with tenderness as he

continues staring at me, not uttering a word more. I'm afraid I'll blurt out my deepest fears if he continues looking at me this way, dipping a spoon into my soul and stirring up things that should be left the heck alone.

I fold my arms, turning my face away.

*Fine. If he wants to play the silent game, I can play too. I just can't look at the magical pools of blue he calls eyes while I do it.*

"Try having fun this next round. Don't focus on winning. Just be in the moment." He steps closer and I frown, my eyes flickering down to his feet and back to his contemplative face. "Enjoy the game and forget about winning or losing," he continues.

My heart is beating so solidly in my chest that I worry he'll see my pulse throbbing in my neck. I want to scoff at his words, make light of his Mr. Miyagi speech, but I can't.

A teasing response sits loosely on my lips, but the words won't spill out. Because deep down, I know he's right. And Colton's gentle approach was probably the best way for someone to drop a truth bomb on me.

How is it that he knew how to help me see a different viewpoint without making me raise my hackles or instinctively declaring to myself and the world that I don't need to be shown how to do something? I'm so used to doing everything myself.

Except, maybe...

Maybe that's not the best way. Maybe it's not the least painful way.

I nod, breaking contact with his too-gentle eyes and turning to face the field in front of me. I force out an exhale, fighting hard not to let the embarrassment permanently brand me.

*Move past it, Ember. Be kind to yourself.*

"Thanks," I whisper.

John blows his trusty whistle, and I feel Colton's hand

curving over my arm as he gives it a gentle squeeze. Then I watch when he pulls away and walks back to his team.

*Dammit.*

If the lingering warmth on my skin is any indication, I'm not sure if my walls are strong enough to protect me from what's coming.

# CHAPTER ELEVEN

## EMBER

Another day, another suspicious pairing with Colton. I have a feeling Ethan has something to do with it. For being part of a team-building exercise, I haven't spent much time with the rest of the team. But I'm the newbie, so I do what I'm told.

I'm in the back of an Uber that pulls into a parking spot at the nursery where Ethan texted me to meet Colton. Neither of us knows anything about today's challenge, but Colton is bringing an envelope that should include all of the details.

"I need a minute before I get out." I tell my driver after he parks, because that familiar twinge of anxiety rears its little head, eager to accompany me again today. If only it listened when I told it to scram.

Yesterday ended better than it began. Though painful to admit, the truth is that Colton's pep talk actually helped me loosen up and enjoy the last round of dodgeball. The girls still lost, but we laughed through the whole thing. Lemon and I even had a semi-pleasant interaction. It didn't last long, and we both felt a little weird after our celebratory high five, but I survived the rest of the day. I crashed when I got home, melting into the couch with Nicolas and spending the evening watching reruns of Bones. It was likely just research for his shenanigans.

Today, I'm refreshed and ready for a new batch of stomach-turning endeavors and a healthy side of *nope*. Because as easy as it is to be around Colton, ignoring the way my heart begins racing every time our eyes meet is tiring as heck. How stupid is that?

And now my pep-talk has taken an interesting turn. One does not engage in smack talk with oneself without questioning one's own sanity.

*I should write for fortune cookies.*

There's a tap on the window of my Uber that pulls me out of my alternate-career thoughts.

I know it's Colton, but I still close my eyes, fortifying my walls and reminding myself what the goal is and isn't, before I turn to face his rugged yet glowing smile.

*Dang it, I'm already failing.*

The plaster on my walls already needs fixing.

I roll down my window, smiling politely at Colton.

"Plannin' on getting out, Flamethrower?" He's upping the ante in this nickname game once again.

"Um..." I purse my lips, looking around the parking lot. "I'm good here. This is a nice spot. I'm actually considering alternate career paths."

That smile just splits wider as he looks at the driver then over the top of the car with a nod. Good, he can do whatever this part of the challenge is without me. I think I need extra time to repair my crumbly walls.

I'm breathing a relieved exhale when the other passenger door is yanked open and a pair of long legs slide their way in.

*Frick! I didn't lock the doors.*

It was a rookie mistake, and I'm paying for it now as Colton stares at me.

Our driver pulls out a newspaper and begins reading, happy to park on my dime.

Ethan's eyes narrow a fraction before he pulls a folded envelope out his pocket and offers it to me. I make sure to avoid any skin-to-skin contact when I slide it out of his hand, then I read over it silently. It's already been opened so I assume he's read it.

"We're gardening for old people?" I ask with a scrunched brow. "The only old people I know are my neighbors, Opal and Gail, and they'd tie me up if I messed with their flowers."

Colton opens the paper that I hold out to him. "It doesn't say old people. It says to find a *retired* couple and plant flowers for them, so we can go to my parents' place. My mom usually does her own gardening, but she hasn't gotten to it yet. Technically, my dad isn't retired, but this will score me extra points with my mom. Ethan took her to see an opera last month, and I'm still trying to catch up."

So much information there. "Catch up?"

"Favorite son status. Last year Ethan won, but only because he redid their porch."

What planet are they from?

"She actually tells you who her favorite son is at the end of the year?"

"Oh, she has no idea we play this game. She'd be mad as hell if she found out. But I like beating Ethan, and this is just another way to do that. Except for last year—that was a fluke."

"O-kay..." The frown on my face will be permanently etched after today. This weirdness will act as a setting agent, and I'll be the girl with resting-frown face, all because of this family.

I glance back at Colton in time to catch another dawning of

a smile. It's an enticing one, and I force myself to turn away from its siren call. I thank my driver, giving him a decent tip and we climb out, walking in silence to the plants that hedge the nursery entrance.

"So, we're buying flowers and soil and stuff, then planting things in your parents' front yard?"

"That's an excellent summary. You should add that to your list of alternate career paths: task summarizer."

"I'm sure I'd be in high demand. Now, look sharp. You get the soil, I'll get the flowers, and we'll meet at the checkout. Oh, and get gloves."

"Ever thought of adding drill sergeant to that career list?"

I poke his side, loving and hating that I've learned his ticklish spot when he crunches forward with a stifled giggle.

The man giggled. Those damn walls are cracking even more.

*Nope. Stop it. He's not for you, Ember. Think of Hawaii!*

We complete our purchases and I'm forced to share a car ride with Colton's masculine scent. Part of me wants to hold my breath the whole drive because I don't think my nose or heart can survive the deliciousness.

Once again, I find myself outside Mr. and Mrs. King's house, which does not in any way look like it needs landscaping, but what do I know?

In all the years I attended committee meetings for such things with my mother, all we did was discuss rumors and address complaints, like the scandalous curves of Mrs. Rigsby's flower beds or the wild nature of Mrs. Daven's roses. Apparently, flower beds should be geometric, not wavy like someone carved them while slurping their fourth glass of scotch. While these matters were debated in great depth, I don't recall doing one second of gardening or even seeing the landscaping they tore apart with their words.

We walk up the steps, greeting his parents. Jeanie insists I call her by her first name after I panic and call her "Mrs. Ma'am." True story. I'm the picture of eloquence. She squishes me in one of her trademark embraces, anyway.

Colton's dad is just as tall as he is, with a few more crinkles around his eyes and a touch of silver sprinkled in his hair. He gives me an equally soul-altering hug, then tells me with a wink that I can call him "Robert" or "Dr. Mr. Sir." I think I'll keep him.

Jeanie walks us to the kitchen for lemonade made with mint leaves and frozen raspberries. She hands me a glass, and I thank her, adding that her hair looks great.

See, I can be normal. I've only embarrassed myself once within the last three minutes.

She waves away my compliment with a gracious smile that throws me off balance. It's beautiful and pure and full of everything storybooks tell you mothers should embody.

Robert bids us a cheery goodbye, promising to return before we leave.

"I'm so grateful you're doing this for us," Jeanie beams. "I've always loved doing the flower beds myself, but I threw my back out last week. Crouching to get to them wouldn't be a good idea."

So that's why Colton brought us here.

It's actually kind of sweet. But that's as far as my Colton appreciation will go today—we've filled that quota.

"Ma, why don't you show Ember where to find the gardening tools? I'm gonna unload everything from my truck."

"I can do that. Then I'll get out of your hair." She smiles warmly as she leads me down a hall into the garage. "I've got a meeting I need to get to, but I can't wait to see what you've done when I get back."

Jeanie points out gardening supplies neatly hung on one

side of the garage. The rest of the space looks like Marie Kondo organized it herself. To one side is a tool bench, the only area that isn't neatly arranged. It's tidy but just cluttered enough to make it look like someone was working here a minute ago and got called away.

Clear, neatly-labeled tubs are stacked with seasonal decor and backups of the things responsible people keep, like light-bulbs and packing tape.

"There's one box up there," Jeanie says as she points to one of the higher shelves. "Wedged next to it are some gardening mats. Trust me, you'll want 'em if you value your knees." I'm wearing shorts, so I'll coddle my knees with a padded mat if I can. "Just get Colton to reach and get everything down. It helps to have a tall, strong man around." She winks.

What is happening here? I nod, still a little weirded out by all this niceness. It's just so...nice. And the strangest part is that it all seems so genuine.

Jeanie gives my hand a squeeze and excuses herself. I shove my hands in my back pockets, doing a slow turn as I exhale a heavy breath.

*Focus on the task, Ember. Get the tools. Plant some flowers. Go home, away from Colton and the tangents that swim in his eyes.*

I grab a few useful-looking gardening tools and carry them to the front of the house. Colton has already laid the trays of flowers out next to the flower beds, but he's nowhere in sight.

I'm about to turn back to the garage when a movement from the corner catches my eye, and I immediately wish I could erase this picture from my mind. Not because it's gross—no—it's every girls' slow-motion fantasy that hits me like a round-house kick to the stomach. But it's certainly not helping me in my determination to shut down the fluttering I feel in my stomach whenever he's around.

Colton struts over carrying a heavy bag of soil on his shoulder, cap turned backward and muscles doing muscly things. It's a picture I'll unfortunately see as I fall asleep at night, mocking me with dreams of strapping, broad-shouldered heroes who don't exist in real life. I blink a few times before I force myself to look away. With a sharp pivot, I hurry back to the garage.

Once I get there, I realize there's nothing else to carry out, so I might as well get the gardening mats myself. I move a step ladder as close as I can get it with the bike rack and stacked kayaks sitting directly in front of the shelf...

*It's a good thing my arms are long. This'll be a piece of cake.*

Climbing up the ladder is no problem, but I momentarily lose my balance once I reach the top step, wobbling for a second before grabbing onto the shelf. I grip the ledge tightly and reach to my left, thinking I'll just knock the mats off and then get them when I get down.

If my arms were only an inch longer, I'd have them, but the mats are still a smidgen out of reach. I maneuver my right hand a little more to the left, making sure I have a tight hold. Rising to my tiptoes, I reach to my left again, one foot going out to the side. I'm starfishing on top of a step ladder, surrounded by many pointy objects.

I grunt as my fingers graze the mats. I shift my weight and manage to pull the first mat off the shelf, just as I feel my body swaying, and I lose the grip I have on the shelf I clung to with misplaced trust. My starfish pose tips to the side until I have nowhere to go but down.

My eyes pinch closed as I brace for impact with the pokey things that I know await my fall. Instead, I slam into something both soft and solid. When no pain registers, I peek an eye open, peering up at a pair of cobalt ones that frown at me with a mixture of concern and frustration.

Colton's gaze glides over my face. A hand caresses my hair

while he continues to inspect me, his other arm holding me in a dancer's dip.

The air is thick and heavy, and I can smell the minty lemonade on his breath as he slowly straightens without putting any space between us. His face is so close that it's intoxicating, and I instantly forget every reason I had for staying away from this man. His nose brushes my temple as his hands continue smoothing my hair.

I'm in shock from the near-death experience, I tell myself. That must be it. That's why I don't take a step back.

But I know that's a lie. There's something else surrounding us, pulling us together. If I name it, I'm afraid it'll vanish. It feels delicate like being wrapped in cotton candy, a fragile sweetness wrapping around our bodies and just as easily broken. And so, so tempting.

"You okay?" Colton's voice comes out in a whisper as if he's afraid to disturb whatever this is that's building between us.

A clang from behind echoes over the walls, finally severing our connection. I step back, brushing my hands down my sides.

"Something fell," I say, refusing to make eye contact lest I get sucked in again.

Those eyes are entirely too dangerous.

"Right," Colton says, a thumb scratching his jaw. And we make a silent pact to ignore whatever just happened.

"Everything's outside?" I ask.

"Yeah. Did you get what you were risking your life for up there?" He crooks his head to the shelf that failed me a minute ago, but his eyes don't leave mine. His jaw tenses, as if he's unhappy with me.

I frown. "I got one mat and almost had the other. I would have been fine, but you startled me. You shouldn't sneak up on people on ladders. It's a rule. Like, never tickle someone in a pool."

"Right," he grunts again to say he disagrees but knows better than to pick a fight with a woman. Wise man. I can defend my ability to get things done till I'm old and pruned. I've had lots of practice.

He glances away for a second, his lips pouting and his hands on his hips, then turns back to me. It's a look that says I'm more of a handful than he bargained for.

"Let's get this over with, Firefly,"

"F—what?" I shake my head, reminding myself that the nicknames shouldn't matter. "Wait, we still need the other knee-mat thing," I say, picking up the one I'd gotten from the floor and following Colton out the side door.

"Don't need it."

I roll my eyes, partially out of annoyance and partially to avoid looking at the jean-clad butt in front of me. It figures that a man like Colton would deny needing a little bit of comfort.

We stand together, looking from the flower trays over to the empty space. "We should probably dig out some of this old dirt, then put the flowers in and fill in the space around them with new soil," I say, mostly to break the silence.

Colton hands me a shovel, and for the next hour, we work side by side, me on my knee pad and Colton looking rugged in his combat boots, jeans, and slightly dirty T-shirt. His hat is still on backward and I have to admit, it works. In a strictly objective sense, I can admit that it's a good look.

He catches me staring at him, and I pretend to be wiping hair out my face with the crook of my arm.

Colton stands, offering a hand to help me up. I could curse the gloves covering both of our hands right now.

*No! The gloves are good, Ember. You don't want to touch his hand.*

I take his hand, letting go as soon as I'm upright. We both turn at the sound of car doors slamming.

"Just in time." Colton's eyes crinkle when he grins. The man is actually happy his parents are back. I still can't grasp that concept.

Jeanie is jogging gracefully toward us, a squeal escaping as she sets her eyes on the flower beds. "Oh, they look so good!" She clasps her hands together, beaming as if we hung the sun for her. "Thank you!"

"You're welcome, Ma," Colton replies, smiling brightly in return.

"Now, come inside and have some iced tea. Y'all look like you need refreshing."

I follow them into the kitchen. Colton, Rob, and I perch on bar stools around the island, and Jeanie makes easy conversation as she works, asking questions about the other adventures we've tried this week. It's still so bizarre having a mother and father figure showing genuine interest in me without any ulterior motives. Colton's parents are completely present in the conversation, and I feel like I'm the only person in the world when they listen to my answers, smiling sweetly.

I ask Jeanie about her lemonades and teas, telling her that I'm fascinated with her flavor additions. I ask Rob what he's been working on at his tool bench, and he shares his little projects while his family listens with pride.

I'm surprised at how pleasant the encounter feels. Rob and Jeanie speak to each other with outward affection, exchanging small touches every few minutes. Watching them even gives me hope that lasting love is possible.

Jeanie feeds us giant sandwiches and more lemonade, then Colton and I pack away the gardening tools and say our goodbyes.

When Colton drop's me off at home, he smiles that smoldering smile. "See you tomorrow, Flames."

I shake my head, amusement lifting my cheeks. It's pitiful how far behind I am in this game.

"Tomorrow, Boss Man." I salute because I'm a weirdo.

## CHAPTER TWELVE

### COLTON

Aster is an average-sized Texas town, with nearly everything situated within a fifteen-minute drive. These short commutes have always been a welcomed chance to clear my head. But over the last week, the silence filling the car has become a roaring monster. It pokes at my happy solitude, jeering snide remarks about my loneliness. Even the country music I've always loved only seems to highlight the fact that I'm a man living without the one thing all these songs were written about.

I lean forward and turn the radio to a sports station. Unfortunately, my brain still wants to use my daily commute to go down rabbit holes that are better left alone. Like, the way I know it's been exactly eight days since Ember started working for me. And how she always walks to work with a homemade smoothie in her hand.

I'm glad that she fits so well within the team. She adds a dynamic we've been missing. Her ideas are insightful and fresh.

That's why I'm in trouble, though. She's distracting. Her presence alone stirs up things I've been happy to leave dormant for a very long time.

Between fielding Lemon's flirting and Ethan's match-making attempts, my head feels like it's trapped in a tumble dryer. As if running a company isn't stressful enough, the universe decided it was a good idea to add some relational angst into the mix.

*No thanks, Universe. I don't need that distraction.*

The trajectory of my life has been carefully built on diligence and focus. I've always imagined myself in a boxing ring, my opponents being the things I'm trying to atone for. But I plan my moves so that it's a choreographed fight scene. Each step requires attention and precision. One slip of concentration threatens to draw my eye away to the things bouncing in my peripheral, distracting me from my opponent. I can't miss a step or my concentration will break, making it harder to ignore the things I convinced myself to forget.

But now, my heart is trying desperately to remind me of a forgotten yearning. A part of me worries that this unplanned peripheral distraction will cause a major misstep, and then I won't be able to ignore that yearning anymore.

I wave away those thoughts about missing out and wanting more. It's easier to continue on the path I'm on. It's one I know well. And my work is fulfilling. I'm creating incredible adventures for others, giving them a lifetime of memories with those they love.

So I tell myself to focus, to ignore the silvery sound of Ember's laugh, the twist I feel inside when she smiles, or the way my heart pounds in my chest when she smiles at me. Ignore the longing for something different. *I've still got time.*

Yeah. As I said, I'm in trouble.

My watch alerts me to my mother's incoming call as if she knows I'm stewing over heavy things. I tap its green button to answer.

"Hey, Ma."

"Colt, sweetie, I'm just callin' to say hey. You on your way to the office?"

I'm thirty-one and well on my way to becoming a millionaire, but this woman will still call regularly to check that I'm a functioning adult. I love her for it, though. If I so much as hint that I'm stressed or, God forbid, missed a meal, she'll swoop in with an armful of lasagna and lick her finger to wipe a nonexistent smudge off my chin. But as much as I love my mama's food, I'm the one who should be looking after her and my dad now.

"Yeah, I'm almost at the office. We're going off for more adventure tests today, just meeting there to carpool. Ethan's planned it all."

"Mm-hmm, and how's Ember?"

That question tells me that Ethan is due for a punch to the arm, which I'll happily deliver in about five minutes. His matchmaking attempts could rival those of a regency mother trying to marry off a handful of daughters.

"Mom, I've got about two minutes before I get to work, so why don't you rapid-fire your questions, and I'll do my best to answer. Because I'm your favorite son."

"Gah, fine," she huffs, her southern accent wrapping those two words in so much righteous indignation that I almost feel like she's doing me a favor.

"Oh, Colt, she's just wonderful! Does she have family nearby? Do you know if she's single? What's her favorite food? Can you tell her we'll be havin' dinner at six on Sunday, and she doesn't need to bring anything, just her pretty self?"

"I don't know any of that, and no."

"Colton Rutherford King, what do you mean *no*?"

My shoulders shake with laughter. "Nice try, Ma. There are so many reasons why that's not happening. I love you, and as much as I wanna delve into this with you"—or not—"duty calls. Tell Dad not to touch the roof until I get around to it this weekend."

"Colt, you don't need to do that, sweetie. Your dad can handle replacing a few roof tiles."

I try not to grunt in response. My dad is a fit guy and still practicing medicine with a sharp mind, but he's too old to climb ladders onto roofs.

"I'm serious, Mom. Tell him you need a shower head replaced or there's a strange smell coming from somewhere. Just keep him off the roof."

She sighs, clearly unimpressed with my constant attempts to care for them. "And you can tell Ember I'm excited to see her again. Bye, sweetheart."

She hangs up before my growl makes it through.

My truck hugs the curve as I glide into The Adventure Project's lot. Everyone stands outside in a small huddle. Ethan gives me a chin lift and a smirk as I park.

That smirk smells of mischief.

I climb out my truck, squinting at the glare reflecting off Lemon's pink, sequin-covered top. Or maybe it's bedazzled? I'm not ashamed to admit that I don't know the difference.

A mantra of thoughts rolls over in my mind as I near the group.

*Avoid Lemon's flirting. Don't stare at Ember. Punch Ethan in the arm.*

Three seconds later, I've already failed at the first. Lemon floats closer, fluttering her eyelashes as she offers me a coffee cup.

It's the figure I notice in my peripheral that earns me strike number two. Because behind Lemon stands Ember. How can I not stare? I could spew fluffy words about how the sun plays with the colors in her hair, but the woman is just plain stunning. She's a beautiful distraction.

*Focus, Colton.*

Lemon mistakes the smile that's crept onto my face without my permission as one intended for her.

*Divert.*

I thank Lemon for the coffee and look over at my brother. "Ethan!" Maybe I'm being a tad loud, but it's a solid plan.

*Throw the focus onto someone else.*

"Run us through what we're doing?"

# CHAPTER THIRTEEN

## EMBER

Colton's deep voice lassos me in, yanking my attention away from Lisa, mid-conversation. Extra weirdo points for me when I just give up on my sentence the moment Colton speaks. I can't even remember what Lisa and I were talking about—hiking shoes, maybe? Something...to do with shoes.

*Ew,* that's too cliche. We may as well have been practicing the *bend and snap.*

*Nope.* Women should be able to gather and talk about shoes without fear of being labeled.

He says something else, scrambling my thoughts again. I want to stomp my foot at my body's betrayal at hearing his voice.

*No. Nuh-uh. We are not going down that path, sister.*

But this betrayal runs deep. The next thing I know, I'm smiling as my concentration shifts entirely to the voice's owner, taking my feet along with it.

*What am I doing?* I will my treacherous feet to abort their mission.

I turn to apologize to Lisa for spacing out on her, but Ethan claps his hands to garner everyone's attention.

"Sorry," I mouth and shrug my shoulders. Because she's a sweetheart, she whispers a quick, "You're fine." And my anxiety lifts a smidgen at the friendly look on her face.

I hate not knowing what we're doing today. Give me a to-do list to complete on my own, and I will show that list who's boss. But I'm a useless ball of nerves when faced with a ton of unknowns in conjunction with so much peopling. And this week has included a lot of that unsettling combo.

Ethan invites the guys to draw names to see which ladies they'll be paired with.

"Mallory can't make it today, so we're evenly numbered. Jed, you're up first," Ethan explains holding up three folded scraps of paper.

I like Jed. He reminds me of a G.I. Joe with his curt nods and buzz-cut hair. He's stoic, but kind. He plucks a paper from Ethan and unfolds it.

"Lemon." Jed looks up and gives her one of his nods, no indication of delight or disappointment at his pairing.

Lemon raises celebratory fists with her hands and gives an unenthusiastic "Yaaay" as she fakes a smile at Jed, then at Colton. Miss Lemon is obviously displeased with this little arrangement. She's made it very clear she has a thing for one Mr. Colton King. But I get it. If I were on the lookout for a relationship-worthy man, my ovaries would be swooning too.

Which—they're not. Because I still have a handful of blind dates to find and an unhealthy determination to avoid dating a coworker ever again. And if I meet a nice, regular man on one of these dates, that's an unexpected bonus.

*Nice. Regular.*

When did I add *regular* to the requirements? Now I can't stop thinking about bran and fiber commercials.

Scratch regular. Nice is the only requirement. Wait, make that nice and not obscenely wealthy.

1. Nice.

2. Normal bank balance.

There. Short and sweet. *Oh, dear God, I didn't mean short is on the list. Let's be very clear about that. Cool. Amen.*

Ethan draws Lisa's name. He turns to Colton, casting a triumphant look his way. He's entirely too pleased about these pairings. I'm almost sure their mom would blame her gray hair on him. Ethan is younger, but something tells me he was the main instigator for most of the trouble the King brothers have gotten up to over the years.

"So, Colton, you've got Ember."

A hairline crack appears in the walls around my heart when Ethan says those words. I'm so mad at what that sentence does to my insides.

For a split second, a crease forms between Colton's brows. He's murdering Ethan with his eyeballs. That granite jaw clenches, the facial equivalent of the Darcy hand flex. I guess someone else isn't happy with our little pairings. I try not to let that knowledge sting.

I glance back between Ethan and Colton. The eyeball daggers are gone, and Colton is smiling politely. It happened so fast that I wonder if I imagined the look they exchanged only a second ago.

Ethan ignores his brother and hands each of the ladies a packet. "These have all the info for the first challenge. We'll meet at Bellini's for lunch. You've got the Polaroids, too, so be sure to take photos."

Lemon gives me the stink eye as I climb into Colton's truck. I offer her a little wave in return because she's too far away to hear a "bless your heart."

That's a lie. That sort of confrontational comeback only

happens in my head. If I ever said one out loud, I'd spend the rest of the day slowly dying on the inside and writing a two-page apology letter.

I'm more likely to send her a text saying I'm sorry for interrupting her and explaining how I didn't orchestrate any of what's happening right now than I am to call her out. Thankfully, I don't have her number so I can't spend the next two hours wording that message.

Workplace drama is the last thing I need right now. If she knew how uninterested I am in challenging her, maybe she'd be less...*lemony?* I want to like her, but the woman lives up to her name. Despite the fit my traitorous hormones have been throwing around Colton, I'm the least likely to sign up for an interoffice relationship.

The next time I venture into a relationship with someone will be on my terms. I want to be loved wholly and wildly.

As appealing as Colton may be, I don't trust myself to be a good judge of character with someone from that upper-middle-class world. I missed too many red flags with Beau. Maybe growing up with old-world money and all its pretenses has contributed to my aversion.

What I do know is that I want something different next time, something real without the blinders and arrogance of wealth.

Colton slides into his seat and looks over at me. His cologne instantly fills the space between us, pushing away any thoughts of *nice* that linger in my brain. It's subtle. Enticing.

The bench-style seats of his old truck are practically inviting me to scoot a little closer. And darn it, I'm being sucked in again. *Stop it, Ember!*

"Ready for some fun?"

There's his real smile. I blink and remind myself that he's

asked me a question, and also that I'm supposed to be immune to his charm.

"Yes!" *Too loud, Ember.* I clear my throat and respond again. "Sure, let's do this."

He chuckles as he starts his truck, and I'm grateful when he doesn't mention my weird response and only nods toward the packet I'm holding.

"Why don't you open that up and read our challenge?"

"Right. Good idea."

I fumble with the envelope before I manage to get it open. I'm in my own head. Can I convince myself not to be attracted to Colton?

I clear my throat again. Why is reading out loud the worst? I begin, hoping it isn't painfully obvious how out of my element I'm feeling.

"Goodwill Hunting:
Find your nearest thrift store and channel your inner stylist.
Each person gets fifteen dollars to find an outfit for your date.
Wear it, flaunt it, own it!
Take a photo and have fud..."

*Dead.*

I reread the last sentence. "*Fun.* Take a photo and have *fun.*"

"Fud?"

This man. I'd hoped he'd breeze over that one, just like he did with my last awkward response. He tries his best not to laugh while I chew my lip and stare outside in an attempt to hide the flaming-red color my cheeks have decided to adopt. I would sell my soul to the person who discovers a cure for blushing.

"Mm-hmm."

"I'd love to have fud. Tell me, Ember, how does one go about having *fud?*"

I growl, but can't hide the smile that overtakes my face. "You're killing me."

*You can redirect Ember, but you're weird, and he'll figure that out sooner or later.*

I was hoping for more later, but my weirdness has no respect. Maybe I should become that girl who wears T-shirts that say things like, *"Sorry. I'm awkward. Sorry."*

I open the glove compartment, distracting the both of us with my unashamed snooping. I'm also surprised Colton doesn't drive some huge new truck with all the fancy bits.

"There's a Goodwill about five minutes away, but I think the thrift store near the community college would be better," I motion with my hand and begin taking things out.

He smiles. This seems to be our go-to encounter. I embarrass myself, Colton tries not to laugh. Except, I'm not sure I like the cycle.

"Sounds good. Tell me where to go, Miss Hayes."

I give him directions and continue rummaging. There are a few napkins, a plastic knife and fork still in the wrapper, and a single gas receipt.

That's it? I wanted something to balance the scales of mortification that are already heavily tipped on my side. But there's nothing. The man is an alien.

Holding up the loot I've discovered, I aim a scowl his way.

"Seriously?"

He laughs, glancing at my stash and then at me before focusing on the road again.

"What?"

"Why is this thing so tidy? Where are the Chick-fil-A napkins, the sauces, the straw cover thingies, the dirty pennies?"

He leans over, and I get a whiff of his scent all over again. I'll have to start wearing noseplugs when he's near. He peeks into the cup- holder that doesnt look like it came with the truck, one eyebrow raised.

"There's a penny in there."

I stick my hand inside and pull out a shiny coin.

"It's clean. It doesn't count."

He shrugs one muscly shoulder. "I like my truck clean." There's pride in his statement, and I get the feeling someone important is responsible for instilling that within him.

My hand goes under my seat as I continue my sleuthing. There has to be something interesting hidden somewhere.

*You've got to be kidding me!*

A first aid kit? Who does that? Everyone technically should have one in their car, but nobody actually does.

"You can't be from this planet. You put one of these in your car. Is it some ploy to secretly shame the rest of us mere humans?"

He smiles and shakes his head. "You're kind of a snoop."

"It's practical experience for one of my backup careers."

"A career in snooping?"

"Never mind that." I flip down my visor, disappointed, but not surprised to find nothing incriminating.

"Well, I'm truly sorry to crush your P.I. dreams, but we're here. You can carry on with your snooping later."

I expect him to get out, but he pauses, holding me in place with a cobalt-blue stare. He gives the tiniest shake of his head.

"Cute," he whispers.

I'm still pinned in place by those eyes. All I hear is his deep inhale like he doesn't know what to do with me either. Then he boops me on the nose and gets out.

*A freaking nose-boop?*

I don't know that anyone has ever booped my nose. My parents weren't exactly the affectionate type. I mentally scoff at myself. That's an understatement I'd need a therapist's couch and a truckload of Red Vines to unravel.

Meanwhile, I'm still frozen in my seat. I'm the dusty mug on a thrift store shelf, and Colton just came along, picked me up, and declared me worth something.

Shock—that's the state I'm in, mainly because this seemingly insignificant act has revealed another fissure in my foolproof plan.

*I am not looking for a relationship with my boss,* I remind myself.

Trust is a fickle beast. Years can be undone in a single moment. In my case, it was a million little moments that grew into really big moments, and that's why I ran. The way things happened with Beau hammered that truth into a hard-packed foundation, one that won't allow me to build anything over it that contradicts those hard-learned lessons.

I don't want to acknowledge the brand new fracture that now threatens that foundation. But that's exactly what a single whispered word and one little boop have done.

My door swinging open interrupts my mini-crisis. "Thanks," I mumble as I climb out.

*Don't let the chivalry deceive you, Ember.*

Colton is still closing my door when I make a beeline for the store entrance, moving much faster than the moment calls for. We all know what happens in a situation like this: he leads me inside with his hand on the small of my back, melting my fragile, romantic heart. Next thing you know, I'm making scrapbooks and shipping our names together.

*Colber.*

Dang it, that's cute.

So, I hightail my hopeless-romantic self and get six feet ahead of Mr. Chivalry before any lower back touching can happen.

I shove the door of the thrift store open with a low growl and stomp inside. I realize all too late that my nerves have teamed up with my low blood sugar to create a classic case of *hangry*. I stop to dig around in my tote bag for a Z-bar. I stand by the theory that wars could be avoided if we simply made it a point to ensure people had happy, full tummies before making big decisions.

The blessed calories chase away the hangry as I chew and smile at the shelves that hug every wall of the thrift store. It's quaint and cramped and smells like old cupboards and nostalgia. It was one of the first places I visited when I moved to Aster.

The air changes as Colton steps around me.

"You okay?" he asks, a hand going to my elbow. We're about two levels from a *small-of-the-back* situation, and I fight the shiver that runs up my arm. He guides me out the way as an older lady enters the store behind us and drops his hand.

"Yup, peachy," I lie, because a woman is never peachy when she uses that term.

I'm not sure if Colton believes me or not, but he doesn't pry.

"So, what's the plan?" I ask, shrugging off the funk I walked in with and starting a back-and-forth swinging thing with my arms.

Colton lifts a hand, and the sudden movement makes me flinch. He narrows his eyes a fraction as he slows his movements, plucking a floppy cream hat from a nearby shelf and placing it atop my head.

My heart rate stampedes in my chest, but I play down my reaction as if I'm moving a flyaway hair out my face.

*Nothing to see here...everything is normal.*

He tilts his head, then readjusts the hat so the bright sunflower on top faces him. His gaze burrows into me, finding a cozy little nook within my eyes.

"Not much to it, Sunshine. You find me an outfit. I find one for you."

*Sunshine.*

My traitorous heart warms at the name. I haven't felt like anything near sunshiney in a long time. Grouchy, pessimistic, jaded—yes. Not sunshiney.

*Focus on the task, Ember.* Be grateful that he didn't ask any questions about your flinchy moves back there.

Task. Right. Find Colton an outfit. I can handle that. This could be fun.

My eyes narrow with a finger on my chin. "I saw a lovely velvet suit the last time I came in. I wonder if it's still here."

"That's cruel."

"There are no rules. I get to pick your outfit."

"You know that goes both ways, right?" He trails behind as I peruse the men's section. He makes a good point.

"Okay, fine. I'll avoid velvet and anything with animals, and you avoid shoulder pads and sequins."

Colton removes a hanger from the rack he's sifting through and holds it up.

"Immediately, no."

"Not a fan of green and purple paisley?"

"That thing would make Joan Rivers vomit." I say, turning back to flip through clothing.

"You've done this before."

"You haven't?" My reply slips out before I can think. *Of course* he hasn't. He's loaded. Why would he ever need to buy a stranger's pre-owned clothes? It's another reason why I should rein in whatever it is that makes my stomach all swirly around Colton.

We're too different. I may have grown up with a closet filled with curated outfits, but breaking free from that world has only affirmed how much I never liked or fit into it.

Besides, thrifting is an exhilarating hunt. It may have begun as a necessity when I needed to get creative with a dwindling savings account, but I actually enjoy it. I'd choose thrift clothes over eating ramen and off-brand Cheerios every time. I know college kids live off the stuff, but my taste buds have standards. And, once I experienced the thrill of finding the perfect pair of designer jeans for eight dollars, I was hooked. Every time I walk into a thrift store, it's like buying a scratch card. Some days are duds, but then you might hit gold and find a gorgeous leather jacket, and all the frumpy dresses you combed through are worth it.

Colton is a few racks away, frowning adorably at every item he sifts through. "I haven't," he says without looking up. "But I kinda get the appeal."

I pause as my eyes dart up to the tall enigma of a man. Beau would have curled his nose in disgust at entering a thrift store.

Why am I comparing them? This is dumb. I barely know the man. Since I'm not looking for a relationship, I don't need to be compiling lists of future prospects.

Wow. I really need to give Regency romances a break for a while. I came too close to buying one of those fold-out hand fans last week. Add a bonnet, and I'll be dropping a handkerchief on my next blind date.

I go off on my own, returning once I've gathered what I think would make a very charming outfit for Colton. It may involve a bow tie. I make my way to where he's standing with a wide grin, clothes draped over his arm.

"Here you go, Sunshine."

My insides melt a little more, but I fight hard not to let an audible groan escape. He's making it so hard to remember all the reasons why I can't allow my heart to get excited.

We swap bundles with a painful lack of coordination. I ignore my rapid heartbeat when our arms brush. Totally a normal response. *Nothing to see, here.*

With jerky movements, I pivot and rush toward one of two changing rooms, glancing over my shoulder and waving as I blurt out, "Okay, have a good day!"

I lock the door of the tiny cubicle, sagging against the wall as my eyes pinch closed. "What is wrong with me?" I whisper to myself.

I know my confidence has been shot over the past few months. I don't know why the tiniest (huge) bit of attraction toward a man has me acting like a teenager who just spotted Taylor Swift.

A throaty chuckle and the sound of a door latching bring my hand to my forehead. There are only two cubicles, which means he *definitely* heard me talking to myself. Where did I think he was going to go?

I hear fabric moving on the other side of the wall, and I hurry to change into the outfit I dropped next to me. I'm still wearing the hat Colton put on my head, and a slow smile grows when I look at the clothes he's picked out: a bell-sleeved, pastel-blue sundress with a subtle sunflower print. Hitting just past the knees, it's feminine and flowy and I love it.

I ignore the strangely intimate feeling of undressing this close to him as I remove my clothes and pull on the sunflower dress. With a hard swallow, I place the silly hat back over my head and remind myself to be professional.

# CHAPTER FOURTEEN

## COLTON

I've just finished changing when an ear-splitting squeal comes from the cubicle that's way too close for two humans to be while undressing in a public place. My hands jerk out, and I'm franticly searching for the exit like a cat in a bathtub. Is she being attacked by the ghosts of second-hand clothing? Clumsily, I fumble with my door latch. After seventy-two tries, it finally unhooks, and I swing the door open.

I rush out and lean an ear to her door, because that will help. "Ember? You okay?"

"Oh my gosh!"

Should I bust the door open? My brain has gone into *must-save-woman mode*.

"It has pockets!"

Another squeal bursts through, making me flinch. It's pretty impressive the pitch she reaches when she does that. Her door swings open, forcing me to take a quick step back.

I'm not prepared for the sight.

Earlier, I plucked the hat I put on her randomly, and the

nickname had just seemed right. *Sunshine.* But seeing her in this outfit sparks a heavy drumming in my chest.

She's radiant. The light in her eyes, the smile, the sunflower theme. All of it. Something has awakened. It's the culmination of things I can't name. I rub the spot over my heart that feels funny.

Hands shove into her pockets and she flaps them like wings.

"You're not being murdered."

"What? No. Look, it has pockets!"

"I take it this is a good thing."

"It's the jackpot!" She beams and then proceeds to twirl. *Twirl!*

If this is what a dress with pockets does, I'll hunt down every one. My smile grows to match hers.

"You look amazing. It was that or the sweater with Bob Ross's face."

"Ha ha." She rolls her eyes. "You made the right choice. If it has pockets, I'm sold. Did you know there are rumors that pockets were banished from women's clothing during the French Revolution to prevent them from concealing revolutionary material? Also, women's pockets essentially disappeared because their husbands would carry all their money and necessities."

I'm still smiling as I continue to take her in. She's a walking encyclopedia, and I'm failing at not finding it adorable. Backpeddle, Colton.

"I did not know that."

"Anyway, pockets are the best." Her shoulders shrug as she sways, making her dress swing gently around her legs. Her eyes meet mine, and she takes in my outfit for the first time.

"Oh my gosh! Look at you!" She whacks the back of her

hand against my bicep. "I think we both hit the jackpot. I knew you'd be able to pull off a bow tie."

I look down at my outfit that I would have deemed questionable two minutes ago. But the way she's biting her lip as she eyes me from head to toe, I'm thinking a bow tie with suspenders might be my new style.

She paired the navy bow tie with a striped short-sleeved button-up shirt that's maybe a tad too small. But then she steps closer, fixing the hem of my folded sleeve. Her fingers on my bicep make me think she picked everything perfectly. She clears her throat and steps back, smoothing the front of her dress.

"Should we head to the checkout?" She questions, avoiding eye contact.

This woman is a puzzle that I'm increasingly interested in figuring out. I'm pretty sure she's one of those 3D puzzles that require a commitment to the task. No half-assing a project like that. But I'm already too intrigued to walk away without figuring this out.

"Let's do it. Just let me know when the fud part of the day begins, okay? I wanna make sure I don't miss the *fud*."

Her eyes widen, and she elbows me, her mouth pouting to the side as she attempts to hide her smile.

"I could change my mind about your outfit, you know. I saw a Wookie costume that you'd look great in."

"I think you're pretty happy with my outfit." I'm skating the edge. Probably very much in the flirting zone, but I'm having too much fun to overthink it.

"Whatever." She rolls those eyes again, but as she turns her head, I see the smile she's trying to hide, which does funny things to my belly.

"Wait—" She pauses, her hand on my arm pulling me to a stop. "Do you think it's okay that we wear the clothes we buy?"

"Aside from the hygiene aspect, I'm sure it's fine." Looking down at her, I take her in. I keep looking till her eyes meet mine.

"You're a rule follower, aren't you?" I ask.

Another piece of the puzzle.

Her face scrunches as she thinks about it. "No. I mean, yes, okay? I like to stick to the rules. It's not a bad thing."

"Never said it was, Sunshine. I'm just enjoying learning more about who Ember Hayes is, that's all."

Her mouth opens, an adorable deer in headlights look in her eyes.

"Come on. I'll pay for this, then we can head to Bellini's."

Yeah. I'm in trouble.

# CHAPTER FIFTEEN

## EMBER

I have this theory that humans tend to take a neutral position on most things, and only when someone pokes at us do we realize we should form an opinion. If not completely neutral, then we at best have a *slightly* more than impartial opinion on any given topic until someone challenges it. It's kind of like how Prince William should just shave his head and embrace the bald look. He'd look good, and he could pull it off. It's a personal viewpoint that I assume most humans would support, but I won't start any bar fights with someone who disagrees.

However, Colton King in a tight shirt, bow tie, and suspenders is *not* the same thing. The man looks *fine*, and I will one hundred percent smash a beer bottle on a counter and threaten anyone who dares to say otherwise.

This realization does not bode well for me and my resolve to ignore my little attraction problem.

We stopped outside the thrift store to take a selfie with the Polaroid camera, and I think that photo might "accidentally" get lost. And by lost, I mean I'm taking it home with me... forever.

I'm torturing myself, but it's been a while since I haven't wanted to gag when a man put his arm around me, and I'd like a keepsake to commemorate the occasion. BO is a surprisingly big problem on blind dates, it would seem. It must be the nerves, but guys tend to sweat a lot on the dates I've been on. I should ask Ivy if she's experienced the same thing.

I spend most of our drive to Bellini's alternating between pondering these odd thoughts and overthinking every second of the past thirty minutes. What in the name of Donald Sutherland's giant head was I thinking touching Colton so much? I should be focusing on this job and praying the next date I go on is a winner. No more low-key pining over my handsome, stinking-rich boss.

My phone vibrates in my hands, and I yelp loudly. I'm not usually this jumpy, I swear. But my nerves feel like I just stepped off a roller coaster I've ridden one too many times. Not to mention, I keep waiting for Beau to call. It's been a few weeks, but my spidey senses are telling me that poop will be hitting the fan blades soon. He isn't supposed to have my number, but it hasn't stopped him before. Hence my phone being a rectangle of anxiety.

Colton looks over at me with a chuckle and a half-smile.

"You okay over there, Sunshine?"

"Yup, my phone just startled me." Because that's a normal thing. I'll have to wait to dissect that whole Sunshine business later and focus on acting less weird for the time being.

I open the text from my hairstylist. "Do you know a place called 'Olive and Vine'?" I ask.

"Yeah, they've got good food."

"Cool."

The silence grows, and I tap a nonexistent tune on my knee. I shouldn't have asked. *Stupid, stupid, stupid.*

"Cool? That's all you're giving me?"

"What?"

"What, *what?* Why'd you ask about Olive and Vine?"

"Oh—" I wince and open one eye as I mumble, "I have a blind date." Cringe. "I'm supposed to meet him there in two weeks. It's...uh, my hairstylist...she...she set me up." I exhale sharply, almost too afraid to breathe in any more of the awkwardness that's lingering in the air.

But there's no rulebook for this sort of thing. *Oh hey, I think there may be some kind of vibe between us, but you're my boss, and I'm actively going on blind dates, so...*

Not to mention the fact that I could one-thousand percent be making up the attraction that's bubbling up between us. There's a genuine possibility this is all one-sided.

Okay, yes, I'm honest enough to admit I'm somewhat (very) attracted to Colton King. But aside from the multitude of reasons why I can't date a man like him, I don't even know if he's seeing someone. So, there. Case closed. The jury can mosey on home.

"Cool."

That's all he says.

What am I supposed to do with that? Does he mean *good-cool, bad*-cool?

Wait, come back! The court is still in session. The jury requests more evidence!

Colton clenches his jaw as he pulls into a parking space outside Bellini's. The jury's request has been granted, but this new evidence may be inadmissible. He's also shooting eye bullets at Ethan, who's standing outside the restaurant, so maybe that jaw clench wasn't directed at me, after all.

Ugh, I'm not made for this level of relationship angst. Are arranged marriages still a thing? Nope, too risky. I'm not a shallow person, but attraction is important. Meeting at the altar is too much of a gamble, even if becoming a mail-order bride is still a viable option. *We'll keep this snippet of inner dialogue to ourselves.*

The truck stops, and I take the opportunity to scurry over to the rest of the team waiting outside. And when I say scurry, I mean I almost trip getting out of the truck because one of my arms is still looped in the seatbelt. It probably looks like the car feels very differently about me running from the bomb I just left inside. But I pop back up anyway, standing straight, shoulders back as I channel all the confidence I don't have.

I am Ross Gellar. I'm *fine. Totally* fine.

*Dear Lord, please let this next activity be a group one. And if minimal touching is required, I swear I'll never leave an item I change my mind about in the wrong aisle at Target again.*

# CHAPTER SIXTEEN

## COLTON

I could kick Ethan for planning this. *So* much physical contact required. He thinks he's a genius.

We're competing in a dual baking challenge. One person stands behind the other, blindfolded, acting as the arms for the person in front, who can only give vocal directions. I'm supposed to wrap myself around Ember like a koala on its favorite branch and feign neutral behavior. I'm more likely to come off like a koala who just found the best spot in the world and refuses to move or let go.

Some distance should help me get my head back on track. I can't do a relationship right now, I remind myself. I can't give a relationship what it needs.

All three "couples" sit on bar stools inside Bellini's, dressed in their thrift-store finds and looking like the cast of an eighties sitcom. Aside from Ember, it seems none of us could avoid the claws of that decade. Lemon is wearing a bright pink, long-sleeved jumpsuit with blue and yellow stars down the arms. She complains about how terrible it looks, but I think she secretly loves it. It has a zipper going down the front that she keeps playing with. It's what I'm beginning to understand as a very Lemon move.

The guys both look like they've been dressed by a denim-obsessed toddler. Ethan's sporting a denim jacket and a matching fanny pack over his jeans. Meanwhile, Jed is wearing —I shudder just thinking it—*cutoff jorts.*

I make a mental note to ask him if he wronged his ancestors somehow because no man should ever find himself with so much leg hair exposed. Lisa looks like a real-estate agent or insurance salesperson in a very outdated purple jacket and skirt. There are shoulder pads, and I'm pretty sure even Gen-Z hasn't brought those back yet.

The garlicky smell that lingers on the walls of every authentic Italian restaurant swirls around us, and my stomach voices its anticipation for Bellini's cuisine. We're seated in a private room that the owner, Luca, keeps for events like this. The large rectangular room houses one long table resembling a kitchen island. The sleek white countertop is furnished on one side with eight red barstools. Plush and cushioned, they match the crimson of the exposed beams that frame opposite sides of the room. Green wallpaper wraps around the countertops, undoubtedly an ode to Luca's Italian heritage, and white, roughly painted bricks create a feature wall behind the center island. The room is earthy and warm, the authentic blend of elements just modern enough not to offend Luca's Nonna, whose smiling portrait welcomes patrons in the lobby.

Ethan walks around to stand on the opposite side of the counter, facing the rest of us.

"Everyone got the outfit mocking out of the way?" He smiles, pausing to make eye contact with each of us. Lisa asks if Jed and Ethan are starting a boy band, and we spend another few minutes ragging on them.

"Y'all wish you could pull off double denim this well. Now, have you got all of it out of your systems? Can I carry on?"

I can't resist one last heckle. "Will you release a pin-up calendar when the band goes on tour?" Giggles eventually die down, and Ethan bows graciously before he continues.

"For the next challenge, we'll continue working with the same partners from earlier."

Great, because I need more one-on-one interactions with the woman I'm becoming more and more attracted to by the second.

Hopefully, by tomorrow morning, I'll have forgotten about wanting to throw up when she told me about her blind date. I'm sure I just ate something weird today.

Ethan continues, explaining that we'll be working in pairs with one person blindfolded behind the other and using their hands to follow our partners' directions to make a pizza.

Lemon scoots her stool closer and wraps herself around my bicep like she's the koala clinging to a branch. "Actually, I thought we could switch partners, mix things up a bit." She scrunches her nose with a little wiggle of her shoulders.

Somehow she's still moving closer. I steal a glance at Ember. Her brows pinch before a smile sweeps over her face, all within a few seconds.

"That's a great idea," Ember says. She's still smiling, but her lips are closed, and the expression doesn't reach her eyes the way it did before when it was just the two of us. "We should definitely mix it up." Her gaze darts from Lemon and me, back to Ethan.

Ethan looks like a kid who's just had his carefully placed figurines rearranged. His little matchmaking plans are fading, right in front of him.

Ember slides off her stool. "I'm just running to the restroom before we start. I'll be right back."

"Ooh, I'll join you." Lemon adds, uncurling herself from my arm.

I watch them walk away, telling myself this switch is for the best.

# CHAPTER SEVENTEEN

## EMBER

I wince as I enter the restroom and notice Lemon right behind me. Group trips to the ladies' room aren't my thing—I'm not fond of the potential for small talk, which all too often leads to awkward eye contact through the wide cracks in the stall doors. History has shown that, in those moments, I tend to overshare, like I'm a guest on an imaginary show called *"TMI from a Weirdo."* Securing the end stall feels like winning the restroom lottery. Equally lucky is having someone flush at the same time you pee—because pee sounds.

Don't even get me started on the nonsense I spew when I'm in there wearing a jumpsuit. It's just you and the good Lord, naked as the day you were born, casually bare-squatting with potential peeping Toms. *Tomettes?*

Lemon goes straight to the sink. I guess she's just here for the girl talk, then.

Except she doesn't say anything. Is this some sort of intimidation tactic? If so, she's good. It's only been a few seconds, and I'm halfway to going insane while the trickle of my bladder emptying is the only sound. I'm on the cusp of breaking my own "no small talk" vow as the echoey sound reverberates off the walls of the small restroom. I pinch my eyes closed, hating that I've sunk this low, but I'll do anything to break this clawing silence. "So how about Jed's legs, huh?"

*Why, Ember, just—Why?*

A haughty laugh pierces the awkwardness. I haven't screwed up a bathroom conversation like this since the Tina-Turner-Lady incident.

"I mean. I guess...if you're into that sorta thing."

Lemon lets the silence stretch again—no doubt step two of her torture plan. She's not quiet for long though, revealing the reason for her tag-along to the restroom. "Thanks for being cool with switching partners, by the way. It's difficult for Colton and I to find time together. You know, just 'cause he's so busy. We've been vibing for a while."

My eyes pop open. *Vibing?*

*The hell?*

I exit the stall in a daze. My brain is busy analyzing every memory of Colton and Lemon interacting. She's always seemed flirty. But she's just the touchy-feely type. Or so I thought. Colton never seemed to reciprocate it.

I guess I was wrong.

"I've already shipped our names. *Colemen*, isn't it just the cutest?"

Lemon is applying lip gloss, and her steely eyes meet mine in the mirror. I've officially been warned off. I don't know why I'm surprised that a good-looking, rich man might flirt with the new employee while *vibing* with another. Beau did the same thing, and it took me too long to realize he was more than friendly with his receptionist.

Colton was flirting with me today, right? Not that I want him to...and the little bomb Lemon just not-so-subtly dropped only makes those boundaries even more clear. I am not interested in Colton. Yes, he's a fine specimen to behold, but that's as far as my appreciation goes.

My type is officially a *nice guy,* not someone I work for or with or near. And it's obvious that I'm not Colton's type. Lemon and I couldn't be more different.

I'm not his type. He's not mine. No problems here.

*This is good. It's great.*

I'll go on my date next week, and then a few more, and I'll focus on Hawaii. I don't need a man right now. This should be my *Hear Me Roar* season. I can't roar with a man next to me. He'd tell me I was too loud or not loud enough.

I didn't wake up thinking I'd be a giant liar, liar, pants on fire today, but here we are. Denial can be a wonderful place.

I finish washing my hands and give Lemon a tight smile. I've gone too long without saying anything. If only I had the guts to embody the southern-sass I've been surrounded by since birth.

Lemon pouts her lips, then lowers the zip on her jumpsuit an inch. She wiggles her fingers in a wave and saunters out.

I give myself a good pep stare in the mirror and take a deep breath. Time to go back out there and be the professional I am...or the professional I'm faking, anyway. Nobody needs to know that I still have no clue what I'm doing. Zac Efron's teenage voice is my soundtrack. "Getcha head in the game."

I can't fail at this. If I mess up, someone will realize I'm a big fraud. I'm underqualified, and this isn't exactly my passion. Effort and hard work will save me, but that's only if I remember the goal.

I'm just trying to prove I can do something on my own, that I can succeed without relying on anyone else. My father's greatest disappointment is that I wasn't born a boy. As much as I tried to please him, it was never enough, and my parents' focus became molding me into the perfect wife for their chosen husband.

That was okay for a long time because all I wanted was to become a wife and a mother. But my parents weren't too pleased when I announced that I wasn't going to be making that happen with Beau...Now, I'm not even sure what my dreams *are*.

I've just been floating along until landing on this path, but I have to prove to my parents that I can succeed in the corporate world, despite the unforgivable fact that I'm a woman. I don't know what else to do, besides going back to school and finishing my degree. And I want to do that as much as I want to get my nose hairs waxed.

I still have time, though. I can do this.

I give my pits a quick sniff. It's not a reliable test, but it gives me some comfort. According to a regrettable Google search, you *can* go nose blind to your own particular stink. Feeling somewhat confident that I don't reek, I take one last look in the mirror.

Time to go be the little spoon to a blindfolded big spoon. I tell myself I'm not in the least bit disappointed that Colton won't be that big spoon.

*Liar, liar, pants on fire.*

# CHAPTER EIGHTEEN

## EMBER

Pre-dawn light glows through my curtains. I'm fighting the pull of sleep while my subconscious is poking at me. There's a hazy recollection of something waking me up—a rattling sound. Awareness slams into the room like a switch being flipped.

It's that loud silence that I wish I could shut up so I can hear. I force every muscle to be still, but my heart is a drum, making me doubt every second of the stifling quiet.

*Did he find me?* He couldn't have—not even my parents know where I live. But there was definitely a sound. My eyes shoot to my alarm clock: 4:53 a.m.

*Think this through.*

He doesn't know where I am. The skeezy weasel wouldn't dare follow me.

A shuffling echoes down the hall, and something crashes to the floor.

Dear God, is someone in my apartment? I'm about to be murdered.

Weapon—I need a weapon.

I sit up, my eyes bouncing around the room. Then I pinch my lips and lean down to unplug the table lamp beside my bed. As far as weapons go, that's as good as it'll get.

*Note to self: buy a baseball bat.*

A shiver runs down my back as I creep to my bedroom door. I force a breath into my lungs before peeking around the corner and down the hallway.

That's when I see the culprit.

"Nicolas Cage, freaking...dammit! You psycho cat!"

He's sitting on the side table in the living room, looking like he's about to have tea with the queen. The admonishing glance I get in return makes me feel like I'm a toddler interrupting a grown-up meeting.

My cat thinks very little of me. I know what the little twerp is up to, though. Last night, I hid the TV remote in the side-table drawer, because I don't like waking up at five in the morning to the obnoxiously loud volume of the morning news.

In his attempt to fish out the remote, he must have knocked an empty coffee mug off the table. It's a miracle he's never attempted to swat down any flower pots.

I should look into cat rehabs.

I return my makeshift weapon before cleaning the broken shards of my favorite mug, the one with Shania's 2005 *The Woman in Me* album cover printed on the side. Ivy gave it to me for my birthday...

I sigh and decide to get ready for work. It's been a week since the staff adventure tests, and I've been surviving on an IV line of caffeine since then. I feel a little like someone who's joined a sports team mid-season. Except I've never heard of this sport, and I'm not appropriately trained.

I guess they're catching up to me, these repeated late nights. I've spent every evening planning and brainstorming for a big presentation we each get to make for new adventure boxes.

Colton gave us a week to pitch an idea that taps into previously unreached demographics. I had to research how to actually give a presentation because, big surprise, I've never done one. I am Jim Halpert, except I can't fax my dad.

The closest I've ever come to a presentation like this was to help my mom demonstrate appropriate lawn decor for the *Southern Ladies Urban Housing and Traditions Committee*. I tried pointing out to my mother how that particular acronym doesn't work. She simply rolled her eyes and said, "Emberleigh Richard Hayes, this committee has been running since our great town was founded in 1903. Do you want to argue with tradition?" Heaven forbid anyone tells my mother we've entered a new century or that women can now wear pants.

Also, yes, my middle name is Richard. My parents were so devastated at having a girl that they gave me a masculine middle name to atone for my inferior gender.

Uterus aside, once I felt confident in my knowledge of how to present an idea in a corporate setting, my ideas began to flow. I decided to focus on families with little kids, so I'm pitching a range of adventure subscriptions for young families to do together. They'd have options for before bedtime, calmer adventures, outdoor adventures, and adventures with extended family or groups of families.

It's like all the things I wished my family did when I was younger just began to pour out of me. And although the satisfaction of seeing so many of my ideas on paper made me smile, the pages mocked me too. It's all evidence of how different my family is from Colton's.

I sigh, unable to deny the ugly truth that my heart can't seem to accept yet. Colton is not for me. Or rather, I'm not for *him*.

Whatever, I might as well start the day.

Today is presentation day. And I won't lie, I'm nervous. I've put so much pressure on myself not to tank this. It's my first chance to prove that I can do more than tread water, that I'm making strides and moving forward.

I choose an outfit that's less formal than what I wore for my interview, but it's also less casual than my usual boho-chic style. I pair navy, high-waisted, flowy pants with a white tank and a tan blazer.

Last night's premade smoothie goes into a tumbler and the blazer over my arm. Taking the remote out from the drawer, I place it where that crazy cat can get to it with minimal destruction.

"Bye, Nicolas. Make good choices."

I blow a kiss to Shania and close my door, humming *"Man! I Feel Like a Woman!"*

A short yelp bursts out when I turn and come face-to-face with Opal and Gail. They're smiling like a couple of door-to-door salesmen, and this is the second time today that I nearly pee my pants.

*Jumpy much?*

I blame the cat.

Although, I know he's not one-hundred percent at fault. I don't think my jerk of an ex would have the nerve to try and find me, but I can't help that this feels like the quiet before a storm.

Opal pats my shoulder. "Oh, I'm sorry we scared you, honey, but we wanted to wish you luck on your presentation today. Also, Gail has a question."

Gail rolls her eyes. "You're just as interested in the answer as me." She turns my way, her sassy expression temporarily replaced by a sweet smile. "Anyway, Ember, honey, we were wondering if you know how to get those TikToks from the Instagram onto Pinterest." She emphasizes the in in Pinterest.

Before I can answer, Opal narrows her eyes at Gail. "Now hang on a minute; I thought we were asking her to make a TikTok with us. What do you want to mix up those socials for, like you're inventing your own cocktail? Just leave them where they are, Gail."

Gail slowly blinks at Opal, then smiles at me. "I found some lovely TikToks about Spain and want to add them to my Pinterest board."

Opal huffs. "What in the world are you doing making a Pinterest board about Spain? Your bones are too rickety to fly all the way there."

"I want my ashes scattered in the Spanish sea after I die."

"Who the heck is this Pinterest board for, the funeral director?" Opal bugs her eyes in response.

More eye-rolling. "Well, yes, if you must know. But you'll have to fly my ashes to Spain if I die before you."

"That's too expensive. I'll tie your ashes to some balloons. They'll get there eventually." Opal straightens with a tiny nod like she's just solved the problem.

There's a lot to unpack here, but if I don't interject, I could be a silent hostage in this conversation for hours.

"Ladies, as fun as this has been, and as much as I'd love to dig into what led to these...ambitious...goals, I have to get to work. But I'm pretty sure the library has classes on social media for seniors," I throw in at the end, locking my door.

Opal hooks her arm through Gail's and gives me an affectionate pat on the cheek. "Of course, sugar. You go on to that fancy job of yours. We'll pop in later to find out how today goes. I see you're wearing pants. In my day, we had to wear a skirt to get a man to listen to us, but I'm sure you'll do just fine with that clever brain of yours."

"Oh-kay...thanks, Opal. I think."

I watch them hobble off, still chirping at one other, and laugh as I begin my walk.

I really hope there are no more surprises today.

# CHAPTER NINETEEN

## EMBER

I inhale a lungful of cool morning air while I walk, mentally reviewing my presentation's key points. It should go well, as long as there aren't any technical hiccups with my slides.

I've memorized everything, so I won't have to look at any notes. Confidence in my idea will go a long way in convincing everyone that I know what I'm doing. It's a good thing I'm passionate about my concept. This opportunity to create activities and adventures for kids and families was like water for the dried soil of a neglected dream. It also reminded me of my jaded desire to have my own family. But finding the right person to spend forever with, while still trying to prove myself in the corporate world feels like wearing mismatched shoes that don't fit quite right.

*Focus on today.*

I can't afford any distractions.

I hitch my bag higher on my shoulder, taking a long sip of the smoothie I almost forgot about. I'm about to cross the street when the flash of a reflection in a storefront window knocks me back. Dizziness hits me like a wave.

*No, no, no, no!*

There's a sudden weight on my chest as I watch a dreadfully familiar figure step inside the dry cleaners in the building across from me. My feet start moving again, but my spatial awareness continues to fade.

*Why is he here? He shouldn't know where I am.*

Panic rises, squeezing the breath from my lungs. There's a fogginess in my ears as I take another jerky step forward, unaware of the need to step down off the sidewalk.

The unexpected decline is my literal downfall.

I lurch forward, and I know this won't end well. Too many things fill my arms and I can't break my fall.

*Dang travel cup!*

I twist to the side in the hopes of minimizing my direct impact with the ground, and my left wrist takes the brunt of the hit. Wincing, my eyes pinch as a sharp pain shoots up my arm.

Tears pool, threatening to spill.

Pain mixes with embarrassment.

It's a special kind of agony, being injured and excruciatingly aware of the added public humiliation.

My hands shake as I brush off the small stones embedded in my skin. I sit up, assessing the damage, and hiss as I roll my wrist, attempting to test its mobility. There's a pretty decent graze, and it hurts like the dickens.

I stand on shaky legs, noticing how my smoothie now decorates the sidewalk. The spill forms a shape that looks eerily like a hand giving a thumbs up.

There's a battle of voices in my head, mockery versus encouragement.

I decide to see it as a *chin up, you've got this!* But as I gather the rest of my things, I can't ignore the sarcastic, *nice one, Ember*, the one that chirps louder.

My eyes scan my surroundings. I never actually thought

Beau would follow me. He's made threats, but I treated them like reminders from the library about an overdue book. If I ignore them, they'll go away. Just like I assumed Beau would stop butting his pompous head into my life again. This potential pop-in has rattled me, though.

Hopefully, there's a forgotten snack bar in my desk, because my breakfast is no more. I know I'm a hot mess as I glance back to ensure I'm not being followed. My shoulder pushes open the doors of The Adventure Project.

Mrs. Sullivan's smile greets me as she turns from the printer beside her desk. She's stacking papers but freezes when she takes in my appearance. I'm hiding my wrist behind my bag, trying not to look like a guilty shoplifter. But I must seem more disheveled than I thought. Her smile falls.

"You okay, honey? You're looking quite pale."

I'm not okay. But nobody needs to know that. I'm the cartoon who just had an anvil dropped on their head but gets up like it's no big deal.

"Oh, yeah. I'm just—I dropped my smoothie. Everything's fine." I point and rush down the hall.

It'll be seriously inconvenient if something is broken. I might need to take an Uber to urgent care during lunch.

I drop my bag at my desk and grab the cardigan I left hanging over my chair yesterday. It'll cover things up.

Stupid Beau. Months later and he's still messing up my life. Maybe I just imagined seeing him, though.

I try to smooth my hair into place as I walk as calmly and as quickly as I can to the restroom, my feeble attempt at, *"Nothing to see here, folks. Look away."* I could find a first aid kit, but I don't need to spark any questions. I'll just sort myself out and get on with my morning.

Standing in the restroom, I run my trembling wrist under cold water, then dab it with a paper towel to stop the bleeding. I vow from now on to carry Band-Aids with me. My Mary Poppins bag is big enough to hold a small medical supply inventory. Too bad it's filled with everything you would definitely *not* need in an emergency. If you ever require a romance novel or the type of bobby pins you can't bend, then I'm your gal. Wound care, not so much.

I'm balling up pink-tinged paper towels when Lemon waltzes into the restroom. She struts toward a stall, her eyes sweeping over me. She's giving me restroom-judgment eyes. Apparently, no one taught her that you're supposed to be more discreet about it.

You know the look, the once-over, split-second assessment that leaves you second-guessing your life choices. Most of the time, it's harmless and probably done on a somewhat subconscious level. The twice-over lets you know you are *definitely* being shredded. That's the look Lemon throws my way before she shuts the stall door behind her. A minute later, I hear a flush, and out she steps.

How did she pee so quietly? It would be weird to ask, right? Is that some skill they teach at finishing schools? I'm sure Lemon went to one and probably excelled at everything.

*And the award for quietest pee goes to Lemon Curdbottom!*

Not her real name, but a girl can dream.

She's applying copious layers of lip gloss when those judgy-mcjudge eyes bounce to me in the mirror. I'm attempting to put my cardigan on, but freak, every movement hurts. Without a bandage, the sleeve catches on the broken skin on my arm, making me wince.

Lemon smacks her sticky lips together. She screws the lid back on her lip gloss and pauses to frown like she's witnessing someone dig through the trash.

"You look weird. Like, weirder than normal."

Not winning any awards for empathy, are we, Lemon? A knot tightens in my stomach, and my defenses rise.

"Thanks...just had a bad morning," I say, pulling at the cardigan sleeves.

"Oh, you poor thing! I hate that for you." She pouts.

Her sincerity is about as genuine as Dolly Parton's you-know-whats. I'm sure she's just heartbroken for me.

"Do you needa go home or something? I'm sure Colton will understand. I could have a word with him?"

*Hmm, yeah, I bet you could.*

I turn to face her. "Thanks, but I'll be fine." A tight smile is all I can manage before I make my exit.

*Tylenol, I need Tylenol.*

Back at my desk, I'm rummaging through my bag for a bottle of pain reliever. But things just continue to tumble around, and I curse my oversized purse.

*Bingo!*

I grab the rattling culprit and pull out a tin of Altoids.

*Frik.*

Time to pull up my big girl panties and ask Mrs. Sullivan if she has a first aid kit. Before I've left my desk, Lisa walks in, peppy and put together in a way that only highlights how out of place I feel.

"Hey, I came to check on you. We're in the meeting room, about to start." She narrows her eyes, looking at me with suspicious concern. "You okay? You look like you could pass out any second."

I'm learning I have no poker face.

"Ha ha, that's hilarious! No. No, no," I say, waving my hand like she just tried to convince me Kylie Jenner wasn't recast without anyone noticing. "I don't faint. I have the constitution of Betty White," I add proudly.

Sure, I get a little lightheaded occasionally when my blood

sugar decides to plummet, but I don't pass out. Women swooning at the literal drop of a hat ended when fashion abandoned the absurdity of corsets and dresses made from five pounds of fabric.

"I just lost track of time while I was going over everything."

"Presentations can be nerve-wracking," she says encouragingly. "But you'll do great. Everyone has each other's back out there."

"Thanks," I respond, grabbing my laptop to follow her as she heads toward the boardroom.

My nerves are swirly and jittery, but not for the reasons Lisa thinks. Sweat trickles down my back, despite the coolness of the room. Of all the days to miss breakfast, today is the worst. A sliver of hope springs that Mrs. Sullivan will bring pastries. It would be nice for something to work in my favor today.

Colton aims a smile my way as I set my things down. I return one with much less enthusiasm because I'm working hard to ignore the pain in my wrist.

I missed his greeting to Lemon, so I have nothing to compare it to, but dang it if his greeting doesn't melt my insides a little. I wish it didn't with everything in me. My little crush will be very inconvenient if he and Lemon are together. And painful.

Whatever, I just need to get through the next hour.

Colton gives me a look like he, too, wants to ask if I'm okay. If this morning has taught me anything, it's that my face has no interest in hiding my feelings.

I walk over on wobbly legs and plop my butt onto the nearest seat before I turn to greet everyone, hiding my traitorous face from Colton. The rest of the team sits, and I jolt when Lemon scoots the chair next to me an inch, creating more space between us. She floats into the seat and leans towards me, saying something about my head being in the way.

*One hour. Get through this one hour.*

Colton welcomes everyone, thankfully oblivious and I concentrate on taking slow, deep breaths as the pain eases.

*Just make it through this meeting, and you can take a little visit to urgent care.*

Lemon volunteers to go first. Opal and Gail must be rubbing off on me, because I try hard not to roll my eyes when she giggles and prances up. She spends the next ten minutes explaining her idea for a late-night edition of The Adventure Project, with all of her ideas centered around bar crawling.

I'll give it to her; it's a bold move. I haven't worked here that long, but going purely off the expressions on everyone's faces as they listen, I'm going to say it'll be a pass on Lemon's idea. She ends her presentation with a summary of demographics and statistics on how millennials spend their money.

Colton clears his throat, his knuckles tapping on the table. "Thank you, Lemon. Great work. Ember, you're up."

Why do I feel like I'm back in middle school and just got called to the front of the class? My hands are still trembling as I stand and smooth them down my thigh.

I can do this.

I place my computer on the table in the front while Lemon gathers her things. I still can't help but fidget, pulling at the cuffs of my sleeves, trying to hide my street-fight look.

Those talking points I memorized are shuffling out of order. My foot bounces nervously while I wait for Lemon to unplug her laptop.

I roll my shoulders and inhale a quiet, slow breath. *In and out.* Those feelings of panic don't go away entirely, but at least I've relegated them to standing in the corner of the room.

Everything will be fine. The information I've memorized will return once I start my slides.

If I perish from unnecessary worry, I hope my life will at

least become a case study for overfunded scientists hypothesizing the patterns of cause and effect resulting in premature, middle-aged death. It's random and overly specific, but there are enough multibillionaires worldwide to warrant funding something as mundane as why some white lady died too soon. I imagine their conclusion reading, "Her downfall was not one thing, but a combination of factors."

My heart rate begins to enter the range of not-about-to-have-a heart attack. At least, I can't hear my heartbeat anymore, so I think that's good.

Lemon is looking positively chuffed, hearts practically shooting out her eyes in Colton's direction as she waltzes to her seat. It's unfortunate for me, not because she represents a rival for the hottest man in the room's attention. I'd actually be fine with that. The more evidence to convince my heart that being attracted to Colton is a bad idea, the better.

Nope, this is unfortunate for me because Lemon is no longer paying attention to where she's walking. The side of her computer clips my left hand, and immobilizing pain stabs my arm.

Sounds fade, and my skin goes clammy. I hear my name being called, but it sounds like I'm underwater. My last thought before everything goes black is that I can never make fun of fainting Regency damsels—because I'm about to become one of them.

# CHAPTER TWENTY

## COLTON

I watch as Ember's face drains of color. Her eyes, wide with distress, flicker with pain before she collapses to the ground, limp as a rag doll. It's as though someone shouted "timber," because she's going down like a felled tree.

My heart is in my throat. I spring from my chair with all the hero-worthy intention of catching her, but I'm not the mom from The Incredibles, and I curse as she hits the floor. Thankfully, she wasn't near the table corner when she fainted. But then again, if she were closer, maybe I would have caught her.

"Oh my gosh! Is she okay?" Lisa gasps, crouching beside Ember.

I frown, carefully lifting her head to slide my folded jacket underneath.

Mallory stands nearby, biting her nails. "Should we call 911? Did she mention not feeling well?" she inquires, looking at each of us.

She didn't seem like herself this morning. I haven't known her long enough to know what's normal for her, but something in her body language said she was out of sorts.

"Could it be lady troubles?" Ethan asks, squinting an eye like he's unsure whether those will be his last words.

"No, you idiot," Lisa reprimands, swatting his leg. "Women don't just faint when they have their periods."

"She could have a concussion. I think we should take her to a hospital," Mallory declares, laying a hand on Ember's shoulder.

"I saw her in the restroom." Lemon adds with a hint of uncertainty. "She was acting a little weird, but I wasn't paying attention." A flicker of concern flashes on her brow. "She was throwing away balled-up paper towels that might have had blood on them."

Straightening a fraction, I narrow my eyes at her. "Explain."

"I asked if she was okay. She said she had a rough morning. That's all."

Mallory lifts the end of Ember's sleeve, revealing a nasty graze and a swollen wrist.

As carefully as I can, I pick Ember up, cradling her in my arms as I stand. She smells like cupcakes. It's a scent that makes me want to bury my nose in her neck long enough to figure out if it's her perfume or shampoo. Thankfully, I have enough sense not to do any of that.

"Lisa, get Ember's emergency contact and medical information from Mrs. Sullivan. Send it to Mallory. Mal, we're taking Ember to a doctor."

# CHAPTER TWENTY-ONE

## EMBER

Waking up in a hospital gown really throws you for a loop. You're left asking yourself stuff like, "Who swiped my clothes?" and "Why does my tongue feel like it's Sean Connery's chest?"

The room is dim, but the pounding in my head makes me wish it was darker. I lift the hem of my gown, relieved to see my tank top is still there.

A sharp, antiseptic smell turns my stomach as nausea and hunger swirl together, forming a weird alliance that I do not support. My throat screams for water, while my mind demands answers. I shift, my movement alerting a brooding figure I'm just noticing.

He fills a room so magnificently that I can only blame the fuzziness in my brain for my lack of awareness. Colton bolts out of his chair, bringing a cup with a straw to my lips.

*Oh, sweet baby Yoda, that feels good on my throat.*

"You know, if you wanted to nap at work, there are easier ways to do it," he says with a smirk.

I clear my throat, the words feeling scratchy as they come out. "Where would the fun be in that?"

"Our ideas of fun are very different 'cause I didn't enjoy watching you suddenly get acquainted with the boardroom floor."

An unusual boldness and lack of inhibition are having an evil laugh together in my head, encouraging me to let out the thoughts that I've been keeping on a tight leash.

"Unfortunately, Mr. Blue Eyes, I can't give a review on the fun factor, seeing as I don't remember what happened," I slur.

Frowning, I examine the cast encasing my arm. "My arm has a home."

"For the next six weeks, yeah, it does,"

Memories from this morning sluggishly return. Beau, the lost smoothie, the fall. The last minutes before everything went black are piecing themselves together. My constant frown isn't helping the pounding in my head, but it feels essential for thinking this hard. "My head feels fruity."

"You mean, loopy?"

"That one." I point then lean forward, staring at his lips. "I wanna be friends with your mouth."

The mouth in question tilts into a smirk. "I'll remind you of that when your pain meds wear off."

"What...happened?"

He pulls a chair closer, lowering himself onto it with a sigh, and his eyes turn to the window. Attractive forearms rest on his thighs, though I suspect I shouldn't be thinking about Colton like that. A tight-jawed silence fills the room.

"Did you hurt your wrist before the meeting?" he asks after a while.

"I tripped...on the sidewalk...I think."

"Why didn't you tell anyone?"

I know I'm a little off my rocker on these pain meds, but I'm still lucid enough to recognize that the medications are the sole cause of my confusion at his question. I've looked after myself for so long that it never occurred to me to tell someone I was hurt. To what end? I'm perfectly capable of getting myself to a doctor, and it wouldn't have been the first time.

"I was fine. I had it handled."

"We could've helped, you know."

The temptation to poke that muscle on his jaw is huge.

*Um, no, Ember. No touchy the boss.*

He's poison oak, and I'd do well to remember that.

*But you could wear gloves...No! Stop it!*

I want to ask more about this fainting business, but a knock on the door and a nurse stepping inside interrupt my thoughts. I can't seem to hang on to one long enough before it fades away.

A bubbly nurse introduces herself as Mary while walking over to a whiteboard on the wall opposite my bed. Man, I have missed some critical details since waking up. Underneath the word *"goals"* she erases the words *"wake up"* and writes *"go home."*

They're such simple objectives that I wish all of my life's goals were just as easy to wipe off and replace.

"Miss Hayes, it's good to see you awake. Are you okay with Mr. King staying in the room while I go over some things about your injuries?"

My eyes bounce to Colton, then back to Mary. "Sure, that's fine. He has a nice face."

Mary laughs with a motherly twinkle in her eyes. "He sure does."

A flicker of a smile tugs at Colton's lips. My heart beats an unsteady rhythm as his eyes bore into mine.

Mary tells me I have a fractured wrist and a minor concussion from my head smacking the floor when I fainted. I want to tell her I don't faint, but I also want to stay on her good side and maybe get an extra pudding cup for good behavior. She asks me questions about what led to the alleged fainting. I give her the details I remember, leaving out the bit about being spooked by my asshat ex. Instead, I tell her my original fall was the result of clumsily trying to avoid stepping on a snail. It's not the smoothest lie, but I've never claimed to be proficient in the art of fibbing, so here we are.

"We're keeping you overnight for observation since there was a loss of consciousness. We wanna get some test results back and ensure everything is as it should be before sending you home. The doctor will also be in later to see you, okay?"

"Sounds groovy, Susie." Fifty percent sure that's not her name, but it felt right.

She bustles off with a chuckle, leaving me alone with Colton.

"Earned yourself a nice wrist jacket there."

"You mean my arm funnel?" I grin, lifting my cast. His smile grows in return, and the full strength of it should come with a warning.

*Caution: May cause heart palpitations and/or swooning.*

My uninjured hand fidgets with the scratchy, bleached blanket covering my legs. There's still something significant about today that I can't quite recall.

"What's going on in that head of yours?" he asks.

"What...what was I doing when I..." I can't even say the word. "When I...*fainted?*" I stage whisper.

"You were about to give your presentation."

There it is.

The rest of this morning's disastrous details come back to me at once and my shoulders sink.

"My pitch. It was so good. Although..." I lean close, probably too close, and whisper next to my hand, "Don't tell anyone this, but I actually have no idea what I'm doing."

I throw my head back and cackle, somewhat aware that my lips are too loose right now. If only I had the self-control to keep them shut.

Colton stands and perches on the side of my bed.

He's looking way too sexy as he takes hold of my hand. He doesn't dress like any boss I've ever known, but his casual style suits him. He's an adventurer at heart, so Colton in a suit, although drool-worthy, wouldn't seem right.

I'm ready to hang on every syllable that might come out of his mouth, the one that's now deliciously close and for which I'd still like the chance to plead my case for friendship.

"You can still do your pitch. Just heal up first. And don't worry about Lemon, she—"

The door to my room bursts open, interrupting Colton, but my eyes are still zeroed in on his lips when he lets go of my hand and stands abruptly.

*You've got to be kidding me! Finish the sentence!*

Nobody likes cliffhangers, and I'm hanging on with one finger. I'm not above begging. If ever there were a sentence I wanted to hear the end of, this is it. Lemon is what? Moving to Zimbabwe? Actually a man? I'm about to ask him when the room burster clears her throat, reluctantly drawing my eyes away from Colton.

*Crap.*

"The nurse said you had a fall, are you all right?" The words are there, but the stiffness in her tone is almost comical. I love my mother, but her level of empathy has never been high.

"I'll be fine, thank you, Mom."

Her throat clears and she casts a look to Colton then back to me.

"Oh—Colton, my mother, Fretta Hayes. Mother, this is my boss, Colton."

"*Boss?*" Her right eyebrow looks like it's attempting to

touch the ceiling. "You call your boss by his first name?" She sounds so aghast, like I've just flashed my underwear before a crowd of men.

Colton tentatively steps forward, offering my mother his hand, the one that was just holding mine a second before we were so rudely interrupted. "It's a pleasure to meet you, Mrs. Hayes. I'm Colton King."

I'm not sure it's ever a pleasure to meet Fretta Hayes, but what's a guy to say when thrown into the drama unfolding before him?

I watch as my mother sizes Colton up, clearly unimpressed with what she sees. "You look very casual, young man, for a work day."

Colton glances down at his outfit, then turns to me with a tiny head shake, the corners of his mouth turning down as his chin scrunches up. It's a look that says, "I don't get it." But I'm way too drugged up to explain that my mother already thinks he should be cleaning her yard, not claiming the title of employer. I'm sure he'd like to run right out of this cozy little room to a place that's more *medical documentary* and less *General Hospital*.

I wouldn't mind watching Colton run. Guys don't run with shirts on, do they? This one certainly shouldn't.

*Oh, Ember, for shame! Look what these meds have you thinking.*

"Mr. King," she says with a tiny sniff and shifts her shoulders back. Her icy gaze returns to me.

"Emberleigh, you really must—"

"Mom, it's *Ember*. For fifteen years, I've asked you to call me Ember. What even is the name Emberleigh?" I'm waving my arms around now, cast included. "Did you and Dad just make up a name?"

"It was your great aunt's name," she replies, sounding as if she's tired of explaining this to me so many times. "A family name, dear. It's nothing to cause a scene over."

Suddenly, it feels like there are too many freaking blankets on this bed. Where is the end of this tube that's snaked around me? With one hand, I lift the sheets and try to follow the line of the IV.

I'm ready to get out of here now. My mother thinks she's witnessed a scene, but uninhibited, medicated Ember doesn't do drama like a normal person. Nope. I'm a toddler getting my face wiped. I will show her *drama*. There's a good chance I'll regret a few things in the morning, but I'm feeling bold enough to tell my mother to shut it.

Colton steps forward, clearly noticing my intention to jump ship. "Hey, what ya doing there?" He takes my hands into his and I lift my elbows, searching.

"I'm looking for the end of this tubey guy so he and I can go home."

"I don't think the tubey guy goes home with you."

"Good, 'cause Nicolas Cage doesn't like men in my home." Not that there have been any men in my apartment, but Nicolas does seem to shun the male species, so I'm counting his vote as no.

"Who's...never mind. Let's leave the tubey guy for the nurse to deal with. Mrs. Hayes, I think Ember needs to rest. Maybe it'd be better if you visited another time?"

My eyes jerk up. Traitor! Don't invite her back! I'm rethinking becoming friends with the mouth that just uttered those words.

"Emberleigh," she begins again. "I understand you needed some time. But I really think you could at least talk to Beau."

So many questions swarm around in my head that I get tunnel vision. All I see is my mother, who has betrayed me, yet again. "You've been speaking to Beau about me? Did you give him my number?"

"He cares about you, Emberleigh."

"Mom, I *specifically* asked you not to give him my number or tell anyone where I was. I told you I needed space."

"I don't know why you need space from people who care about you, but I can see you need to calm down. I'll let you have a nap, and we'll talk about this later." She pats my foot, barely acknowledging Colton as she leaves the room.

"We won't! We won't talk about this, Mom!" I shout as she retreats to her ice castle. "Well, that was quite the show, wasn't it," I say after a second of awkward silence.

Colton is still holding my hands. He releases them, and I almost groan in protest. But then he's scooting closer, and the next thing I know, his arms are wrapping around me in a tight hug.

If I made a list of all the possible responses to witnessing what just happened, this would be at the bottom, the least likely. But I can say without a doubt that I never want to leave this spot. Someone bring me a lease agreement because I will sign my soul away to take up residence in the warm embrace of Colton King's arms.

*He has a girlfriend, Ember. His arms are not for you!*

*Shhhh, just let me have this.*

Much too soon, he's leaning back, ducking slightly to make eye contact.

"You okay, Sunshine?"

That question seems heavy, asking more than I want to give away right now, maybe ever. So I deflect.

"You keep using that word, and I don't think it means what you think it means." I'm anything but "sunshine" at the moment. I am Oscar the Grouch.

Then I realize that things are still a little swirly in my head, but not the fun kind, like when you've been dancing too long. This kind makes me want to hurl.

That grin emerges as his hands slide down my arms, gently cradling my fingers. I sincerely hope that this blip of attraction will disappear when I'm no longer tripping on the meds. Because if not, then I am in for a heap of pain.

# CHAPTER TWENTY-TWO

## COLTON

There's just something about sports mascots that triggers a bizarre impulse in me—I actually kind of want to see one get punched. I know violence isn't the solution, but if I found myself next to a guy in a giant duck costume, I might be strangely tempted to sock him just out of pure annoyance. And if this guy Beau ever showed up in that scenario, I'd secretly hope he'd throw the first punch, just so I'd have a good excuse to hit him back.

I realize my disdain for sports mascots is a bit much. During my college years, I was on a fast track to making baseball my career; local mascots were the glue that everyone rallied around. Sometimes I wonder where I'd be if I'd made a different choice ten years ago. Now every time I see a mascot–I'm reminded of the career I almost had and what it cost me.

I blink away those thoughts that feel too heavy to resurface while holding the hands of a girl like Ember.

There are so many things I want to ask, things I want to say. Nicolas Cage is one of them. But she's still too out of it to give any reliable answers. I don't like that I know nothing about the situation with her ex, except that he did a number on her and that's why she ran. And that I want to punch him.

Her glazed eyes stare at my chest. "Button is a weird word, right? Butt-ons." She carries on enunciating the one word like it's two. "Butt ons..."

I'm beginning to wonder if the pain meds they gave her were too strong, because this doesn't seem like a normal reaction to what I'm guessing one needs for a broken wrist.

There's a soft knock on the door, then a petite, blonde around Ember's age walks into the room with wide eyes and her mouth hanging open.

"Vee! You came!"

"The heck, Hayes? I'm getting ready to text you about your pitch when I get a call that you're in the HOSPITAL!" She lifts and drops her arms. "Are you okay?"

"Peachy," says Ember.

"She's not peachy. She has a concussion and a broken wrist."

"Minor concussion. Colton, this is my Ivy. Ive, this is my Colton. Mmm...nope, that wasn't right." She flaps her hands like she wants to wave away her last sentence. "My boss, Colton."

"Ooh, Hi," Ivy says, holding her hand out with a smile and an eyebrow wag at Ember. "I'm the best friend."

I think for a second that I might not mind being Ember's Colton. *Don't go there.*

I shake Ivy's hand and give her a summary of what happened. "The doctor should be in soon to go over everything. They should check her medication dosage, though. I think it may be a bit too strong for her."

"Eek, yeah, she reacts weirdly to medication. I'll mention it. Hey, thanks for staying with her."

"Of course." My gaze moves back to Ember. I'm contemplating stalling, but I have no reason to hang around now that her friend is here. She's safe and taken care of, and I'm not Ember's Colton, after all. I squeeze her uninjured hand. "I'm gonna head out, but if you need anything, let me know. And don't worry about your presentation. You can do it when you're back at the office."

"Thank you, Colton. Sorry 'bout the drama with my mom."

"Wait, your *mom* was here?" Ivy shouts. She seems to operate at a volume that's louder than most.

"Ugh, yeah, I didn't think through adding her to my emergency contact list. Parents should be on that list, right?" She stares at a random spot in the room, her expression sad.

Ivy pats her foot with regret. "Not your parents, sweetheart."

I hate leaving her like this.

The urge to hug her again is strong, but I settle for giving her hand one more squeeze. "I'll check up on you tomorrow," I promise as I stand.

It's for the best that I'm leaving. I don't need my head any more distracted than it already is, yet I relish the way Ember's eyes follow me to the door as I wave goodbye.

The events of the morning replay in my mind all afternoon, like a news recap showing the same footage of a local disaster over and over again. My thoughts are all over the place.

Superspeed! That's a way better superpower. Why was the stretchy mom from The Incredibles the first superhero I thought about instead of the Flash or literally any other manly superhero? Even Hulk would have saved the girl from face-planting the floor.

Back in my office, I fight the urge to text Ember. I'm sure she's resting, as she should be. She's fine and doesn't need me to hover.

I reassure myself that she's being cared for and that she's happy. It doesn't matter that my stomach twists a little at the thought of not being involved in that happiness.

# CHAPTER TWENTY-THREE

## EMBER

"This is stupid."

"It's not stupid."

"I'm still recovering from a concussion. I should rest."

"That was a week ago. You've rested enough. You know you want to see Mr. Delicious."

A growl escapes as I flop back onto my bed and cover my face with the dress Ivy just handed me. I'm still getting used to having a cast on my arm, and I accidentally whack myself in the head. "Ow. I'm pretty sure those were your words, not mine."

"Potato, potah-to." Ivy waves me off. "I live a boring life as a second-grade teacher. I've gotta get my drama fix where I can, and currently, you are the source of said drama. Your life is better than the current season of The Bachelor. I must know what's happening with Lemon and Colton, or I'll wilt like a sad, floppy flower because nobody watered me with scandalous information." She turns her big doe eyes my way. "Come on, Em. Don't let me wilt."

"You can find better drama at a poker game with Opal and Gail."

She carries on rummaging through piles of clothes, making it feel like we're stuck in a nineties rom-com gearing up for a montage. Clothes and shoes cover my bedroom floor, and Ivy inevitably trips over something every few minutes. She's the clumsy to my awkward. If there's something to bump into or trip over, or even nothing to trip over, Ivy will find it. She's also a little sensitive about her height, so you'll almost always find her in heels, which makes her tendency to wipe out that much greater.

"Let's find something to wear to this Halloween party so we can go out and get the scoop!" She does a slow turn my way. "Or...you could always just come straight out and ask him if he's seeing Lemon."

The past week has been ridiculously confusing. Lemon disappeared for a few days, and Colton was tight-lipped, offering nothing that could help me determine if they're an item. Frustrated, I vented to Ivy, who then devised a bolder strategy for us to dig up more information.

"I'm not asking him! In what world do you think that's something I'd do?"

Ivy sighs and begins rummaging through the mounds of clothes piled around her like haystacks in a field. "Fine, but it would solve the problem," she mutters. Meanwhile, more clothes come flying in my direction.

"Why didn't we plan outfits earlier? There's nothing here that'll work."

"Because you, sweet Em, procrastinated your ass off and only told me about this party two hours ago."

"I like procrastinating. It lets me temporarily avoid the feelings that come with the task."

"That's rather bleak, Freud. But it still doesn't solve your problem, which is that you have a crush on your boss and need to check out the competition."

"It's also a terrible idea 'cause I don't *want* to like him. I can't date another coworker. I've learned my lesson."

"That lesson was that your parents don't always know what's best, and they shouldn't have shoved Beau at you because he's a terrible human. It's not a workplace problem you have."

A crease that I'm worried might become permanent forms between my eyes. Before I can dive into Ivy's claims, she squeals, clapping her hands excitedly. "I know what we can wear! Wait here!"

I flop back, staring at the popcorn ceiling, finding shapes and faces in the ugly dots. I tilt my head, staring at one that looks like a unicorn when Nicolas Cage jumps onto my bed. "Hey dude, you watch anything interesting today?" He rubs against my side and then kneads the clothes scattered around me.

A minute later, Ivy's voice interrupts my ceiling hobby with a throat clear. I ease up on my elbows to see her holding up two sheep costumes.

"Why do those look like a bunch of seven-year-olds made them?"

"Because they did," she says, looking way too happy as she tosses one my way, hanger included. "Put it on."

She's already undressing, so I give in, knowing I can't get out of this. We spend five minutes laughing hysterically as we try to find the correct openings for the right limbs, pieces of cotton falling off around us.

"That's the wrong arm hole," Ivy giggles. "Let me help you."

"Hang on, I've got it. Why do you even have these? We look..." I can't breathe, I'm laughing so hard. I catch a glimpse of our sad forms in the mirror, setting off another round of hysterics.

"We look like sheep that were an experiment gone...gone wrong!" I finally manage to say as I wipe the tears from my eyes. We're basically wearing large burlap sacks with chunks of cotton glued to them, except the brown of the burlap and the many missing pieces of cotton make us look like sheep that were attacked by a set of shears.

Ivy and I have reached the drunk stage of our delirium. It never takes much to set us off, and now we're like the floating tea party in Mary Poppins, and it'll require just as much effort to bring us down from this high. Unfortunately, we don't have Mary Poppins as our voice of reason.

Ivy's fingers massage her face. "My cheeks are so sore." She tries to stand, but trips over the wardrobe explosion around us. "They were so proud..." she clutches her stomach laughing, "they were so proud of these outfits." She takes a deep, calming breath before attempting to speak again. "I told them that my teacher's aide and I would wear these on Monday if they all finished their book reports. Oh my gosh." Another deep breath. "Okay, this is clearly a fail."

"I wish I could be a fly on the wall, y'know, just see what's happening without having to do all the socializing stuff. I don't have the energy for all that." I almost never have the energy for that.

Ivy smacks me on the arm, her eyes wide. "We could go full Kim Kardashian!"

"I don't think a celebrity getup is the solution right now, although I could be talked into making her weird crying face from that meme."

"That sounds fun, but no. I mean we should dress all black, head to toe, a la Met Gala Kim. Nobody will know who we are. We go in, observe, and leave."

If I were less laugh-drunk, I might see how terrible this idea really is, but my bestie has always been able to talk me into crazy stuff I'd never do on my own.

"How do you see this coming together, exactly?" It's concerning how the idea seems less and less ridiculous as I stare at Ivy's excited face.

"Okay, we both have black jeans and a black, long-sleeved shirt. We could swing by a store and get black ski masks, gloves, and ball caps. It's genius!" She doesn't give me time to reconsider before she drags me off the bed. "Come on! This is gonna work."

# CHAPTER TWENTY-FOUR

## EMBER

We're parked alongside the dirt road leading to Ethan's house, giggling like thirteen-year-olds. An oversized black sweater hides my cast and a men's glove covers my hand.

"I can't believe we're actually doing this. Is this a bad idea?" I turn worried eyes to Ivy with a hand on my forehead.

She adjusts her cap, not looking at me when she responds. "It's genius. And we're already in too deep. We've gotta go through with it."

"Okay," I breathe, smoothing my hands over my thighs. "Remember, we can't talk to each other, or someone might recognize my voice. And make sure your ski mask is tucked under your cap. Maybe you should take your glasses off first?"

"I may as well close my eyes then! It's bad enough with the ski mask. How will I witness the drama with ten-percent vision, Em? It's fine, see?" she asks, covering her face and glasses with the mask.

"Okay. Find Lemon and Colton. Observe. Exit." I remind her of the plan.

"I feel like a badass spy. Let's do this." We fist bump to seal the deal.

We climb out of the car and head towards the house, trying to blend in as much as possible. Ethan's driveway is packed with cars, yet since he lives just outside the suburbs, it doesn't feel overcrowded. I reckon this might be the only time I'm actually thankful for such a large crowd at a party.

Luckily, it only takes us two minutes to reach the door; any longer and I might have second thoughts. Just as I consider making a quick dash back to the car, Ivy catches on and grabs my arm, pulling me forward. We weave through guests dressed far more appropriately than us as they mingle on the wraparound porch.

And then the realization hits me: this may be the best way to go to any social event. It's oddly comforting knowing my identity is hidden and that I won't have to talk to anyone. I'm only here for answers, after all. Not sure what I'll do with those answers, but I feel like I'm stuck in limbo until I have them. My bruised little heart seems to need them.

Ethan's home sits on a large piece of land, glowing with its tasteful Halloween decor. I wonder if someone helped him or if he's the one responsible for the ambiance.

I lead Ivy inside, and familiar faces dot each room as we walk through the house. There are still a decent amount of partygoers I don't recognize—which is good for us.

We make our way into the farm-style kitchen. It's unfinished, with exposed cabinets and unfinished surfaces, but the bones are good. The large living room has all my shiplap-filled Pinterest boards crying out at me.

Ivy bumps into someone, but we're maintaining a vow of silence, so we only bow in apology. I make a mental note to debrief later on that simultaneous response with zero choreography.

I'm starting to notice the weird looks, although I shouldn't be offended. I'd stare, too, if I were a witness to our freak show. The last bit of sanity taps me on the shoulder, but I've already committed, so I shoo it away. I'll undoubtedly question my actions later, but in the words of Mama June, "It is what it is,".

Neither Lemon nor Colton seem to be among the crowd in the kitchen, so I signal wordlessly to Ivy, and we slink through a passage into the main living area. However, it's becoming clear that our vibe is less "badass spies" and more "escaped backup dancers from a Lady Gaga music video."

I spot an open space near the corner of the large living room, squeeze Ivy's elbow, then nod toward my intended surveillance area. Looking eerily like Peter Pan's psychotic shadows, we awkwardly make our way through the mashup of guests. How does Ethan know so many people? Surely a gathering of this size violates some building codes or would at least annoy the fire marshal.

And somebody should open a window. The air is humid and warm inside like the old AC can't keep up.

We finally reach the wall that I've now designated as our stakeout zone for the remainder of the night. I'm in the nightmare version of my wallflower dreams. Instead of being approached by a handsome duke, I'm the subject of whispers behind the glares of confusion and maybe even fear.

I lean towards Ivy's ear. "People are scared of us. Also, I'm sweating so much."

"Right? Did *not* anticipate so much sweating," she whispers back.

We continue to hold up our wall like a couple of gas-station lurkers for another fifteen minutes. A few brave guests attempt the world's most awkward one-sided conversation, but they all give up once they realize that all we can do is nod in response.

It's quickly becoming the cringiest moment of my life.

Then, I feel a line of moisture dripping down my back, the final straw. I grasp Ivy's wrist, pulling her down a hallway. "Bathroom meeting. Now."

Ivy trots behind, her muffled laughs escaping through her ski mask. I'm trying to stifle my bark of laughter as I open a few doors until I find the bathroom. I swing Ivy inside and shove the door closed behind us. We pull our masks down, gasping at the semi-fresh air.

"Why did we do this?" I fan my face with my hand.

"We can't even drink or eat anything," Ivy moans while washing her hands and splashing her face with water. "Did you see the charcuterie table? I swear, I nearly gave in when I spotted the bacon-wrapped dates. Bacon, Em," she pleads, gripping my shoulders.

"This was your idea! We're ridiculous. This plan was ridiculous. I'm sweaty and hungry."

We glance at each other in the mirror and erupt into laughter all over again. I'm a grown woman. Why do I find this situation so hilarious?

Then I realize it's not the situation. It's my friend, who brings a lightness to my life that I so desperately need. If not for Ivy, I'd probably be a reclusive cat lady by now, one with whom not even Opal and Gail would want to associate.

Smoothing our sweaty hair down, we reluctantly don our Kim K coverings again.

"Maybe we should go hang outside for a bit. It'll be cooler." Ivy suggests, fanning her face.

I take one more look in the mirror. "Okay, but we never tell anyone about this."

"Agreed." She nods, and we creep down the hallway until we reach the door leading outside.

Floating skull candles bob around in the pool, and I'm so

tempted to join them. Nobody would even notice. We'd blend right in.

Ivy pulls me to the far end of the yard, our bodies a pair of dark forms slithering in the night. A brave man in a Greek toga makes his way toward us. I wonder if we've become a bit of a mystery for the others to solve, as a growing number of guests attempt to draw us into conversation.

Toga dude self-assuredly struts closer until Ivy shakes her head, kindly informing him he's not worthy. His shoulders drop, and he pivots to rejoin the group he left before. Failed mission, buddy. I bite my lip and press my face into Ivy's shoulder.

Poor, courageous toga guy. "He walked over so confidently," I whisper through a silent laugh. Ivy's gloved hand covers her mouth. She's trying just as hard to maintain a semblance of control over the traveling circus we've become.

A slight breeze blows, and just as my flaming cheeks cool down, a sight across the yard makes my heart thud inside my chest.

Colton is standing amongst a small gathering, his back to me but easily recognizable with his tall frame. And aren't I the picture of a Regency damsel, noticing a man's physique?

Ivy's elbowing stops me from going further down that rabbit hole and taking too much notice of his tapered waist or the thickness of his thighs.

*That's it. I'm packing my Regency novels away tonight.*

"Colton. Over there," Ivy warns me.

"Thank you, Captain Obvious," I rasp.

In a perfectly timed movie moment, Lemon emerges from the crowd and sidles up beside him. She hands him a drink and stands on tiptoes, whispering something in his ear. The moment looks intimate, and I wish with everything in me that I could see his face right now.

He leans closer, his hand reaching the small of her back and giving me my answer. I can't watch any more. Dejection, shame, and disappointment all find a place in my chest as I pull Ivy towards the house, weaving through people.

This was a bad idea.

What am I doing, acting like a teenager, spying on my boss? *My boss!*

There's obviously something going on between Colton and Lemon. Besides the fact that I don't even want a relationship right now, I won't pine after someone whose interests lie elsewhere.

"Em," Ivy whispers harshly as she tries to slow us down, but I have a firm grip on her arm and a walk of shame to finish.

I whip my head around. "It's fine," I barely choke out.

People try to engage with us, but Ivy only has time for quick salutes as I drag her along with me.

We're both silent until we're back in the car.

"Em."

"I'm fine. It's fine. Really," I ramble, gesturing too much with my hands for someone who claims they're fine. "We did what we came to do. Now I can move forward. It's good. This is good. I'll continue with the blind-dating thing, as much as I hate them. You said the blog is doing well, right? So let's carry on with the plan."

There's a long beat of silence while I expect Ivy to ask if I'm really okay, but she doesn't, probably because she already knows that I'm not. I couldn't dream of doing something this bold without her. I'd have precisely two friends if she didn't constantly push me out into the big, bad world. And although I'm truly grateful for her support, I can't ignore the feeling of foolishness that makes my skin crawl.

Why did I think someone like Colton would be interested in me? I'm a mess. My life is a mess. Everything seems neat on the outside, but inside, anxiety rules most of the decisions I make. Heck, if it weren't for Ivy, I'd probably still be trapped in an abusive relationship and living with my parents.

Ivy stares at me, seeing so much. Like the good friend she is, she notices when something is threatening to wrap around me. Every sensation has me on edge, everything feels so stifling.

She gives a quick nod. "Let's eat ice cream and watch TV with your weird cat."

My nostrils flare, and I fight back the tears threatening to open a floodgate of emotions that have been patched closed. "Thank you, Vee. You're the best. You know that?"

"That's what I keep telling people." She smiles.

# CHAPTER TWENTY-FIVE

### EMBER

Who would have guessed that water coolers actually live up to their stereotype of being a beacon for office-gossip central? You'd think it would be the coffee machine or the box of sinful pastries Mrs. Sullivan puts out nearly every morning, but we're a hydrating bunch at The Adventure Project.

As far as random spots go, this one rates high on comfort and aesthetic appeal. A large fiddle leaf plant cozies up next to the cooler, and the temperature is just right in this little nook. It's not directly under an air vent and still catches some of the soft morning light from the window beside it. It's the little things, I tell you.

It's a no-brainer that most people come to fill their water but stay for a chat. I'm not exactly the chit-chatting type, but sometimes hydration is a powerful motivator, so I brave the water cooler today.

Today's hot goss? Ethan's Halloween party.

Lisa, Jed, Ethan, and I stand in a half-circle around the cooler, reusable tumblers in hand. All we need is someone to toss out a hacky sack, and we'd be reliving our high school days before smartphones kept our butts on benches.

I look at my banged-up metal cup, some of the newer divots serving as a reminder of my smoothie-sidewalk debacle. Lisa's is glittering and shiny in comparison, like it came from a unicorn swag bag, and Jed and Ethan hold polished cups, no dents in sight. It's the adult equivalent of lunch box envy.

Ethan lifts his tumbler, one finger uncurling as he points at me. "Ember, we missed you at the party. I thought you were planning to come?"

*Oh, if you only knew.*

"Yeah, I'm bummed I couldn't make it. Anything interesting happen?" I'm fishing, I know.

"Nah, not much."

Lisa snorts at his reply. "There were a few randos there. You should up security for entrance next time, Ethan. Those two in all black were a little...strange." She arches an eyebrow and takes a sip from her tumbler, its sparkles nearly blinding me.

Ethan's eyebrows crease. "That was a bit weird."

It's somewhat satisfying to know we creeped some people out.

Lisa's gushing about the food when Lemon struts over, her disposable coffee cup in direct defiance of our unofficial water-drinking club bylaws.

"Hey gang," she trills, then turns to me, scrunching her nose. "Oh my gosh, Ember, my Nana has that same sweater! That's so cute."

"I like it," Lisa adds, coming to my defense. The guys are oblivious to what's unfolding, even though it's one of the oldest tricks in the book.

But I'll be damned if I let someone else fight my battles, so I smile sweetly at Lemon. "Thanks, old lady was just the vibe I was going for this morning." I'll relive this moment of public sass later on, but for now, I keep my guard up.

Lemon lets loose a sound that's something between a laugh and a scoff, disappointed when her attempt at a dig doesn't quite land how she thought it would.

*I've got claws too, sister.*

Not that they come out often, but I won't let her sour juju get to me. I'm grateful for this job, and I will do it professionally.

She's not too happy that Colton decided to go ahead with my family box idea. If she thinks she can subtly embarrass me in front of coworkers to reassert herself, I've got news for her. I do that job just fine on my own.

Colton chooses that moment to step out of his office, looking like the cover model for an outdoor magazine. I roll my eyes at the wayward thoughts.

I don't want to find him attractive. He's a taken man, dammit.

It's fine, though. Eventually, the sting of seeing him and Lemon together will ease up, and the butterflies in my stomach won't party like they're on spring break every time Colton walks into the room.

His eyes meet mine for a second before he looks at Lemon.

"Lemon, can I see you in my office, please?"

"Of course." She smiles brightly at me.

"Well, back to the ol' grind. Maybe we'll bump into each other again sometime," I offer the rest of the water-cooler crew in an attempt to diffuse the awkwardness. I could be a spokesperson for those progressive ads about not becoming your parents.

Lisa laughs at my dad joke, and we disperse as if the end-of-recess bell just rang.

The rest of the day goes by rather pleasantly, maybe

because I don't see Lemon again. By four o'clock, I'm closing my computer and straightening the things on my desk, placing everything just how I like it. I throw away a stack of papers and grab my bag as I turn to leave, then jolt to a stop at the broad chest that suddenly appears in front of me.

"Mother of pearl, Colton! Did you take a class on sneaking up on people?" I exclaim, my hand flying to my chest.

A sheepish smile greets me. "Sorry, I swear I don't mean to keep scaring you."

*Avoid the eyes, Ember. They'll suck you in.*

I focus on his chin, which isn't any better because now I'm noticing that his jawline is also quite appealing. It's rugged. Not, like, Gaston-rugged, but it's definitely giving Chris Evans vibes.

It would be too weird to snap my own fingers at myself, right? I need to do something to break the spell his presence has on me.

His gaze bounces over my face. "Are you walking home?"

"Huh?"

"You're heading out. Are you walking? Can I give you a ride?"

"Um...okay. I mean, yes. Thank you. That would be great."

I'm such a sucker for punishment.

We walk side by side toward the parking lot, and it's like the hallways hold their breath as we pass. The tension is thick, but it's not the good kind. Maybe he's using this as an opportunity to speak to me about my mediocre job performance. I knew it was only a matter of time before he caught on to the fact that I have no idea what I'm doing.

Colton opens the passenger door for me, and I regret saying yes to his offer to give me a ride home. I live only a few blocks away. Why am I submitting myself to this mega pint of awkwardness?

Oh my gosh, if he's about to bring up something I said while I was more than a little tripped up on pain meds, I'll legit have to move to Mexico.

Colton clears his throat, and I watch his hands tense on the steering wheel. "Do you have any plans tonight?"

"Yeah, I have the blind date my hairdresser set me up on. Thanks for offering to give me a lift. It actually helps a lot." *Stop rambling.* "If I'd have walked, I'd probably get all sweaty, 'cause it's still hot as Mordor even though it's November. Then I'd have to figure out what to do with my hair, and it's not a hair-wash day. Anyway. Yes. To...your question. That's my place over there. You can pull into that parking spot."

*Like a baby's cheek, Ember.* Honestly, sometimes I shock myself with how smooth I am. He stares straight ahead as he nods, his lips flat. Finally, his gaze meets mine. "I hope it goes well. I'll see you tomorrow, Ember. Stay safe."

"Okay, thank you, Colton...for the ride." I wave stiffly after fumbling my way out his truck.

I walk up to my apartment and try to avoid overanalyzing every second of that interaction with Colton by putting on my all-time favorite Shania song, "Queen of Me," while I get ready for my date.

Shania always helps. This song has become my anthem, summoning the level of confidence I aspire to reach one day, to be in that place where I'm in total control of my life, breaking glass ceilings and all that. I'm not exactly crushing it just yet, but at least I'm nobody's punching bag. I guess I could do with some more empowering goals. Because if Shania can do it, I know I will too.

Nicolas curls his body around my ankles as I finish touching up my makeup in the bathroom. "I wish I could join you on the sofa tonight, buddy, but I've gotta go meet a stranger so I can eventually get to Hawaii. You understand." I recap my mascara and rub his head. "Don't wait up for me." I smile at him.

It's nice to have someone to talk to, even if it is the world's strangest pet. His quirks are weird, but at least he doesn't walk on his back legs like some spawn-of-Satan cat. I draw the line at that level of creepy.

The sun is about to set as I climb out of the Uber outside Olive & Vine. My phone lights up with a text from Debbie, my hairdresser.

DEBBIE

Enjoy your hot date! Cliff said he's wearing a red shirt and he'll meet you at the bar.

*Here we go.* I take a deep breath and lean back on the head-rest. Please let this guy be normal.

I walk into the restaurant and tell the hostess I'm meeting someone. The vibe inside is like an Applebee's with a touch more class, like it's casual enough but that they won't feed you and have you ready to leave in under twenty minutes. It's a good sign. A guy wouldn't bother to set up a date at a nice place if he was a deadbeat. I hope.

Cliff's red shirt is easy to spot. His rather tight red shirt. I weave through the tables, admiring the couples enjoying their romantic dinners as I head toward the crimson beacon. My first impression is that he's generically handsome, despite a nose that's possibly too big and the over-gelled, nineties-spiked hair.

Lord, I hope that hairstyle isn't making a comeback. Can Gen-Z not leave anything in the past? Some trends don't deserve resurrecting.

Nineties Cliff sees me approach, giving me a head nod and a slimy grin. I guess Debbie told him what I look like.

He stands when I get closer. "Amber?"

"Ember. Hi. You're Cliff?"

"Oh, right. I thought maybe that was a typo on Debbie's part. Yeah, I'm Cliff. You look hot." His gaze travels down to my shoes, mapping my body way too slowly. "I ordered you a drink," he offers, lifting a pink cocktail from the bar and handing it to me. "I figured chicks dig colorful drinks."

*Presumptuous. Also, ew. Chicks?*

This guy is stuck in another decade. He attempts a sheepish look, but it smells too much like arrogance. And he's sadly mistaken if he thinks I'm drinking something a stranger just handed me. I've overheard enough of Nicolas Cage's true crime shows to know that's a big no-no.

"Uh, thanks. Actually, I'm not too fond of pink drinks. I'll order something at our table." He shrugs and scratches his head like I've just asked him the distance from Earth to the sun.

*Don't overthink it, dude.*

"Okay. Our table's this way." He gestures over his shoulder with his thumb, and I follow. This is going splendidly. I mentally roll my eyes. Ivy is going to lose her crap over this one.

Cliff leads me to a booth in the back and slides onto the bench ahead of me. An ankle weight around his leg catches my eye as he scoots over to make room. This guy must really be into fitness. His muscles have muscles, but they're doing nothing for me. His arm stretches across the back of the bench, a barbed-wire tattoo on display. A grin slides onto his face like he wants me to think I've just won the lottery.

Oh, this poor man. He actually expects me to sit on the same side as him.

*Not happening.*

I take a seat opposite him and thank the waitress as she sets a basket of bread and butter on the table. "I'll be back in a minute to get your orders."

"Thanks." I smile at her before turning my focus to my date. He's shifted back to the middle of the bench, looking slightly annoyed. It's a pity that he's so unaware of his lack of charm.

When he clears his throat and leans his elbows on the table, I brace for the unfortunate small talk to begin.

"So, are you one of those girls who looks up your dates' criminal records?"

"No." I frown.

"Good,"

What in the actual heck? Is this guy seriously an ex-convict? I'm all for seeing a date through till the end, but now I'm slightly concerned he'll do something crazy if I piss him off. *I'm going to kill Debbie.* That is if I'm not murdered first.

Is it uncouth to ask if he's the one who brought it up? There's a big difference between sitting opposite someone who dabbled in light embezzlement and someone who drives around with a shovel and duct tape in their trunk. What would Shania do in this situation?

My heart plays jump rope as I try to tame my thoughts. How nice do I need to be to hit the sweet spot between not angering the possible serial killer in front of me and giving him false hope about this little date leading to anything past the confines of our table?

*I should say something to keep the conversation going, right? Keep it light. Don't laugh or smile too much. Hold back the sass.*

I swallow. That bread looked delicious a minute ago. Right now, anything I eat will turn to stone in my stomach.

# CHAPTER TWENTY-SIX

## COLTON

I'm sitting alone in a booth at Olive & Vine and I realize the case against me for stalking is not looking good. But I'm just here for the burgers. Couldn't get them out of my head since Ember mentioned this place. That's the only reason.

I'm on the opposite side of the room from Ember and her date with a clear line of sight, but my booth is more in the shadows, so she can't see me doing my Aragorn-brooding-in-the-corner thing.

I've been sitting here for thirty minutes. I'm so focused on Ember that I even reject a call I've been awaiting from a realtor in Salt Lake City. I need to decide what type and size of property I'd need for a shoe-manufacturing factory. An old baseball teammate and friend who went pro recently contacted me about going into business with him. He has some ideas about creating his own brand of shoes, and I like the notion of a product that's manufactured in America. My grandad and dad always had a thing about wearing the right shoes for the right activity. Designing and manufacturing hiking and adventure shoes sounds like a great business opportunity, and my grandpa would have loved it.

I don't know if I'll move there permanently, once everything is running smoothly, though if I wanted to start another business, Utah could be the place. Time will tell, but the tax incentives alone make the move a worthwhile consideration. Still, I've been putting off any big decisions. I'm not ready to face those thoughts yet.

I'll deal with it later. It's good to take a break from work stuff once in a while. I could have gone kayaking or hiking, but today the burgers called to me. They're great burgers, I swear.

I'm here to enjoy good food. Ensuring that Ember's date behaves himself is a bonus.

I was so proud when she refused the drink Red-Shirt dude ordered.

He's a piece of work. Pretty sure he's wearing an ankle monitor, which is another reason why I'm not letting Ember out of my sight.

She looks uncomfortable. She's hardly done any talking and barely touched her food, although I doubt her date has noticed. I'm guessing he hasn't stopped yapping about himself since they sat down.

I sip my beer, eyes zoned on Ember's face. Red Shirt weasels out his side of the booth, and I watch Ember frown when he sits next to her. The move has my hackles rising.

He scoots way too close, setting off a million sirens in my head.

From under the table, I watch as he puts a hand on her thigh. Now I'm seeing red. The move is obviously unwelcome, but he doesn't seem to care. That's when I can't stand back any longer. Later on, I'll wonder how I made it to their table so fast, but right now, I'm too angry to process anything besides a desire to punch this guy.

Ember pushes his hand away, and the sleaze-ball laughs. He doesn't know that it might be the last sound he ever makes.

"Easy, babe. I'm just being friendly." His douchey response cancels out the last sliver of guilt I felt over spying.

Ember looks like she's ready to give him a piece of her mind. Her green eyes meet mine, widening in surprise when I grip her date's shoulder with a painful pinch to the nerve in his neck.

"Colton." She whispers. I think I hear relief in her voice, but a scowl takes over her expression.

I lean down to her date's ear, barely holding back my growl. "Time's up, buddy. Just walk away."

I make a point of glancing down at his ankle monitor. He can't afford to ignore my threats, because he and I both know the last thing he needs is his parole officer hearing about any trouble. I straighten and give him a hard slap on the back. "Don't worry about the check."

"Whatever, man," he raises his hands, scowling. "I wasn't gonna pay for any of this anyway."

Ember's jaw slackens when she watches him go. She moves a trembling hand to tuck a strand of hair behind her ear, making me want to follow that jerk outside and leave him with a parting uppercut to the jaw.

"You didn't need to do that, you know. I had it under control," Ember says, scowling and actively avoiding my gaze. I take her hand in mine. There's no way she's leaving this place feeling even an ounce of embarrassment.

"Are you okay?" I ask, ignoring her protest. I'm expecting her to freak out. Maybe cry a little? The guy violated her space.

Except she doesn't do any of that.

She closes her eyes, releases a huge breath then squints at me through one eye. "He was an ex-convict, wasn't he?"

"Without a doubt, yup."

"Cool," she nods. "Ivy will love this one. Yay, Hawaii." She sings the last words and shakes her fist in the air in mock celebration.

"I'm kinda pissed at your hairstylist."

Her nose scrunches and her eyes finally meet mine. "Right? She said she cut his hair last month, and he was *charming*."

That guy was a tool." I clench my jaw, remembering the moment he touched her.

She nods with wide eyes. "Yeah. He was."

I stand, not letting go of her hand. "Come on, let's get out of here." Uncertainty flickers across her face, but she doesn't argue. I lead her to the front of the restaurant, settling the bill on our way out.

That adorable frown deepens. "You didn't need to do that,"

"Wasn't gonna let you pay for that idiot's food."

She grimaces, but she doesn't let go of my hand, so I'm counting this a win.

I decide to continue walking since it's a relatively warm evening. We make it a block away when Ember suddenly stops, shaking our linked hands apart.

"What's wrong?"

Her eyes bounce everywhere as she wraps her arms around herself again.

"Nothing. We shouldn't be holding hands. It makes me uncomfortable."

*Wow. Cue the "whomp-whomp" sound effect.*

The last thing a guy wants to hear is that he makes a girl uncomfortable. Red-shirt guy could do with hearing it a few times, but I didn't expect to be the one on the receiving end of those words. I at least thought Ember trusted me enough to know that she's safe with me and that my intentions are good.

*Suck it up, Colton.*

This moment isn't about me. Ember's had a crappy

evening, and if there's anything I can do to change that, then I will.

"I'm sorry I made you uncomfortable. Would..." Man, putting myself out there is scarier than I thought. I clear my throat awkwardly before trying again. "Would you like to join me for ice cream?"

The tiny freckle on her brow lowers as she frowns, and it almost seems like shock flashes across her eyes. But another expression quickly takes its place, like she's trying to solve a puzzle.

"It's just ice cream."

"I'm kind of a mess. And grumpy."

"That's why you should say yes. Anyone would have the grumps after dinner with that convict ding-dong, and there's no mood that ice cream can't fix." I pause, hoping like hell she'll give me a chance. And then I realize that my intentions aren't strictly platonic, and she's probably figured that out. Time to back up. "Just ice cream."

She nods, but I can still see the apprehension on her face.

"Tell me about Hawaii."

There's a tinkling in her laugh when she explains how she and Ivy came up with the blind-date idea to boost the traffic on their blog and earn enough money for them to take a beach vacation. It's creative, but I also want to go all grizzly bear and growl at all the men she's dated. It's a very telling new feeling for me since I'm not the jealous type.

We walk into the creamery, noting the modern amenities that keep it from being called an ice cream shop. The shiny white counters, Edison bulbs, and hanging plants suspended in those rope things give it a millennial touch. It's empty, besides the preppy-looking server behind the counter, who looks like she's twelve.

I lightly guide Ember with my hand on her lower back as

we approach the counter. Her wide eyes dart up to mine, and I shove my hands in my pockets.

*Play it cool, man.*

The server interrupts with a cheery greeting, "Welcome in. What can I get for you?"

I smile at Ember. "Order for me?"

"What? I don't—what?"

"Order for me." I tip my chin to the display behind her, my eyes still locked on hers. "Or are you too scared?"

Her spine straightens before she answers. "I'm not scared of anything." The moment stretches while she tries to determine my angle again. After a sharp inhale, she quirks her lips. "Okay."

*Atta girl.*

I stand behind her as she turns to study the long list of flavors they offer. It's purely coincidental that I get to enjoy the smell of her perfume while she peruses the menu.

This need to be near her is weird. It's like my brain has suddenly decided to ignore all the reasons I've never allowed myself to get close to anyone.

A minute goes by, and she's still staring at the display, biting the corner of her lip. She glares at me and then waves toward the seats behind us. "Go, get us a table. You're making me nervous."

*Why is she so cute?*

I take a step back, lifting my hands in surrender. "Noted," I laugh gently. "But I'm paying, so I'll just stand over here." I stop about two feet away and fold my arms.

She grunts and mumbles, "Fine," then looks at the server with a forced smile. "Can we please get two cones with a single scoop of cereal-milk ice cream?"

I swipe my card, and we wait for our order in silence. We're both trying to hide the grins on our faces, and I'm struggling not to laugh at her overthinking.

The server hands our cones over, and we make our way to a table in the corner. I wait for Ember to sit, then take the seat opposite her. Minutes pass quietly, each of us holding out for the other to speak. But watching her squirm while she waits for me to comment on her flavor choice is fun. Finally, I give in when she pulls a funny face at me.

"This is my favorite flavor."

"Stop." She sits up straighter and hits her palm on the table, wincing when she realizes she did it with her injured arm. "Seriously? I picked your favorite flavor?"

She's looking so pleased, but then I see her catch herself and force the smile away, and that frown creeps back.

I lift her cast with my free hand and lay it on my upturned palm.

What? I'm just being a gentleman.

Her dainty fingers rest on the sensitive skin below the crease of my elbow, momentarily short-circuiting my thoughts. Then she glances down at our arms and slowly removes her hand, tucking it under the table. Her hand may be gone, but I still feel the burn where her fingers were before.

*What the heck is that about?*

I clear my throat and bring my focus back to her question. "Yup. But you can't mix it with anything besides chocolate. I've tried."

"You come here often?" she questions with a raised eyebrow.

"It must be hot in here...cause you're making me melt."

"Huh?"

"I thought we're doing pickup lines."

"Ha ha!" She scrunches her nose at me.

"I don't come here too often, but often enough to try every flavor they have."

"So, a lot then?"

"Pretty much." I nod. She tips her head back, belting a laugh that warms my insides. I decide right then that I'd do anything to see her laugh like that again. She thinks she's grouchy, but she's a bundle of sassy sunshine I want to scoop up and carry around with me.

I mean, I can appreciate her pleasant disposition from a platonic distance.

*Liar.*

We eat our ice creams while chatting lightheartedly about our favorite things and memories from our pasts. I mostly say the cheesy things I can think of, just to make her smile. Although she never fully relaxes, some of the tension from an hour ago has faded.

But by the time we make it back to her apartment, she's regressing. Regret colors her expression as if she's chastising herself for letting her guard down again.

She turns to open the passenger door but then pivots sharply, taking a deep breath before speaking. "Colton, I think it's best if we keep things professional. Thank you for coming to my rescue and for the ride home. But from now on, we should stick to workplace interactions."

*Wow, I didn't see that coming, either.*

Sneaky little what-ifs have already begun worming their way into my mind, bringing those stomach flutters that could technically be called butterflies along with them. But I'm a grown man and owning to that feels weird. Regardless, Ember's words are like a can of toxic bug spray, killing off the entire swarm. It's worse than the friend zone—I'm being work zoned.

My forearms, resting on the steering wheel fall to my side as I look across the street. She's right, though. She's my employee—my new employee—and I should be focusing on my company. That's always been easy for me. It would be crazy to start something with anyone right now when I plan to move in a few months.

My eyes return to her, and I almost wince at the sight that still causes my heart to beat faster. "Right. Of course." Forcing a cheerful smile takes more work than it should. She climbs out , turning to me after closing the door. "I'll see you on Monday, Ember."

"Goodbye, Colton."

It takes even more effort to ignore how those words sound so final.

# CHAPTER TWENTY-SEVEN

## EMBER

My cubicle looks less like a corporate workstation and more like the site of a plant convention. Seriously, why is there so much greenery around here? I'm half-convinced it's some sort of secret test to see if we can keep this jungle thriving. Joke's on them, though—I've never managed to keep a plant alive.

I'm a serial plant killer. There's a reason why Opal and Gail take responsibility for the flower pots they've transplanted around my apartment.

I puff my lips, blowing out a breath as I scan my desk, procrastinating about my decision to leave the safety of these three half-glass walls.

Okay, fine. What I'm really doing is trying not to think about Colton, specifically the dejected look in his eyes when I told him we should keep things professional.

Why would a man in a relationship be so taken aback by that? Are all the other women he flirts with just okay with being a side piece?

Whatever. I'm staying in my nook as long as I can, although I know I'll be forced to go out and socialize at some point today.

Unfortunately, there are people associated with the work part of this job.

*Lip balm. I need lip balm.*

A hit of my favorite cupcake scent never disappoints. Plus, digging through my purse to find it will buy me at least two minutes of busy time. I reach under my desk for my handbag, but retrieving it isn't as easy as it seems when wearing a calf-length pencil skirt. Thank goodness I opted for my trusty white sneakers this morning with the skirt and black Shania tee, because this whole maneuver would be impossible if I had heels on. I don't know how Ivy or Reese Witherspoon do it.

I grab the strap of my bag, but my momentum is halted when it catches on something, and I'm forced to stop with a sudden jerk. I almost topple over, but I barely manage to catch myself. The last thing I need is to be found on my back, like a bug wiggling its legs in the air because it can't turn over.

I'm blindly grasping for whatever my handbag is hooked on when I wrap my hand around something squishy. And that's when I yelp.

A big, high-pitched, terror-filled yelp.

The kind that carries a pitch strong enough to pierce walls and what my mother would deem, "screaming like a banshee."

In the two seconds since the aforementioned unladylike screech, I've gone through a myriad of emotions: fear, because of the icky thing I thought I saw; relief, once I realized what it actually is; and a healthy dose of trepidation, because there's no way anyone missed that shriek.

"Ember?" As if summoned by the embarrassment gods, he appears at my desk. He's slightly out of breath, because, of course, he ran. Colton's brows draw together in concern.

The butterflies in my stomach band together to perform a synchronized wave. It's messed up that I'm still so annoyingly attracted to a taken man. But at least the knowledge that he'll be laughing at me soon keeps me from appreciating the full force of Colton's handsomeness.

"You okay? I heard you scream." His eyes dart around the room, still frowning as he checks the area for potential threats. Sensing none, he turns those navy blue soul scanners my way, sweeping over me from head to toe.

He's only checking to see if I'm injured, yet my insides have gone all swirly and swoony under the scrutiny of his gaze. It's a wonder I'm not a puddle on the floor. On the outside, I'm the picture of calm and innocent, but my heart beats wildly in my chest, contradicting the chill vibe I'm faking.

"Yup...I'm fine...everything is just perfectly normal here."

*Go away now, Mr. Blue Eyes.*

He stalks towards me with that smirk on his stupid, handsome face.

He's a flirt, and I don't condone a man getting more than friendly with multiple women. It was bad enough that he kept trying to hold my hand last week. But his show of concern is messing with my brain.

"That doesn't sound suspicious at all." He lifts an eyebrow, and it looks like it's capable of conducting its own investigation.

I look down and busy myself with shuffling papers around my desk, while I plead with the universe to save me from just *one* embarrassing moment. I don't think that's too much to ask.

Part of me knows he won't drop it. He's a hound who's caught a scent, and he's on a mission. The man seems to have made a hobby of teasing me any chance he gets.

I don't hate it, though I know I should.

I wave my hand casually as I attempt another deflection to spare myself the embarrassment I know is coming if this hound doesn't back off soon. "It's nothing. I thought I saw something under my desk. Don't you have meetings to frown over or Ethan to terrorize?"

"Wait, Little Miss '*I'm not scared of anything*' was startled by something? This is too good. Making fun of Ethan can wait."

He stalks intimidatingly in my direction, and my hands can only stack so many things on my desk. I'm scrambling for another diversion tactic and making a strong mental note to avoid the stapler. All bets are off if my hands get a hold of that sucker. There is no way to appear cucumbery cool while failing at attempts to staple random piles way too thick to get a staple through. That level of multitasking requires more brain function than I can successfully garner at the moment.

His annoyingly deep and sultry voice interrupts. "What do you think you saw, Em?"

*Oh no.*

It's the first time he's shortened my name, and I like it way too much.

He sucks in his cheeks, and I decide I'll file a complaint against the universe for still having to think he's hot while he's trying to suppress a laugh at my expense.

"I don't know the English word for it." I shrug a shoulder.

*There. That'll throw him off.*

"Do you know a word for it in a different language, then?" I swear, those eyebrows could have their own PI show. It's only because his flirting has short-circuited my brain that I'm not confessing everything.

"Danger noodle."

*Smooth, Ember. Real smooth.*

"That still sounds English."

*Mother Of Pearl!*

I roll my eyes and growl.

"Fine. I thought I saw a snake, okay. Or I thought I grabbed a snake. There. You gonna grow a ridiculous mustache and call yourself Poirot?"

He shakes his head. "I don't have the growing power to push out a stash like that. Best I can do is Ace Ventura hair."

"How nice for you." I smile, still hoping he'll drop the topic.

He steps in closer, making me want to throw my hands up and shout, "Whoa, buddy!"

But there's also a part of me that wants to ignore the voice that's angry whispering in my ear, reminding me he has an almost girlfriend. Acknowledging that urge is another cold splash of shame. I need to tattoo the backs of my eyelids with "Colton is unavailable."

His eyes pierce me as he asks, "What did you grab that you thought was a snake?"

And the hound continues its search.

*Frick, what did he ask me? Come on, brain. You're better than this.*

"A Red Vine." I say with fake confidence. I turn and resume reorganizing my desk, still unable to look at him while I make a fool of myself for the millionth time. "It felt squishy and gross, and my mind just jumped to snake. It's a perfectly normal response."

"Not a fan of snakes?"

"Is anyone a fan of snakes?"

"Some people." He shrugs, throwing around that grin that does things to my insides.

"Not the sane ones," I respond, walking behind my desk. I need some space for my brain to remember how to operate. "Now that I've confessed to my very human moment of weakness, you can scurry back to the important things I'm sure you must do." I wave my hand, shooing him away.

He looks like he's getting ready to tease me more when Lemon walks into the room, her head easily visible over all the cubicles because of the sky-high stilettos that she seems to float around in.

I straighten, even though I'm already standing as stiff as a board. The wide eyes I'm aiming Colton's way don't seem to translate, as he casually leans on my desk with his hands in his pockets. Does he not feel guilty about getting caught loitering with me? The way his girlfriend is trying to murder me with her eyes implies that he should.

Her voice is syrupy and sweet as she glances between us. "Ember, I came to get you so I can show you the supply samples. Jed is setting up a table in the boardroom. Can you meet me there?"

Well, it looks like I've officially been dismissed.

"Right." I nod. This has been a sufficiently excruciating encounter. I try to avoid eye contact with either of them as I straighten random papers on my desk for the third time. On my way past the imposing form that's still leaning against my desk, I catch a narrowing of Colton's eyes, like he's trying to figure something out. If it's a way to get alone time with Lemon before she joins me, I'll happily make myself disappear.

I blink back the tears of embarrassment as I walk across the office space with my head down. Is it possible for a heart to physically ache from being trampled? I'm so tempted to shut the dang thing off and say "stuff it" to everything. It feels so enticing, the thought of going a little numb.

Instead, I reach the boardroom and stop to take a breath before entering, with a new wave of determination forcing my chin up. I won't become that cold, jaded person, the girl I almost lost myself to a few months ago. It might hurt to hope, to feel the flickers of possibility, only to have them repeatedly extinguished. But I'd much rather feel pain than feel nothing at all.

# CHAPTER TWENTY-EIGHT

## EMBER

Jed sets up the table and kindly shows me the sample boxes in the corner of the room before he leaves me alone to wait for Lemon. I don't know how this sample-selection process is usually done, but rather than having to picture Lemon and Colton canoodling in my cubicle, I make myself useful by unpacking the boxes into categories.

Five minutes later, I'm setting out the last of the products when Lemon's heels click into the boardroom, a satisfied curl to her lips.

"Sorry about the wait." She wipes at the corner of her mouth, and I fight the urge to hurl. Can I fast-forward until my heart doesn't skip a beat whenever I'm forced to think about him? It should be against the laws of physics and chemistry to feel drawn to someone who's so clearly unavailable. Let's not forget that this man is possibly flirting his way through every female employee, for all I know. His red flag needs to appear a shade more crimson, so my insides can catch up with my brain and warn me to back the hell away.

"Oh good, you've unpacked everything. I have the list of

supplies here." She opens a spreadsheet on her iPad and gestures to the products. "For some of these, there are multiple brands to choose from. We need to decide which is best, and also check the quality of the items with only one option."

Her chin remains dipped when her eyes run over my clothes. A hand reaches forward, briefly assessing the fabric of my sleeve between her fingers. "Is this polyester? Paint will wash out of it I'm sure. You can test the messy things. This is silk," she announces, sweeping a manicured hand over her blouse. "I can't get anything on it."

Again with the outfit digs. I happen to love my boho-chic style. This skirt was two sizes too big when I found it, but Gail's sewing skills solved that problem.

"That's fine. Should I grab a bunch of things and get started?"

"Well, I'm not gonna blow a whistle. Just keep the messy stuff in those pans over there." She nods her head to a stack of plastic trays under the table. "The list outlines which products go together. Stick to that, and mark off which ones you choose on the iPad."

I roll my bottom lip over the top, then make a popping sound. "Got it."

She doesn't know what to do with my weird, blinking before turning her back to me. Lemon is the cool older sister, and I'm the nerdy, nose-in-a-book younger sibling with a secret crush on her boyfriend. I know I said it feels like a work-family around here, but I'm strongly against the part I've been cast in. It would be nice to be the big sister, for once.

I grab all the fun-looking things that Lemon calls messy, including fabric and body paints and a tie-dye kit. While I disappear into a more colorful world, I hear Lemon sigh occasionally, as she switches between typing on her phone and hammering letter stamps to etch words onto leather samples.

I've tested and marked off ninety-five percent of the pieces, satisfied that every product has a good, quality option. I'm grateful since Ethan explained before that requesting and waiting for new samples is a pain.

Lemon dusts her hands off, even though she's touched nothing remotely messy.

"You can email that list to Jed. That's all I needed you for."

I feel so valued. She's done wonders for my self-esteem.

I make it back to the safety of my desk and text Ivy. This time with Lemon has left me a little depleted, but Ivy's abundance of enthusiasm should balance things out.

EMBER

So Lemon is a real peach

Pretty sure her and Colton were making out in my cubicle earlier

IVY

Ew. Shout "Get out of my nook, Dwight!"

EMBER

I need sanitizing wipes, not an incentive to sound more weird

I can do this, right?

IVY

You've got this babe! Just picture those white sands of Hawaii and forget about your sexy boss

EMBER

Not helping

IVY

Sorry. You could always get Nicolas to make Lemon disappear

EMBER

Tempting…

IVY

I've gotta go. My class is due back from PE soon. Think of me when you interact with other adults today!

EMBER

You're the best teacher ever, Vee. Love you!

Gratitude swells in my chest. I don't need a man. I have friends who love and appreciate me. So what if two-thirds of those friends are in their seventies? They add comedy and wisdom to my life, and that's enough for now.

# CHAPTER TWENTY-NINE

## EMBER

On my walk home, my phone thankfully rings, interrupting my replay of Lemon wiping her lips after what seemed like a pretty intense make-out session with Colton.

"Hey, Mom."

"Emberleigh," my mother's voice returns, slightly too loud. I stifle a groan. "You shouldn't answer a phone call with 'Hey'."

"My humblest apologies. Hello, Mother."

"Are you walking? You sound out of breath."

"Yes. I'm walking home."

"Well, that doesn't sound safe, Emberleigh. You should be aware of your surroundings."

"I'm sorry, I'm still working on my teleportation skills. Would you prefer I hang up so I can keep an eye on the vagabonds that might accost me?"

She sighs, clearly frustrated with my sarcasm but sometimes it's the only way to survive a conversation with her.

"What is this company you're working for exactly?"

I stifle a groan, deciding it'll take less energy to just explain everything to her rather than trying to avoid this conversation.

Though there's no doubt in my mind that her tone will turn judgemental soon.

"I was rather shocked that the casually dressed man I met at the hospital was your boss, but hearing that he's just making up games for people puts it into perspective, I guess. Are you sure you won't come work for your father again? No one will judge you for this little self-discovery detour."

My jaw slackens for a second before I clench it tightly, trying to rein in the explosion of words that want to escape in defense of Colton and the huge success he and his company have become.

"Yes, Mom, I'm quite sure I don't want to work for Dad again," I say through my teeth.

"Well, you don't have to decide right now. Anyway, I know you don't want anyone to know where you're living, but Beau is very concerned. I think you should call him, just let him know where you are. It's the least you can do."

My hand forms a tight ball at my side and a wave of nausea overcomes me at the thought of ever speaking to him again.

"Mom, I have nothing to say to Beau, and he has no right to any information about me. Please *keep* it that way."

"What am I supposed to say to the poor man, Emberleigh? He's coming over for dinner tonight, and I know he'll ask. I don't like lying to him, and I don't see the harm in telling him where you are."

"You don't have to understand it, Mom. You just need to respect my wishes. Please. I don't ask you for much. Ever. But I need you to give me this."

"At some point, you'll need to grow up, Emberleigh, and face the people who care about you."

Talking to her requires the patience of a saint. Throwing a fit isn't worth the emotional blackmail that will follow, though.

So I grit my teeth, wondering for the hundredth time whether I should have told them the truth about Beau.

I say goodbye, ignoring the disappointment that coats my mother's voice.

Maybe I should have told them a long time ago, but I couldn't face the possibility of them taking his side over mine. Right now, I'm just their difficult daughter, and I can live with that. I don't know how I'd handle the alternative. Because, no matter how contentious our relationship is, I've never given up hope that we could have a smidgen of a normal relationship.

# CHAPTER THIRTY

COLTON

Ember and I stand elbow to elbow at my desk, and each accidental brush of our arms sends a zap of warmth shooting through me. Yet, despite the proximity, she's avoiding eye contact, just as she has all day.

"We've been staring at these for too long. Let's grab coffee before we make our final decisions." I nod towards the breakroom.

I pull two mugs from the cupboard, and Ember reaches out to take one.

"What are you doing?" I ask.

"Making coffee."

"I'll do it. You sit."

"I can make my own coffee."

"I know you can, but right now, I'm making it for you."

There's a war raging in her eyes. She's so intent on doing everything herself. But why?

I can see the effort it takes for her to give in. "Fine—thank you."

I resume making her coffee, mimicking the way she adds an

offensive amount of maple syrup and half-and-half then sticking it in the microwave for thirty seconds, like I've seen her do before.

When I turn, she's looking at me like I've just sacrificed a herd of cattle in her honor.

"How—how'd you know I take my coffee like that?"

I could laugh it off and avoid looking like Creepy McStalker, but I'm trying to put myself out there. "I've seen you make it a few times. It's cute how you hum when you add the syrup. Like just the anticipation of the sugar makes you happy."

She shakes her head gently with an exhale, peering out the door. She mutters, "Of course," and rolls her eyes my way.

I want to ask if I did something wrong, but then I overhear her whispering, "Dang, that's good."

And I get lost all over again, staring at her dainty fingers and the way she's trying so hard to scowl while enjoying her drink.

We sip in silence, Ember looking everywhere but me, while I stare unashamedly. Minutes pass before she eventually stands up with a huff. Something is ticking her off, and I'm going to figure out what it is.

She opens one of the higher cupboards, reaching on her tiptoes to put a box of coffee pods on a shelf.

"Those don't have to go there," I say, standing and taking a careful step toward her.

Without turning around, she continues her attempt to elongate her body past its limit. "Well, I think this is a great spot for them."

So stubborn.

"Emie."

"Don't call me that." She whips her body around to face

me. Anger, pain, and confusion appear in the crease of her brows.

I hate that my words have caused the hurt I hear in her voice. I know she asked me to be professional, but hell, I feel something here. And I might be crazy, but I could swear she feels it too. Despite calling her a name that clearly doesn't hold good memories, there's a different kind of tension between us that I can't seem to ignore.

Her chest rises and falls as she breathes heavily, and I bring my hand up, achingly slowly, and tuck a strand of hair back, lightly brushing my fingertips against the shell of her ear.

For a second, her eyes flutter closed, like she's savoring the moment, then that flash of anger returns, and her arms are folding in front of her.

She takes a step back, turning her head away to speak. "I can't do this, Colton. I can't fall for someone I work with again. It's not right, and it's not wise. Lemon isn't my favorite person, but I still won't do that to another woman."

Lemon?

She takes my silence as encouragement, her hands going to her hips. She's just upped a level in her shredding. I'm being laid into for something I'm not even sure I've done.

"What is it with you men? You think you can just flirt your way through every skirt." She waves a hand to the side, her eyes bugging out as she continues, "With no consideration for each person in the skirt. I'm a *person*, Colton. We're all people with feelings and hearts. And sometimes those hearts are tender and vulnerable, and all you do is stomp on them."

Oookay. I think I'm beginning to see what's happening here.

Ember continues, her hand gestures growing more haphazard.

"You think you can do whatever you want without consequences, but I'm done. I won't be that girl again. Lemon deserves better. *Women* deserve better—"

"Ember," I interrupt.

"We deserve to be valued and cherished, not treated like today's flavor, only good until the next one comes along."

"You're right."

She finally stops, and her emerald eyes meet mine.

"What?"

"You deserve to be treated like the most valuable thing in a man's life. Not for a moment, or a time, but for all time. As long as he breathes, he should live with the knowledge that in his care is the heart of someone to be treasured."

Almost robotically she says to me, "You're doing it again."

"Doing what, Sunshine?"

"Making me want you."

It's my turn to inhale a giant breath of oxygen. I'm on the precipice of something.

"Why is that a bad thing?"

We've both been still, frozen in the timeless fog that surrounds us. But my question breaks the spell, and she lifts her hands in frustration again.

"Because you're taken, Colton." Her eyes seem to get even wider as she waits for my response like she's caught me red-handed in something.

"Taken...where?" I force a frown. I'm pretty sure I know what's going on here, but she's so damn cute when she's frustrated. I wouldn't be surprised if she stomps her foot soon.

"Ugh," she growls, moving hair away from her face. And there it is. The foot stomp.

I cross my arms, bringing one hand up to cover the smile that wants to erupt on my face.

"You..."

"Yeah?" I prompt, making her work for it.

"And Lemon..."

"Are we just naming employees?"

"You're *vibing*...dating...whatever you wanna call it. I will *not* be a side piece, Colton." She points a finger at my chest, glaring fiery daggers.

I settle back against the kitchen counter, crossing my feet in front of me, and she drops her hand.

"Em, there is not currently, and never has been, anything romantic happening between Lemon and me."

"What?"

"I've always had a personal policy not to engage in romantic relationships with any of my employees."

Her lips roll in and something else flashes across her face.

*Wait, is she disappointed?*

"But you and Lemon were...*canoodling* in my cubicle."

"Canoodling?"

"Um yeah...so my imagination might have gone to a weird place. But just so I'm clear, you're not in a relationship with Lemon or interested in a relationship with Lemon?"

"That's a very strong no."

A hand goes to her forehead as she turns away, pacing.

"And you've never been in a relationship with anyone at the office?"

"Again, no."

"But I saw you at Ethan's party. You two were—"

It's my turn to frown. "You were at Ethan's party?"

She swallows, and I watch as her cheeks darken.

"Um, so...I've gotta go," she squeaks. Then she's just a blur of fabric, and I'm suddenly alone in the break room.

*What the hell just happened?*

# CHAPTER THIRTY-ONE

## EMBER

It's official. I can never show my face around here again. I'm spiraling as I speed walk home. I don't even care that it's the middle of the workday.

My phone vibrates, eliciting a sigh before I can even check who's calling.

"Oh, thank God. Hey, Vee."

"Is someone chasing you?"

"No, I'm just walking."

"Oh. You sound out of breath. I'm on my lunch break, so I called to tell you about my blind date last night." She pauses while I continue my heavy breathing, checking my surroundings. "Okay, but it sounds like you're really struggling there. You sure you're okay?"

"Yup, just speed walking home after embarrassing myself beyond repair. I'm serious, Vee. I really did it this time. There's no coming back from this. I'm quitting. I can't go back there. I'm gonna look into that teaching English online thing. I can work in my sweatpants. That's enough of a reason to do it."

"Em, back up a bit. What are you talking about?"

The mortification isn't lessened as I recount the events of the entire day for Ivy. It feels worse hearing myself retell the story.

"I'll email my resignation and tell them I had to relocate. I think I might need to *actually* relocate, though. I live too close. There's too much risk of seeing someone from the office. I'll miss Opal and Gail, but it has to be done. It's my only option. Colton must think I'm the biggest freak on the planet. I behaved abominably, Vee. You know I don't use that word. But this was truly *abominable*. You can't even make this stuff up. You should have seen—"

"Emberleigh!"

I gasp at her audacity. She's bringing out the big guns. "You didn't," I seethe, pausing at the top of the steps to my apartment block.

"Oh, yes, I did. The occasion called for it. Now listen up missy, you will not resign! You'll put your big girl panties on and walk in there with your chin up."

"What if my big girl panties are the granny kind, and I'll only die more?"

"You can't '*die more*.' You're either alive or dead, and you are very much alive and capable."

"I hate when you're right," I admit with a sigh. "But I'm avoiding everyone for the rest of my life. I'll find a closet to move my desk into. My skin might turn vampire white, while people refer to me as '*the weird one who works in the back*,' but it's a sacrifice I'm willing to make."

"Atta girl!"

"I interrupted your story about your date. I'm sorry." When I unlock my door, Nicolas is on the arm of the couch watching TV.

"Eh, your thing was more urgent. You're fine. What's my boy Nicky watching?"

I slump down next to him on the couch, gently stroking under his chin. In response, all I get is a flick of his tail.

"NCIS," I tell Ivy.

"I'm so proud of him."

"His dedication is admirable. Now, tell me about your date."

Ivy shares her blind date escapades before saying goodbye. I melt into the sofa, determined to avoid thinking about the fact that Colton is single and how much I would have loved to mingle, had I not embarrassed myself enough to account for the entire human race.

# CHAPTER THIRTY-TWO

## COLTON

Ember has been dodging me lately. Every time I spot her, she disappears so quickly that I start to wonder if she was ever really there. She's like a ghost, her flowing skirts haunting me throughout the day.

Just before lunch, I decide enough is enough. I'm hunting her down today.

The bullpen is buzzing as I walk in and catch sight of the elusive beauty hunched over her desk, her eyes darting around, poised to vanish. Our eyes meet, and she quickly straightens up, absently wiggling the mouse on her desk and frowning at her screen.

Oh, she's good.

When I reach her cubicle, she's performing her usual routine, shuffling and stacking papers, clearly gearing up for a quick getaway. But I know for a fact she's just stapled a Wendy's brochure to a receipt from our paper supplier.

I did some thinking last night, and I realized that the lady doth protest too much. She likes me. She fought it and probably stacked up a whole list of reasons why it wouldn't work.

As far as I'm concerned, there's no good reason not to see where this could lead. There's something here, something unique that I've never felt before.

"Where you off to with your stack o' papers?"

For just a fleeting moment, her eyes meet mine before she quickly clutches her paper props to her chest, her gaze shifting to look over my shoulder.

"Recycling."

I step closer, quickly counting the spectators around us. Privacy would have been preferable, but waiting for the perfect moment could mean not speaking to her until I'm eighty. She's like a flighty bird, always vanishing just as I try to get close enough for a real conversation.

"You stapled them *before* taking them to recycling?"

I carefully draw the stack of papers from her hands, bringing us closer than what's deemed appropriate for coworkers. Yet, I find myself indifferent to the breach of social norms. Captivated by her upward gaze, those vivid green eyes and slightly parted lips, I'm using every ounce of restraint not to draw her even closer.

"Yup, I keep them together until they're ready to be recycled. It prevents any papers from flying off," she says, fluttering her hand for emphasis.

She's rather good at making things up on the spot.

"You're avoiding me."

The only denial she can manage is a tiny head shake. The rest of the room disappears as I stand before her, locked onto her gaze. Background noises fade, and all I hear are her heavy breaths.

There's no way she can deny what's happening here.

Without breaking eye contact, I reach for her hand, brushing my thumb along the inside of her wrist.

"You like me."

"That's beside the point." She tries to pull away, but I give a little tug, and she relents. "We both agreed that an office relationship isn't wise," she whispers.

She lifts her chin defiantly, that stubborn spark igniting once again, and it's so endearingly cute that I can't help but smile. This, of course, makes her frown—but I find that adorable too.

"Stop smiling."

"I can't help it."

Her frown is now a full-blown scowl.

"You said you have a rule too. What's the point, Colton?"

"It's not an official rule, more of a personal policy. In the past, it's just been simpler to keep those two worlds separate."

I inch back slightly, yet I keep a firm hold on her hand. The room buzzes with activity around us, making our exchange appear like nothing more than casual conversation to an outsider. However, within the confines of this small cubicle, a fire ignites, fueled by the growing tension between us as my thumb gently strokes back and forth over her wrist.

She nods, eyes falling to the floor as fleeting disappointment lowers her shoulders. It won't be there long, but it's welcome information.

The air is electric, charged with the energy of new beginnings as we stand facing each other. Uncertainty flickers in her eyes. She attempts to withdraw her hand from mine, her gaze darting about restlessly. It's endearing, almost like she's playfully resisting, yet her body language tells a different story, not quite ready to let go.

It only takes another slight tug, and we're back to standing close enough to see that tiny freckle above the arch of her left eyebrow.

Finally, she lifts her chin, her emerald eyes piercing

through me. She smells like cake again, igniting my curiosity about the source of her delicious scent.

"Ember, I like you. I haven't felt this drawn to someone in..." I pause, wanting to tell her that I've never felt this way about anyone, but worried it might be too much. I shake my head slightly, searching for the right words. "In a long time."

This time, she takes a small step back, but I instinctively move closer, unwilling to let the space between us grow.

My gaze flits between her eyes as I find the words. "I'd really like to get to know you better. There's no pressure, though. If things get too complicated, we'll step back and keep it professional. I know this might seem sudden, considering what you thought was happening before," I manage a nervous laugh, "but can we just see where this might lead us?"

She's silent, only giving me a slow nod.

"Need to hear you say it, Em."

A small curl of her lips. "We can see where this goes."

*This woman.*

"Good." My smile eases wide. "But can you do something for me? No more blind dates?"

Her lips purse in thought.

"It kills me to think of you on a date with anyone else. Give me a chance to show you this can work between us."

She's biting the corner of her mouth again, and it's nearly my undoing. But then her eyes spear right into mine, and she gives me the cutest barely-there smile I've ever seen. And another nod, like it helps her reshuffle things in her mind.

"Okay. No more blind dates."

If I had to describe the feeling of relief, this moment would be it—the moment when what I've hoped for shifts from dream to reality, almost too good to be true.

"Thank you." Tension seeps from my muscles, and I squeeze her hand. I want nothing more than to pull her into my arms, but I settle for rubbing my thumb on her wrist one more time before letting go.

She has some catching up to do. I've only just admitted my feelings to myself, but I think she's had me under her spell since the first day I saw her hopping on the sidewalk.

I'm so screwed. But I couldn't be happier about it.

# CHAPTER THIRTY-THREE

## EMBER

I love grocery shopping. It's a bit embarrassing to admit, but I haven't had much practice with many of the mundane errands and chores that most adults are used to. However, I can't really blame myself for something I wasn't permitted to do growing up.

There's a large grocery store nearby with great fresh produce and self-checkout. It's like hitting the jackpot on the same level as getting the end bathroom stall.

I find a unique kind of calm in being in a large building without the crush of a crowd. It's refreshing to wander the aisles, enjoying the ample space between me and other shoppers. Another bonus is the self-checkout; it spares me the usual cashier small talk about weekend plans. Trader Joe's, I'm looking at you.

I nudge the cart through the store exit with one hand, while the other wrestles with the stiffness of the cast on my arm, struggling to pull my phone from my back pocket. With some hesitation, I finally open the newly arrived text message.

All I can muster is an eye roll as I delete Beau's text and start loading groceries into the trunk of the Uber that's waiting for me. Suddenly, a throat clearing behind me makes me jump, sending me into a clumsy dance with airborne freezer boxes.

"Ember, wow, that's a lot of pizza for one person."

I tug my hoodie off my head and turn around. Is the universe hitting me with a one-two punch? Another text from Beau, and now her too?

"Hey, Lemon."

She circles her hand around my groceries. "I love this party-food vibe you've got going on. It makes you seem...fun."

Okay, I will *not* be pizza-shamed. One-handed cooking isn't at the top of my to-do list right now.

"Yup, I do love to party." I'm not even sorry for the lies spewing out of my mouth. I just want to get this interaction over with.

"That's so cool!" She wrinkles her nose, sporting the same face you'd make when a child tells you something random and you fake an enthusiastic response.

I lift my hand, shading the sun from my face so I can continue looking at her. Always keep a hostile in sight. Another nugget of wisdom from my cat's true crime shows.

"Okay, well—it was nice seeing you." The lies just keep flowing. I've always thought of myself as a decent person, but lying through my teeth to dodge awkward small talk has definitely revealed a new side of me.

"We should totally plan Colton's going away party together!"

*Say what now?*

She must read the shock on my face. "Oh, you didn't know? He's moving to Utah to start a new company. It's a shame 'cause I would've loved to see where things could have gone with us. Anywho, I'll let you get back to your...party food."

She says this, but she remains rooted in place. I keep my eyes locked on hers as I hastily back toward the car, her intense gaze following me every step of the way. The Uber driver must think he's picked up a crazy person as I hurriedly plop down inside and swing the door shut, much like I would if I were dodging a bee determined to sting. But it isn't her actions that deliver the sting today; it's her words, casually spilling over and darkening my sunny Saturday morning. I know she doesn't always stick to the truth, but this time, there's enough reality in her words to make them hit home.

She knows nothing will happen between her and Colton. Any insecure woman will tell you the next step is to ensure no one else gets the guy.

It's a bluff, and she's taunting me until I show my hand.

But she doesn't get to see my weak spots.

For good measure, I lock the doors and crack the window open just an inch.

"I'd love to help with that. Let me know what I can do." I'm ready for my honorary doctorate in bending the truth. We'll call this a "distant cousin" of the truth because there's no way in hell I'm signing up to plan anything with Lemon. I'm growing increasingly okay with the idea of Lemon and I being the relatives in this weird work family that passive-aggressively ignore each other.

As I'm driven home, the news of Colton's possible move finally seeps in. I give myself one minute to feel all the fear and doubt it brings, then push it away.

I'm a woman capable of existing and flourishing without a

man. If nothing comes of this little road bump in my plans, then I'm all the better for it. Recalibrate and resume initial route to destination.

I have a home, a good job, and a small nest of friends who care about me. Colton is a nice guy. I'm just not sure he's meant to be *my* nice guy.

# CHAPTER THIRTY-FOUR

## EMBER

"Knock, knock."

"Vee? What are you doing here?"

Ivy's blonde hair bounces playfully as she strides toward me in the boardroom. Her spirited walk is endearingly cute, although it frequently causes her glasses to slip down her nose. As a result, she habitually pushes them back up, gently nudging the rim with her fingers.

"I got out early this afternoon and just stopped by our favorite thrift store. I found some shoes for my date next weekend and couldn't wait to show you, so I thought I'd surprise you at work."

She looks around the room, her chin jutting up with an impressed arch to her mouth. "This is really nice. What is this room?"

"It's like an informal boardroom, I guess. Show me the shoes!" I widen my eyes at her in anticipation. Ivy has also taken to shopping at thrift stores, which puzzles me, considering her decent salary. Teachers may not earn a fortune, but she's only supporting herself.

She pulls a pair of boots from a tote bag, miming a silent squeal when she gets another eyeful of them.

"Ivy June. These have heels. I thought your date was a hike?"

"So?"

"So? You can't hike in these!"

"What? No, look, I'll show you. They're fine."

She effortlessly slips off her heels and steps into a pair of wedge-style combat boots. Striding over to a bench cloaked in greenery by the half-glass wall near the boardroom entrance, she catches my eye. I purse my lips, watching as she playfully leaps up and poses atop the shelf nestled between the plants.

Someone with her reputation should not tempt fate this much, since Ivy's already been given all the chances she'll ever get, and I'm afraid she's close to running out. Her near-major accidents are bound to turn into serious ones pretty soon.

"Ta-da!" She throws her palms up at her sides, smiling like she's just validated her point.

I'm about to inform her that this proves nothing when I catch Ethan prowling down the passage with an uncharacteristic scowl in his gaze. His eyes scan over Ivy, and she takes my silence as further need to continue convincing me.

"Em, these are fine to hike in. I'm used to wearing heels, plus I'm sure we won't go far. Look, I can do all the normal things, maybe even better than before, 'cause these have great ankle support."

She starts spinning, all while perched on a bench that seems barely strong enough to hold a few potted plants, let alone support the weight of a moving person—even someone as petite as Ivy.

Her back is to me when Ethan slinks into the room, his glare so intense it leaves him momentarily speechless. As Ivy completes her turn to face him, she's met with his eyes, blazing with fury.

She shrieks, jolted, and the small bench beneath her wobbles perilously. Instinctively, my hands shoot up, but it's futile—I'm too far away. All I can do is watch, helpless, as the impending catastrophe unfolds.

Time seems to slow down just as I see Ethan sprint forward and catch Ivy in his arms. My hands fly up to cover my mouth in surprise. Lady Fate is certainly smiling on my friend today. Maybe Ivy should consider sending her a thank-you card after this.

Ethan has Ivy encircled in his grip, slowly lowering her, though his incinerating frown only deepens.

"Tell me you're not dumb enough to wear those boots on a hike."

Oh, noooo!

Ethan has a tendency to put his foot in his mouth, but unbeknownst to him, he's just hit a sore spot with my BFF. His comment is like acid over old wounds.

Her defenses are up as she shoves Ethan away.

"I'm perfectly capable of judging my own abilities, thank you very much!"

She impales Ethan with her own take on the death glare.

I've gotta say, being a third wheel to this much tension is kind of weird.

"Make sure your date has the muscles to carry you before you start your hike. He'll need it when you twist an ankle in those ridiculous boots."

"Excuse me? Eavesdrop much?" Ivy's hands go to her hips as she steps closer to Ethan. Even in her heeled boots, she's nearly a foot shorter than him and has to tilt her head back to meet his eyes.

I jump in before one of them attacks the other. "Okay kids,

let's play nice." I'm not too sure which kind of attacking might happen, because the tension here feels equally love/hate, but it's best to get a handle on things now, just in case.

"Ethan, thanks for your quick reflexes. Vee, let's go to my desk."

I grab her other heels and handbag, herding her out the door while their narrowed eyes track one another's movements.

By the time we get to my cubicle, Ivy is muttering the word "jerk," amongst other less polite terms.

"What the heck was that?"

"What? That guy was out of line, Em. Who is that?"

"Colton's brother, Ethan."

"The guy who's party we—"

"Shhh!" I hiss, darting my eyes around to ensure we're not overheard. With all these plants around, it's the perfect place for eavesdroppers to hide.

"Yes, *that* guy. Now explain yourself, ma'am."

"He started it, manhandling me! Spewing accusations!"

"Mm-hmm. Okay. Well, I guess we'll see how this plays out." I fold my arms with a smirk. If these two had started differently, I suspect there might have been romantic sparks instead of a crackling TNT fuse.

"Whatever," she rolls her eyes. "I'm keeping the shoes. They were six dollars, and they're cute. Gran said this guy is tall. I don't want to feel like an elf next to him. Plus, I don't actually know if we're hiking. She only said he's outdoorsy and that we're going for a walk near the boat pier."

I continue to stare, squinty-eyed, so she feels my judgment.

"What? There'll be lots of people there. I wouldn't trudge off into a forest with a strange man, no matter how long Gran said she's known him."

"And how does she know him?"

"He's a therapist at the retirement village—the one with that therapy dog."

"Right. Well, you're adorable with or without heels, Vee. You know, eventually, especially once you're married, you'll have to allow yourself to be flat-footed in the presence of a man?"

"Yeah. But I don't plan on marrying this dude, so why go through the schlepp of confronting my insecurities about my height deficiency? I'll save it for a man who's worth it."

"That sounds perfectly healthy." I laugh while her eyes twinkle with humor. She's good at deflecting. "Call me later and I'll tell you about my run-in at the grocery store over the weekend."

"I can't wait," she sings, grabbing her shoes.

Ivy hugs me goodbye and I continue plotting ways to get her and Ethan in the same room under less hostile circumstances. I'm not sure how things will play out with Colton's time in Aster apparently on a countdown. But that doesn't mean I can't hope for a romance for my friend.

# CHAPTER THIRTY-FIVE

Colton walks into the bullpen and catches me humming to my little tub of Lunchables. Nearby cafes are too expensive, and I have a lot to do, so lunch at my desk, it is.

"It's not just syrup that elicits a serenade. It's lunch too?"

"I guess, but it's probably anything sweet. I may have a sugar problem."

He steps closer, softly grasping my left arm and inspecting the cast.

"Did you steal that lunch from a kid?" he asks, though he seems very preoccupied with my hand, running his thumb over the angry red skin that's slightly chafed. His gentle touch is a flame to my icy exterior, melting me faster than my brain can comprehend.

How did I go from upholding an anti-relationship, *casual-blind-dates-only* policy to seconds away from wilting at the slightest touch of this man? Given, he's not just *any* man. Heck, he's not just a handsome man. He's the sweetest, most attractive male I've ever met, and his attention turns me into a speechless mess. I'm the phone left outside in the sun, refusing to function due to extreme heat exposure.

"Lunchables have no age limit. My mother never let me eat them so I'm rebelling."

A deep, rumbly sound escapes from his chest, filled with enough Roy Kent gravel to make a girl squirm. I can't tell if he's thinking of his own childhood or just unhappy about mine, though I suspect it's the latter after having met his ridiculously charming parents.

He reaches across my desk for a Sharpie and inspects the splatters and flecks of paint covering my cast from when I tested products last week.

His eyes map the space like it's his very own canvas, and then he's writing something, causing my stomach to dip with giddiness. I feel like the dorky girl whose high school crush just noticed her. Seconds later, he's recapping the Sharpie and dropping it back into the pen holder.

He releases my arm, so I turn it over, grinning at the smiley face with his initials underneath.

*He drew a freaking smiley face.*

How am I supposed to function like this?

Colton puts his hands in his pockets, then removes them a second later, fidgeting with a plant's sad-looking leaf. He bumps over my pen holder and fumbles to put everything back in place.

Nervousness busies his fingers, and it's adorable. He's always so confident and sure of himself, and this new side is rather delightful.

Hands slide back inside his pockets, eyes meeting mine. Suddenly, he's flipped a switch, turning off unsure and hesitant and turning on knowing precisely what he wants.

"Ember, would you like to go to dinner with me?"

*Oh.*

"On a date," he clarifies.

I'm still playing catch-up. When Colton told me he wanted to see where this went, my head was still spinning after finding out nothing was happening between him and Lemon. Since then, I've spent the past five days replaying everything he said in that conversation, wondering if I imagined his request for me to stop dating other guys or if he only wants something casual since he's leaving so soon.

I'd almost convinced myself he wasn't serious when I didn't see him Thursday and Friday, and Ivy and I spent Saturday debating whether I was ready for another relationship, as well as the merits of my whole "no romance at work" motto.

After a weekend of extreme overthinking, and much to Ivy's horror, I decided it was best to keep things professional and pretend last week hadn't happened.

When I got to work this morning, Mrs. Sullivan told me Colton was returning from a trip to Utah. That word—*Utah*—has become a trigger word, reminding me that regardless of what could have been, this situation with Colton has a time limit.

Since then, I've ping-ponged between acting casual, telling him I'm not ready for a relationship, and saying "What the heck, let's see where this goes."

And now I'm staring at him while my thoughts attempt a flash dance in my head, except none of them have rehearsed a single step, and it's a total disaster.

"Yes." The word escapes without my permission.

*That settles that, then.*

The man continues killing me with his smile as I stand here contemplating how my obituary should read.

*Emberleigh Richard Hayes. Deceased. Overexposure to sexy grins. She died happy.*

His eyes bounce between mine while the air feels like it's being squeezed. "I'll call you later with the details."

And then he turns and walks away, taking all the oxygen with him.

# CHAPTER THIRTY-SIX

The last rays of the evening sun sift through the towering oak trees surrounding Ember's building. I absentmindedly rake my fingers through my hair, though I'm not feeling nervous. It's been a while since I've taken anyone out on a date, but the fluttering in my stomach is probably just hunger.

I might be a bit nervous, but mostly it's because I hadn't planned on asking Ember out so soon. The idea was to take things slow, to gradually win her over. She's like a wary rabbit; too sudden a move and she might dart back into her burrow the moment I look away.

I should have given her time to warm up to the idea of us dating. But when I saw her, I had to act.

It took ten minutes of listening to her insist that she could get to our date on her own before I finally convinced her to let me pick her up at her apartment.

I swiftly make my way to the gate that opens into the garden patio at the heart of the complex. Just outside, there's a quaint wrought iron table where two elderly ladies sit, dressed as though they've just returned from high tea at a country club. Mischief twinkles in their smiles as they size me up, simultaneously lifting frosted martini glasses, and taking a slow, synchronized sip.

"Mm, Gail, this must be him. Lord, look at the shoulders. I bet his hips don't squeak when he walks."

"Mm-hmm. I bet those hips don't squeak at all. He's a ten, but I can tell he likes women his own age."

"Pity."

"Ladies." I nod with a smile as I intend to pass them.

"Hold up there, young man." The shorter one raises a finger at me. Gail, I think.

She tilts her head, pausing to examine me in a way that makes me feel like a teenager picking up my prom date. "You must be something special for Ember to give you the okay to pick her up at home. You should know she doesn't do that."

"Yes, ma'am. I appreciate the warning, and I certainly won't take that fact lightly," I reply, squaring my shoulders.

Gail elbows her friend, passing the interrogative baton.

"Young man, I'd apologize for our brashness, but we say what we want at our age, and we're never really sorry about it. This, here, is Gail, and I'm Opal. Now you should know that, despite how this looks, it would be effortless for us to dispose of a body. We've had years to devise the best way to do it. All this to say, Ember is the sweetest person you'll ever meet. If you hurt her, we will find you." Wrinkled eyes narrow in my direction, and Opal sets her glass down, hardening her stare. "I'll save you the guessing—that was most definitely a threat. Lord knows we're too old to be hinting at things. So, you be sure to treat her right."

I clear my throat, working hard to hide my smile.

"I'm happy Ember has two caring, and slightly scary,

friends looking out for her. I promise not to do anything to hurt her."

Gail nods, seemingly satisfied, then lifts her martini glass. "Alright, Opal, let this handsome man go so we can stare at his tush after he passes."

"Excellent." Opal hums, wiggling her fingers at me in dismissal.

I hope I've passed the test. As I wave goodbye, there's a slight worry that I might get a cheeky pinch—and I don't mean on my face.

"Seriously, Nicolas? Why now?" I hear Ember whining before her door swings open.

My thoughts are scattered, but one word is illuminated among the others: *radiant.*

The only other thought that's clear enough to be coherent is that I want to ask her what she's doing for the next sixty years.

"Hey," she beams.

Her smile is everything. I'm hit with a warmth in my chest that begins to spread the longer she grins at me. It's the feeling of lying in the sun after a cold swim, and I want to soak up every ray as it warms my body. I'm greedy for it, ready to shoo away anyone who blocks the toasty glow from falling over me.

"Who's Nicolas?"

"He's my cat. Nicolas Cage," she replies, hitching a thumb over her shoulder.

"There's a story there. Tell me about it on the drive? You look beautiful, by the way."

That's an understatement. She's stunning. She looks amazing in high-waisted, wide-leg jeans with a fitted, cream tank, and she gifts me another colossal smile that sends a wash of that warmth all over again. I want to roll around in this feeling. Like a cannoli dipped in chocolate, just cover me up in her colorful, sprinkled goodness.

The drive is comfortable, despite my first-date jitters. But who wouldn't feel nervous with a date that looks so huggable?

I laugh as Ember tells me about her cat and how he got his name.

"He sounds like he's slowly gaining enough knowledge to murder you."

"What? Nicolas is a weirdo, but deep down, he's a teddy bear."

"A teddy bear who's trying to kill you."

She eyes me narrowly. "I take it you're not a cat person?"

"I think cats that think they're dogs are cool."

"Explain."

"When you get a dog, you research the breed, knowing what kind of personality you're getting. But a cat is a gamble. You could end up with one that's a total jerk, like the cats that sit on the top of doors, waiting to attack when you walk into a room. But the ones that think they're dogs and follow you around are the best. They're companions, as opposed to the ones that just sleep on your freshly washed clothes or drop dead mice on your lap."

"I take it you speak from experience."

I shake my head. "I'm not carrying any trauma from a past experience at all."

Her melodic laugh fills the truck, and I've already found another thing I want bottled or recorded to take with me. Just until I can convince her to spend forever together. No big deal.

We're still talking when I park in front of an arcade center, and Ember stops mid-sentence when she looks up and sees the sign above the entrance. Her smile grows as she glances at me and points at the sign, and my heart stretches just the same. I'm starting to get a high every time she throws one of those dazzling grins my way. I'm afraid it could very quickly lead to an addiction.

"We're going to an arcade?" she asks incredulously.

"Yeah but you need to know something. There's no chivalry in a place like this. I'm gonna kick your butt at every game."

"I'm glad we've set the ground rules 'cause I will own you."

I nod. This woman is amazing.

"What happens in the arcade stays in the arcade." I hold my hand out so we can shake on it.

We climb out of the truck, Ember opening her door before I can get to it. She glances at me over the roof. "I'd appreciate it if you went back to being a gentleman once we're done," she says.

I click my tongue and wince. "You'll have to wait for me to recharge. Tomorrow, there's a ninety-nine-percent chance the chivalry will return."

She meets me on my side of the truck, lips pursed. "I like chivalrous Colton."

I tuck a stray strand of hair behind her ear, momentarily losing track of our joke. Her dazzling green eyes capture all my attention. Taking a deep breath to calm my nerves, I'm enveloped by her scent, reminiscent of the honey my gran used to keep on the table during those leisurely summer vacation mornings, with slow starts and hearty breakfasts. Everything about Ember just feels like coming home.

"Don't move," I say, reaching into my truck to grab a Polaroid camera. She stands there, haloed by bright lights that cast her in a dim silhouette. With a playful pout and folded arms, she strikes a pose while I step back to frame the shot. The camera spits out a photo, but I barely glance at it—the real scene before me is too mesmerizing to miss. I tuck the camera and the undeveloped photo back, lock the door without looking away, and keep my eyes fixed on hers.

Then I step in closer, trailing my hand down her arm. The sleeve of her cardigan is pushed over her cast, and my fingers glide until my pinky hooks around hers. Tonight is about fun, something I'm guessing Ember doesn't make a lot of time for.

As our fingers intertwine, I see a spark in Ember's eyes, a fleeting glimpse of a carefree spirit usually tucked away. Tonight, my goal is to see that side of her bloom.

# CHAPTER THIRTY-SEVEN

## EMBER

As we step into Zane's Arcade, a blast of eighties music and neon lights hits me, immersing us in a vibrant sensory overload. Behind the kiosk, a grizzly man with long, frizzy black hair and square glasses oversees an array of prizes hanging from hooks and displayed in cases—trinkets most people wouldn't think twice about tossing. Yet, something tells me that tonight, I'd go as far as selling a kidney for the largest stuffed animal in the collection.

Teenagers make up most of the room, and I'm not at all embarrassed to be here as a twenty-five-year-old.

My parent's idea of appropriate teenage fun involved learning how to use a napkin in a ladylike fashion or polite simpering over tea. Boys were permitted slightly more reckless entertainment, like racing a golf cart or practicing being mini-jerks in preparation for becoming full-fledged jerks, like their fathers. My parents would never have allowed me to frequent a place like this. I'm sure the words "Arcade Center" alone would cause my mother's eye to twitch for twelve hours. Tonight my excitement overrides my anxiety, even in this sensory-overloaded environment.

Colton flinches when I pinch the back of his arm, and I decide the tiny yelp that follows is my favorite. He turns towards me. "What was that for?"

"Sorry, just getting this feud going," I reply, wringing my hands. "Okay, confession time."

He drops his hands to his side as his face pales. "You hate arcades."

"No. It's not that..." I clear my throat and cringe. "I've never been to an arcade." Once again, I'm revealing too much about my lame upbringing.

"Oh, you are so dead," he grins.

He's right. The smile he's giving me has set the butterflies in my stomach into a state of hysteria on par with a tween who just touched Harry Styles. They're trying to signal to my heart that my time has come.

"You talked quite a big talk out there, Hayes. Don't worry. I'll go easy on you." He nudges my shoulder before stepping forward and buying a tap card for each of us.

I thought these places used coins you put into slots, but apparently, I missed that whole era.

"What do you wanna do first?" Colton asks as we near the noisy machines.

"Whatever I can decimate you in the quickest."

"That took a dark turn." He smiles, then lifts his chin toward the first machine in front of us. "How about this one? You shoot targets, and sometimes zombies show up."

"Sounds like dinner with my parents."

"That's frightening."

Again with the smile that makes the room spin a little.

"Whoever gets the most points wins," he declares, grabbing the handle of the gun in front of him and taking a seat.

"You're going down, King." I'm admittedly talking a lot of smack talk for a girl who's never played an arcade game in her life.

We tap our cards, and the music starts. My squeals can't be contained. I'm like a kid in line for a bag of cotton candy.

Colton looks over at me. "You okay holding that with your cast?"

"Yeah, I can manage." I wiggle in my seat as the countdown begins. "Get ready, King. You're about to eat dust."

He shakes his head, casually leaning on the gun in front of him. "The sheer number of threats I'm getting is concerning."

"You started it with all that '*chivalry has no place in an arcade*' talk." I elbow him.

The timer starts, and it takes a few seconds to acclimate to the way the targets move so quickly.

"The purple circles are worth the most points," Colton says without looking my way.

"Are you mansplaining this to me?" I retort, though my heart is racing like crazy, and I've hardly blinked before the round ends. "Another round?"

He lets out a chuckle and taps his card again. "As you wish."

I think I hear the ovaries of every woman in the room sigh. Granted, that's probably only four other ovaries because most of the females present are thirteen and too young to get a *Princess Bride* reference.

We play two more rounds, and by the end, Colton swivels on his seat to face me, lips turned in and nostrils flaring.

"Just say it," I grunt jokingly while I narrow my eyes his way. "And what happened to '*no chivalry*'? You helped me!"

A burst of laughter bubbles out. "I felt sorry for you. You were terrible."

Okay, yes, he owned me. I improved with each round, but he'd still nearly doubled my score by the end.

"The night is young." I wave my hand, looking around. "What's next?"

The next thirty minutes consist of Colton obliging my every whim, while I'm freshly enamored with each new machine. Every time I get the hang of a game, another one catches my eye by reminding me of a movie or TV show. It's not my fault that I experienced most normal teenage things vicariously through a TV screen.

I laugh as Colton beats my score in yet another game. I've exhausted both of us with the adrenaline high I've been running on.

I wipe a few hairs away from my sweaty forehead. "We need water."

"I'll grab us some if you want to find a table?"

"Perfect. I'm gonna run to the ladies room first. I'll find you."

"Sounds good." He winks, and I try to ignore what it does to my insides.

Once again, I find myself in a line for a restroom, only this one has a big neon sign pointing me in the right direction and making me wish every toilet was so obnoxiously advertised. This isn't a huge building, but I've gotten lost in smaller spaces.

I dig out one of my favorite flavored lip balms and wait silently with the three pubescent girls before me.

I wish I was that cool when I was twelve. Unfortunately, I was a lanky kid sporting a middle part before it was fashionable to do so.

"I love your pants!" one of them exclaims, and I check behind me to make sure it's me they're talking to.

"Oh, thanks," I say with a genuine smile. "I got them at a thrift store."

*Is it uncool to admit that?*

Evidence would prove otherwise because they collectively squeal their approval. "We love thrifting. Sasha found her satchel there," she gestures to her tween sidekick, "and I got this jacket."

My momentary cool status is threatened when I feel the urge to draw them a map and label all of my favorite thrift stores, but luckily, I'm saved when the restroom opens and all three of them disappear inside.

I hum Shania's *"Life's About to Get Good"* while I wait, imagining her smile at my half-decent interaction with scary tweens.

How can such a bustling place have only two restrooms? Thankfully, they're private, enclosed rooms, which keeps my usual restroom anxiety at bay. When my turn arrives, I appreciate the solitude as I do my business, grateful for the privacy. After exiting, I set out to find Colton, but pause when my phone vibrates. Checking it, I don't see him nearby. Maybe he's texted to say he's found a table elsewhere?

Except it's not from Colton.

UNKNOWN NUMBER

I know you're in Aster. We need to talk.

*No, no, no, no, no!*

All the blood drains from my face.

I'm frozen, my brain a few seconds ahead of my body. I'm telling my feet to move and my lungs to inhale, but they're not responding.

*How does he know where I am?*

My hands feel clammy.

I wrote off that little sighting of Beau a few weeks ago as an optical illusion, a mirage, my subconscious's excuse for my perpetual jumpiness and the need to check that my doors are locked twice per night. But then I painted over that image, telling myself it was all in my head. Everything was fine. He was supposed to stay in my past. Why will this man not leave me alone?

Until now, when reality rains down, dissolving the neat little watercolor I created in front of me. Colors bleed as I mourn the illusion of freedom.

I shove my phone back into my bag and pull at the collar of my shirt when it suddenly begins to feel too tight.

*It's too hot in here.*

I turn, heading for the door. Not that I can tell which direction that is while I feel like my head is being smothered with pillows.

*Not this way.*

I pivot, colliding with a hard chest. Solid arms hold me upright.

"Whoa." The smile on Colton's face fades, and a crease forms between his brow. "What happened?" He looks around like he's searching for an assailant, and I adore him for it. He scowls at passers-by, then darts his eyes back to mine. His face softens slightly. "You're pale. You okay?"

Hands fall gently on my shoulders, and he moves us out of the way of the foot traffic.

My instinct is to tell him, "Of course, I'm okay." But I wasn't okay every time Beau swung verbal and occasionally physical blows at me. Eventually, I was okay. But it was through my own strength that I managed.

I scan the room, afraid I'll see Beau emerging from every corner. "Yeah. Um...I just need some air. Can we go outside?" I finally look up at him, still feeling the need to pull at my collar.

"Of course." He leads me to the exit with a hand on my lower back. If I were less unsettled, I'd go mushy inside at the move that seeps warm liquid into every romantic crack of my heart.

The cool air soothes my nerves as we step outside, and my heart rate slows.

I got so comfortable living in my semi-happy Aster bubble, thinking I was out of reach of the ugly claws of a past I'd like to forget. I was only fooling myself into thinking that bubble wasn't as fragile as it really was.

The sun has just dipped and the evening colors are a welcome respite to my neon-assaulted eyes.

Colton leads us to his truck and opens the passenger door. I sit, and before I can swivel my legs in, he ducks so we're eye to eye, hands gently resting on my shoulders.

"What's going on, Em?" His thumb moves back and forth on my neck, distracting me from my freakout.

I sigh heavily and look out the windshield, staring vacantly.

*You need to tell him.*

I know I do. But it's not easy sharing that weakness, the way I allowed the people in my life to control me. I wave my hand, intending to tell him everything, but the gnarly, twisted story feeds on my doubt. I come with a lot of baggage. What if he regrets starting this with me once he knows about my past that won't seem to stay in the past? He's also apparently moving to another state, which still hasn't come up.

I tell myself it's better to sort this Beau situation out alone. I'm good at that. Dumping it on Colton's shoulders doesn't feel fair.

"I got a text from my ex. It freaked me out a little, but I'm fine." I force my face to shed any lingering trace of unease.

A slight wind blows, and I shiver when it reaches the truck's cab. Colton stands, squeezing my hand. "Let's get something to eat."

"Yeah, that sounds good."
I can fix this Beau stuff. Everything's fine.

## CHAPTER THIRTY-EIGHT

### EMBER

Colton announces we're off to a food truck that supposedly has the best tacos ever. As he drives, he gently lifts my hand, cast and all, resting it on his leg and plays with my fingers in the quiet of the ride.

When he parks and comes around to help me out of the truck, I find myself too caught up in checking him out to even think of beating him to the punch.

"You don't needa that, you know. I can get in and out of a truck just fine," I say nonchalantly, but a little sass clips my words. I'm no damsel in distress. I don't need to wait like a puppy to be let in and out of the vehicle.

He steps closer, hands bracketing me on the side of his truck. "Listen, Sunshine, make no mistake about it. When a man walks his lady to the car or holds the door open for her, it's not because he thinks she can't do it herself. He does it for those extra few seconds—to place his palm gently on her back or to let his hands linger on her waist. It's all just an excuse to be a little closer to her."

I need an audible gulp button. I'm melting like a marsh-mallow after a run-in with a blowtorch.

"You're gonna love these tacos." He steps back with a smile, graciously opting not to draw attention to my gooey, bubbly state.

"All that lack of chivalry at the arcade must have taken a toll. I think I'd eat whatever you put in front of me."

"You paid a steep price but learned a valuable lesson, Hayes."

"Yeah?"

"I'm the master at shooting things. Also, you're too easy to tease, so that's probably not gonna stop any time soon."

"Is this a pulling-on-pigtails thing? Because I've already admitted I like you,"

We join the line in front of a taco truck with Mexican music gently playing in the background and twinkle lights strung on the overhang. Colton lifts a hand, twirls a strand of my hair around his finger, and then lets it bounce away.

"You'd look cute with pigtails, but no." He pauses, eyes reeling me in. "You're fun to laugh with."

He says it casually, but I feel his words washing over all the insecure parts of who I am. For as long as I can remember, I've been told I'm not enough and that I need to do better, that I should take things more seriously. So I stifled all the parts of myself that once felt free to find joy in anything.

It's not like I've been walking around like angsty Avril Lavi-gne. But being near Colton and hearing his words makes me realize how much I've forgotten who I truly am and who I've always wanted to be.

I'm deep into contemplating life when Colton offers to order for us. Out of instinct, I bristle at the feelings wafting in with that question. But they're faint and easily waved away once I remind myself that Colton isn't Beau and he's offering out of kindness. I nod absently, drifting as Colton gives his order at the counter.

Our food arrives quickly, and I'm grateful because my stomach is about to stage a coup. We grab napkins and carry everything to one of the square tables that dot the paved area in front of the food trucks.

Colton takes the seat perpendicular to mine, using his foot to scoot my chair closer. I chew my lip to hide the ridiculously huge grin fighting to overtake my face.

The enticing smell of the food dulls the rest of my senses, including my worries about my ex following me. Beau's harmless. I know he is. He'd never actually do anything crazy. He just has a hard time hearing "no."

The first bite of steak taco is delicious, and I hum with delight. My eyes bug out, and I cover my lips to speak with a mouth stuffed with flavor. "This is incredible." Colton nods triumphantly when I add, "These tacos should be added to the list of recommended food groups."

"Right? I discovered them last year. It's another place I'm happy to frequent a fair amount."

I grab a napkin to wipe the sauce that escapes my face hole and decorates my cheeks. My mother would be mortified to see that those ladylike napkin lessons didn't take. According to her, if you need to use the napkin, you've already failed and are now a savage.

In my fervent rejection of cutlery tonight, I end up channeling my inner Neanderthal and clumsily knock a fork off the table. As I bend down to retrieve it and straighten back up, I notice Colton's arm extended, shielding me from the table's sharp corner.

*This.*

This is why I'm a goner.

I have the urge to start a slow clap with all the women-folk nearby. I want the world to know he's one of the good ones.

And now he's looking at me like that.

I'm on a fast track to falling head over heels, and when he does stuff like this, I'm only more inclined to fall harder. At this point, he's making it difficult to do anything but tumble down the hill toward him.

My trust in my judgment of people might still be growing, but taking it slow with Colton still won't be easy.

Deep down, I know that every cell in Colton is good and honorable. But I remind myself that there were a lot of red flags I ignored in my relationship with Beau. I ignored things I shouldn't have, made excuses for the horrible way he treated me. It wasn't love that blinded me, but rather my insecurities about pleasing my parents.

I console myself by thinking that at least I didn't pull a full Padme Amidala, overlooking the glaring, Death Star-sized red flag of someone massacring an entire tribe, women and children included. If I were her, Anakin and his Padawan braid would have been history. I mean, Padme ignored so many red flags she could have decorated the entire galaxy with them. But then again, the rosy tint of new love has a crafty way of turning your head when you really should be keeping your eyes wide open.

But I refuse to be Padme this time. Even though I know Colton is nothing like Beau or Anakin, slow is best.

Slow is good.

Colton lowers his hand from the table corner. His smile is tender and gentle, revealing the laugh lines and creases in his eyes.

He places his drink down and pushes his plate in. "You said you lived in Magnolia. Why'd you move to Aster?" He leans back, a hand resting on my chair.

I wipe my mouth with a napkin. I'm not a barbarian, but I refuse to pat my lips like I'm dabbing at a spritz of facial mist.

"I needed a clean break from everything back in Magnolia, and Ivy seemed like a safe place to land," I start, my shoulder lifting as I muster the courage to reveal more. Opening up about my vulnerabilities doesn't come naturally to me. "At the time, I was working for my dad's company, but things turned sour with my ex, and i needed a change. I assured everyone I was safe, but I kept them at arm's length—that's all the access I allowed them. That is, until the hospital incident." I pause, the memory bitter. I still wish I could erase that day from his memory—and mine.

"That was brave of you, to make those changes."

I shrug. Ivy's told me the same thing so many times, but escaping doesn't feel courageous. "I guess. It felt like running away from my problems. But I knew I couldn't stay."

A few seconds of silence follow, and he turns his hand to lace his fingers with mine. I watch his jaw tick, focusing on that solid muscle. He clears his throat and seems to brace himself like he knows the story gets ugly. "Tell me about your ex."

The steady heart rate I'd settled with a good meal kicks into overdrive again. This is the moment. I can at least give him the backstory.

"To everyone else, he was the picture-perfect gentleman. But he was a terrible boyfriend. We dated for just short of a year." I sigh again, knowing I must get the rest of the story out. "My parents set us up. He works for my dad. It's your typical old-money business deal. Families planning for their kids to unite and magically create unbreakable dynasties through arranged marriages. Unfortunately, Beau started showing me another side. Within a few months of dating, the pile of red flags grew too tall to ignore."

"He started controlling every aspect of who I was,

becoming angrier and angrier when I did something he didn't like. He never hurt me, but he'd threaten to. Raising a palm occasionally then pulling back and apologizing profusely. But he got so good at making me feel like I'd provoked him. I've read enough novels to know how that story usually ends."

I look up, finally making eye contact with Colton. "I refused to be the woman who tried too late to get away. So I packed a few bags and made my way to Ivy's."

Colton's face is the picture of controlled fury when I look up. I've seen his jaw tick when he's been upset before, but it was nothing compared to the way his facial muscles are pulsing now.

"Your parents didn't do anything about how he treated you?"

"They don't know." My eyes fall back to our hands. "I only told them I was unhappy and that Beau wasn't the man I thought he was. I felt ashamed because I'd let him treat me like that for so long. And they loved him, so I guess I doubted they'd believe me. So, I ran, before I became someone I couldn't recognize. I love it here, though. Being near Ivy has been a godsend."

"You have nothing to be ashamed of when a man doesn't treat you the way you deserve. That's all on him, Em. Not on you."

"I know. I mean, I know that *now*. When I left Magnolia, all I had the strength for was getting away. I couldn't deal with trying to tell my parents the truth, only to have them say they didn't believe me."

He's quiet for a while before he speaks again. "You'll tell me if he continues to bother you?"

I nod, not able to say the words. I want to tell him. But there's a naive little girl on my shoulder whispering that if I just give it time, Beau will find someone else to focus on.

Colton stands and offers me his hand. He grabs his jacket,

draping it over my shoulders. The air is only a little cool, but I'm wrapped in his masculine scent, so you won't hear me complaining.

He gently pulls at the lapels, locking his eyes on mine. "You're brave, Em," he says with finality, then places a kiss on my forehead. I don't think there's any coming back from this. I'm falling fast, and I'm almost positive I won't recover if he breaks my heart. I also can't help but worry about how serious this thing between us might get if he's leaving.

I push those thoughts away. There'll be time later to rein-force my defenses. Right now, I'm soaking up his words and his warmth.

Colton drives me home, and his hand stretches over to clasp mine. Would he be mad if I happened to superglue our hands together? He'd have to take me everywhere. That sounds like a cozy plan.

Wait, scratch that. I didn't think the toilet situation through. I love holding his hand more than the royal family likes shooting birds, but I already have issues with toilet noises.

He parks and jogs around to my door, and I take the opportunity to sniff his jacket, knowing I'll have to part with it in a minute.

I'm not a weirdo. You are.

With my handsome boss's help, I climb out, and he curls his arm around my waist as we walk. Our steps are slow. Neither of us is ready for the evening to end.

Walking through the courtyard of our apartment complex is like stepping into an enchanted garden, thanks to Opal and Gail. Their floriferous efforts make this prolonged ending to our date even more magical.

Sadly, we reach my doorway too quickly. Colton turns, pulling me into him, and I go willingly. The wind wraps around us, and he tugs me closer, his jaw resting against my head.

I think I've found my new home. The feeling of security he gives me is almost overwhelming. Before I get too emotional about the fact that I haven't had a good hug in too long, I lean back a fraction, looking up at him. "Thank you for today. For tonight I mean. It was amazing."

He smooths my hair, smiling lazily down at me. "So, I didn't lose points for the part where my chivalry went MIA?"

"Nah, I can't hold that against you. You've got mad skills. Chivalry would have given you a huge disadvantage."

"I'm glad you understand. It's not something that most people would handle so gracefully."

I reward him with a goofy smile. "Colton King, you're not what I expected."

"You're welcome," he jokes.

Then he steps back, his arms unraveling from my waist, and I want to haul him back to me in protest.

He holds his hand out like he's waiting for me to give him something.

"Oh, right," I say, pulling his jacket off.

With a slow smile, he shakes his head. "That's not what I wanted."

He fishes out a Sharpie from his back pocket, drapes the jacket over his shoulder, and tugs my hand closer. He moves to stand beside me, half-tucking my cast under his arm, and I watch, slightly stunned, but mostly loving the gentle way he's handling me.

I use the time to study his face. It's a welcome distraction to the barrage of texts I can feel coming through on my phone. I'm not about to waste the opportunity to be close to him without his ridiculously enchanting eyes casting a spell on me. A shadow of a beard dusts his square jaw. The outdoor lighting casts just enough light that I can see the pulse point in his neck. And I'm barely saved from doing something crazy, like leaning in and kissing him on that spot, when he replaces the marker cap with a click and snaps me out of my ogling.

I'm a kid with a present, dying to rip into the wrapping. I lift my arm, eager to discover what he's drawn, but his lips are pressing against my cheek, zapping the thought away. Before I can blink, he's pulling away. It happened so unexpectedly that I want to ask for a redo. I wasn't prepared, and I want to feel it again. I almost moan aloud.

"Sleep well, Sunshine. Text me when you wake up."

He steps back but doesn't turn away. By some miracle, my brain regains an ounce of functionality, and I nod in response after realizing he's waiting for me to enter my apartment.

With awkward, jerky movements, I unlock my door and turn. I attempt to wave but look more like a cat swatting at a toy.

He returns the gesture, and I'm jealous of his ability to do it like a normal person. Then I dart inside and close the door, leaning against it and flinching as Nicolas Cage curls around my leg. The TV is on, but the volume is thankfully low. I glance at the screen. History's Greatest Heists with Pierce Brosnan. That tracks.

My head is in a daze. I smile at my cast when I see the smiley face with long hair and the letters "*E.H.*" that Colton added beside the tattoo of a boy's smiley face with his initials. It's silly and sweet at the same time. What grown man doodles on a cast?

*The one who's slowly knocking down all the heavy brick and plaster around your heart, that's who.*

# CHAPTER THIRTY-NINE

## COLTON

Sunday morning, I wake up smiling like an idiot and feeling happier than I have in as long as I can remember. But I'm happy to be that idiot. It takes extreme self-restraint not to text Ember as soon as I open my eyes.

I head to the gym to meet Ethan for our usual kickboxing session, where he thoroughly kicks my butt. Noticing my distraction, he seizes the chance—like any typical younger brother would—to exact some playful revenge for all those years I was the bigger one.

We walk out of the gym sweaty and puffing our chests like we've left a heap of bad guys in our wake. Something about beating the crap out of a punching bag, and sometimes a sibling, makes a man feel on top of the world.

Ethan catches me off guard and flicks the back of my leg with his towel, making me groan and shove him back. He laughs, eyeing me as we near our trucks.

"Dude, where's your head today? You look like you drank sleepy-time tea instead of coffee. And there's a goofy smile on your face. It's creeping me out."

I hoped I'd make it to my truck without Ethan bringing it up, but I guess I was too optimistic. I fooled myself by thinking he wouldn't notice the way I'm floating. The guy is too observant. I'm surprised he waited this long to bug me about it.

"Dunno what you're talking 'bout. I'm just in a good mood."

"Colt, don't be the trial period of Babble. It's a girl, isn't it?"

And this is what I was hoping to avoid. It seems innocent enough—just a brother inquiring about his sibling's life. But Ethan is the biggest gossip ever. He's Michael Scott with a secret. If I so much as hint about my date with Ember, I'm likely to get a million texts and freak-out GIFs from my mom, before I can even make it home.

I love them. I do. But we all understand that pressure from meddling, albeit well-meaning, family is never a welcome ingredient in a relationship, especially a new one. And I have no doubt the avalanche of questions will only be made a hundred times worse because they haven't seen me date anyone in years.

I can't avoid telling them about a relationship forever. And I'm seriously hoping this thing with Ember can go the distance —weddings, babies, rocking chairs. The whole thing. But that doesn't mean I'm excited for the pitch of my mom's voice when I officially tell her I'm dating someone.

I reach my truck and throw in my gym bag. There's a tiny squeak when I put my full weight onto the seat. Ethan stares, waiting while I rub the spot between my eyebrows.

*Might as well get this over with.*

"I took Ember out last night, and it went well." I inhale deeply, then fold my arms, unable to fight the spread of my grin. "I really like her. But I've gotta take things slow. She had an ex who was an absolute ass. She's skittish. Literally and figuratively."

"But now she's got you," he says, smirking back at me. "I also gotta boast because I called it."

Pulling my door shut, I scoff, hoping to escape after dropping that bomb.

"You did not."

He's a salivating dog, and I've just dangled a big, juicy steak in front of him. I'm surprised he's not texting our mother right now.

If I were a meaner brother, I'd make fun of him for being a mama's boy, but we're both pretty close to our parents, and I'd never want to shame him for that. Even when I'd like to tape his mouth shut and tie his thumbs down so he can't use his phone like the little snitch he is.

"Dude, I called it the first day I saw you together." He folds his arms, sniffing proudly. "I'm ready for your apology now."

"Apology?"

"I recall someone making fun of me for suggesting he ask out a certain fish in a pond."

"That analogy is weird. I've always wanted to avoid an office relationship 'cause it gets complicated. Not to mention the possible move—" I gesture haphazardly with my hand. "But with Ember, it's different." I lift a shoulder, feeling a twinge in the spot where Ethan got a good punch in earlier. "I just couldn't imagine not knowing her better. It hurt too much to think about that."

There's a stretch of silence while Ethan stares at me and then shivers.

"Too Hallmarky?"

"Yeah." He shakes his head, mock pity in his eyes. "Tighten it up. I can't be seen with you if you say stuff like that." He wiggles his phone at me, then runs to his truck, giggling his stupid head off.

I'm older and an inch taller, with a couple pounds more

muscle. He's a wise man to run. My love for him runs deep, but I'm not afraid to give him a dead arm when the occasion calls for it.

"Eth. Please...Don't. Just give me a week before you say anything."

"No can do, brotheroo. Mom rewards me with baked goods. That's a deal I can't back out of. Think of it as payback for making me wait two hours before you spilled."

"You have issues. Fine. But your time for falling head over heels for someone will come."

I close my door, glancing at Ethan as his thumbs type their gossiping little hearts out. I begin a slow countdown in my head back from thirty.

*Twenty-nine, twenty-eight...*I reverse, checking to make sure my watch has enough battery to take a call. *Twenty-three, twenty-two...*I pass Ethan McChatty Fingers, still parked outside the gym. He glances up, flashing me a cheesy smile. I return one, in addition to a hand gesture or two. *Fifteen, fourteen, thirteen...*

I make it to seven when my phone rings, and I've got to say I'm impressed with the speed. I tap the answer button on my watch. I love this old truck, but I miss Bluetooth for taking calls while driving.

"Hey, Mom. How are you this morning?"

"Colton Rutherford, Don't you '*how are you*' me! Why am I hearing from your brother that you took Ember on a date?" Her Southern accent gets really thick when she's angry. She's so sweet ninety-nine percent of the time, making it hard to take her seriously when she ups the sass a level.

She resumes talking before I can answer her. "We're doin' a family hike next Saturday and havin' lunch after. I expect both you and Ember to be there. Tell her to wear good shoes; you know how your Dad is with shoes. Actually, sweetie, give me her number. We'll just cut out the middle man."

My eyes bug out, and a clipped chuckle escapes my throat. "Mom, no. I'll ask Ember about Saturday, and you can talk to her then, like a sane person." This time a real laugh bubbles up. "You know you and Ethan have a problem. Can't you two join a bingo league or something? Channel all this nosey energy into something...more productive?"

"Well, you may as well suggest we pick out my coffin! I'm certainly not at bingo age, Colton!"

I wince. I should have known that comment would come back to bite me. "Your brother is being a good son, giving his mama the information she craves. Bring your Ember on Saturday, okay? I have to go. Judith from across the road is picking me up for bridge."

"You should invite Ethan."

"Don't be smart. I love you, sweetheart."

I tell her I love her, too, and we say goodbye. A slow smile creeps over my face as I shake my head. As much as their meddling is a pain, I'm grateful to have a family that cares.

I get home, flopping onto the couch with my phone. Surely, a normal amount of time has passed for me to text Ember without it being weird.

COLTON

Hey, I miss you.

I erase it, not wanting to come on too strong, too soon, and type out:

COLTON

Hey Gorgeous. You were supposed to text me this morning.

I only have to wait a minute before a reply comes through,

but it feels like hours. Where's a teenager who's fluent in texting when you need one?

EMBER

New phone, who dis?

COLTON

Cold *winking emoji* Fess up, Casper.

EMBER

Casper?

I love giving this woman nicknames.

COLTON

Like the ghost...

EMBER

Ha ha *laughing emoji* I turned my phone off last night then forgot about it. I'm sorry. I'd never ghost my boyfriend

COLTON

Boyfriend, huh?

I shoot back a playful reply, wondering why she'd need to put her phone on time out. The only explanation I can think of is if someone was pestering her. Before I can delve deeper into that thought, those three dots flicker on the screen, only to vanish, and then appear again.

A minute goes by. Then two. Crap. She's freaking out. I hit the call button, muttering "*please pick up*" to myself.

"You're one of those that talk on the phone."

My muscles relax. "Yeah, clearly, I'm not great at the texting thing. And to clarify, I am one-hundred percent your boyfriend."

"And I'm your girlfriend?" she asks, and I can hear the smile over the phone.

"Hell, yeah."

"Okay. Good...so what's up?"

"My parents do this family hike and lunch about once a month." Suddenly I'm nervous, worrying she'll think this is moving too fast. But there's genuine excitement in her voice when she speaks. "That sounds fun. I'd love that."

We spend the next two hours talking. Ember does laundry and chores, while I putter around doing nothing, just enjoying the sound of her voice. I'm an addict of all things Ember. We chat about everything and nothing. It's perfect. I can't get enough of learning about her likes and dislikes.

What we don't discuss is my pending move to Utah. It's become the elephant in the room that neither of us wants to acknowledge, assuming she's heard the rumor by now. I haven't kept my plans to start a new company in Salt Lake City a secret, but I also haven't made an official announcement, yet. But now it seems I have important decisions to make.

Eventually, we agree I should shower before my sofa permanently assumes my *eau de* gym sweat, and Ember has to help Opal and Gail. Apparently, there's a feud going on between them and the lady across the road.

I hesitate to say goodbye, unsure if it's too soon to ask her to meet again. What did I even do with my weekends before meeting Ember? Now, every moment seems filled with thoughts of her. Unable to resist, we end our call with plans to go out for lunch tomorrow.

I lie on my sofa, staring at the ceiling for another minute. There's no denying that Ember has turned my life upside down. My priorities are shifting. I'm sure there will be hiccups, but there's no way I can go back to before I met her. My heart is already hers.

# CHAPTER FORTY

## EMBER

Saturday morning arrives all too soon. Colton could have been a lawyer, given how long we debated the merits of me taking an Uber versus him picking me up to go to his parents' house. Eventually, I caved, agreeing to let him come get me.

Now, I'm sitting in his truck, fidgeting with everything in sight. I open the visor, make a goofy face, and flap it closed. My lips puff out a noisy breath of air. It's not sexy.

Colton glances over, a hint of a smile curling the corner of his mouth. He rests his hand on my leg, giving it a reassuring squeeze. "Stop being nervous," he says softly. "There's no pressure here."

He may as well tell Shakira not to use her hips. If there's one thing I excel at, it's overthinking. I'm quite proficient at it. He's unaware that I don't know how to do "nice family." The man witnessed a level of dysfunction at the hospital that I'm still unclear about, but it's so much more than that one incident. I spent half my life rinsing and repeating some extraordinary, therapy-worthy cycles of trying to earn my parents' approval and the other half trying to avoid them.

I'm about to witness something different. I'm not sure how I'll respond, how I'm supposed to respond.

Should I have brought a gift? Are there topics I should avoid? Did I pick socks with no holes?

"The last time I saw them, I was in the employee category. This is a new category. There are different standards."

His family is all so happy and outgoing, and I'm Wednesday Addams. What if I forget how to greet his dad again and end up saying "howdy," or shaking his mom's hand when she goes in for a hug, and we look like we're making up a secret handshake?

"Em, I've seen you with people. Everyone likes you. You could convince a stranger to sign up to sell essential oils without even trying." Another squeeze on my leg. "There are no expectations, and they already love you. My mom keeps telling all her friends about your bacon milkshakes. They made them at her book club last week. "

A deep breath in. "I'll be fine. I'm just a little nervous, and I don't wanna do anything weird. But if I ever get sucked into an MLM, I give you permission to Britney Spears me and take control of my money, 'cause then you know I've lost my mind."

He taps his head like he's making a mental note. "MLM, red flag. Got it."

He's given me a pep talk, but the knot in my stomach is a stubborn rock that refuses to budge. Fidgeting continues. My arm nearly disappears as I rummage through my overstuffed tote bag.

"Watcha doin' in there, Mary Poppins?"

"Looking for emergency supplies...Ew," I grimace. "Definitely felt something sticky."

A partially opened toffee candy sticks to the hem of my sleeve when my hand emerges.

"You have a sugar problem."

"Harmless self-medicating."

Colton parks, pulling me closer when we meet on the side of his truck. I do let him open my door for me sometimes, but my tiny stubborn streak still likes to make an appearance now and again, and I jump out before he reaches my side. It affirms my independence and earns me a little head shake from Colton.

He links our hands and kisses the back of my hand before pulling me toward the front door. He's slowly getting me hooked on his touches. I'm quite happy to be addicted to this man, but the withdrawals might kill me if this thing doesn't pan out.

Two minutes later, I can confirm that the Kings are all legit huggers. The past couple times I've met them weren't flukes. The tight embraces happen every time. Warm arms engulf me in a hug that soaks into neglected spaces. This hug whispers, "I'm proud of you. Everything will be okay," and then wraps me in a fluffy blanket. It squeezes at the tightly wrapped need for motherly affection that a jaded child has kept stuffed at the back of the junk drawer for years.

A fogginess blurs my eyes. I desperately want to appear normal instead of on the verge of asking for another hug, because that one should be on Oprah's Favorite Things list.

Robert hauls his son in, and they swap manly slaps on the back, but the gesture is filled with an affection that further tightens my throat.

After he pulls away from his father, Colton leads me into the house with his hand on my lower back. He doesn't know how close he is to having to go everywhere with me.

As soon as we walk inside, Jeanie eagerly grabs my arm, bubbling with excitement about all the compliments her neighbors have given her on her flower beds. She guides us into the kitchen, where an assortment of snacks and water bottles are neatly arranged on the sprawling island. Nearby, Colton edges closer, loading his backpack with supplies for our hike.

Contentment swims in his eyes as he looks at me, and he playfully nudges me with his elbow as I hand him things. I'm getting stuck inside my head again, and he knows it. But every bump from his arm stops my internal freakout. We will have words later about how he's trying to *Cesaer Milan* me. I hate that it's working.

Jeanie has definitely shifted me into the girlfriend category as she peppers me with questions about my interests. I handle those fine. They're the ones I expected. But the question about my family has my stomach dropping like I walked into an exam unprepared. It's innocent, and it shouldn't shake me like it does. All she asked was if I had any siblings. But that question is Pandora's box and will lead to answers that leave me feeling achingly lacking. My family doesn't operate like this one.

"Nope, no siblings. Just me. What's the plan for the day?"

Nobody blinks an eye at my not-so-subtle subject change. It's easier than explaining my very formal relationship with my parents.

They continue discussing the day's logistics, and I remind myself of what Ivy told me when I moved to Aster: my relationship with my parents does not define me.

Ethan's booming voice interrupts, as he and Rob join to stock their own backpacks.

"Hey, Ember. What's up, brother boss." He gives me a smile and Colton a chin lift before he begins throwing supplies into his bag.

"How's the house going? You get the roofing done yet?" Colton casually inquires.

Before Ethan can answer, Jeanie holds up a hand, looking apologetic. "I'm sorry to interrupt you boys, but if we wanna make it back in time for lunch, we'd better get a move on." She taps her hands on the island, and Ethan and Colton reply with a chorused "yes, ma'am." I want to ask if she's had a good look at them recently because they're more like flirty giants than boys.

"I shouldn't need my phone, right?" I ask Colton.

"I've got mine with me, just in case."

I don't want the distraction, especially in the form of a text from Beau, and I'm with the only person I'd be sad to miss a call from, aside from Ivy.

# CHAPTER FORTY-ONE

## EMBER

We shuffle outside, and I discover that our hike begins right from the backyard. The property is nestled at the edge of a nature reserve, crisscrossed with walking trails. Colton mentions that some trails are steep, but he assures me that he and Ethan have tackled them all before. Watching them bound up the incline with the ease of a nineties Air Jordan commercial certainly confirms it.

I guzzle an entire bottle of water before we've even left the property. Surely, hydration is number one on a basic survival list.

Colton takes my hand, interlacing our fingers as we pass through a gate at the back. We follow a winding stone path that seamlessly merges into the rugged forest terrain. Our trail, beautifully organic and shaped by years of adventurous footsteps, meanders ahead of us. Longleaf pines rise sharply from the mountainside, standing tall like pins on a cushion.

Colton and I lead the group, Ethan and his parents following. My unfit glutes scream at me, but they appreciate setting the pace.

While we walk, Ethan tells us about the house he's renovating. I'm grateful I don't need to participate much in the discussion because, let me tell you, the walk-and-talk part is not as easy as it sounds. Cardio and conversation are not friends. It's not a good look on me. I play it safe by sticking to one or two-word responses.

Every few minutes, I glance over at Colton for a quick read of his expression, checking for signs of frustration at our lack of speed. I don't find any, but upping the pace a fraction can't hurt. I'm not trying to break any records, just letting my legs know they've been slacking off the past decade.

I don't even regret that decision once I start to sweat. I won't say I love sweating, because gross, but I do find a slight sense of pleasure in it. According to my mother, intentional physical exertion is a cardinal sin. Southern ladies should never perspire. There are hand fans and pool boys with palm fronds for things like that. How dare a lady show evidence of a beating heart.

My moment of inner rebellion spurs me on.

*Watch me sweat, Mother!*

Nope. That didn't come out right.

But seriously, why have I avoided outdoor activities for so long? I'm owning this hiking thing.

This positive outlook doesn't last long though, because ten minutes later, my lungs are screaming, yet I'm too stubborn to risk slowing the group down. Where are the Planet Fitness "zero judgment zone" wall decals when I need them? Logically, I know nobody is judging my lack, nay, deficit, in fitness. But I'm also the only one panting like I just wrestled an alligator.

Colton slows, putting space between us and his family. He jiggles my hand. "You okay?"

I wave the question away, nodding as I finish my second bottle of water. Hydration: tip-top. Lung capacity: substandard.

He takes a step closer and runs a thumb over my cheek, causing my already flushed face to heat further. I fan my cheeks while locked in a gaze with those denim eyes that always see too much.

"Yup, I'm great. I do this all the time." I'm putting my honorary fibbing doctorate to good use again.

He only smiles that megawatt smile in response.

I warned Colton beforehand that ventures like hiking and camping have never been an area of interest to me. But maybe that's because I was led to believe that most outdoor activities were a waste of time or unsuitable for women. My forehead creases as this revelation becomes clearer in my mind.

"What if I am an outdoor enthusiast, but I've never been given a chance?" I step back, swiping away the hair sticking to my forehead.

"I could have the potential of a gold medalist in nature things and just not know it."

A rumbly laugh erupts. "If there were a gold medal being given out for 'nature things,' then I'm sure you could win it if you wanted to." He's laughing at me, but his genuine encouragement is adorable.

"I'm serious. There could be so many things I'm potentially amazing at but would never know because I've been kept in a pretty, doilied-up box my whole life. What if I was born to be a race-car driver or a hotdog-eating champion, but I've missed my calling, and now I'm too old?"

A raspy sound emerges as Colton rubs his thumb across his chin, his cheekbones becoming more pronounced as he tries to suppress a smile. While I can appreciate the humor in my little rant, I won't hesitate to pinch the back of his arm if another one of his growly laughs breaks free from that handsome face.

I step toward him, my lips pressed into a thin line and my

eyes wide. Sensing the threat in my stance, he straightens up, coughs awkwardly, and rubs the back of his arm.

"Come on, lovebirds. Breaks over," Rob calls.

Colton slides my empty bottle into his bag and grabs my hand again.

"I don't think I like the idea of a racing career. But with enough training and a strong gag reflex, you could go for gold in a hotdog-eating contest. I'll even dunk them in water for you."

"Ew, is that what they do? Why? It doesn't matter, and I'm too many steps away from a racing career" I swat my hand.

"What do you mean?"

I've given away too much. I had been planning to address this shortcoming by myself, but I suppose he'll find out eventually, especially if we keep spending more time together.

"Uh...I don't have my driver's license."

We walk side by side as my eyes venture over to Colton to check his reaction to my confession. He looks like he's practically bursting with questions.

"You just need to renew it with a new address or something?"

There's a clawing desperation building inside, urging me to play this down. It's no big deal, right? So I haven't gotten to an essential right of passage. I've managed just fine.

"No. I don't know how to drive. I've never driven a car."

"You haven't wanted to learn?" There's gentleness in his voice. He waits patiently for my answer, no humor on his face, no teasing.

My pulse quickens as the fear of exposure tingles up my arms. With every confession, I lose another piece of the armor I've built around myself. If I continue to disclose this next piece, I'm afraid I'll be leaving myself too vulnerable.

Colton traces small circles on the inside of my wrist with

his thumb, goosebumps chasing the motion. But his touch is soothing, reminding me that he's safe. If there were ever a person I could reveal those parts of myself to, it would be the man walking next to me, the one anchoring me.

I untangle our hands to dig through the pack on Colton's back for another water bottle, needing the distraction. I uncap the bottle and take a few gulps, crinkling it in my hands when it's empty.

"My parents had drivers that took me where I needed to go. I was told there was no need for me to learn when I'd never have the need. And I naively obeyed." I continue, and a heavy sigh escapes my chest. Living with your parents until you're twenty-five isn't exactly an Instagram profile-worthy flex. I could have moved out earlier and gotten my own place, but my parents threatened to disown me if I dared to spit in their faces by drawing a perfectly healthy boundary like that.

"It's on my list of things to do. Ivy said she'll teach me over the summer when she's off school. Ubering around isn't so bad."

I release a noisy exhale, my mouth suddenly feeling too dry after divulging how utterly lame I am. I'm dying to fill the silence that grows after my admission, when Jeanie, my savior, calls out a two-minute warning. We both turn to see Rob bending down to tie her shoelace.

Colton returns his warm gaze to me, giving my hand a quick squeeze.

"Thanks for telling me, Sunshine."

A light thump on Colton's back makes him flinch. He whirls around, scowling at Ethan.

"My bad!" Ethan yells, his face betraying no real apology. "I thought you said to toss you a stick."

Colton narrows his eyes, the slight raise of his lip the only sign that his murderous glare doesn't hold any weight. "I'm thinking you're being something else that rhymes with stick."

Ethan grins like Colton just handed him the keys to a Ferrari. "Mom!" he yells, and I smile at his attempts to tattle on his brother.

Colton's parents are sharing a cozy embrace, and Jeanie places one last peck on Rob's cheek before she turns to face us. "Ethan—stop tattling. Colton—manners."

They share a grin before we all form a line and resume our hike. Rob promises it's not long until we reach our stopping point before heading back.

Apparently, the view from the spot we're heading toward is beautiful. I'm new to wilderness walking activities, but I thought that was a 'goes without saying' kind of thing. I can't imagine traipsing up a mountain just to get to some random spot and turn around without a visual reward or a flag-planting opportunity. Americans love to stick a flag in a bit of dirt whenever possible.

Ten minutes later, we still haven't reached our destination, and I'm starting to feel the three bottles of water I guzzled earlier, like a camel loaded for a long trek across the Sahara. Clearly, I overestimated my hydration needs.

I fiddle with Colton's fingers, dreading the walk back. Because right now, I'm using every ounce of concentration to send calm, zen thoughts to my bladder. When I start to trumpet a tune through my lips, Colton shifts closer as a frown flickers across his face.

"You okay?"

"Mm-hmm," I respond too quickly, rolling my lips in. A groan escapes as my bladder protests the jolting motion I'm forcing it to endure.

Colton moves us to the side so his family can pass. "We'll

catch up with you," he says with a chin lift when Ethan over-takes us. His big hand rubs at the base of my neck as we wait for them to gain some distance.

I pinch my lips, bracing. Look, I know I'll have to tell Colton about my little predicament. But admitting that I'm a grown woman about to pee my pants isn't how I imagined the afternoon going.

The concern in his eyes has me fighting off another groan, because this sweet man is about to find out that the only thing I need is an adult diaper.

"We're about five minutes from our stop. Can you make it? I can carry you if you're too tired."

It should bother me that he thinks I'm this unfit, but I can't even muster together the energy to be slightly offended. Every brain cell is too busy sending a Mayday alert to the rest of my organs.

*We have a bladder threatening to burst. All teams on standby!*

I squeeze my eyes shut, wincing as the agony finally over-takes my dignity. Sneaking a glance at him through one half-open eye, I brace myself.

"I really need to pee! Like, find me a bush in the next minute, or you'll have an interesting third-date story to tell."

The tension melts from his brow, and he laughs. He laughs at me! "I thought you were in pain from a stitch or something." He nods behind him and starts leading me with his hand. "Come on. I'll find you a bush."

I freeze, pulling us to a stop. My eyes go wide, and honestly, I'm surprised my body can spare the energy to activate any of the muscles in my face with the effort it's taking to test the limits of my pelvic floor. "You can't come with me."

"I'll turn my back."

"You *cannot* listen to me pee, Colton." He doesn't know how strongly I feel about pee noises. I'm bouncing on my toes, doing the toddler potty dance. I pat his chest gently, then hold my hand up in a staying motion. "Wait here. I'll go...make friends with a tree. Or whatever. Just don't follow me."

I spin and let out another loud exhale—sweet mother of pearl! I've got another minute of holding power in me, tops. Colton's voice fades as I put more distance between us.

"Don't go too far!"

But I don't think I can go far enough. The thought of accidentally mooning my boyfriend urges me a few trees further. I locate a small shrub that doesn't look like it'll kill me and do my thing. This level of relief must be akin to that of women after childbirth. Slight exaggeration, but I'll wager it's close enough. I don't even mind the long stalk of grass that violates my butt cheek. What happens in the bush, stays in the bush.

I suffer through the drip-dry process, breathing a sigh of euphoric relief when I stand.

Trees are greener. Birds sound chirpier. My bladder isn't being tortured, and I have a new lease on life.

Cheerful rays of sunlight cut through the trees, warming my shoulders as I make my way back to Colton. I look down, enjoying the sound my shoes make as they crunch on the drying leaves that carpet the ground. I took the beauty of my surroundings for granted while trying to avoid wetting myself.

Five minutes later, I start calling for Colton, surprised that I haven't found him yet. I pass tree after unfamiliar tree. Not that I would notice one I'd passed before, but suddenly nothing about my surroundings feels recognizable.

I turn in circles and only succeed in confusing myself more.

*No, no, no, no, no.*

I know my sense of direction is lacking. But seriously? I'm

sure this was the direction I came from…said every waylaid person ever. I refuse to even think of the L-word.

My heart rate echoes in my ears. It taunts me like my very own Jaws theme song.

"Relax, Ember. Think."

How did this happen? Just ten minutes ago, I felt like Cinderella, surrounded by friendly woodland creatures in a sunlit forest where everything seemed to sing. Now, I'm more like Belle, lost and alone, with unknown creatures eyeing me like I'm their next meal. Things have taken a drastic turn, and I'm well aware that alligators have been spotted in these woods.

I spin around a few more times, desperately searching for something familiar or even a squirrel to point me in the right direction. Fifteen minutes slip by, and I'm still quietly repeating to myself, "It'll be okay," though it does little to ease my growing anxiety.

*Dang it.*

I finally admit that I am very much lost.

What exactly is the protocol when you're lost? Should I have stayed put instead of wandering even further from where I started? And to top it off, I don't even have my phone with me.

*Crap.*

At least it's nowhere near sunset. I'd be ten steps ahead in the freakout trajectory if I faced spending the night taunted by nature and her beady-eyed minions.

I despised all the water I guzzled earlier, but what if I do become dehydrated? Someone tell Alanis Morisette that that is irony. Just as I'm contemplating shelter structures, I hear my name drifting in the breeze.

"Ember!"

"Colton!" I call back, thundering toward his voice like the dramatic Disney princess I am.

"Ember!" His voice grows, and I pause, frantically trying to pinpoint its origin. The sounds of heavy footfalls and branches snapping draw my eyes to the world's most deliciously welcome view. Within seconds, I find myself once again engulfed in arms that have definitely formed my favorite place.

Ethan breathes heavily as he emerges from the same direction as Colton (the direction I should have gone), with their parents not far behind.

"Oh, thank God! You found her." Jeanie affectionately rubs my arm, sits on a nearby rock, and sighs.

"You had us worried there, kid," Rob says, laughing as he places his hands on his hips. Seeing the relief etched on everyone's faces nearly brings me to tears—it's touching to realize they care enough to worry. It's a warm, new feeling, and I want to bask in its fuzzy goodness.

Colton inches back, cupping my face. His eyes bounce between mine, and I watch as worry is slowly replaced with a touch of humor. "I told you not to go too far."

"I'm never drinking water again."

The last dregs of strain drift away with his deep chuckle. "Let's try some navigational skills first." He kisses my temple and whispers, "You okay?" into my hair.

I give him an extra tight squeeze. "Yeah. I was about to set up rabbit snares, but you guys saved me the effort." I won't admit that I'm infinitely more relieved than that.

"Maybe I should add an Airtag to your shoes next time, in addition to the navigation lesson."

"I was born with a directional deficit. I should've warned you. It's in contrast to my snooping skills, so at least I'll always know what your neighbors are up to."

"That's an invaluable skill," he teases in response. He hands me a sandwich and bottle of (evil) water, at which I scowl but reluctantly accept.

I nibble at my food on the walk back to Jeanie and Robert's

house, recounting my twenty-year forest escapade like the dramatic reenactment of a pioneer woman.

We arrive at the Kings' back gate, and I have to stop myself from flopping down on the manicured grass and hugging it.

I may need to ease into this whole outdoorsy revelation I just had.

# CHAPTER FORTY-TWO

## EMBER

I'm drained and feeling the effects of an emotional morning. I'm a boneless chicken, ready to be marinated. Except my marinade is a bubble bath and an episode *of The Office.* I need space to decompress safely.

Colton plonks me down on the living room sofa and tells Ethan not to be weird.

"I'm gonna help my mom with lunch. Send Ethan if you need anything," he says with a wink and a squeeze of my shoulder.

I give him a lazy thumbs up and curl my legs on the couch.

Ethan turns the TV on to re-runs of Seinfeld, and we chat intermittently about his house flipping while I gather the courage to ask what I really want to ask. I clear my throat, and Ethan looks at me expectantly. "So, um..." This is going to come out so weird. "You're Colton's brother. And you know him better than anyone, I assume. What...What is *wrong* with him?"

A burst of laughter erupts, and I shush him, looking over my shoulder to ensure Colton doesn't walk in.

"Oh, man." He has tears in his eyes, like I'm freaking Will Ferrel and just performed the world's funniest bit.

"Okay, I don't mean *wrong*-wrong, like there's something really wrong with him. He just seems too good to be true. Is there anything he can't do? Because so far he's a storybook hero, and that scares me, because I keep waiting for the other shoe to fall, you know?"

He sobers and wipes his eyes, folding his arms when he leans back with one leg propped on the other. He frowns in thought, then raises his eyebrows in delight. He's so excited to share a fault of his brother that you'd think he's one correct answer from winning a million dollars on a game show.

"He can't cook. Or sing. It's kinda like singing...but not. He also squeezes the toothpaste from the middle, like a psychopath."

This is good. He can't sing.

Things have been going so well between us that I was starting to worry I was entering another relationship with blinders on.

Listen, I know it's weird to want to find a fault in someone. But this insignificant imperfection, this nugget of information, settles something in me. It smooths out my reservations about cracking open the door of one of the many gates around the fortress I've locked my heart within. Some people defend their choice to eat gas-station food. I'll defend my self-protection methods, thank you very much.

I rest my head on the couch, satisfied with Ethan's answer. "You were very quick to offer up Colton's faults," I reply with a laugh.

He looks at me with sincerity, which has me paying attention to whatever he's about to say. "If it means you feel more secure with my brother, I'll write a whole list for you. He really likes you. And I want him to be happy."

The idea that a family member would wish for another's happiness feels foreign, like trying to make sense of a jumbled mess of cutout magazine words that were haphazardly thrown together. The concept is so bizarre to me, yet I want more of it.

There's a purity in Ethan's wishes for his brother that makes me envious since I've never had the experience of knowing that someone truly wants what brings me joy, instead of just enforcing what they believe is best for me.

I want to bottle this feeling and keep it with me to twist the cap under my parents' noses to show them *this*. This is what family feels like.

We spend the rest of the afternoon eating hotdogs, and I listen to Colton's family debate the best garnishes and the correct order for applying toppings. They banter and tease one another until my cheeks ache from smiling.

Family.

That's the thing I want.

# CHAPTER FORTY-THREE

"Sorry to deprive you of my presence, but I've got a house that needs work." Ethan salutes us, kissing Jeanie on the cheek before she walks him out. Rob pats his tummy, telling us he and Jeanie will be in their room watching sports, but we can hang around if we want.

"Did you bring your swimsuit?" Colton turns to me after Rob leaves.

"Yeah, it's in my bag."

"I know you can't swim because of your cast, but there's a hot tub out back. Do you feel up to chilling in there? You can rest your cast on the side."

"You'll be able to hold yourself back from splashing me?"

"Normally, no. But I will. Only because of the cast." There's so much troublemaking behind that smile.

"So kind of you." I laugh. "Hot tub sounds good."

Colton shows me where I can change, then tells me he'll paint arrows on the ground so I don't lose my way.

"Too soon, King." When I make a move to pinch his side, he jumps back with a high-pitched yelp.

He turns, speed walking down the hall as he looks back at me. "I'll draw you a map and leave it outside the door."

The cheek of that one.

There are no eggshells about the getting-lost thing, but internally, I'm sighing with joy because he knows when to make light of things and when to be more gentle. It's the feeling of being known that hits the deepest.

I make it to the hot tub without incident, eternally grateful to Ivy for forcing me to buy a new bathing suit. It's not exactly something you want to get at a thrift store. The white-and-navy-striped one-piece I'm wearing today puts its chlorine-eaten predecessor to shame.

I step onto the deck just as Colton is lifting the hot tub cover. He folds it and leans it against the wall, revealing muscles that look like they belong in an anatomy textbook—holy abdominals! He catches my gaze and flashes a nonchalant smile, seemingly unfazed that he's causing my brain to malfunction like one of those fembots in an Austin Powers movie.

He sets a few chilled water bottles nearby, then climbs in, fiddling with switches and buttons. The noise snaps me out of my ab-induced brain freeze.

I should have covered my cast with a waterproof bag, like I usually do in the shower. But let's be honest, nothing kills the mood during a romantic hot tub session like the crinkle of plastic every time you move. That's definitely not the vibe I'm going for. Instead, I'll rely on Colton's promise not to splash and hope to snuggle up to my boyfriend without any distracting noises.

"Let me know if it's too warm, and I'll turn it down."

I take off my sweater and silently curse. I stared at his abs too long. I didn't use my time wisely, and now I need to climb in when all his attention is on me. A smug little smile sits on his face, even though I'm dying to tell him to look the other way. My arms and legs are second-guessing every move they make. Is it like climbing on a horse? Just throw a leg over?

"This hot tub seems taller than it should."

Colton leans back, arms resting on the sides. He lets out a laugh as he observes my graceful movements. "Need any help there?"

"You're enjoying this."

I finally slide in, moving to sit across from him.

"Very much, yes," he says, looking like the Cheshire Cat.

I watch the water drip from his triceps as he lifts an arm to press a button near the controls. Country music plays softly, and I spring a grin. "Smooth."

"You're welcome."

"I really wanna splash you."

The smirk morphs into a grin that's wide and loose. "But you won't, 'cause I can't splash you back."

I twist my mouth into a smug grin, mirroring his own. That confident look of his won't last long—he's just sealed his fate. Lately, I've discovered a certain thrill in breaking the rules when it comes to this man.

But I have to play this smart. I might manage one, maybe two splashes before he strikes back. He can't get my cast wet, but I'm sure he'll find some kind of loophole.

I casually drape my left arm over the side, keeping it out of the way. He watches my movements intently. When I clench my hand into a fist in the water, his eyebrows shoot up, a silent, "Really?" etched across his face.

My hand opens, forming a small cup for water to gather in. I tilt it towards him and give a squeeze, sending a jet of water splashing right into his face. I try again, but this time he dodges with cat-like reflexes, and my aim misses. In an impressively fluid motion, he's suddenly by my side. The guilty expression on my face as he wraps an arm around my waist is purely theatrical—I'm not feeling guilty at all. In fact, I have him right where I want him: *deliciously close.*

Our breaths mingle as time seems to stretch around us. We're both aware that any sudden movement could get my cast wet.

Colton reaches behind me to grab a water bottle, his arm still wrapped around me, holding me close to his side. Not that I'm complaining.

He uncaps the bottle with his teeth, spitting the lid over the edge and taking a few long gulps.

Crystal blue eyes are locked on me. His Adam's apple bobs, and I wonder if he'll down the whole thing. But he pauses halfway through, poised to initiate more mischief.

He tips the bottle over my head as icy water soaks my hair. The cold contrast with the hot tub's warmth sends a shiver through my body.

I attempt a shriek, but annoyingly, no sound comes out. I'm left sucking in air, with my mouth gaping like a fish. I hunch my shoulders while water runs down my face.

"You did not just do that." I swipe at the droplets, even though it feels futile. A scowl forces its way onto my face, but the amusement in my voice betrays me. I can't stay mad. After all, what woman could remain upset while in the arms of a gentle, muscled man?

Colton tosses the empty bottle to the floor, and I follow its descent, ready to make some wise remark about littering. But when I return my gaze to him, the smoldering look he's giving me is hot enough to cause all of my thoughts of joking to evaporate.

"I'd really like to kiss you, Hayes."

I don't answer him or give myself time to think. Instead, I move my lips an inch forward, obliterating the space between us, and it's the best spur-of-the-moment decision I've ever made. The lingering droplets of water on my face soak into his short beard. Colton's free hand rests against my head, his fingers weaving through my wet hair. And the way his lips seem to just melt into mine so perfectly is warming me up more efficiently than a hot tub ever could.

We spend so long sharing intoxicating kisses that by the time we finally emerge from the water, we're both sporting rosy cheeks and wrinkly skin.

I can't imagine a more perfect ending to a third date.

It's late afternoon when Colton parks outside my apartment. He shuts off the engine but doesn't rush to open my door the way he usually does. Those arresting eyes lock with mine. "Thank you for trusting me with the hard stuff today."

Gooey things stir at those words, the acknowledgment that today was a big step. It was good, and my soul sighs dreamily at the fact that he recognizes that it wasn't easy to reveal those parts of me that still feel tender. But a woman in her mid-twenties shouldn't carry this much baggage from their parents.

He lays his palm face up next to my cast, a silent request for me to put my hand in his. When I do, he pulls down his visor and removes a Sharpie tucked into the sleeve. My heart rate picks up at the feeling of his skin on mine.

I'll never admit to my growing affection for my cast and the little doodles he's been slowly adding to it. Casts are gross; I know this. They're a breeding ground for ickiness, and a big part of me can't wait to be free of it. But I'm also trying to work out a non-creepy, palatable way to immortalize the sentiment Colton has etched there.

I watch him, entranced. He uncaps the marker, leaning closer while he draws a heart around the two smiley faces that I definitely have not spent hours staring at.

My smile swings free. He's so unassumingly sweet and

romantic—this incredibly hard-working, determined man. I don't think my face has ever had to work this hard, because I've never smiled so much. I nibble on my lip, trying to give my aching facial muscles a break. Dropping my gaze to the doodle, those warm fuzzy feelings threaten to elicit another toothy grin.

I launch myself at him. Thankfully I remembered to unbuckle myself, but getting my arms around him and my lips on his involves a few knocks and giggles. Eventually, I'm where I want to be.

Smooshed next to Colton. Melting into a silky kiss.

My fingers thread through his hair, and he pulls me closer, wrapping his arms around me.

I never want to stop kissing this man.

It might be what I was born to do. Could I make this my calling? Kissing Colton King? Because I will unalive the person who tries to stop me.

# CHAPTER FORTY-FOUR

Monday morning finds me scrambling to catch up on work that's piled up since Ember began occupying every corner of my mind. I smile as I recall our day yesterday. During our hike, there was a heart-stopping moment when I nearly dialed 911 after twenty agonizing minutes without any sign of her.

My dad wasn't exaggerating when he said she scared us. After losing my grandad, we've all become a bit jumpy in stressful situations. Ethan encouraged me to push on for another five minutes before we considered making an emergency call. She managed the situation impressively, looking unexpectedly adorable with her wind-swept hair.

My desk is a battlefield of urgent tasks clamoring for attention. I need to review the final drafts for next season's subscription boxes and follow up with suppliers. To add to the chaos, Mrs. Sullivan just informed me that our social media manager has handed in her two weeks' notice; she's expecting her first child and plans to stay at home.

The pressure to ensure the continued success of my company pushes at me, begging me to give it all my attention.

Not to mention everything in Utah that needs at least a small amount of my time if I want it to go anywhere.

This week, I'll pick up the slack.

Five seconds later, I decide I've waited long enough and pull out my phone to text Ember. She's in the building. I'll also see her in an hour. But here I am, a man besotted.

Rag on me. I don't care. After our kiss yesterday, I'm fighting the urge to yell out the "L" word. But I reminded myself it's too soon to feel things like that. I won't do my company any favors if I lose my head over a woman.

In one hour, I'll be seeing her beautiful face. I need to maintain at least a semblance of professionalism for this meeting, despite telling myself earlier that I'd focus solely on work this week. Focus. Thankfully, I'm not in charge of the meeting.

Ember will be leading the session to discuss the details for the family boxes. She's proposed reaching out to the local school for volunteers and beta testers.

*Crap.* Ember is leading the meeting. I'll stare at her forehead so I don't get distracted by her eyes. Yeah, that's a solid plan and a totally normal thing to do.

Just a quick text, then back to the grind. I'm a professional, I swear.

COLTON

Hey, Sunshine. See you in an hour.

Killing this text game.

EMBER

Stop distracting me at work. I'm a professional. *Gif of Jim Carrey's sellotaped face from Yes Man*

> Also FYI, it's widely considered uncouth to end a text with a period. People will think you hate them. You're too nice to insult your texting buddies unknowingly, so you're welcome for this PSA

COLTON

> What? That doesn't make sense.

EMBER

> I don't make the rules *shrugging emoji*

COLTON

> What are your Thanksgiving plans?

EMBER

> You're late to the game, King. Your mom already invited me

Of course she did

> I see that lack of period *clapping emoji*

> Now, get back to work. My boss is a real stick in the mud, and I don't want him catching me flirty texting my boyfriend

The sides of my mouth draw up and I shake my head, forcing myself to be productive. I may have already lost my head to this woman.

A week goes by where I constantly remind myself to keep my brain in the right lane and do my job. It's not just a job. It's my company.

A month ago, I would have bled for this place. But now I finally realize there are other things worth my attention. Okay, one thing, and that thing is Ember.

Being around her is like tasting food with salt for the first time. The passion I had for The Adventure Project when I started it is nothing compared to how I feel about her. It scares me.

I don't know how to care about both things and give them what they need. Delegating feels like handing my baby over to others, trusting they'll care for it how I would. My heart rate jumps just thinking about it. I've planned to hand more to Ethan and Mallory, but that doesn't feel easy. How will I entrust the whole thing to someone else when I move to Utah?

I don't want to hurt Ember by not giving her all the love and attention she deserves.

Ethan strides into my office and deflates into the chair that faces my desk.

"Everything ready for next week?"

His head falls back with a sigh. "Mostly, yeah. A few last-minute things to hammer out. Then we send everything to them."

"I still don't know how you did it, but getting us on The Morning Show is huge, man."

He waves away my words. "It wasn't too hard. I sold one of my renos to the sister of a producer on the show. I gave her one of our boxes. I guess she loved it." He lifts his head and smiles at me. "It's a good thing I check that email now and again, or I wouldn't have seen hers till it was too late."

The evidence of long nights is clear on Ethan's face, likely from spending less time in the sun. For the past three weeks, he's been indoors rather than his usual work of climbing roofs.

He and Mallory have put in a lot of the work. Samples, videos, and photos that The Morning Show requested. We fly out to New York for the interview the week before Christmas. After that, I can work on delegating more. I just need to make it past that interview. It feels like the culmination of years of hard work. Being recognized so publicly, not to mention the free marketing of being on America's number one morning show.

"I appreciate it, Eth."

All too knowing eyes squint my way. "You know it's already a success, right?" A hand that hangs off the armrest gestures around us. "All this. It's successful. You don't have to prove anything. You took his dream and made it into something. It's okay to enjoy it for a little while. You can let me help more too. My houses are calming down for the season. Let me help."

The chair squeaks when I lean back, scrubbing my face. "I know you can handle more. It's me that struggles with handing it over." I shake my head, staring out the window. "I dunno..." My chest expands but the heaviness still niggles after the deflate. "I know I can't keep going at the pace I have."

"You can't."

"Yeah." We're silent, both knowing this need to cling to the embodiment of my grandpa's memory is something only I can let go of.

Ethan taps his chair and then stands. "I've got a few more things to tie up. I'll see you at Mom and Dad's tomorrow."

Tomorrow. Thanksgiving. Where I get to focus on my family and Ember guilt-free.

It's early afternoon, and I've already sent everybody else home. I jump in my truck, eager to get to Ember. We're hanging out at her place tonight to watch TV with Nicolas. I'm told sometimes she waits to see what catches his fancy and watches whatever show he settles on. I'm still not convinced her cat isn't a shapeshifter who's angry he got stuck in his cat form.

I stop at a grocery store for snacks and dinner ingredients. I've stalled at the dairy section. Why are there so many cheeses?

I frown at a block called Timberdoodle when my phone vibrates in my pocket. The phone gets propped between my ear and shoulder when I answer. I return the cheese that sounds like a dog breed to its friends, and the wine bottle in the basket rolls to the other end, causing the whole thing to hang sadly off balance.

Ethan's voice shouts at me through the phone. "Colt?"

Failing at multitasking. "Yeah, I'm here."

He sighs, and I wonder when we turned into a couple eighty-year-olds. "Colt, I'm sorry. I'm...I'm gonna need you to come back to the office."

"What? Why?" Disappointment pounces heavily on my shoulders.

"The show called. Another segment dropped out, so they want to extend ours. They're asking for a demonstration of one of our adventures, which triples our airtime," he says, followed by a heavy exhale. I can almost see him rubbing his forehead in frustration. "I can handle most of it, but there are decisions I can't make by myself. If I get a head start tonight, I can at least take it easy tomorrow. I'd call Mallory, but she's currently on a plane to New Jersey."

I let the basket handle slide down my arm, catching it in my hand as I stare at the contents. "Of course. Yeah, give me a few minutes to call Ember, and I'll head back."

"I'm sorry, man."

"It's fine. I'll be there soon."

This is why handing my business over to someone else feels like parting with a limb. Making my grandad proud, even from his grave, has sewn me and this business together. I've lived and breathed it for so long. Its success is my success. Who am I if I hand it over and it tanks?

I hang up the phone and begin returning the ingredients to their shelves. The clink of the empty basket taunts me as I place it back with the others nestled at the store entrance. As I pull my truck door shut, I hit call on Ember's number.

"Hey."

"Sunshine. You okay?"

"Yeah, I just have a stomach ache. I think tonight might just be me sleeping this off on the couch."

"Sleeping what off?"

I hear shifting, followed by a groan. "I made a lunch decision I think might come back to haunt me."

"What did you do?"

"The shame is too much."

"Em."

"Okay, but in my defense, my stomach has been coddled most of its life, so no judgment."

"Never," I promise. I'm in her corner and she'll never get judgment from me.

"I learned the hard way that not all hot dogs are created equal. The one I got from the food truck by the mall seems to have it out for me. Looks like I'll be spending my evening curled up on the couch."

"Em, I'm sorry you're feeling rough. I just got a call, and I need to head back to the office for a bit—Ethan's got something urgent that popped up. Hopefully, it won't take long. You okay to be on your own for a while?"

I know I can't be everywhere at once. But not being with her shreds my insides. If I can help Ethan get a head start, I can focus entirely on Ember tomorrow. My palm massages the tension building in my neck.

"Don't stress. Seriously. I'm probably just gonna pass out on the couch. I'll call Opal and Gail if I need anything. Take your time and help Ethan."

The pull to be in two places at once has never felt so strong. The company I grew from the ground up is stomping its feet, demanding a piece of me while the sweetest woman I've ever met blinks her giant doe eyes at me.

"Okay, but call if you need me."

"I'll see you later," she yawns.

I will the time to fly by so I can get to my girl, make her some tea, and hug her.

It's midnight when Ethan and I finally decide that we've done enough to give The Morning Show a rough outline of the changes they requested. Mumbled good nights are swapped, and we climb into our respective trucks. Ethan drives off, and I pull out my phone, checking if Ember replied to my last message. The bitter taste of guilt sours my stomach at the realization that I couldn't make it to her before she fell asleep. I smile, reading the last text she sent around ten pm.

Hot dog not friend. Going sleep *peace sign emoji* *devil emoji*

I text her again, telling her I'll call in the morning. It's late, but I reply to my mom about what time we'll be at their place for Thanksgiving. The smile on my face cannot be stopped as I drive home with thoughts of the future swimming in my head. I just need to manage the juggle of things pulling at me over the next few weeks.

# CHAPTER FORTY-FIVE

## COLTON

I've texted Ember five times. That's probably the limit before I cross over into the creeper category—a place I find myself too often, now that I think about it. But I'm freaking out. She wasn't feeling well, and now I'm wondering if her last text yesterday wasn't as funny as I originally thought. I assumed she was just tired, but what if she was seriously out of it and delirious?

My mind begins trailing a hundred different scenarios, including scenes of her accidentally mixing the wrong medication or forgetting to lock her door.

Predators. Murderers. My thoughts have gone to a dark place.

Do you even take medication for an upset stomach?

My dad's a doctor, not to mention, I'm an adult. I should know this.

It's 9:00 a.m., and I'm white-knuckling the steering wheel while I drive way too fast for a cozy Thanksgiving morning. I'm in uncharted territory. To prove it, I scowl at the leaves hitting my windshield.

I always thought I was good under pressure, but now, I'm falling apart. Ten minutes ago I even growled at a bird. I'm not sure who I'm becoming, but the thought of Ember not being okay feels like accidentally pulling a loose thread on your favorite sweater—the whole thing starts unraveling, and there's nothing you can do to stop it.

I park haphazardly and run toward Ember's unit. Not even the obscene amount of flowers in the courtyard diminishes my sense of panic.

I knock and wait a full sixty seconds in agonizing silence. All my murderer worries are loud in my ears, but I wait because I'm holding onto the sliver of hope that I'm a helicopter boyfriend with an overactive imagination.

A second later, her faint voice pierces my heart. It's groggy and slurred, but at least it means she's alive. "Gail?"

I turn the knob, ironically grateful that the door is unlocked, and my chest thunders as I step inside, discovering the woman curled up on the couch. I rush forward, dropping to my knees.

Her face is too pale. She's struggling to open her eyes as I palm her forehead. It's too warm. My skyrocketing heart rate has me doubting everything.

"Em, Sunshine. Look at me."

But she doesn't. She only mumbles incoherently, whispering something that sounds like "Nicolas drinks tea."

*Crap.* She's dehydrated.

I put my fingers on her wrist, feeling her pulse. Too fast.

She groans and leans forward. That's when I notice the bucket next to me. I grab it and hold it for her as she dry heaves.

My heart breaks when she moans and attempts to wipe her mouth, but her movements are pathetically sloth-like.

I rub her back and pull out my phone, shakily tapping "call" and switching to the speakerphone.

"Colt, you and Ember on your way? Mom was just about to text you."

"Dad. I'm freaking out." My voice is rough and jittery as I continue, "Ember's sick. I think she's dehydrated. Could you come check on her? Please?" The desperation in my voice sounds foreign to my ears.

He asks me questions that I dazedly answer. Somehow, despite my brain freaking out at how white her normally peachy skin looks and how weak she seems, I'm able to convey to him that Ember has food poisoning. He takes down her address, and I hear him getting in his truck.

He continues his assessment as he drives over, getting me to check her heart rate and responsiveness. I don't know how reliable my answers are. My heartbeat feels like it's hammering too loudly to count hers.

I should be better in this kind of situation. Ethan and I have seen our fair share of accidents and injuries growing up. My mom fell off a kitchen ladder two years ago and got a minor concussion. I got the call from my dad and rushed to meet him and Ethan at the ER. In those moments, I was worried. But I managed to maintain a sense of calm throughout the ordeal. However, none of those events have prepared me for what I'm feeling right now.

The air is thick with panic, and I'm at the center of it. My dad promises he'll be here in eight minutes before hanging up. Meanwhile, Ember dry heaves a couple more times.

Time seems to drag, aging me by years, but finally, my dad, Opal, and Gail all arrive at the door at the same moment.

I rub her back, holding her hair away from her face.

Opal shuffles near, cooing sympathetically and rubbing a veiny hand up and down Ember's shoulder.

"Poor thing."

Gail mentions grabbing some broth before she hurries out.

She's back in under two minutes, breathless and clutching a jar filled with a murky, brown substance.

"This'll fix our girl up. Give it to her soon as she can keep something down." She bustles around, placing things in the fridge while my dad measures Ember's pulse.

"She's barely opened her eyes since I got here."

A frown pushes Opal's glasses down her face. "Stubborn girl. She texted earlier. Didn't say a word about feeling ill. Just asked if we had any coconut water. Like we'd have something so disgusting in our kitchen. Why can't water be water and milk be milk? Do we have to milk every damn nut under the sun?"

"Opal!" Gail shouts sternly, which seems to help Opal refocus.

"Right, sorry. Anywho, we were at the nursery and only just got back. If we'd known, we would've tended to her sooner."

She glances at me, and her brows crease with worry. "Oh, sweetie. Sit next to your girl while this handsome doctor does his thing. I'll fix you some tea." She pats me on the arm, her face full of kindness, but I'm too wound up for it to calm me.

I'm on the edge, and fear is poking at my back. I want to yell at everyone for acting like all she has is a paper cut. She's too pale, too lethargic. I want to hear her snarky responses, see her sunshiny smile. It's tearing me up seeing her like this.

In the three minutes they've been here, Gail has managed to tidy the room, putting things away and wiping down surfaces. Opal putters around, watering plants and talking to flowers while the kettle whistles obnoxiously in the background.

When she sets a cup of steaming tea in front of me, Gail hooks her arm around Opal's and tilts her head toward the door. "Now, come on, Opal, the lovely doctor has a ring on his finger and a patient to help. Let's leave 'em be and give them some space to breathe."

Opal rolls her eyes as she's reluctantly dragged toward the door. "Colton, dear, you know where to find us if you need anything. I'm sure Ember will be fine in no time. Nothing a little brandy won't fix." With a wink, she pulls the door closed behind them.

I turn to my dad. My mouth hangs open, but I have no words for the whirlwind that just departed.

He shakes his head, eyes softening sympathetically with a smile. I try to return one, but my anxiety still overwhelms me. "Do we need to get her to a hospital? Maybe she needs an IV. What can I do?"

His smile is still there, his expression too at ease. "Firstly, son, you needa calm down. She needs your head in the right place. We'll give it another two hours before making the call about the hospital. Pour some of that apple juice in a cup and bring a spoon. Give her little sips every five minutes. If she can keep that down for an hour, we should be in the clear. She's dehydrated, but her pulse is good. I think she's more exhausted than anything."

A minute later, I'm kneeling beside Ember, tilting her head to coax some apple juice into her mouth. She tries to take the spoon and do it herself but begrudgingly relinquishes when more liquid ends up on her clothes than anywhere else. She sighs sleepily when I sit beside her and rest her head on my lap.

Another thirty minutes passes with my dad occasionally checking her pulse and me getting most of the apple juice into her mouth. My nerves gradually settle when we reach the one-hour mark and she hasn't thrown up.

My dad tries talking to me but gives up after my fifth grunted reply. All I can do is sit here, threading my fingers through her hair, staring at her beautiful face. How did I come to care for someone so deeply in such a short time? It snuck up on me, like an enchanted vine tangling its way around me. And there's no desire to untangle myself, even just a little bit. She's a gorgeous, funny, slightly prickly tendril that's taken possession of my heart, and I'm ecstatic to proclaim that it now belongs to her. There's a burning compulsion to figure out all her dreams and spend the rest of my life making them come true.

My finger traces the contours of her chin, and my dad's giant grin has me looking up.

"I'm happy for you, Colt."

Emotions bubble up, the past hour making me feel raw and exposed. My dad has supported me in every stage of my life, and I'm so grateful he can be here now.

"Thanks, Dad." I clear the lump in my throat. "Thanks for being here. I don't know what I would have done."

Ember stirs, and my dad stands up, placing his hand on my shoulder. "She's gonna be okay, son. Remember, I'm just a phone call away if anything changes. I'll let your mom know you'll be here today, and we'll swing by later with some food."

He gives me instructions on what to do and what to look out for before we say goodbye, and I hear the click of the door closing. I lean further into the couch, pulling Ember closer.

Today didn't go the way we'd planned. I'm not with my family, celebrating Thanksgiving like we usually do. But looking down at Ember, being able to care for her—I realize there's nowhere I'd rather be.

# CHAPTER FORTY-SIX

## EMBER

I wake up encased in strong arms, a welcome sanctuary from the chaotic Black Friday crowd rampaging through my head.

Still, this beats waking up in a hospital bed, dazed on pain meds. I ten-out-of-ten recommend finding a strong set of biceps to surround yourself with and a manly scent to inhale when you hear death banging at your door. I don't even mind that my bones feel like they've been liquified while I'm snuggling up to this deliciously solid chest. I should suggest this to the hospital; it's a revolutionary new form of therapy. I'm not even a little ashamed when I burrow my nose and inhale another hit of my favorite brand of pain management.

"Hey, Sunshine."

And that voice. I have no idea how I ended up in this delightful scenario. I could do without feeling like I've emerged from a sweat lodge, but I'm here for the rest of it. Reality can float on back at a leisurely pace, thank you.

I don't want to open my eyes. I'm not ready for the pieces of the last day to reassemble themselves.

My senses continue to return, and I can't ignore the fact

that I feel...how can I put this delicately...not fresh. Sticky, like I have two-day-old sweat percolating my clothes and pores. I bolt up—and when I say bolt, I mean move with the speed of a hungover sloth, because that's my energy vibe at the moment.

Colton looks at me with that sexy creased brow. "Easy. What do you need? Do you need to throw up again?"

My eyes bug out.

*Oh, no, no, no, no, no.*

"*Again?*"

He reaches for the bucket I became all too well acquainted with yesterday.

"I'm fine." My hand finds his arm. I look around, taking in the tidy room. "What happened?"

Colton sits up, blinking sleep away. "What do you remember?"

I pinch an eye closed. Thinking hurts. I lie back down on his chest, and he covers me with a blanket. "Not much. I remember talking to you on the phone, and then I started throwing up." My mouth turns in a grimace. "A lot." Understatement. "At some point, I think I texted Gail and Opal. Am I imagining things, or was your dad here?"

"You were pretty out of it by the time I got here." He laughs, but there's no humor in it. The poor man looks haggard. "I kinda freaked out, then called my dad, who came over to check on you." Soothing strokes brush up and down my arm, threatening to lull me to sleep again.

He's here. I'm sick and he's here. Something about that fact rocks me. I lift my head to face him, noticing the shadows under his eyes. "What time is it?"

"Almost five a.m."

I flinch.

"It's Friday," he clarifies.

"I missed *Thanksgiving*? How'd I lose a whole day?"

"I think I lost five years." He breathes out.

Colton fills me in on the rest of what transpired, and I'm now ready to book a flight to Mexico and disappear forever. I cannot fathom the level of grossness that he witnessed.

How is he still here? Never in my life have I had someone show this much care when I've been sick. My parents treated any ailment or illness as an inconvenience and a cry for attention, leaving the housekeepers or drivers to begrudgingly attend to me. I once had a severe ear infection when I was sixteen and had to call a friend's mom to take me to urgent care. My parents were out of town and couldn't be bothered. They told me to simply lie down and rest with a window open.

Colton missed Thanksgiving with his family to be with me. I recalibrate our relationship status while his sacrifice sinks in. He's found the secret lever and dislodged the massive stone blocks that have formed a fortress around my heart, and now the walls are tumbling down. I can no longer deny that this man has crept into the crevices of my heart while I wasn't looking, successfully evading all the booby traps and dragons along the way.

My loud sniff has Colton's eyes popping open. He must have fallen asleep while I was busy wrapping my mind around all this.

Before he can ask if I'm okay, I wave away his growing concern, which he's made apparent by the way his eyebrows squish together.

"I'm okay. Promise. These are happy tears. I just...I'm not used to someone doing something like this for me. Thank you."

He pulls me in tightly. "You never have to thank me for caring about you, Em."

Fresh tears spill over. I have to keep pinching myself because I'm still not entirely sure this is real. How is it that this amazing man not only exists, but has stayed single for so long?

"We need to get some food in you. My mom dropped off chicken soup. That should be easy enough on your stomach."

"Your mom was here?" More tears well up.

"Yeah, she and my dad came over with Ethan to bring Thanksgiving dinner for me and the soup for when you woke up."

"I'll text her in a bit to say thank you." I sniffle.

Colton kisses me on the forehead, then stands and does a few stretches. "Your phone buzzed a few times last night, but I didn't check it. I did have to plug it in to charge. I'll bring it to you before I heat some of that soup."

"I can heat the soup."

"I'm just gonna pretend you didn't offer to do that." He hands over my phone and walks to the kitchen.

"I don't feel too bad anymore. I'm well enough to press a few buttons on a microwave."

"But you don't have to because you have me."

He winks and busies himself with reheating the food. I'm mesmerized as I watch him move around my kitchen. It feels nice to see him here.

My phone vibrates in my hand, and I notice the stack of unread texts.

There are two missed calls and three texts from my mother, and another from a number I don't recognize.

I open the messages from my mom first.

MOM:

Emberleigh, this is your mother. Your father and I are concerned about your well-being and must insist you return home.

Emberleigh, please return my calls.

Beau is worried about you, Emberleigh. Just speak with him so that you can sort this out.

It amazes me that my parents are still holding onto the archaic belief that I'm to blindly obey their every command, even as an adult. God forbid I have my own plans for my life. It sounds like they're gearing up for another intervention.

They had reacted this way once before when I painted my nails too dark. It was my one act of rebellion at fifteen. I had chosen my own outfit for a charity function, but my mother declared that my dark navy dress and matching nails made me look like an "emo deadbeat on the brink of self-destruction." She promptly reminded me that proper southern ladies wear pastels, and my black nails were practically an alliance with the devil. I rolled my eyes internally but complied, knowing it was easier than fighting a losing battle.

I was young and didn't dare to rock the boat. But now I understand that freedom might just be worth the risk of capsizing.

And boldness can become addicting. When the fruit is confidence and liberty, it'll make you hungry for more. Moving to a new town was my first taste. The decision to go off on my own served to disturb the balance, but as many parents do, mine ignored what they thought was simply an oppositional-behavior phase and assumed I'd eventually outgrow my need for independence. As scary as it feels, sooner or later I'll have to commit and go all the way, overturning my family's whole power dynamic. My parents need to know they can't keep treating me like they do, but I still dread initiating that level of conflict.

I open the last text.

UNKNOWN NUMBER:

Ember, we can help each other. Meet with me and let me explain. B

I blocked his last text, which he must have figured out, as this one is from a new number.

I manage to evade the imminent bubble of anxiety when I switch off my phone. I'm not ready to deal with Beau at all, and certainly not in my current condition.

Colton brings me a steaming bowl of soup but hesitates before handing it to me. "You're pale again."

A Beau-related confession almost slips out. My defenses are sluggish, weakened by sickness.

But this is my battle, and I won't be dragging him into it. I I wave my hand, assuring him I'm fine and hoping he won't pry any further.

The ongoing drama with my parents and Beau isn't something I'm ready to unload on him. I'm a mess right now—visibly and emotionally. Between my extensive baggage and the recent chaotic events involving far too many bodily fluids, I'm hardly in a state to be promoting myself as a great catch in a budding relationship.

The reality is, I come with a lot. My past relationships have been highlighted in a more sour light after being welcomed so lovingly into Colton's family.

Is it wrong that I'm praying Beau either gets bored or eaten by a shark so I can move forward?

I'll tell Colton the whole truth about Beau, eventually. But I want to ensure I don't scare him away before there's an actual chance at having an eventually.

The morning flies by after we finish eating. Colton looks on as I wrestle with sealing a bag over my cast so I can take a shower.

"You think this is funny? I've gotten better at it. The first time I went through an entire roll of tape."

He's leaning against my tiny kitchen island, arms folded, humor in his baby blues.

"Need any help?"

"Nope." I smile triumphantly once I'm finished. Then I pull a rogue piece of tape from my shirt and stick it on Colton's nose. "That's a good look for you."

"Thank you," he grins, watching me walk slowly to my room. This man is dangerous to my currently weakened state.

The first thing I do is brush my teeth. After showering and washing my hair, I feel completely rejuvenated—until the act of getting dressed nearly depletes my energy. Unfortunately, I still need to dry my hair to avoid catching a chill from the dampness.

Standing feels like too much of an effort, so I sit on the toilet lid and lean forward to hold the dryer over my head. Through the curtain of my hair, I notice two manly feet appear in the open doorway of the bathroom.

"Need any help?"

"You keep asking me that," I shout over the noise of the hair dryer. There's a flash of light in front of me, and then I spot the Polaroid camera on the bathroom counter.

"And you keep resisting it." I can hear the frown in his voice. What's the bet I'll find those muscly arms folded when I look up?

Judging by the way my heart is thumping loudly with the effort it's taking for me to hold the dryer, it's probably a good time to take a break. As soon as I straighten, blood rushes to my head, and I curse the wave of dizziness that hits me. Perfect timing.

"I can do it," I say with pinched eyes and a strained breath, willing away the black dots in my line of sight.

Hands gently push my shoulders down until I lower my head. "Breathe, Em."

I slowly sit up when my hearing and vision both clear

again. "I'll just finish the rest without leaning down this time. I'm almost done."

He's crouched in front of me, looking so eager to be of use, and I really want to accept the offer to borrow some of his energy.

"You don't need to do everything yourself."

It's so tempting, this gift, offered so freely, yet it feels like I'm asking too much of myself by attempting to hand over the independence I've worked so hard to gain. I want to reach out and accept help, but tethers from old habits continue to hold me back.

Colton places a hand on my knee, and a new wave of exhaustion drains the last dregs of my energy.

"Okay," I say, relinquishing the hair dryer and my stubborn streak. I may be hardheaded, but I have enough sense to realize I'm risking another close-up with the floor if I keep insisting on doing this myself.

My arms are propped on the counter as Colton runs his fingers through my hair, drying it completely. I'm on the verge of dozing off when a glimpse of myself in the mirror sends me into a fit of laughter. "Electrified hedgehog" is the first thing that comes to mind.

"You should keep your day job."

"You look beautiful," he says. Such a guy thing, having no clue how to wield a blow dryer and thinking nothing of my current appearance.

"I look like I have a perm that got wet." I can't care enough to do anything about it, though. I'm running on emergency reserves at this point.

I stumble back to the couch, while Colton shadows me like a robot with its arms permanently stuck out.

The feeling of his lips brushing over my forehead is the last thing I remember before falling asleep.

# CHAPTER FORTY-SEVEN

EMBER

By the time I wake up, light is dancing across the room, bathing it in the glow of early afternoon. Beside me lies a form decidedly less masculine. I blink lazily, gradually emerging from my nap.

"Ivy?"

"Afternoon. Nice hair," She lowers her phone, smiles at me, and then casually places her palm on my forehead. Leaning back, she gives a satisfied nod.

"What are you doing here?" A yawn escapes while I scan the room.

"I showed up to pick you up for our Black Friday thrifting trip and was met by your worn-out boyfriend. He briefed me on your crazy hot-dog escapade before I sent him off to shower,"

"Oh."

Her face splits with a giant grin. "That man is smitten, Em. He only agreed to leave 'cause he got a call from Ethan about some mini emergency at work." She shrugs. "I had to promise to text him as soon as you woke up."

My phone vibrates on the table next to me as if on cue. I reach over and open the text.

COLTON:

Hey, Sunshine. How you feeling? Sorry I had to leave. Ethan needed help with The Morning Show prep. I'm still at the office, but I'll call you soon

"Look at your face! You're just as gone as he is."

Ivy shakes her head, a touch of sadness in her expression as she begins examining her hands.

"Ivy."

She looks up at me with raised eyebrows and a forced smile. "Can I get you some tea? How's your stomach?"

"Don't deflect. What was that look about?"

"Nothing," she sighs, smiling at me. "I'm really excited for you, Em. You deserve to be happy. And I can tell that Colton makes you happy."

"You know he won't replace you, right? You're still my person."

For the first time, I see how my relationship with Colton could seem threatening to Ivy. When I was with Beau, she and I hardly saw each other. I hid so much from her for so long, and it wasn't great for our friendship.

"Colton isn't Beau. I won't lose myself again."

She squeezes my hand, her head falling back on the couch. "I know. But you can't blame me for worrying."

"I know. And I love you for it. This kind of messes up our deal with the blind-date blog, though, huh?"

"I'm guessing Colton isn't okay with you dating other men, even if it's for a good cause?"

"You'd be correct." I laugh thinking of how he reacted to

my last blind date, and we weren't even together then. "Speaking of, how was your hiking date?"

She does a slow blink while her jaw juts out. "Oh my gosh. How have we not discussed this?" Her fists bounce on my knee. "Em. This dude," she begins with a head shake. Then she covers her mouth and blurts out from behind her hand, "He brought a pet."

"So?"

"His pet chameleon."

"Yikes. Okay."

"Then, we spent our hike walking around and looking for flies for said chameleon. I can't even make this stuff up. I literally spent a date catching flies!"

We fall back against the sofa in a fit of giggles. How we find the world's strangest characters is beyond me.

"It's fine. Maybe I'll go on a few more dates, but I'm also researching other ideas to make a quick buck."

"That sounds frightening."

She pops up from the couch and skips to the kitchen. "We won't need to do anything crazy. It'll be fine. By the way, I've been told you may only leave your current position to go to the bathroom. Otherwise, you are confined to your throne on the couch. I was also instructed to feed you and keep you hydrated. You're basically a plant."

"That's not gonna happen. A walk will be good. I don't want my muscles to shrivel up."

"Deal with it. You're staying on that couch."

I know she has to meet her brother later, so I just smile, telling myself I'll visit Opal and Gail after she's gone.

Nicolas jumps into my lap, finally done giving me the cold shoulder. He's been salty after being denied access to the remote for over twenty-four hours.

"Hey, Mr. Cage. What you wanna watch?" I give him a rub behind the ears, which he hates, but it's good for him to be reminded that he's a cat.

Then I flip through channels with Nicolas's tail flicking impatiently in my face. I pick a romantic comedy, finding the genre less repulsive than I had a few months ago.

# CHAPTER FORTY-EIGHT

## EMBER

"Oh, Ember, you look terrible! You sure you're fine to be working?" Lemon's fake concern pierces the silence I've been enjoying in the break room.

I don't give in. Again, she underestimates the toughness of my skin. Her words do nothing to me—a shopping cart with a bum wheel bothers me more than she does. I'm the poster child for "I am rubber; you are glue."

"You look lovely, too, Lemon." I blow into my coffee mug, watching the ripples fade.

I catch the curl of her top lip out of the corner of my eye. "You know, I didn't realize we were from the same town. Imagine my surprise when I went home a few weeks ago, only to discover our parents are old friends."

She has an angle here. But I refuse to sign up for whatever she thinks this information will do to me.

"Huh," I reply because I don't know what else to say to that. My parents will call the mailman an old friend if it means they can get something out of the connection. I abandon her in the breakroom, giving up on my plan to enjoy my coffee in peace.

I steal a glance into Colton's office, where he's sitting with Ethan and Mallory, deep into the final details for The Morning Show.

The man fills a room unlike anyone else.

An unexpected chord of sadness hits me at the thought of how much I'll miss him while he's in New York. Then the absurdity of that thought whacks me on the head. We haven't even known each other very long, and he'll only be gone for three days.

Three days in which I won't feel the bristle of his beard in the crook of my neck. Three days in which I won't have to fight a blush as his blue eyes whisper to my soul. And three days in which I won't get to see the smile that unravels me so easily.

I blow out a breath, resolving to figure out how to occupy myself for those three days. I should probably use the time he's away to sort out this Beau business, once and for all.

My phone rings as I sit, an involuntary grin springing loose when I see Ivy's name on the screen.

"Vee, what's up?"

"Keep an open mind, okay?" She says without a greeting.

"Promising way to start a conversation."

"I've found some options for our Hawaii fund. Just hear me out, though."

"You're not setting yourself up well, here."

"Everyone cuts their toenails, right?" she continues, ignoring me.

"I'm legitimately afraid of where this is going."

"It's not weird if you don't think about it too much."

"Tell me the rest, and I bet I'll beg to differ."

She stifles a sigh, her sales-pitch voice coming in strong. "All we have to do is send this dude our toenail clippings. I mean, you'd be throwing them out, anyway, so what's the harm?"

"The harm is that it's gross."

"Party pooper. Okay, fine. This next one is fun. We just try on clothes."

"That's it?" I know there's a catch. I can hear it in the inflection she adds to that last word.

"Well, no. They send you clothes to try on."

"They?"

"Just a couple guys from Latvia."

"Some bros from Latvia want us to try on clothes for them?"

"Okay, fine, they send us their Latvian girlfriends' clothes, we try them on, take a few photos, and send them over. Apparently, Latvian women are huge compared to Americans."

"And they get off on seeing tiny American women in their giant women's clothes?"

"Don't judge someone's kink, Em. It's harmless."

"You keep using that word...but I do not think it means what you think it means."

"Don't *Princess Bride* me when there's nothing dangerous about this plan."

"This is the part where I beg to differ. I'd argue it's harmful to society to encourage someone's tiny American women fetish."

"So, that's a no?"

"It's a hard no."

Ivy makes a fart noise. "You're no fun."

"I love you, Vee. We'll get there, okay? I promise. Preferably without ending up on the creeper wall of some guy's underground bunker."

"The search continues!"

"That's the spirit."

After we hang up, the rest of the afternoon drags. I ignore three more texts from Beau, each one more threatening than the last. I block them all, thinking the dude must have gotten some crazy bulk deal on burner phones.

In the back of my mind, a voice is whisper-shouting at me to confide in Colton about my problem with Beau, but isn't that tiny angel on your shoulder just there to be flicked away and ignored? It'll be fine. Beau will give up eventually.

I keep myself busy by focusing on finalizing the family subscription boxes, using my to-do list as a handy distraction from that nagging little voice in my head.

We're almost ready for the test run. I've had several meetings with the admin and principals of two local schools, getting their input and their permission to try out some of our boxes with their students. A glow of pride warms my chest, and I'm overcome by all the "*I knew I could do it*" feelings when I think of what I've accomplished in the last two months. To an outsider, my small accomplishments may seem trivial, but to the woman I was four months ago, the one with the bruised confidence, these things I've said "yes" to are proof—proof that when fear told me I couldn't, or shouldn't, I chose to fight for a life that was my own.

# CHAPTER FORTY-NINE

## EMBER

"What if a bee flies in while I'm driving?"

"Keep the windows closed." Colton answers patiently.

"What if it's hot and I need fresh air?" I ask, my sweaty palms gripping the steering wheel.

"That's what AC is for."

"You're right. Okay. I can do this..."

A stretch of silence settles over us as I gaze out the front windshield, hunched over the steering wheel as if it's my lifeline. Colton, ever patient, waits quietly, giving me the space to gather my courage.

"You gotta turn the key, Babe. The car won't bite you."

"I know, but why are we using your mom's car? What if I crash it?"

"My truck's too big to learn. She needs a new car anyway, it'll be fine."

"Colton, you can't just buy someone a new car 'cause I crash one."

"Do you wanna buy her a new one?" He laughs.

"Well, no..."

"You're overthinking this. One step at a time. Keep your foot on the break and turn the key."

I stare at the empty parking lot in front of me. *Come on, Hayes. Where's your grit?*

With a heavy sigh tinged with frustration, I mentally brace myself. Turning the key, I proceed to follow Colton's instructions, making a tortoise-paced lap around the lot.

"Look at you! You're driving!" He beams with pride.

"Can I go faster?"

"For the love, *yes!*"

"Hey!" I turn, elbowing him but still keeping my hands glued to the wheel. The silence in the car is broken by my phone vibrating loudly between us.

"Just ignore it."

"You sure?" Colton asks.

"Yup." I reply, recognizing my mom's name on the caller ID. "This is actually kinda fun. We should go somewhere."

"Slow down there, Hamilton. You needa learn to park and pass your learners test before taking on public roads."

"Right. Got a bit carried away there." I let out a deep exhale, feeling the tension melt away from my shoulders. I'm frustrated with myself for putting this off for so long and not fighting for it sooner. I've allowed my parents to dictate my life far more than I should have.

Colton's question snaps me out of my regret. "You wanna do another lap and then practice some reversing?" he asks. Instead of dwelling on the past, I decide to focus on being grateful for the man sitting next to me.

"Yeah." I pull to a stop, stretching my aching hands as I look over at him. "Thanks for doing this with me. I could've waited for Ivy's summer break, but having such a hot Driver's Ed teacher definitely doesn't hurt."

"Is it okay for your teacher to kiss you?"

"I encourage it." I say with a cheesy grin before Colton pulls me in for a kiss that's just as hot as he is.

By the time we get back to my apartment, my phone starts buzzing again, making me slump in annoyance. I lean against the kitchen counter, steeling myself for the call I can no longer ignore. The last thing I need is for her to show up in person.

"Hey, Mom." I answer and Colton steps near to wrap his arms around me in silent support.

"Emberleigh. Finally. I've been trying to contact you all day. Your father and I would like to see you."

My jaw drops in confusion. They don't usually seek me out. Normally, I'm on the receiving end of verbal reprimands for inappropriate behavior or summons to various charity events, but requests for quality time? That's new.

"Wh—uh...why?"

"Is it so unusual for parents to want to see their daughter, Emberleigh?" Always with the full name. "We'd like you to meet us for dinner. Can't we all share a nice meal together?"

Colton rubs a finger at the crease etched between my eyes. I relax my face, which is hard to do when talking to Fretta Hayes.

She must sense my hesitation, because she adds, "We'll stop pressing you about Beau."

This feels like a trap. But the carrot she's dangling seems too good to ignore. If they stop pushing Beau on me, maybe the asshat will stop blowing up my phone.

"If I come to dinner, you'll lay off the other stuff?" My eyes bounce to Colton and then to my feet. This is a weird conversation to overhear.

"Yes. We just want what's best for you." That's the problem. Her "best" and mine are very different.

"Okay."

"Splendid, I'll have my secretary forward you the details,"

she beams, and I can hear it in her voice. I don't remember the last time I saw her smile.

"That was weird," I frown after hanging up. "I'm pretty sure my mother was smiling."

"I can't picture it."

"Right? They wanna have dinner. With me."

Colton seems like he has questions, but discussing my parents or Beau would only cast a shadow over an afternoon that's been bursting with color. I'd much prefer to savor every last minute with the man wrapping his arms around me.

A slow smile grows on my cheeks, and I burrow my nose into his chest before I lift my chin and gaze up at his gorgeous face.

"Wanna watch a movie and snuggle?"

"Those are my two favorite things," he replies with a smirk.

"Liar." My fingers find the one ticklish spot I've discovered on his side, just above his hip bone. He laughs, and I continue my mission. Knees and arms try to form a barrier as he makes a half-hearted attempt to defend himself from my prodding hands. He takes a few steps back, humoring me by allowing me to poke his muscled side before grabbing my right wrist and the elbow of my casted arm. A gentle hold pins them behind me, and goosebumps ripple down my spine when he brings his mouth to my neck.

"With you, anything is my favorite," he whispers.

His raspy voice caresses my skin. I melt toward him, but he surprises me by hoisting me over his shoulder with a sudden movement. I'm not proud of the squeal that comes out of my mouth. Goodness, the man is carrying me like I weigh nothing.

He gently lowers me onto the couch, his lips smacking a kiss on my forehead. I'm becoming addicted to those.

Arms cage me in, and dang it, I could get used to this. He's so close I catch the glint in his eyes as they map every freckle on my face.

"You get that blanket and choose a movie. I'll make the popcorn," he tells me.

There's a slight pout of his lips as he hovers over me, teasing and baiting me to make the first move. I don't know when we started playing this game of who can make the other initiate a kiss first and who can hold out the longest while the other shamelessly flirts within inches of their lips. But I'm happy to be the loser every time. especially if losing means this gorgeous man gives me every ounce of his attention. If all I have to do is close in a little bit of distance to meet his soft mouth, then make me a T-shirt and sign me up. I'll happily give in because I'm not a loser for long.

I lick my lips and he watches intently as I make my move. Tilting my head, I grasp his shirt, pulling him close until our lips meet. The kiss deepens in just a heartbeat. Time blurs—seconds, minutes, hours, it's hard to tell. We're wrapped in a happy bubble. Arms explore, soft noises escape.

Eventually, he breaks the kiss, his chest rising with heavy breaths. "You're gonna be the death of me, woman." And then he's smiling, shaking his head as he struts to the kitchen.

# CHAPTER FIFTY

## EMBER

I wake up cocooned between the couch and something warm. As I attempt to lift my arms, I quickly realize that only one responds—the other has gone numb from lying on it all night. Grasping the back of the sofa with my left arm, which is awkward given the cast encasing it, I struggle into a sitting position. By the time I'm upright, I'm completely exhausted from the effort.

There's a deep grunt as I hoist my body up, making me flinch as I squint to see in the dark room.

*What the heck?*

I rub my eyes, moving my hair out of my face. "Colton?"

"Hmm?" A deep hum resounds.

Okay, I'm ninety-nine percent sure it's him, but my racing heart settles when I confirm Colton is the warm body I nearly impaled with my elbow. I'm beginning to understand why Opal and Gail use them as weapons.

The last thing I remember is drifting off during Kate & Leopold. Colton had never seen it, but he didn't make a peep when I insisted we watch it. Honestly, a man who's happy to watch chick flicks is a keeper in my book.

His eyes remain closed as he draws me closer, gently rubbing my upper arm. "Morning, Sunshine," he murmurs, his smile gradually widening.

I've heard his professional, concerned, and playful tones, but this sleepy, gravelly voice might just be my favorite. It's deep and rumbly, carrying promises of slow kisses and lazy mornings.

I lay my head back down, soaking up the euphoria of this perfectly snuggled state. The last time Colton stayed over, I was sick, but this time, things are different. There was no emergency keeping him here, but he doesn't seem weirded out by the fact that we've woken up tangled on my sofa, so I sigh contentedly, enjoying the moment.

"Tell me about your truck?"

"My truck?"

"Yeah. There must be a story behind it. You can afford a new one. I wanna know why this one is special to you."

He inhales a breath, deep and slow, allowing old memories to take shape. It's as if this history holds weight, and unearthing it requires courage.

I wait. His fingers rake my hair before he clears his throat.

"It was my grandad's. He passed away eight years ago."

Saying I'm sorry seems so trivial. It's such a throwaway response to hearing about a loved one's death. "That must have been hard."

He gives a little squeeze of my arm, and his fingertips burn a trail up and down my back.

"We were close. Up until my late teens, Ethan and I spent every weekend with him, hiking, fishing, building things. He taught us so many life lessons. I think he knew he was getting older and always talked about that one big adventure he still needed to go on. He'd started dreaming about it with us. In my last year of school, I decided to make baseball a career, so I threw all my time and effort into the game. I gave it everything, and when I was twenty-three and stupidly self-centered, my grandad said he was finally ready for his big adventure, that he wanted to take Ethan and me on a two-week hike through the Grand Canyon. I told him it wasn't the right time, and I told myself there'd be another opportunity, one more convenient for me. Before I could pull my head out of my ass, he was gone."

I feel his chest rise with a deep inhale like a small weight has been lifted now that he's verbalized those things, and he's finally free to fill his lungs completely.

"Colton—" I want to tell him so many things. That it's not his fault. That he's incredible, and his grandpa was proud of him, because how could anyone not be proud of the man he is?

"It gutted me that I hadn't made time for him. He said he'd wait for me, but he died without ever going on his big adventure. I know I made mistakes. Anyway, the truck was his. My parents gave it to me when we got rid of some of his stuff."

"He's the reason you started The Adventure Project?"

Another deep inhale. "Yeah."

This sweet man. I lean up, gathering his face between my palms. My trademark awkwardness heightens the moment, with my clumsy cast and the way I'm lying on top of him.

With a soft gaze, my eyes bore into his with all the comforting reassurance I can muster. "You're a good man, Colton. And he'd be proud of you."

He pulls me in tightly, smooshing my body against his. Long, quiet minutes go by as my breaths fan his neck until I'm feeling brave enough to ask for more.

"What about Utah?"

He exhales heavily. Again, the silence grows, but this time

it's loud, carrying none of the gooey content like before. It's scratchy and stifling, clawing at my heart.

I don't want to hear that he's leaving. But I need to know. Seconds tick by before he finally clears his throat and tells me his plans.

It all sounds exciting, starting a shoe manufacturing company with Jaxon Tate. I don't know baseball, but I guess he's a big deal. If it didn't affect my heart so personally, I'd be gushing about how sweet Colton is for wanting to continue his grandpa's legacy in such an impactful way. It really is so beautiful, but I selfishly want him to stay with me, and can already feel my heart buckling with stress fractures.

"Why Salt Lake City?"

"Jaxon's there. He has a wife and kids, so it makes sense. It's a good location, business-wise."

Well, that's that I suppose. Almost as an afterthought, he continues, "You and me, though, we'll work it out, okay?"

I don't know what that means, but I nod anyway. I'm already too far gone for this man, on a train headed one-way toward him. If it ends in heartache, then so be it. There's no going back.

"What time do you fly out today?" I ask after another tight squeeze.

"Seven." He lifts my fingers to his mouth, kissing gently on the tips. He curls my hand around his and kisses my knuckles peeking from my cast. I swear his eyes get even bluer when he stares at me with that look of awe and bewilderment. It's the same look someone gets when standing in a museum in front of artwork they've studied for years. After his vague response about moving, it only confuses me more.

"How do pancakes sound?" he asks.

"You make pancakes?"

He lifts a solid shoulder. "It can't be that hard. Do you have the ingredients?"

There's so much I love about this morning, but I'm already sad that I can't spend the rest of today with him. He told me yesterday that he and Ethan have to finalize some things at the office before they fly out.

"I think so, yeah." I reply, absorbing every bit of the picture before me, his mussed-up hair and a slightly scruffy jaw.

He pats my arm, a plan for our morning already forming in his mind. "You go shower; I'll handle breakfast."

My lips brush his cheek in a quick peck, and we extricate ourselves from our cocoon with an amusing amount of clumsy elbows, old-person huffing, and unrefined grunts.

After showering, I dress comfortably and check my phone. I stifle a groan because Colton will probably come marching in to look for an assailant if he hears me. Two increasingly ugly texts from Beau stare back at me, threatening the first bit of happiness I've allowed myself to feel in ages.

*Stupid jerk.*

I add the new number to the increasing list of blocked contacts and ignore the texts.

My feet silently pad to the kitchen, and I find Colton standing by my stove, his cap on backward. I watch as he lifts my cast iron pan and flips a pancake.

*I am not okay.* The man is trying to kill me. A grin pulls at my lips when he curses at a pancake.

A burnt smell reaches my nose, and I creep forward. I'm up on tippy toes to get a better look. I bite my lips, trying not to give myself away, but the laughter is already bubbling up.

What I see is so delightfully terrible that it fills me with joy. I never thought a pile of crispy pancakes would dust away the last cobwebs that had been stringing my doubts together, but they've done it. The small fact that Colton cannot cook hints at an imperfection, and I love him all the more for it.

If I'd walked into the same scene but with a perfectly cooked breakfast, I would have come stupidly close to swooning, because it doesn't take a lot for Colton to have that effect on me. But knowing that he's terrible at something and not afraid to show it is another swipe of healing balm on my heart.

He's not too good to be true. He's beautifully human. He has faults, just like everyone else. No pretending he's perfect.

He's not Beau.

And he's not my father.

My throat is thick. I swipe a tear off my cheek before making my presence known. Colton's eyes find me, and humor dances in his gaze.

"I could blame it on the pan, but the truth is I suck at cooking. As you can smell." He gestures toward the pile of broken pancakes that look like they've been mauled by a toddler. I roll my lips in, fighting a laugh again.

"I see that." So many mangled pancakes. "Those do look rather sad." I lift one mostly black piece, bringing it to my mouth.

He winces. "You don't have to do that..."

"Oh, but I do." I smile back at him.

It looks like a heavily charred and flattened potato, but I take a tiny nibble. I'm still holding the very suspect pancake as I choke back a cough.

Colton's smile is everything. He shakes his head and unfolds his arms. "Don't move," he grins at me.

Half a minute later, he's back, pointing his Polaroid camera my way, and a flash goes off.

"You do that a lot." I smirk, returning the pancake to its incinerated friends.

He shrugs like it's not a big deal. "Life goes by fast. I wanna remember these moments."

My heart stirs at the beautiful sentiment, and I'm about to gush over him when my phone buzzes loudly in my pocket. I don't even need to check to know it's Beau. Again.

Colton looks curious, but I can't allow him to ask any questions. I don't want to lie to him, and this is my problem.

"Why don't you go shower," I say, poking his chest, "and I'll run across the road and get us something from the bakery."

He curls an arm around my waist and nuzzles my neck. "That's a way better plan." He steps away, walking backward towards my bathroom. "I wouldn't expect you to eat those pancakes without second-guessing my boyfriend status."

What he doesn't know is those pancakes have done the exact opposite.

# CHAPTER FIFTY-ONE

## COLTON

"I'll see you in four days," I murmur, kissing Ember's temple. I linger, unable to pull away with my mouth content to rest against her skin for as long as possible.

Eventually, she's the one to step back, but my lips don't like the current lack of contact.

"I thought it was three days?" she frowns with an adorable crease between her brows.

"I won't be back until late Tuesday night, so I'll only see you on Wednesday." As my thumb brushes against her hip, I find myself questioning this whole idea of expanding the business. Do I really need a job? I'm not afraid to be the sidekick. I'll be Ember's cheerleader and watch her shine. A niggling voice reminds me that it might be a relationship damper if I implode her career by not actually doing a good job with this business that's quickly moving to second place in my life.

*Focus, Colton.*

Once I'm back from New York, I'll have the chance to let go of some things. However, this feature must go well first. It feels as if everything I've been working towards hinges on this one moment. Gaining broader recognition for our company feels like a personal redemption, and there's no bigger stage than The Morning Show. Additionally, there's a deep sense of responsibility that comes with creating opportunities for others to make lifelong memories with their loved ones. It's essential that we do this right.

I remind myself that there's no need to make any rash decisions. I'm just love-drunk and don't want to be more than two feet away from this woman at the moment.

"After a moment, she reluctantly steps back from my embrace, a playful pout on her face tinged with a trace of anxiety. "Fine," she says, "but let's do something fun Wednesday night, if you're not too tired."

I take it back. Forget feet—I'm unhappy with more than a few inches between us. "Wednesday, I'm all yours," I promise, wrapping her in one last hug. "You'll be okay at dinner with your parents?"

She sighs, resting her chin on my chest, and points those tropical green eyes at me. I'm so gone. I need to buy this woman a ring and officially make her mine.

"Yeah. I mean, it won't be fun," she begins. Her fingers fidget, and her eyes study the space next to us. Things are stewing in that beautiful mind of hers. Then she shakes her head like she's pushing the thoughts aside. "Hopefully they behave. They're mostly harmless, especially since I've learned to tune out ninety percent of their criticism. It's nothing new."

She shrugs as if that kind of relationship is normal. There's an ache in my chest from knowing she's had to learn how to control her emotions and deliver that response. Parents should encourage their kids, not break them down.

"What time are you meeting them?" I ask, hating that I can't be with her.

I'm fiercely protective of those I love. There isn't much I

wouldn't do to defend those closest to me. But with Ember, it's already so much more than that. I want to beat my chest and growl at anyone who looks at her the wrong way. Knowing how her parents wield their words against her kills me.

"I'm meeting them at Capelli's at five. Lord knows why they want to eat so early."

The timing sucks. "I'll be on my way to the airport around then, but call me after. Are they still pushing you to meet with Beau?"

"My mother said they'll drop the whole Beau thing in exchange for this dinner. We'll see if that actually happens, though," she says with a smile.

I don't want that jerk anywhere near her. I know she said he's never hurt her, but his behavior seems like that of someone who's becoming increasingly unhinged.

I squeeze her a little tighter, making the moment last as long as possible and prolonging the goodbye.

When I can't put it off any longer, I kiss her deeply, storing up the feel of her lips against mine. I climb into my truck, and Ember blows a kiss as I pull away.

*Get New York out of the way. Then make her mine.*

# CHAPTER FIFTY-TWO

## EMBER

Here's a tip: If you're ever looking to truly challenge your dignity, try cutting a steak with a knife and fork while your arm is in a cast, especially in front of people who have been disappointed in you your entire life.

I'm Edward Scissorhands, struggling with my elbows up in the air like I just don't care while I massacre a beautiful cut of meat. Except, I do care.

Mortification seems to be the axis my body gravitates toward. If I had a say in the matter, I'd choose a more subtle form of degradation. But the universe cares not for my dwindling dignity.

If a situation holds the possibility of humiliation, I will find myself in it. I've become the equivalent of Pin the Tail on the Donkey, where I'm the Donkey and the Tail is a myriad of disastrous experiences ranging from, *"Yikes, that's awkward"* to *"Kill me, now."*

So, to recap, I'd rather not be demonstrating the fine motor skills of a two-year-old while cutting a steak, but here we are.

I wonder if pre-cut steak is an option?

The fact that we're sitting in an elegant restaurant with cloth napkins and servers who shine their shoes only highlights how out of place I am. I glance around the restaurant, at the luxury that seems to mock the façade my parents and I are putting on.

A pianist plays slow-tempo jazz, haloed by soft lighting. Nearby, patrons quietly wield their cutlery, their hushed conversations barely noticeable over the music as they continue to sip on wine that costs more than everything I own. It's a beautiful restaurant, and if it weren't for the knot in my stomach, I'd venture to say I wouldn't mind returning, perhaps with better company. But the impending fallout will probably tarnish my memories of this place forever.

I admittedly downplayed my anxiety over this meeting for Colton. I didn't want him to worry, especially since I knew he'd be away. But I suspect my parents have something up their sleeves. What they promised in return for my appearance was too tempting to ignore, and likely too good to be true.

But I'm not the same submissive daughter who ran away from her problems months ago. I've gained enough self-worth and boldness to set my own boundaries.

My mother daintily picks at a salad, her sharp eyes reprimanding my cavewoman behavior.

My parents have an agenda for this dinner, and because of said undiscovered intentions, my dearest mother is attempting to be civil. By civil, I mean she's holding back from commenting on my choice of clothes or the barbaric nature of my table manners. It's taking everything in her not to subtly inform me I could have done any number of things better.

My dress is fine, but I should avoid it with my skin tone. There are more flattering hairstyles her stylist can help me to find. Her yoga instructor is also available to help with my posture. I've heard every variation over the years.

Although she's momentarily reined in her criticism, no doubt due to some ulterior motive, she still wields her eyes in a manner that conveys her message. I could write a fifty-page essay describing the disdain and disapproval she's able to project with her gaze this evening.

My father cups his fist in front of his mouth, swallowing a bite of food. For a moment, all I see are the eyes I used to stare into while sitting on his lap, thinking the world of him.

He clears his throat, chasing the memory away.

*This is it.*

He's looking at me when his eyes refocus on something in the background.

"Now, Ember, please don't get hysterical," he begins.

Yeah, because nothing terrible ever follows those words. I roll my eyes, but just a fraction. No need to give my mother more ammunition. She's about to boil over with all the chastising she's been bottling up since I sat down. Her tell-tale eyebrow twitch is a giveaway.

My defenses are ready, my walls reinforcing themselves. I prepare myself, awaiting their next move.

"Hello, Ember."

*And there it is.*

I thought I was ready, but I'm completely blindsided.

A shiver begins in the tips of my fingers and crawls up my arms. My mouth hangs open, and there's a slight tremble in my lips.

"How could you invite him here?"

The question is ignored. My father turns to Beau and the tall woman standing beside him whom I'm only just noticing.

"Thank you for joining us. Have a seat." He gestures toward the two extra chairs I didn't question until now, like he's inviting them to participate in a boardroom meeting. But there's also gratitude in his eyes. They're doing him a favor by being here. "Beau. Dr. Pratt," he nods at each of them.

There's a burst of hope when I think this woman and Beau might be together. I don't envy any woman who's been fooled by this man, but if his focus is off of me, I'm not complaining. But my optimism is quickly replaced by alarm bells as soon as I realize my father just called her "doctor."

Here's a tip: A wave of nausea washes over me as every face at the table turns in my direction. I scan their varied expressions—determination, smugness, arrogance. Dr. Pratt, whom I've never met before, offers a half-smile filled with pity, and it irritates me more than anything.

*This is an intervention.*

Just a minute ago, I felt out of place in such a posh restaurant. But now, this has "Jerry Springer vibes" written all over it.

I'm faced with two choices: I can leave now and resign myself to perpetuating this cycle of dysfunctional behavior, or I can bide my time, let them show their cards while I gather all the confidence I've been building for months, and finally set some boundaries. I could throw in a few truth bombs, drop the mic, and then make my exit.

"It's lovely to meet you, Emberleigh," the doctor says, snapping me back to the present. Her dark bob and shiny pearls catch the candlelight flickering from the table.

A waiter appears to take the additional drink orders. Beau orders his usual glass of scotch, then he turns the slightest of sly smiles my way as he tells the server that I'll have a red wine. It's such an ass move, letting me know he's in control here. Like he's done countless times in the past, he's dictating my life.

But before the server can walk away, I do what I should have done the first time he ordered for me without asking. "Actually, I'll have sparkling water instead. Thank you."

The table is blanketed with silence as a half-dozen conversations occur without anyone uttering a word. Eyes squint, eyebrows raise, and heads tilt like we're each playing a separate telepathic game across the table.

"Someone better tell me what's going on," I demand, piercing the silence that's slowly suffocating me.

My mother folds her hands elegantly over the table, glancing at Dr. Pratt and Beau before she speaks. "Ember, we're concerned about you. We love you, but your behavior since you left Magnolia has been..." She pauses to look at my father. "Well, to be honest, dear, it's a little troubling."

"What are you talking about?"

I can feel my mouth flattening into a sour line while a giant neon question mark hovers above my head. I've clued on that I'm the subject of an intervention, but Dr. Pratt's presence is like that annoying missing puzzle piece.

"Ember," she exhales like her patience has thinned. "Running away from one's problems isn't a healthy response to anything. And your behavior at the hospital was erratic and rather concerning. We just want to help you."

"I was on pain meds. The dosage they gave me was too strong."

If my parents had ever taken the time to know me, I wouldn't have to explain this. What child has to defend her medical history to her own mother?

She continues, disregarding everything I've said. "On top of that, you've been acting unbalanced from what we've heard, stirring up relational issues amongst your coworkers and dating your boss? This is all beneath you, Emberleigh. And it doesn't paint a good picture."

"How would you know any of that?"

I narrow my eyes at Beau. He's sitting there calmly, looking suave, like this little game is playing out just the way he planned.

"You had something to do with this, didn't you?" I accuse him.

"Beau has been nothing but supportive and shares our concerns about you, Ember," my father's stern voice declares.

"Your coworkers are worried, too, Emie," Beau adds, his words dripping with false concern.

I hate that he gave me a nickname. I want to rip it out of his mouth. He doesn't get to fake tenderness after everything he's done to destroy my self-esteem, especially now that I know that he's just a cruel narcissist hiding beneath a pleasant facade. I want to wipe away the memories of him calling me that name affectionately from both our minds.

He doesn't deserve to call me by a nickname.

The pianist begins a new piece, the tempo quicker than before. Its haunting melody, punctuated by eerie, low notes, feels strangely out of place in the tranquil setting of an upscale restaurant. Whether it's the unsettling music, the circumstances, or a mix of both, every instinct in my body screams for me to run, to retreat. But I recognize that there's more at stake here. Leaving now would only postpone what's inevitable. This war has dragged on for far too long; it ends today.

My brows pull together. "What coworkers?"

"The Simmons's daughter. Clementine? No, that's not it." She waves her hand casually like we're discussing the latest handbag designs. "Different fruit..." Again, a pause. Her nonchalance while she racks her brain grossly contrasts the fuse inside me that's slowly burning.

"Lemon," she says. "It was Lemon Simmons. She's such a sweetheart. Regardless, Emberleigh, Dr. Pratt is here because we're concerned about your state of mind. She runs a very discreet clinic. It's more like a spa, really. But we all feel it would be best if you accepted her help."

So this is the card they're playing.

The haunting piano soundtrack fades with all the rest of the noise once I realize I'm that girl—the one whose parents tried to declare her insane.

Dr. Pratt raises a milky palm to speak and I almost expect her to pass around a conch or a unity stick.

*Screw it. I'm not sticking around for this.*

Before she can start, I grab my handbag and push away from the table.

"I don't have to put up with this," I declare. "I'm leaving."

I hear my name called in a variety of condescending tones, but I don't turn back.

My limbs are trembling so badly that it takes a couple tries to press the elevator button. But I can't still myself long enough to wait, not when it feels like the ugliness I left at the table is clawing its way behind me. I go for the stairs instead. They're carpeted and well-lit. Whatever gets me out of here the quickest.

I wish I could call Colton. I regret not telling him that Beau found me. If only I had been brave enough to share the whole story, I'd have someone to lean on right now.

I haven't even opened up to Ivy about what's happening with Beau. She'd definitely point out that withholding such significant news isn't wise, reminding me that relying on friends is a strength, not a weakness. Right now, I could really use that extra support, as my own strength is wearing thin. A hug would be ideal, but I'll have to endure a few more days of this agony before I can experience the bliss of Colton's embrace again.

My hands are still trembling as I fumble with my phone to order an Uber, but before I can finish the request, a voice calls out from behind me.

"Ember, wait!"

*You have got to be kidding me.*

# CHAPTER FIFTY-THREE

## COLTON

Mallory knocks as she enters my office, a massive smile on her face. She's been an invaluable part of the team, and I realize for the first time that I'm confident I could hand things over to her. I return her smile and inhale a deep breath, struggling to shift mental gears again.

I rub the spot on my chest that still feels uneasy.

"You with us, Colt?" Ethan asks, snapping me out of my thoughts.

"Yeah, yup. Sorry. Did you ask something?"

He laughs, shaking his head. "Mal asked if you checked the email from The Morning Show liaison. They said to review all the visuals again and give them the final go-ahead to submit it to production."

"Right, yeah. Let's go over that together. Then we can run through the script before we head to the airport."

Ethan and Mallory share a look like they're amused and not entirely sure I'm present.

"I'm fine. I'm here. I'm distracted, but I'll get my head in the game," I reassure them.

Ninety minutes later, we're all tired and ready to relax, but we've still got a late-night flight to catch. I stretch my arms behind my back, trying to release the tension that knots my muscles.

"I think we've done all we can do," I breathe out.

Mallory opens her mouth to say something when footsteps echo down the hall.

"It's Lemon with the sample books she picked up from the printers," Ethan explains after poking his head out the door.

We watch through the glass walls as Lemon trots over. "Hey, y'all. Here are the samples. That was cutting it pretty close," she says with a laugh. "We found a typo in the first batch, so I had to rush order the reprints."

Ethan and Mallory start gathering things on the coffee table, and I bend to pick up a sheet of paper from the floor. When I straighten, I find Lemon perched on the arm of the sofa. She seems to like that spot.

"You know, Colton, I think it's pretty cool that you're okay going out of town while Ember's meeting with her ex."

I frown as I step back, wondering how she knows any of this.

"She's meeting her parents. Not her ex."

"Oh. I talked to my mother this morning, and she mentioned Beau was joining their dinner."

Ethan pauses in his movements, stepping closer to me. "That's not the ex who—"

"Yeah. It is." I clench my jaw so hard my teeth ache. My stomach turns with the thought of him somehow cornering her. If he so much lays a finger on her...Ember's parents don't know how Beau treated her, so they won't think twice about leaving the two of them alone.

Ember can handle her parents, but she shouldn't have to

deal with Beau. It feels like there's another layer to this plan, an uglier motive hidden beneath the surface.

There's steel in my voice when I ask, "Lemon, are you sure about this?"

She shrugs again, but her mask is slipping. Uncertainty grows in her eyes, and she must be reading my panicked expression because a flicker of regret casts over her face.

"My mother mentioned it. I'm sure it's not a big deal."

She finally seems to understand that there's a real threat of danger for Ember after seeing Ethan's reaction, as well, and I can see her genuine concern growing, though it may be too late.

I'm about to fly to New York for three days—this is the break I've been working toward, the big hoorah before I pull back, but how can I lighten my responsibilities at work without the hoorah? I've got to make sure the business is set up before I can rest.

But gradually, my priorities begin to shift, almost like watching a 3D rendering morph right before my eyes.

Ethan's eyes meet mine. "I can do it, Colt. I know this presentation better than any house I've worked on. Let me take this off your plate."

Mallory steps forward. "He's right. We've got this, Colton."

But it's like white noise. My brain swirls with questions. How do I let go of this? How do I uphold the promise I made on my grandad's grave? How can I make amends and honor his memory if I'm not the one making sure the adventures happen?

Meanwhile, the urge to run out and protect Ember is overwhelming my thoughts. It's like a curtain's been opened, revealing the need to be near her over everything else. The realization crushes my nice, neat plans, like a piano falling from the sky.

I've spent years fighting to give others their grand adventures, but I haven't gone on many myself, starting with the ones

I missed with my granddad. But ever since Ember came into my life, she's been the best part of every day. Being with her has been the ultimate adventure. It's time to fight for that—fight for her.

It's a big sacrifice, but it's also an easy one.

"Thank you," I tell them before I turn and immediately begin packing my things. "I'm gonna try to make it to the restaurant."

"We have everything under control. Besides, everyone knows I'm the more handsome King; it only makes sense that I'm the face of the company," Ethan says, trying to lighten the mood, but I still have to swallow the lump in my throat.

Mallory gives my arm a quick squeeze. "Don't worry about New York."

Ethan sticks his hand out to shake mine, but I grab it and pull him in for a hug. "You'll have to call Dad if you need to be bailed out of jail," he says from over my shoulder, finally getting me to smile.

I glance at my watch as I pull away, then grab my phone and slip it into my pocket. I only manage a nod at Lemon on my way out.

The restaurant where Ember is meeting her parents is thirty minutes away. It's a little after five.

*Crap.*

Ethan may have been joking about me ending up in jail, but if driving twenty miles over the speed limit or punching some loser ex of hers who can't take no for an answer means risking a night behind bars, then I'll be happy to do it.

# CHAPTER FIFTY-FOUR

## EMBER

I quicken my pace as I head out into the parking lot, searching for a well-lit spot to wait. It's dark, and a twinge of unease stirs in my stomach. They say you should heed those little warnings when something feels off, and I definitely don't feel comfortable being alone here with Beau. My best bet is to defuse the situation and make a quick exit. I'd try to threaten him with fake karate moves, but he'd see right through that.

If only I had my driver's license and a set of car keys to fist in my palm. I could stick the sharp end of the key out the way I once read in a BuzzFeed article.

There are so many cars but no people. The *one* time I want people around, and there aren't any.

"Emie, I just wanna talk," his clipped voice booms at me.

"Beau, please don't call me that." I'm like a petulant child, stomping my foot. But I've had enough of this man and my parents not listening to me.

I keep my back to him, pretending that I have a car in my sight. I tell myself everything is okay and that he won't do anything. We're too easily visible here.

But the closer his footsteps get, the less confident that voice sounds. I never thought I'd be a candidate for one of those *what-went-wrong* shows, but here I am, running away from a crazy ex-boyfriend.

I'm inches away from grabbing the cold handle of a random car door when a bruising clamp on my arm pulls me back, the intensity taking me by surprise. His grip tightens, and I'm forced to turn and face him.

"Ember, I can make all this disappear, if you listen to me." His teeth are bared, and he tugs my body close.

I hiss at the pain sinking into my upper arm.

"Let. Go."

*Calm. Keep your voice calm. Don't upset him further.*

But he doesn't seem to hear. Eyes shadowed with anger stare back intensely, making me shiver while his hand acts as a vice. My only line of defense is the cast on my injured wrist since I can't even get a knee to his man parts with the way he's holding me. Feelings of helplessness and vulnerability burn at my insides. I hate being powerless like this.

I catch the slight curl of his mouth, and my face blanches. He's starting to remind me of a horror-movie psycho, following his prey at a leisurely pace. He doesn't run. He walks because he knows he'll get his victim.

This is all a game to him. He's been maneuvering all the pieces to secure what he wants, while I've lived in mostly blissful ignorance for months.

My stomach turns again as real fear scrapes its way in. He wouldn't dare hurt me in such a public place, right?

The reassuring voice from before doesn't answer this time.

He finally speaks again, his unnaturally calm tone putting ice in my veins. "Come on, Emie. You and I could be so good together. Just like we were, once upon a time. I'll tell your parents this was a misunderstanding, and we can all move forward. But you have to come with me."

Where the heck does he want me to go? Does he have his own brainwashing camp now? Because there's no way I'm willingly doing anything with this man.

The situation has escalated at an alarming pace. The voice in my head is back, screaming that I'm not safe.

I remember the mace in my bag, but there's never enough time to get mace out when you need it.

I try to form a response, yet my words are bottlenecked, mixed with fear and fury. I should be lashing out, but I'm frozen at the audacity of his actions, of his words. How could he think this would convince me to return to him and the town that only promises more pain and heartache for me? He must be as delusional as my parents to think I hold their opinion of me so highly that I'd sell my soul to gain their approval.

I'm never going back to him.

Why can't I remember any self-defense moves? Nose, throat, groin? It's like someone turned the volume up in my brain, and I'm too overstimulated to sort out my thoughts.

Stop, drop, and roll? That's definitely not the right move, but it might catch him off guard and give me a chance to either run or scream. If this were a movie, this would be the moment I'd be yelling at the TV, "Why isn't she screaming?"

That's it. I'm going to head-butt him. It might leave me with a concussion, but I won't go willingly.

"You have two seconds to let go of her arm."

That voice.

The growl is instantly soothing, lessening the whooshing in my ears and it's like my body knows I'm safe.

"Colton?" I ask in disbelief. I've never experienced more gratitude at seeing anyone in my life, but I also can't fathom why he isn't on his way to New York.

Beau doesn't let go right away, a look of irritation marring his face. He must take longer than two seconds, because Colton is suddenly moving with that flash-like speed, twisting Beau's arm until he lets go of the death grip he's been using on my bicep.

Beau curses loudly, preparing himself to take a swing at Colton.

It's a stupid move, though. Colton is faster, throwing a hard uppercut into Beau's stomach, and a shriek echoes from behind as Beau hunches over and sinks to the ground. It's so satisfying to watch him take a hit.

I turn to see my parents frozen, my mother's mouth hanging open. They arrived just in time to see their golden boy beaten up by my boyfriend.

*Splendid.*

"What is going on here?" my father belts out furiously.

Beau is lying on the concrete now, playing the wounded victim. But I know without a doubt he'd be lunging at Colton if my parents hadn't shown up.

"I'll have you arrested, young man," my father growls out.

His eyes flicker to me for a second before he rushes over to help Beau stand. It doesn't surprise me that he's the one they're concerned about, though it's no less soul-crushing than all of the other times they've picked someone or something else over me.

The truth is, they have no reason to think Beau is anything but innocent in all of this. That's on me. But I'm not making that mistake again.

"Colton did nothing wrong here, Dad. He was defending me because Beau couldn't take no for an answer. *Again.*"

As all of this unfolds, the only expression on my mother's face is one of sheer weariness. She isn't worried about me; she's just tired of my antics. "What are you talking about, Ember-leigh?" she sighs, her eye roll barely contained.

"He's not the man you think he is," I tell them. My chin quivers as sadness coats the lens through which I see my parents. There's also regret for the relationship we could never have.

"Don't do this, Ember," Beau whispers a warning while he glares at me.

I return a stare, hoping he'll sense my resolve to never let him control me again and then I shut him out, taking a small step toward my parents.

He must finally see it, because he shakes his head as he walks toward his car and drives away. I have no idea where Dr. Pratt has disappeared to, but I'm just relieved that there's one less person around to witness the chaos unfolding in the restaurant parking lot.

"I ended things with Beau and moved away from Magnolia because he was controlling and emotionally abusive. Leaving was the only way I knew to stop that cycle without causing more drama."

It feels like I've finally set down the heavy weights I've been carrying for so long. Confessing this secret is unbelievably liberating, especially one I never imagined I'd have to keep.

My parents both utter their disbelief, issuing fresh lacerations to my heart. I hate that it hurts so much, that I was stupid enough to hope for something different this time.

"That's ridiculous, Ember," my mother repeats.

But Colton presses a kiss to my temple as he stands behind me, his support softening the sting.

"You know, it should hurt that my parents tried to send me to an institution instead of talking to me like normal people do. But I'm not surprised, 'cause you've only ever shown me this same disappointment and disregard for who I am."

I force a steady inhale as I continue. Tears once again threaten to escape, but I push them back. "But you don't get to shove me in a box and tell me who to be anymore. I love you both, I do. But from now on, if you want any relationship with me, it'll happen on my terms."

Before I turn, I look at my father. "Beau only wanted to marry me to get a leg up in your company." A bitter laugh seeps out. "It's so damned cliche, and you let him get away with it."

I stare at the sky for a second, then return my gaze to their solemn faces. I think they might actually be starting to question their beliefs, especially the ones about Beau, but I know it'll take time and a willingness to see the truth for themselves.

Tonight may have been the worst, but I can picture Shania giving me a proud wink.

Colton urges me on with a gentle hand on my back, walking me to his truck and holding the door while I climb inside.

I watch him circle to his side of the truck, unable to face my parents, so my eyes stay fixed on him. A lone tear escapes, trailing down my cheek as the night's adrenaline begins to ebb. I quickly wipe it away with my sleeve, suppressing a shiver just as Colton opens his door. He starts the engine, flips on my seat warmer, and cranks up the heat, bringing some comfort to the chill of the moment.

The drive back is wrapped in silence. Colton holds my hand the entire way, a gesture we've grown accustomed to despite my cast. As usual, he rests my arm across his thigh, curling his hand underneath mine, our fingers intertwining perfectly.

We drive to his house, which I've only ever visited during the day. The outdoor lights create an inviting glow as he leads me inside, bringing me to his sofa and waiting for me to sit.

After the quietness of the drive, my mind finally jolts back to reality. "Why aren't you in New York? You should be on a plane!"

He remains silent as he drapes a blanket over me, then strides to the kitchen and comes back with an ice pack for my arm and a water bottle. Moving with a graceful motion, he hands me the water and settles next to me on the couch. Pulling me gently towards him, I lean back into his chest as he wraps his arms around me, enveloping me in warmth.

"No, Em. I'm right where I'm supposed to be."

Questions are stacking up in my mind, yet my heart clings to those words. Growing up, I was never anyone's priority—not my parents', not my few allowed friends', and certainly not Beau's. But in just a few short months with Colton, not only has he made me feel valued, he's also consistently tended to the fractures and wounds I've carried for so long.

Tonight's decision to finally be honest with my parents took boldness, but it also gave me courage. I made a move for myself, another step towards feeling whole. Colton's words and actions have helped heal me in ways I never knew I needed.

He places a lingering kiss on my temple. "Tell me about tonight," he whispers softly while his thumb rubs over my wrist.

I choke out a laugh and wipe away the tears that have gathered. "My parents tried to stage an intervention. They were going to check me into some kind of psychiatric clinic."

Colton halts his movements then shifts our position so he's meeting my gaze. There's a storm brewing in his eyes.

I lift a hand and smooth over the jaw muscles he's clenching tightly before I skim my finger over the crease between his brows.

"They even brought a doctor, as if they expected me to just agree to be whisked away, willingly slipping my arms into the straight jacket they were holding out for me."

I can't help but smile at the growl he lets out. Having

someone in my corner, ready to fight for me, is an incredible feeling—one I wish I'd embraced much earlier. Ivy, Opal, and Gail would have gone to great lengths for me, even hiding a dead body if needed, but I never shared with them just how bad things had gotten. I haven't been completely open with Colton, either. If I'd told him about Beau's harassment, we could have avoided tonight's ordeal. Moving forward, that's going to change. I've come to realize that showing vulnerability isn't a weakness; it's a true sign of strength.

"Em, baby, that's messed up." Colton's eyes bounce between mine. I know he has questions, so I put on my big girl panties—no more secrets.

"Beau's been texting me. And calling. A lot, actually. The texts were kinda scary. I thought he'd get the message and eventually leave me alone, but I think he's gone wrong in his head or something. He said I had to go with him. It doesn't make sense, but he's clearly unhinged."

Who knows what Beau would have done if Colton hadn't shown up when he did? That's an icky thought.

I sigh when I meet Colton's eyes and see them filled with fury and the remnants of fear. This is the last thing I wanted—him stressing over me.

My lip trembles while I stare, caught in his gaze as he processes. We both know things could have gone very differently tonight, but I need to own up to my part in that.

"I'm sorry I didn't tell you. I kept hoping he'd get bored and move on. I didn't want to place all this on you. I know that was stupid."

A finger tucks my hair behind my ear, and his eyes roam over my face and shoulders, caressing, grazing, adoring. "I wish you'd confided in me, but I get it. And I forgive you. I'm here for all of it, Em, the good and the bad. You can lean on me and still be the independent woman you are."

He pulls me in tight, and my body relaxes as his fingers glide over my arms and back.

"Thank you. How did you know to come tonight, anyway?" I ask.

Colton tells me about Lemon showing up at the office and not-so-subtly trying to cause drama. I'm barely awake by the end, still cuddled in Colton's arms. His feet are propped on the coffee table, and he turns on a show about home renovations. I laugh sleepily at his choice. When he digs his fingers into my ribs, I squeal and regret the convenient placement of his hands for only a second.

"Okay, okay, truce!" I yell. "I actually think it's cute that you and Ethan watch these shows. I like listening to your commentary on their reno methods. It's like when Ivy and I watch a Hallmark movie."

"I've heard some of your Hallmark commentaries. Y'all are ruthless."

I shrug. "The characters are begging us to comment on their life choices."

"I'm glad I'm not a Hallmark character, then."

"Don't worry. You'd totally be the sexy lead we'd swoon over while being madly jealous of your love interest."

He pats my head and pulls me in tighter. "Go to sleep. You're becoming delirious."

*Delirious for you,* I think as I snuggle closer.

# CHAPTER FIFTY-FIVE

## COLTON

I wake up with Ember in my arms, thrilled at the thought of making this a habit. We're still nestled together on the sofa as the first rays of sunlight peek through the curtains. Sometime during the night, Ember began unbuttoning her shirt. I laughed and told her I wasn't that kind of guy; she playfully swatted me and sleepily explained that the buttons were uncomfortable.

Now she's left in a cream tank top, squished against my side.

The most beautiful woman I've ever seen is pressed tightly to my body, and I'm suddenly grateful she's on my side, if you know what I mean. I'm trying really hard to be a gentleman, and this scenario isn't helping.

I *am* only human, for goodness sake.

And this situation is way too tempting. Before my hands can wander, I count to five and begin my extraction plan.

I don't want to wake Ember, because I'm not sure I can resist her getting all cute and snuggly right now, but I'm failing at my subtle attempts to slip my arm out from beneath her when there's no feeling left in it. The inevitable pins and needles will be a treat.

Ember frowns, keeping her eyes shut. "Hmm, nope. Not ready to get up yet," she mumbles, snuggling in closer.

*Maybe I can handle snuggling, just for a little while longer...*

Nope. Snuggles lead to cuddles, which will certainly lead to more clothes coming off.

I may have handled things differently in the past, but I believe that kind of intimacy is best saved for a committed relationship, preferably when there are two rings involved.

"Em, I love you, but my arm is gonna fall off if I don't get the blood supply back to it soon."

She lifts her free hand to wave off my concerns as she squirms even closer, and I stifle a groan.

*Why am I being tempted like this?*

"You'll be okay. Just...breathe through it," she says sleepily, probably thinking the tingly arm is the only source of my discomfort.

Still, I can't hold in the bubble of laughter that's been brewing. She's just so freaking cute.

She surprises me when her head pops up, and she's instantly awake. Giant green eyes stare at me, shock written all over her face.

"What?"

"You said you love me."

*I did.*

I said I loved her.

I might have messed up by saying it so soon, but it's the truth—I love her more than I ever imagined possible. Yeah, call me sappy if you want. But just try staring into those emerald eyes and see if you don't end up spilling your secrets or scribbling down a poem or two.

I smooth some of the wild morning hair out of her face.

"I do love you, Sunshine, so much. You're my everything."

Those words aren't enough though. I feel so much more deeply about her presence turning my life upside down in the best way. But without having planned it, I've uttered the words in this beautifully raw moment, and that simple truth feels right. My stomach dips as I wait for her response. I don't need her to say it back; I just want to make sure I haven't freaked her out and blown our progress.

"I-love-you-too," she says on an exhale that's still filled with awe. Enchanting eyes roam over my face. A huge grin slowly overtakes my shocked expression. The next thing I know, she's burrowing her face in my neck, her arms tightening around me.

"I love you, Colton," she whispers, her breath warm against my skin. As she raises her arms to wrap them around my shoulders, her cast accidentally nicks my ear. "Sorry," she mumbles, her face still pressed close to mine.

The smile on my face is ridiculously cheesy. "I might lose an arm, now you're threatening to take out an ear, too?" I joke although internally I'm still freaking out over hearing those three words said back to me.

"Crap! Sorry," she squeals and jumps off the sofa, unpinning my hand.

"Worth it." I shrug while flailing my limp arm around. I can't put a price on waking up with the woman I love curled beside me.

She gazes at me thoughtfully, then shifts her eyes downward to her lap. "So, how do I fit into Utah?" she asks.

"It's a big state; I'm sure you'll fit."

She's giving me serious eyes, but her mouth still splits with a wide smile. "You know what I mean!"

"I'm not moving to Utah," I say, returning a grin.

"You're not?"

"Nope. Already texted Jaxon. I told him that if he wants

me to be a part of his idea, we'll need someone else to be more hands-on."

She takes a small step closer. "Why'd you tell him that?"

"I've decided I don't like rectangular states. Utah looks like the block version of Pac-Man trying to eat Wyoming. It's disgusting."

We're standing toe to toe now, and I get a pinch in the ribs for my teasing. "Colton," she reprimands me.

"I think you know why, Sunshine," I say, softening my tone.

"You're staying for me?"

"It's certainly not for Ethan."

Her face lights up, and I pull her in for a hug. Then her stomach rumbles, and she groans. "You didn't hear that."

"Let's feed that thing before it threatens to remove more of my limbs."

"Shut it."

"I'm glad I'm finding out so soon that the woman I love gets hangry in the mornings. I'll have to remember to hide the heavy pans and sharp knives before you've eaten."

I've already learned that she gets hangry all the time, but I won't be telling her that.

Our hands are still linked when we reach the island in my kitchen.

"Colton King, it's unwise to make fun of a hangry woman before feeding her."

I step forward, walking her back until she's pressed against the counter. "I'd never dream of it."

I lean in, bringing my mouth inches away from hers, never breaking eye contact. She doesn't know the inner strength it takes not to kiss her first when we play this unspoken game. But the tiny sound she makes as her eyes darken right before she kisses me is cute as heck, so I persist. Just as I hoped, she makes the quietest noise of frustration before her lips meet mine. I settle into the kiss, tilting my head to the side and bringing my hands up to her hair when her stomach growls loudly between us. I pull back, my eyes bugging in mock fear.

"I could kiss you for hours, baby, but for my self-preservation, I gotta feed that noisy thing." I nod toward her stomach.

Ember digs her fingers into the only spot I'm ticklish, making me yelp like a three-year-old.

"Stop!" I hold my hands up. "Such violence," I tsk. "Let me hide the heavy pans, first."

"You're the worst," she grumbles.

"But you love me."

"I do. Now feed me. Please."

"As you wish." I wink at her.

I whip up a batch of scrambled eggs while Ember supervises my every move. The pancake incident has earned me a rep, and I'm fighting hard to redeem myself. Luckily, Ember says my eggs are better than my pancakes. We load our dishes in the dishwasher together, since she refuses to let me do all the cleaning.

She rinses her hands and flicks her fingers, splattering drops of water my way. I distract her with my best crazy face while slowly reaching for the extendable faucet handle.

"No, no, no, no! I didn't mean it!" She laughs, but she still looks guilty as hell. "It was an accident. It wasn't me—there's a leak in the ceiling!"

She rounds the island, and I aim the nozzle at her. I raise my eyebrows, waiting for more of her excuses, but the doorbell rings. Ember straightens, tilting her head in confusion.

"Who's that?"

"That would be my parents saving your butt, Miss Hayes." I laugh as I replace the faucet trigger. "I texted them last night. They're coming over to watch our segment on The Morning Show." I tag her waist and pull her close. "Is that okay?"

Her hands go to my chest as she begins kissing along my jaw. To be honest, she could tell me anything she wanted right now, and I'd agree if it meant she'd keep her lips on me like this. "Of course. I love your parents. I'm gonna ask them about adopting me."

"Baby, I think there's a better and more fun way for you to join the family. Besides, I don't wanna marry my sister," I say, waggling my eyebrows at her.

She steps away, looking all flustered and cute. But I value my life, so I refrain from telling her she's adorable when she's mad.

"You can't just drop a bomb like that while your parents are at the door!"

The knocking begins again, so I turn to wink at Ember before opening the door and greeting my parents. My mom has her phone out, barely glancing at us as she walks in.

"Quick, put the TV on! They're about to end this segment, then Ethan and Mallory will be on. Oh, hi, Ember, sweetie." She squeezes Ember in a motherly hug, looking away from her phone to link arms as they sink onto the sofa together. My dad shakes my hand as he reassures my mom. "There'll be another five minutes of ads before they're on, love. We're fine."

My mom holds onto Ember's hands as she speaks. "Sweetheart, I'm so sorry to hear about what happened last night. I didn't wanna bring it up in the middle of the show, but seeing as we have the time..." She waves a hand in the air before resting it on her chest.

My mother is the walking embodiment of love and tenderness and will fuss over anyone wronged.

"I am so glad Colton got there when he did. I can't even imagine what might have happened if he didn't. How are you doing?" Her eyes flicker over the slight bruise on Ember's arm.

My jaw tightens when I think of that ass laying his hands on her. I really should have punched the guy in the face.

"Thank you, Jeanie. I'm okay," Ember answers. "Still a little in shock over everything that happened, but overall, I'm good. My ex was horrible, and my parents admittedly went too far again, but I'm proud of myself for finally setting some boundaries and telling them how their actions have affected me. Enough about me, though." She turns to face the TV and hooks her arm around my mom's again. "Let's watch Ethan make America swoon."

I smirk because my girlfriend is amazing.

My dad and I hand out coffees, and I perch on the arm of the couch, my hand on Ember's shoulder while we watch the show. We alternate between my mom's squeals and Ember's shouts of "ooh" before she rapidly explains the backstory for each bit that Ethan and Mallory share.

My parents are as captivated by listening to Ember as they are by watching their son on one of America's longest-running television shows. She fists her hands under her chin and leans her elbows on her knees when Mallory describes the family boxes we'll release next year.

The segment ends, and we all cheer, drunk on the high of seeing our work so beautifully summarized and presented on a screen for millions of other viewers. My parents pepper Ember with questions about the family boxes, and she comes alive under their attention.

*This.* This is the woman I wish her parents could take the time to see. She's killed it with the family-box idea, but it's the affection and interest my parents show in her ideas and who she is that have her blooming. Her soul is kind and loving, and she has so much of both to give. I'm pissed at the stunt her parents pulled all over again, and I vow to do my best to protect her from them, indefinitely.

But damn was I proud as I watched her stand up for herself last night. Still, until they start treating her with the respect and decency she deserves, I'm the guy they'll go through. For now, that means protecting her from more hurt.

Hopefully, they'll make the right choices and begin repairing the damage they've done. I doubt her relationship with them will become Disney's next happily ever after, but there's still a chance they'll swallow their pride and own up to their faults, someday.

All I want is the best for Ember. Skipping out on New York to be with her was an easy choice, and changing my plans for Utah was a no-brainer once I saw Beau's hand around Ember's arm.

I know I can't shield her from everything, but hell, I want to try.

I want forever with her.

I will make this woman my wife and do my damndest to ensure she's happy.

# CHAPTER FIFTY-SIX

## EMBER

"I can't wait to get this stupid thing off," I say, scratching at the seam of my cast. Tree limbs with spots of brown and red shade the car as we drive to my doctor's office. Fall has scurried away as winter gently makes its appearance. Cold, sunny days are my favorite in Aster. Magnolia's climate was similar, being less than two hours away, but something about this town makes everything more magical.

Today is the day that I'm finally getting rid of this cast. Thank goodness it's winter because my skin is Marylin Manson white under this thing.

"Ivy and I need to figure out how to get to Hawaii so I can rectify the pigment discrepancy on my arm. Still a 'no' from you on the blind-date-blog thing?" I squint one eye at him. His only response is a growl that goes right to my toes.

A wave of sadness hits me when I trace a finger over the heart on my cast. As much as I'm ready to have my arm free of its cannoli case, a tiny ache lingers at the thought of not seeing the doodle with our initials every day. I chew my lip as an idea dances around in my mind.

I fumble behind our seats, searching for what I need. Colton parks the car and hands the Polaroid camera to me, placing it gently on my lap.

"Could you take a picture for me?" I ask. "The thought of never seeing this again is heartbreaking. This way, I can keep it with me forever."

"Of course," he returns with a wide grin.

He readies the camera and lays my arm across his lap. I'm once again really grateful for the proximity these bench seats allow. And excuse me, how haven't I noticed these thigh muscles before? I could get very used to this.

*Don't mind me, just making myself at home here.*

The camera flashes, and a Polaroid buzzes out. Colton holds my arm gently, and another flash goes off before the camera spits out a second print. I reluctantly resume my previous position and simmer down from my thigh-high. Fingers pretzeled together, we soak in the silence, goofy smiles pasted on our faces as we wait for the photos to develop. My heart settles when we're together. These moments are everything my introverted heart could have dreamed of.

He flips the Polaroids over, and I swallow the lump in my throat.

"They're perfect." I rub my nose with my free hand, my eyes stinging with happy tears. His hand curls gently around my neck, and I feel his lips on my temple. Then he tucks one photo into the visor in front of him and hands me the other.

An hour later, I leave the doctor's office with a pasty-white wrist and a set of instructions for strengthening my skinny arm. Not having to support the weight of the plaster feels strange. It seems symbolic like I've let go of the baggage I used to protect myself for so many years.

The cold air bites at my nose when we exit the building. There's a sting in my cheeks when I smile at the Christmas decorations outside. Christmas is two weeks away, and I'm ready for the break. The adrenaline crash after the work projects and family drama of last week have me aching for some down time. By "down time," I mean uninterrupted hours with Colton. And if I don't have to wear anything but sweaters and sweatpants, I won't complain either.

He pulls his coat collar around his neck before opening my door. The man can wear the hell out of any outfit and has convinced me that every man should own a navy peacoat.

He gets in, unaware that I'm checking him out like he's my favorite dessert.

"We hanging out at your place?" he asks while he ruffles his hair, nearly sending me into cardiac arrest. Thankfully, I walk a lot, so I don't embarrass myself by needing him to call 911. I'm young, though. I should probably tell him that if he pulls those moves when I'm over sixty-five, he'll need to get me one of those fancy watches that warns you when your heart freaks out.

I clear my throat before answering. "Yeah, Nicolas has been particularly moody lately. I probably need to spend more than a few minutes there during the day."

Colton's place is quickly starting to feel like home to me. Plus, his furniture is a lot more comfortable—it doesn't try to swallow or stab me every time I sit down. Other than having tea with Opal and Gail last week, I've really only been to my own place to sleep. These days, I spend my work hours at the office and my evenings relaxing with Colton at his house.

"Sounds good," he says, starting the car and pulling out of the parking lot.

While he drives, his eyes ahead of him on the road, he gently lifts my hand and brings it to his mouth. My wrist looks like it belongs to a scrawny ten-year-old with his giant fingers, but he continues anyway.

Dang. This is what I've been missing out on this whole time

I had a cast. He presses his lips to the back of my hand in feather-soft kisses that send a shiver all the way to my toes.

Okay, so we can agree I'm a goner regarding this man. He turns my insides to mush. I should ask him to sing. Maybe his out-of-tune voice will bring me down to earth—even the playing field. My ovaries need a break from all the swooning.

I reach for the radio, finding a country station.

"Do you ever sing?"

*So much tact.*

Colton laughs, tapping his thumb on my knuckles. "Sometimes. I'm pretty bad at it. You?"

I guess it was too much to hope he'd start belting to the song that was playing.

"I'm okay. I can carry a tune, but I'm no Shania Twain."

He parks outside my apartment complex and turns his body to face me with an assessing gaze. He leans forward, and I fight another shiver when his nose grazes my neck. "You tryna tell me I don't impress you much, Sunshine?" I feel the curl of his smile when his lips trace a line to my earlobe.

"Qui—quite the opposite." I pull back, cupping my hands on his handsome face. "I wanna say I was thinking more '*Any Man of Mine*'." I smile when he tries to tickle my side. "But when it comes to you, our Shania song can't be anything but '*Love Gets Me Every Time*'."

Colton's face sobers, and I watch his cheek muscle jumping.

"Dang, woman. I didn't want to risk Gail and Opal catching us making out in my truck, but...ah, stuff it." And then his lips are on mine, tilting my head back as he deepens the kiss.

My heart thumps loudly in my ears, and in the next second, his free hand is cupping the back of my head as his mouth does delicious things to mine. A fuzzy feeling wraps tightly around me as the warmth of his nearness intertwines us.

Lips glide. Moans escape. It's heated and intense, stamped with the urgency of his words, like neither of us can deny the tension we'd both created. Minutes pass, and eventually, the intensity fades as we settle into a softer and more gentle kiss.

I melt into his touch while his kiss brands me, tattooing something beautiful and unspoken onto my soul. He nips my bottom lip, trailing kisses along my jaw. Forget being peppered with kisses—I want to be smothered, *marinated*, in the feeling of his lips on my skin.

Somewhere in the recesses of my make-out-addled mind is the thought that this is a little indecent. But that thought is hastily silenced by the silky feeling of his mouth returning to mine.

I could happily continue like this for hours, entangled in each other's arms. But a sense of being watched finally pushes through with enough force that I lay my palm on Colton's chest. Reluctantly, I break the kiss. I struggle to open my eyes and emerge from the bubble of bliss surrounding us, but as soon as we both return to consciousness, we jolt at the two figures standing a foot away from the car.

"I think you'll needa take extra blood-pressure medicine today, Gail." Opal smirks, taking a pistachio from the bag that Gail is holding. She cracks one open, popping it into her mouth as she nods toward us and elbows her friend. "That sure got my heart rate going."

I stifle a laugh, burying my face in Colton's arm as my hand covers my mouth. My cheeks burn with embarrassment as I groan out muffled words, "I'll never hear the end of this."

Colton palms the back of his neck and clears his throat. "Ladies," he nods in greeting. He then opens his door, with Gail and Opal barely stepping back an inch, allowing him just enough room to squeeze out. Circling around to my side, he arrives to help me out.

"He's a gentleman too," Gail croons.

Colton's cheeks flush pink as he shuts my door. Seeing this rumpled, slightly embarrassed side of him is incredibly endearing, leaving me perpetually in need of smelling salts.

I unlock my apartment door, and we both erupt into laughter. "That wasn't embarrassing at all," I say.

He shrugs like it's no big deal. "Worth it."

He's said those words to me a few times, and they seal a truth more permanently into my heart each time: that I am worthy of love. I'm worth being someone's focus. I'm worth having someone's full attention.

# CHAPTER FIFTY-SEVEN

## EMBER

I'm having tea with my mother. For many, that's just a regular day. But for me, choosing to meet with her voluntarily is nothing short of a miracle.

She orders a garden sandwich tray and a pot of lavender rooibos from the server, then turns to me with a slight smile. "What'll you have, dear?" she asks. I can tell she's making an effort, and I appreciate that.

I rattle off my order, then clear my throat uncomfortably as I slip my hands under my thighs. My mother may be making progress, but I can't help the anxiety that wants to resurface, like an old friend who's always been invited to the party.

An awkward silence lingers, but it's different from before. I can sense a change in her; the judgmental arch of her brow has softened, and her tone carries less bite.

"Your father and I watched The Morning Show segment," she blurts out, and for the first time, I can sense that she's just as nervous as I am. This is a new and weird dynamic in our relationship.

She uncharacteristically plays with a fork on the table. "It was very impressive. Who would have thought something like that would become so popular?"

Are we making small talk?

"Oh, um...yeah, the segment was a huge success. Colton's done an amazing thing, growing this company. And his brother has gained a lot of attention since the show. I think some TV networks have approached him after hearing about his house-flipping business." I ramble, thinking this is the longest we've gone without one of us uttering a sarcastic response.

"That's just wonderful." She smiles back.

*Who is this woman?*

"Ember, we also found out that Beau was stealing money from your father."

I raise my eyebrows, but I can't say I'm surprised.

"I'm sorry. Is Dad gonna be okay?"

"Oh yes, he's fine." She waves her hand then smooths out a napkin. "But we've clearly been wrong about a lot of things."

A glistening in her eyes has me leaning forward, a little in shock that my previously cold mother is producing real tears.

"Mom, are—are you *crying?*"

She blinks rapidly, but there's a quiver in her voice when she continues. "I'm very embarrassed by the way we treated you. I...I never had a great relationship with my mother. And, well, I suppose I didn't really know what to do with you when you were born. I thought you'd be the son your father always spoke about training to follow in his footsteps one day. And acting out of the fear of disappointing him, I failed you."

"Mom—" I begin, ready to brush off her speech, so completely out of my element with what's happening here.

"I'm sorry, Ember. For a lot of things. Your father wants to apologize, too, but I wanted to speak with you first. I'm sorry for not being what you needed all these years."

"Mom," I whisper, my voice thick. "I forgive you," I add,

clearing my throat. I'm so used to not allowing any emotion to slip in during our interactions. The thawing of that response will take a while.

We get through the rest of our lunch by continuing with the same awkward small talk. But the important thing is that we're both trying. My mother only makes one comment about my appearance before she catches herself falling into an old habit.

I know it will take time to repair the years of walls we've each built up. But at least there's hope that we can have a somewhat pleasant relationship, maybe even a healthy one.

# CHAPTER FIFTY-EIGHT

## COLTON

As we lounge on my couch watching *"The Princess Bride,"* I gently comb my fingers through Ember's hair.

She arrived an hour ago, emotionally drained from having tea with her mother. To add to her day, on her way home, her father called to apologize and informed her that they were pressing embezzlement charges against Beau and initiating a formal investigation.

That little fact made me very happy.

"They asked if they could see us on a regular basis. I think it'll be good."

"I'm proud of you Em."

That's an understatement. Seeing how she stood up for herself and for me, I actually couldn't be prouder.

It makes me even more determined to make all her dreams come true.

"What would you do if money wasn't an obstacle?" I ask after a while.

"Like, for work?" she questions.

"Yeah."

She purses her lips in thought, but when she starts chewing at the corner, I push for the answer I sense she's hesitant to give.

"You wanna adopt a hundred cats and raise them to be as evil as Nicolas, don't you?"

She swats my arm and laughs into my chest. "No, you weirdo. I...I don't want you to feel any pressure. Like seriously, *zero* pressure from me saying this..."

"Spill it, Hayes."

"Okay, but don't freak out." She stares at me waiting for my acknowledgement.

A chuckle slips out before I feign a serious face. "I swear not to freak out."

"I do like having something to do. I couldn't do *nothing*. But I think I'd eventually like to be a stay-at-home wife and mom."

My heart is a stereo inside my chest.

"Em..."

She has no idea how her words make me want to go all caveman and find a ring and fly to Vegas immediately.

I'm undone. There's nothing left. Every part of my heart is now hers.

Forest green eyes bounce between mine like she's looking for a sign that she's scared me off. But I lift my hand to cradle her face while I rub a thumb along her cheekbone.

"Tell me I'm the man you want those things with, Sunshine. 'Cause I've been waiting for you to catch up since the day I met you. I don't care if you work or not. I just want you to be happy."

A watery smile lights up her face. "Colton King, you are the only man I could ever want those things with. Now, kiss me."

"As you wish."

# EPILOGUE



"Where are you taking me?"

"It's killing you, isn't it?" Colton grins.

"My funeral plan's ready and the casket is picked out. It's a rich mahogany. You'll love it."

"Wow. That got dark pretty fast. You just had that one ready to go?" His brows crease for a second, but he still manages to put a smug smile on his face, which continues to be stupidly handsome. He peaks at me from the driver's seat and sets his eyes back on the road like a responsible little driver. There's nothing little about this man, but I'm a teensy bit hangry and feel I've earned the right to complain at this point.

"I will implode if you don't give me a hint, at least!" I beg.

"Baby, I've been giving you hints all week."

"What? When?" I gasp, giving him an indignant look before playfully swatting his bicep. He pretends to be annoyed, but we both know he secretly enjoys it when I admire his muscles.

After all, he's worked hard for them—it'd be rude not to appreciate the effort.

"What's been different this week?" he prompts.

I lean forward, peaking inside the cup holders in front of us. "You added a penny to your one other penny."

He leans back and lets loose a rumbly laugh, and I watch his Adam's apple move with the sound. It seems crazy, but every time I hear him laugh, my heart still races.

"That's specific. And yes, I did, but that's not the hint. That's just some change from Chick-fil-A. What else?"

My eyes narrow as I rack my brain for any clues I've missed.

I lift my hands and drop them down in defeat. "I'm on the verge of malnourishment. It's almost three p.m., and I didn't have lunch today. I can't think when I'm so hungry, and I know there's food in the back. I can smell it." I tip my head to the seats behind us.

His only response is another laugh as he leans across the cab and pops open the cubby in front of me. He takes out a protein bar, one of the chocolate ones that are mostly dessert, as they should be, and hands it to me.

"Eat this, then you'll find out more. I can't have you passing out or attacking me in the middle of your surprise."

"Thank you," I say indignantly, taking the bar he offers. It's just the hangry talking, but I love the way he's so ridiculously thoughtful. I should have known better and brought my own protein bar, but we all know the perils of changing a handbag. I sorted through the contents and decided "I won't need this today. It can stay in my regular bag," leaving my emergency snacks in a pile, so here we are.

I wolf down the bar in a grossly unladylike way. Colton knows there is no space for manners when I'm this hungry, bless the man.

He boops my nose, giving me flashbacks of the first time I rode in his truck. I take a huge breath, feeling my limbs waking up now that my body doesn't think it's a prisoner of war. Colton is already out of the truck, jogging around to open my door. It swings open, and eyes like two cerulean crystals pin me in place.

"You checking me out again?"

"Unashamedly,"

He plants a quick, sweet kiss on my lips, full of love. Then, reaching behind my seat, he pulls out a picnic basket. "Come on, Sunshine," he says with a wink, leading me toward the most stunning house I've ever seen. This place is the epitome of beauty, with its wrap-around porch, large windows, and the kind of electric bill that comes with making your neighbors jealous.

"Whose house is this? Shouldn't you knock?" I begin slowing my steps, but he tugs me along and pushes the front door open.

Colton steps inside and flips a switch to his right, illuminating an open-floor space that could comfortably fit fifty people. I gasp for the second time this afternoon. Beautiful dark-wood floors softly reflect the light from outside. My brain is a jar of bees as I take everything in and those little hints he's been dropping all week come to mind. I do a slow spin, preparing for a squeal, but decide to find out what's going on before jumping to conclusions.

"Colton, why—what's going on? Whose house is this?"

He places the picnic basket in the middle of the room and holds his hand out to me. I slide my palm over his, and he leads me to the only piece of furniture in the room. On the far right of the open living space is a giant dining table pushed up against the wall. There are samples for paint, cabinets, and countertops scattered around brochures with pictures of more houses, houses that look like the only people who can afford them are the ones who can also buy themselves a small island. Toward the end of the table is the same Polaroid camera that Colton carries along everywhere he goes.

His eyes sparkle with mischief and the tiniest hint of nerves.

"Before I answer any questions, have a look at something first." He turns me toward the table, pressing his chest lightly against my back. I catch a hint of his delicious scent when he reaches an arm around me and places a small Polaroid photo album in my hands, then he opens it.

"The first time I beat you in a competition," I tease, grinning at the photo he took when we made milkshakes in his parents' kitchen.

"That's the day I decided to make it my mission to help you take risks. After watching you come alive when you stepped out of your comfort zone, I knew I had to see that look on your face again."

A feeling of breathlessness warms me as a smile gleams on my face.

The next photo is one I didn't know he took. It's me, leaning in the garden bed in his parents' yard, placing a daffodil into the ground.

"This one was selfish. I was in denial about my feelings for you."

"Really?" I gasp.

He continues with a sultry voice in my ear. "But I felt compelled to capture your beauty. I told myself it was for the challenge, but I kept it in my desk at work."

I smile, turning the page.

"Aw, I love this photo!" I gush at the picture of the two of us in our thrift-store outfits.

He chuckles behind me, and I feel his breath on my ear. "I learned something significant that day."

"Yeah?"

"I learned that pockets in dresses are like finding gold."

"It's true," I say with a huge grin.

"It's also the day I realized fighting my feelings for you was pointless. When you squealed in that dressing room, I knew I had to get to know you better."

I want to say something light and teasing, but the words get clogged in my throat.

On the next page is the photo he took outside the arcade on our first date. I stare down at the picture of my face branded with elation.

Colton leans closer, his words more intimate as he continues speaking next to my ear. "That's the day I decided I'd do whatever it takes to have more fun with you, to go on adventures with you."

Another bubbling laugh escapes as I wipe away a tear, turning the page.

"This one," he says, leaning over me to touch the photo of me blow-drying my hair in my apartment bathroom, "is when I knew it'd be worth the fight to break through your defenses. To get past your walls and help you realize you didn't have to do everything yourself."

My heart.

It's like someone handed him a care manual labeled "Ember." In the next sleeve is a photo of his doodles on my cast. I rub a finger over it, remembering the roughness of the material.

"This was the day I decided," he says.

"Decided what?"

I feel him step back a fraction, but before I can face him, he's reaching around me for the Polaroid. I'm still facing the table when he places the camera in my hand, whispering his words into my ear. "The day I decided I wanted forever with you."

My heart is melting. He turns the page again, then steps back further. I lean in to read the note in the sleeve where the next photo should go.

Em,

Turn around and take a photo

—Yours, C

I whirl around with the camera still in my hand, laughter mingling with tears of joy as I spot Colton on one knee, ring in hand. It's oversized and dazzlingly sparkly, but it's the earnest look in his eyes that completely overwhelms me. Covering my mouth with my free hand, I blink back the tears.

"Take the photo, Sunshine." He beams at me.

"Oh, right." I sniff and quickly capture the most beautiful moment of my life. The photo spits out, and I place it and the camera on the table before I face Colton again.

"Em, I'd like to fill that book and a hundred others with the memories we'll make together. I love you with everything in me. I'm no longer content making adventures happen for other people; I want a lifetime of adventures and memories with you. Will you marry me, Sunshine?"

"Yes! Yes!" I cry out, launching myself into his arms. He stands firm, holding me tightly as my feet dangle off the ground.

Eventually, he gently lowers me until my feet touch the

ground again, but Colton's arms remain wrapped around my waist.

"So, the house?"

"It's ours."

"You bought me a *house*?"

This man could teach university classes on how to be swoon-worthy. My cheeks sting with happiness. I stare up at the man who's become my everything.

Once, during one of our late-night TV binges, we debated whether Pam from "The Office" should have been more upset that Jim bought a house without asking her first. I argued that Pam was so thrilled to be with Jim that the location of their home didn't really matter to her, and she could always decorate and renovate to make it her own. Still, I never imagined Colton would take that conversation to heart, let alone surprise me with the most picture-perfect house I could ever dream of.

"Yeah, Sunshine. I bought you a house. You can even hang Shania wherever you want. This is where our forever begins."

Another smile ambushes my face as I picture Shania on our wall, winking at me with that magical glint in her eye. Because I finally get it—I get what she meant when she wrote "*Queen of Me*."

It's not about fitting some man-crushing mold of a woman whose version of success only looks like one thing.

Being the "Queen of Me" involves embracing support from others. It means pursuing my dreams without any shame and choosing paths that resonate with me, whether that's being a mom and a wife now, and something else later. It's about allowing myself the grace to dream freely and accepting that those dreams might evolve over time.

Colton takes my hand and doesn't let go while he gives me a tour of our home. I almost faint at the sight of the ensuite bathtub and closet space. I don't, because I'm still adamant about not having that weakness, but if anything could bring me to admit I came close to passing out, it would be the beauty of that bathtub.

"I could fit a small family in there!" I point to the walk-in closet that's more like its own room.

"That would be weird. I'm definitely planning to walk around in my birthday suit on a daily basis, so let's not do that," he says, making me laugh and blush at once.

By the time we return to the living room, I'm giddy and drunk on happy hormones. Colton lays down a picnic blanket, and we eat sushi while laughing about the "hints" he'd been giving me all week.

"Okay, I admit, the paint swatch as my bookmark was good. But a house and then a sushi emoji? I one-hundred percent thought that was another one of your old-man texting disabilities like maybe you thought they meant something else."

He snorts. "Like what?"

"I dunno, like how your dad thought LOL meant 'lots of love.' I thought it was cute the way your old soul was struggling to figure out technology."

Colton moves my plate out the way, mischief in his predatory gaze. In a quick lunge, he's hovering over me, speaking against my neck. It's my weak spot. "I understand emojis, Em," he rasps while his short beard grazes the area behind my ear. "I think you're just mad you missed all my clues."

"It's okay. I'll still marry you, even though you can't cook or sing and you're terrible at giving hints."

A giggle escapes my mouth when he growls against me, tickling me and sending a shiver down my back.

"I just..." I'm distracted as his lips continue, leaving a trail of heat along my neck. "I just hope our children don't suffer from these shortcomings," I breathe out.

Colton finally relents and lifts his head, bringing his eyes to mine.

"They'll be okay 'cause they'll have you."

I drink in the view of him hovering over me, eyes swimming with affection.

"What do you think of your ring?"

I lift my hand between us, tilting it back and forth while it glitters. I could not have picked out a more perfect ring. It's a simple-yet-elegant cluster ring on a gold band, and I will be doing the queen's wave to showcase this beauty for the rest of my life.

"It's the most beautiful thing I've ever seen."

Colton's eyes are still on me when I look up at him.

"Yeah. It is," he says.

"Why do you call me that?" I ask gently.

"Sunshine?"

"Yeah. You called me that when we barely knew each other."

Colton shifts over his elbow, tucking a strand of hair behind my ear. My question hangs in the air. He pins me with an intense gaze that nuzzles its way into the depths of my heart, warming the last lonely nooks. He lifts my hand, gently kisses my palm, and presses my open hand on his cheek.

From the moment I first saw you, I knew you'd become the center of my universe. Watching you switch your shoes and hop around, and then meeting you in my building, I realized I was utterly powerless to resist you.

Heaven help me. Somebody bring the gurney. How am I supposed to think straight? What do I say to those words? My breath catches, and I blurt out the only thing I know that communicates how much I adore every fiber of who he is.

"I love you, Colton King. You're my favorite."

"You're my everything, Ember Hayes," he replies with

another kiss to my neck. "Soon to be Ember King," he whispers against me.

"You'll still need to make friends with Nicolas, you know. He's used to being the man of the house."

"Nicolas Cage and I will come to an understanding because we both love the most gorgeous girl in the whole world."

"I bet that's a sentence you never thought you'd say." I wiggle my eyebrows at him.

"I have a feeling there will be many more of those. As far as Nicolas goes, I'll turn a blind eye to his murderous vibes, and he'll eventually, but begrudgingly, come to see that I love you and want to make all your dreams come true."

"You're my dream come true, Colton King. I can't wait to become Mrs. Ember King."

"By the way, I hope you're okay with that happening soon, 'cause my mother is already looking at venues."

"I'm good with soon." I pull him close and hug him tightly. We lie back and stare at the ceiling while planning our forever.

In my wildest dreams, I couldn't have imagined finding someone so perfect for me. The past year has been crazy, but it's also been the best change of plans.


The End

# BONUS CHAPTER
## IVY

I just can't deal with my brother right now. I let out a loud sigh, adjusting the corner of my gold-rimmed glasses as I pull my phone from my pocket.

Dwight Schrute's "*Idiot*" repeats three times, alerting me to my brother's text. I assigned the unique alert to his contact because, although I love him dearly, Ross can be an idiot. It's also a reminder for myself, not to be an idiot by letting him take advantage of me.

I fail repeatedly, so I can't recommend my methods.

I pull out my phone to read over his text and immediately regret it.

He knows I can't say no to him, and that's the crux of the matter. He's the older one—I should be the one relying on him to help get my life in order. Except we've never fit those roles, and I'm always stuck being the responsible one who fixes his mess.

But this time, his mess has become my mess, and I'm a little out of my depth.

I ignore his plea for now. I only have a few minutes to get to my newly engaged BFF before school. My second graders are the best, but I need a silent cup of coffee before the minions stampede into my class.

I spot both Ember and Colton's cars when I pull into the parking lot of The Adventure Project.

Gah, I love that my bestie has found the most perfectly amazing man. I could not have designed a better match for her. Unfortunately for the rest of us, I think he was the last of the good ones.

At least, I have yet to meet my own Colton King.

Ethan's cocky grin affirms my hypothesis when I pass his office. How that man is related to Colton, I have no idea. They may look like brothers, but they're Scar and Mufasa when it comes to personalities. No matter how amazing Ember tells me he is, Ethan will always be the enemy in my mind. He has to be.

"Knock, knock," I say, plastering on a giant smile as I walk into Colton's office, where I know I'll find Ember.

Just seeing her so happy affirms that I'm making the right decision. This gesture is as much about blessing them as it is for me.

I'm going to be fine. My bestie is getting married, but it's not like everything will change, right?

*You're not being replaced, Ivy June.*

"Vee!" Ember squeals and pulls me in for a hug. "What did you have to speak to us about so early on a Tuesday?"

*Yeah, it's random as heck for me, too, sister.*

But if I don't do this now, I'll chicken out and do something crazy, like return these tickets for rent or grocery money. And as much as I need those things, this decision gives me a sense of peace.

Ember's forehead creases questioningly with a tiny frown, while her lips still flash her beautiful smile.

Colton gives me a side hug, then perches on the desk, curling an arm around his fiancé. My eyes mist up just looking at them.

*You're important, Ivy.*

For the longest time, It's been me and Ember against the world, and seeing her knight in shining armor swoop in to whisk her away has admittedly triggered my abandonment issues.

I pull an envelope out of my bag, gripping it while I beam my happiest grin at these two love birds.

"Em, I know we started planning for Hawaii together, and it took some blood, sweat, and tears to reach our goal, but...I did it."

Ember's hands slowly cover her mouth. Those green orbs of hers flick between my hand and my own eyes, which are misting up again. "Wha—what, Vee? How? I thought we—"

I laugh at her reaction, hoping this lands well. "I spent the last few weekends driving to yard sales, looking for things I could resell. We only had about a thousand dollars to go. I found a set of golf clubs that made the biggest chunk. But, anyway..." I hand the envelope to her. "This is my gift to the two of you."

Ember glances at Colton, frowning, then opens the envelope. She pulls out the tickets, shaking her head in confusion. "Vee, I don't understand—"

"It's an early wedding present. Tickets for you and Colton to go to Hawaii. Seven days, all expenses paid."

I know Colton could very much afford this, and that's why it feels awkward. But it also feels right, because it's my choice to set my own seal on their relationship and not let the doubts and fears tell me what to do.

Tears spill over Ember's lashes. She knows the sacrifice behind this gesture. Together, we started this dream as a way to get over her ex and to have some fun. Then it became the light at the end of my tunnel.

Through all Ross's drama, I always had Hawaii to look forward to. But I tell myself there will be other Hawaiis. I'm young, and I'll reach that goal again.

*Someday.*

First, I'll have to dig myself out of a hole, but it'll be fine.

"Thank you, Vee. This is incredibly generous of you. I know how much this trip meant to you."

"I love you guys," I croak out, and Colton pulls us both in for a hug.

"Thank you, Ivy," he says, squeezing us tightly. "We love you too." He's too much of a gentleman to embarrass me by refusing the gift, and I'm so grateful for it.

I step away after a few seconds, dabbing the tears away and saying a quick goodbye. I've got a school day to get through and an apartment to pack up.

# ACKNOWLEDGMENTS

It took two years, mostly stolen moments during nap times, to turn this book into what it is today. I couldn't have done it without my husband, Dean. Babe, thank you for believing in me and helping make this dream a reality. I love you.

To my three beautiful children—may you discover the joy of perseverance and chasing your dreams. Thank you for your patience when I disappeared into my writing.

Esmée, without your insightful feedback and suggestions, this book would have been nothing. Thank you for caring so deeply about these characters. You are incredibly talented and a true gift.

To my hype team—Tina, Amber, Lisa. You endured the rough drafts, and for that, you have my deepest thanks. Your support throughout this daunting journey has been invaluable.

Libby and Louise, you're the best celebration partners anyone could ask for. Thank you for being there to cheer every achievement along the way.

To my Instagram friend and favorite line editor, Katie S—I hope we can meet in person someday. Your friendship and understanding of my humor have been a highlight of this project. Thank you for everything.

And finally, to my entire family—your encouragement and excitement have buoyed me through this process. I hope you find as much joy in reading this book as I found in writing it.

# ABOUT THE AUTHOR

Cindy Ras is a South African living in Northern California with her husband and three sons. She's survived motherhood without any caffeine and much prefers a good cup of tea. This is Cindy's first book but she plans to write more when she isn't drawing covers for other amazing authors. You can connect with her on Instagram @cindyras_author or check out her cover art @cindyras_draws

Thank you for reading and reviewing! Reviews are incredibly helpful to indie authors and yours would be very much appreciated.